Touching the
Brilliance of
Sunrise

Touching the Brilliance of Sunrise

a novel of faith, love, and second chances

by Lisa J. Lehr

A special thanks to
Natalie Dodd for her technical assistance
and Noelle Dodd for her artistic assistance
with the cover art.

The characters in this story are fictional.
Any resemblance to any real persons,
living or dead, is purely coincidental.

The author apologizes for the potentially
misleading references to a "Braille Bible."
The author would like to clarify that a
Braille Bible actually comprises several
volumes, and that a person would not
normally carry around an entire Braille
Bible. These references were made for
the sake of literary simplicity at the
expense of factual accuracy.

See www.justrightcopy.com/books
for other titles.

Contact the author at
lisa.justrightcopy@gmail.com.

I dedicate this book
to the people of
Grass Valley-Nevada City, California,
who encouraged me to write.

Lisa J. Lehr
January 2009

The sun was already well above the horizon. She could tell by the slant of the sunlight streaming through the windows of the sleeping porch, illuminating the raised sailboat pattern on her bedspread, spilling down onto the worn floorboards.

What time is it?

Melissa looked over at the bedside table. It wasn't really a table, but a stool, its chipped paint revealing layers of colors, a testament to its years of service to generations of cottage dwellers; now accommodating a reading lamp, her Bible and some other reading material, and an alarm clock.

I've missed the sunrise.

She'd thought that choosing the sleeping porch, with its abundant, uncurtained windows, would ensure an early awakening. But the previous day's transcontinental flight had ensured something else—deep sleep.

That's okay. There will be other sunrises—two whole weeks of them.

Slipping on a pair of plaid shorts and a new sweatshirt, Melissa tiptoed past the quiet bedrooms, through the kitchen, with its smell of old wood and well-scrubbed linoleum, to the big picture window. There, the living seascape begged her to become part of it—the clouds, feathery brushstrokes against a pale-blue canvas, floating above the diamond-strewn surface of the Atlantic. She could almost feel the coarse, ivory-colored sand beneath her feet.

Looking around the cottage's cozy main room, Melissa discovered a vintage radio on the table next to the door leading out to the beach, but decided not to turn it on just yet, rather to relish the quiet. She opened the door, inviting in the music of crashing waves and the cry of gulls. *Ah, and the sea smell.*

Her eyes then fell upon her art folio in the wicker chair where she'd dropped it the night before. She was determined to take home a finished work suitable for framing. It had been far too long since she'd created anything for fun—it was always work. Now, she had a new pocket sketchbook, pad of canvas paper, and brand-new supply of watercolor pencils in colors to capture her impressions of Maine—greens, blues, teals, purples; periwinkle, gray, gold, coral—and keep her ever mindful of her goal.

She turned toward a sound behind her. "Morning, Emily."

The mumbled response could have been either "morning" or "m-hmm"—Melissa wasn't sure. Emily rubbed her eyes, trying to make sense of the display on her watch.

"Whatever that says, it's three hours later," Melissa said.

"Oh. The time difference. No wonder it's so light." Emily fiddled with her watch, then looked dazedly out the window.

"Is Jessica awake?" Melissa asked.

"Yeah. She's coming."

A moment later, Jessica appeared, pulling from her hair a sky-blue headband that had gone askew during the night. She sat down at the table with a bemused squint as she gazed out the window.

"Good morning," Melissa offered.

"Why is it so light? I feel like I just went to bed."

"The time difference," Melissa and Emily said together.

Jessica nodded absently. "Are we going anywhere today?"

"Well, into town, to get some groceries. Other than that, I thought we'd just stay here. Maybe go for a walk on the beach. It *is* Sunday."

"Sunday!" Emily repeated. "What about church?"

"Oh…it was too late to look for a phone book last night. Besides, you never know what a church is going to be like in a strange town."

"Has Matt been up yet?" Jessica asked.

Melissa glanced around the tidy little kitchen. "I think we'd be able to tell if he'd been here. He'll probably come out as soon as we leave."

Jessica nodded, smirking a bit.

"What's there to eat?" Emily asked.

"I see they left us some 'gourmet blueberry muffin mix' and some coffee and tea."

"I'm not hungry. It's too early," Jessica said. "Let's do the walk first."

Melissa looked at Emily, who shrugged and nodded.

Melissa scribbled a note for Matt—"Went for a walk— Mom, J, E"—and fixed her gaze on the seascape while the girls changed. Something about this scene was musically evocative…as if the ivory-colored beach could be the keyboard of a celestially scaled piano.

Growing up in California, Melissa had visited the coast nearly every summer of her life. Yet, nothing stirred her imagination like the coast of Maine. At this point in her life, she felt the pull of her Yankee roots more than ever before. Somewhere on this trip, she hoped, she would find that special place—a quaint coastal village, a friendly farming community, a relaxed lakeside resort—that felt like home. Maybe *now* was the right time, the right set of circumstances, the right degree of freedom from complicating attachments to make the move she'd so long dreamed about. The fortnight stretched before her, as vast and full of possibility as the ocean itself.

§

Melissa curled her toes as the frothy water swirled around the straps of her sandals.

"That's *cold*!" Emily shrieked.

"I'm awake *now*!" Jessica laughed.

"I think we'll have appetites when we get back," Melissa said. She drew in a lungful of the damp, salty air, and felt herself fill with gratitude for her daughters' company. It was one of those perfect, freeze-frame moments. At fifteen and ten, Jessica and Emily had sailed over some pretty big bumps in life with their sweet spirits intact.

Matt was a different story. Now on the brink of adulthood, he'd always been the independent one, and his blasé attitude about being part of the family was a constant source of conflict, as well as sadness for Melissa. She tried to give him his space, and the girls more or less filled the void. With his departure for college two weeks hence, she looked forward to the shift in their relationship—having him as a fellow adult. All three were academically gifted, and none had ever given her any real trouble. Overall, she felt abundantly blessed.

Melissa closed her eyes and took another deep breath. She longed to recapture the magic of childhood summers at the beach, and things looked hopeful indeed.

§

3

Melissa was startled back to reality as a flock of seabirds suddenly took flight. She hadn't even noticed when her daughters left her side. They appeared to be on a course toward a young man walking a dog; that is, a man probably younger than she, and she did not yet think of herself as middle-aged.

Not terribly surprised, Melissa reflected with a smile that all her kids had become animal lovers like herself. The girls especially had been known to cast aside any tendency toward shyness upon encountering a stranger accompanied by an animal of any sort.

Her amusement turned to dismay as a second glance revealed something extra in the picture. *A harness...with a long handle...like those used by guide dogs for the blind.* Melissa cringed at the realization that her daughters were about to interrupt a guide dog at work.

She toyed with the idea of simply walking on, of letting the girls make fools of themselves without her help. They certainly should have known better.

But something, a sense of duty perhaps, compelled her to try to catch up with her daughters. "Girls, wait," she called out breathlessly, but the breeze blew her words away. "I'm sorry," she tried again as she drew nearer. "They should have—"

"That's all right," the man answered with a smile that set her at ease. "They asked first."

Melissa looked down at the golden retriever the girls were fussing over. "Beautiful dog."

"Thank you. And Shanna loves people, don't you, Shanna?" He stroked her head, and she panted and wagged harder in response to her master.

"Girl dog?"

"Yes. And I'm Kraig." He offered his hand, and Melissa was struck by the strength and warmth of his handshake.

"I'm Melissa. My daughters—" she nudged them, "Jessica, Emily."

"We've met," he said simply. Fortunately, he did not offer his hand again, as they weren't paying attention to *him*.

An awkward silence followed. "Are you on vacation?" Melissa asked, a bit lamely.

4

"Yes." He nodded toward someplace behind him. "I'll be here a week. You?"

"Two weeks. We're renting a cottage. Do you live around here?"

"I'm from Portland—"

"Oh, we flew into there last night," Emily interrupted.

He laughed a little. "Portland, *Oregon*."

"Really! We're from California!" Melissa exclaimed.

"Is that right! I once lived in southern California."

"Well, we're from *rural, northern* California."

"Ah, the *other* California. What town? Past Sacramento, I know nothing."

"Oak Hill."

"Sorry," he shook his head.

"Most people haven't heard of it. It's in the foothills. *Far* from the beach. Although I grew up in the Bay Area, and used to go to the beach all the time."

"Mm," Kraig nodded.

"Well, you were probably on your way somewhere...."

"No hurry," he said, taking a deep breath, and Melissa found herself doing the same, and feeling relaxed.

"Well. What kind of work do you do in Portland, Oregon?"

"I'm a writer. I write for a small, conservative newspaper."

"Thank God for conservative newspapers!" Melissa blurted out.

"Are—you Christians?" Kraig asked, his face lighting up.

"Yes," all three answered.

"How wonderful to meet you, so far from home." He held out his hand again, and Melissa put hers in it again. This time, he seemed to release her hand rather more slowly.

She took a closer look at this friendly stranger whom serendipity had brought across their path. He was perhaps forty years old; and, judging from the angle at which even she had to tilt her head to look into his face, tall—probably taller than Matt, who was over six-foot-two at last measurement. He was clean-shaven, although perhaps overdue for a haircut; his madras plaid shirt didn't appear to have been ironed since it came out of the suitcase, yet he wore pleated khaki pants and deck shoes to walk on the beach.

Melissa suddenly realized that no one had spoken in several seconds, and her silence probably sounded like staring. "So! You'll be here through next weekend?"

"I fly home Saturday," he said with an ambiguous sigh. *Relief? Regret?*

"Well. Maybe we'll run into you again."

"I hope so." And the way he emphasized *so* made her believe he meant it.

Melissa signaled "wrap it up" to Jessica and Emily. They poured their goodbyes all over Shanna, and again and again, and after several rounds of that, Melissa nudged them and jerked her head in Kraig's direction.

"Bye—Kraig," they both said.

"Melissa, Jessica, Emily." Kraig bent to pick up the harness handle.

They continued on their way, he on his.

"I'm surprised you remembered his name," Melissa scolded as soon as they were out of hearing range.

"Why? He was cute," Emily said.

"Cute?" Melissa laughed. "I never even saw you look at *him.*"

"Didn't you think he was cute, Jess?"

"Oh, well, yeah, but..." she turned away to hide a smile. "You know, like Mom says, *that's* not what's important."

"Well, he was *nice*, too, wasn't he, Mom?"

"Very nice. And a Christian."

"And from Oregon!" Jessica said. "And he liked you. I could tell."

"That's ridiculous. How could you tell?"

"By the way he shook your hand. *Twice!*"

"He would've shaken your hand, too, if you'd been paying attention."

"We were paying attention," Emily said. "We noticed things. Didn't we, Jess?"

"That's ridiculous," Melissa said again, nearly tripping over a piece of driftwood, but not really believing herself. "I think he's younger, anyway."

"So are you, Mom," Jessica said. "You know what I mean. Everyone says you seem younger."

"Well, okay. But he needed a haircut."

"Mom, that is *so dumb*," Jessica said with the scornful look that all teenagers seem to have practiced to perfection.

Melissa decided not to say anything about the wrinkled shirt, or the oddness of wearing pleated khakis and deck shoes on the beach. *Maybe he's going to church later...maybe he doesn't have a travel iron...maybe I would wear shoes on the beach, too, if I couldn't see to avoid broken shells and beach glass....*

"Well, anyway," Emily said, "that was a really neat dog."

§

Jessica and Emily were still discussing how neat it would be to have a dog like Shanna, or *any* dog, as they stepped back into the dim light of the cottage.

"If I were a dog, I'd want to be a guide dog," said Emily. "I bet he takes such good care of her."

Matt was at the table, eating something out of a crumpled grocery bag he must have brought in his suitcase.

"Morning," Melissa said, attempting cheerfulness.

"Who are you talking about? What dog?"

"Good morning to you too," Jessica said sarcastically.

"We met a man on the beach, and he had a dog, which happened to be a guide dog, and we thought it was a really neat dog." She refused to react to his rudeness, and at this moment it was easier than usual. She turned to the old radio, hoping to find a Sunday sermon being broadcast. As she fiddled with the knobs, the static subsided, music poured forth, and she immediately recognized a song she used to hear on the radio as a girl. She settled into the window seat and let the memories flood over her.

That was before I knew life doesn't always turn out the way you plan.

As the song faded away, Melissa was surprised to see Kraig's face in her imagination. *Broad forehead, deep-set eyes, strong chin.... What color eyes?* She was sure he hadn't been wearing dark glasses, yet she had no impression of eye color. She couldn't complete his face until she knew this, and it bothered her.

"When are we going to the store?" Emily interrupted her thoughts.

7

Melissa sprang from her seat. "We all need to eat something first. I for one want to take a shower. And I need to make a list." She started to leave the room, then remembered her new bag of art supplies. She took out the large drawing pad, opened it to the first page, and set it on the tabletop easel on a small marble-topped table. "There."

§

• Chapter 2 •

Monday morning. A little better than yesterday. But I still missed the sunrise.

The day trip she had planned lured her out of bed—art galleries, craft shops, a museum or two—but first, a walk on the beach, certain to begin her day in her right mind, primed with fresh air and a fresh outlook.

Matt was in his room, studying to get a head start on his fall classes, haven risen and eaten earlier. Jessica and Emily were in the window seat, Jessica reading a book, looking up periodically to gaze intently out the window, and Emily doing nothing *but* gazing intently out the window. Melissa did the breakfast dishes alone, thinking it somewhat unusual that *neither* of them had offered to help with clean-up, but not especially annoyed. *They are on vacation, after all.* For Melissa, washing dishes by hand brought back memories of childhood summers at beach cottages without dishwashers, but Jessica and Emily made no such nostalgic connection.

She thought of the folk art exhibit she would see at one of the museums. Perhaps she would be inspired to lend a folk-art touch to her own seascape. *Especially the clouds. Primitive. Naïve. Innocent. But not too.*

The door leading out to the beach was open, and through the screen drifted the muffled crashing of waves. She could just see the ocean, too, from where she stood. How lovely her daughters looked with the ocean as a backdrop—Jessica, with a storm-blue headband in her hair, the color of strawberry applesauce, and Emily, hers the color of warm honey, now shimmering in the sunshine. Melissa was wondering if perhaps she should try to get Matt interested in a walk on the beach when suddenly Emily jumped from her seat. "There he is!" She bolted for the door. Jessica tossed her book aside and followed, trying not to run.

There who is? Melissa was about to ask, but before she could formulate the question, the answer came to her. *Kraig. Of course.*

Melissa snatched the towel to dry her hands, called to Matt that they were going for a walk, and slipped out, closing the screen door with a screech. In the fraction of a minute it took her to reach the beach stairs, she had time to start worrying. *What if he isn't*

9

really glad to be stopped again? What if he was just being polite yesterday? What if....

From the top of the stairs, she could see Kraig motion toward each girl in turn, and each of them nod in response. While she couldn't hear their exchange, it appeared he was recalling their names correctly. She had an apology all prepared, just in case, but just then Emily turned to her.

"Mom! Look!" Emily bent and hugged Shanna, who probably would have loved to jump all over her new friends, only her thorough training preventing it.

And then, Kraig turned toward Melissa with a smile that nearly outsparkled the sun, reassuring her that he really, truly was glad to have been stopped again.

"Good morning, Kraig."

"Melissa." He held out his hand to her, and he didn't so much shake it as just squeeze it warmly, letting her fingers slip softly out of his grasp.

Jessica gave her a see-I-told-you-so look, and Melissa hoped she didn't look as flustered as she felt. As she mused on the fact that she had now shaken this man's hand for the third time in barely twenty-four hours, it occurred to her that it was probably his favored means of connecting with a world full of people who were, to him, otherwise invisible.

"Were you just starting out, or just getting back?" he asked.

"Just starting out," the three of them said almost in unison.

"Shall we, then?"

"Which way were you going, before we so rudely interrupted you?" Melissa asked.

Kraig laughed. "Not rudely at all. We are most delighted to have company. South."

As he reached for Shanna's harness handle, Melissa saw that he was not only tall, but big—he moved with such grace, the observation came as a surprise. He wore khaki pants again—though not the same pair—with a striped polo shirt. He signaled Shanna forward, Melissa fell into step beside him, and the girls jockeyed for position on Shanna's other side. She soon saw that, as a team, Kraig and Shanna kept up a good pace, and that she'd be getting a workout.

"So," Melissa began, "you're here on vacation; you told me that yesterday. Have you been to Maine before?"

He smiled. "I try to come back every now and then."

"You mean—you used to *live* here?"

"I was *born* here."

"You were? Why did you leave? And when? Do your parents still live here? I'm sorry—too many questions at once."

He laughed again, a warm and reassuring laugh. "Not at all. Starting with the last one—my parents are no longer living. But they *did* live here, after they retired."

"Oh. I'm—"

"No, don't be. They were older. My mom was thirty when she had my brother; nearly forty when I was born."

Melissa set aside her questions for a moment to do the math. *Kraig and his brother must be nine or ten years apart in age...I wonder if he comes from a large family, with a lot of siblings in between.* She filed the question for later.

"Now, your second question. My family left Maine when my brother went away to college. And that leads to your first question— why. There were a lot of things happening at the same time. My dad's business was expanding; he'd started with a vegetable stand, which grew into a corner grocery store, then a chain of small grocery stores, and finally to a major supermarket chain. You'd know of it if you lived in southern California. Also, my parents thought the educational opportunities would be better for me there than in rural Maine. That's where I stayed until I was an adult myself."

"Oh. Wow." The pace of their walking in the shifting sand left Melissa with little breath for conversing. "Were all your ancestors Mainers?"

"My dad's parents were Russian Jews who emigrated here after World War I. So he was a first-generation native Mainer."

"Russian Jews. That reminds me—you haven't told me your last name."

He hesitated only a moment. "Dobrovsky."

"Oh."

"Everybody does that. Then they ask how to spell it."

"Well, it would help if you didn't do it with a Russian accent. But I bet I can figure it out. I was always a good speller." She wavered over whether to use a "v" or a "w" in the middle, but settled on "v" and spelled it out loud.

"I think you're the first person who's ever gotten it right on the first try." He looked genuinely impressed.

Melissa beamed.

"You might have a more difficult time with the way it was before someone shortened it. It used to be *twice* as long."

"Are you serious?"

He laughed. "No. Kidding." He then said nothing, and the silence sounded like a question.

"Melvin. That's my—that was my married name."

"Melissa Melvin. That has a nice sound to it."

"People say that. But I always liked my maiden name better."

"Which was?"

"Crane."

"Melissa Crane. Well, that has a nice sound to it, too."

"Thanks. What about your mom's family?"

"French Canadian, from Quebec." He pronounced it "Kebec." "My parents met in northern Maine, where they were both living then, but settled in southern Maine. That's where I was born, in a rural suburb of Portland."

"Oh. Wow." So absorbed was she that she suddenly realized she'd heard nothing from her daughters for the last half-mile. She looked past Kraig to check on them now. They were neither distracting Shanna nor waiting for a chance to talk. They just smiled back and kept walking.

"Well!" Melissa let out a big breath, lightheaded from all the fascinating tidbits she'd just learned about Kraig. "My story's not nearly so interesting. My ancestors came over on the Mayflower. I'm a sixth-generation Californian, but before that, we came from Maine, and I come here as often as I can, which isn't *nearly* often enough, and now I want to move here."

She half-expected him to announce that he, too, was planning to move back to Maine, to which she would reply, "How nice. We'll move to Maine and we'll already know someone"…but he passed right over the opportunity.

"Don't say that, Melissa. I minored in History. Being able to say your people have been here for almost 400 years is no small thing. So what brings you here now? Family reunion? Genealogical research?"

"A little of that, yes, but mainly it's our last family vacation before Matt leaves for college."

Kraig raised his eyebrows. *Oops!* He didn't yet know about Matt. "I take it Matt doesn't like to go for walks on the beach."

"At home, he runs and goes to the gym. Here, he mostly studies, or gives the appearance of studying. He didn't want to come on this trip, and he doesn't like to travel, and he hates having other people make decisions for him."

"I see." Kraig was quiet, and Melissa wondered if her description of Matt had done some damage to his image of her. She studied his face, and having noticed that his eyes were usually half-closed, she realized it would be difficult to determine eye color.

"So Matt's a runner," Kraig said after a while. "I like to run, too, when I'm at home."

"Oh." Too late to stop it, she heard her "oh" lilt upward, making it sound like a question.

"It's all right to ask me questions, Melissa. My buddy Dave got me into running. He's made my fitness sort of his personal mission. I do owe him, though. I've lost about twenty pounds since I started exercising with him."

Twenty pounds! Even considering Kraig's sturdy frame, a twenty-pound loss must have been significant. She looked again at her daughters; they seemed content to let her hog Kraig's company. "So, what kinds of things do you write for your small, conservative newspaper?"

"Social and political commentary; movie reviews; pieces about movies as social and political commentary. I'm trying to get my column syndicated. And I've had some pieces published in magazines. You may have seen some of them."

"Wow. *Interesting.*"

"It is. But," he said, turning toward her, "I haven't heard what *you* do."

"I'm a graphic artist."

"A *graphic artist.*" He repeated each word as if holding it up to the light for inspection. "Tell me. What exactly do you *do?*"

"I work for a small advertising agency. Logos, letterheads, pamphlets, things like that. We do jobs for a lot of the other small businesses in town."

"That sounds interesting too."

"Yeah, it is."

"But?" he prompted.

"Well, sometimes I wish I'd chosen something…different. I was a good student. I chose art because I enjoyed it. But I could have done something else."

"*Could* have. But does that mean you *should* have?"

"I just never anticipated being the sole support of a family."

"It's important to do something you like."

"Yeah. It's worked out okay."

Kraig suddenly signaled Shanna to stop, and Melissa was relieved to have that conversation be over. He reached for something on his belt, touching its surface with his fingertips. Melissa leaned in for a closer look. "We've walked about a mile," he said, turning the thing toward her, which appeared to be a pedometer with a tactile display. "What do you say we turn around here?"

"Sure, fine," she answered lightly, recognizing that their time together was now half over.

As it turned out, executing a 180-degree turn involving four people and a dog was not exactly simple. She ended up on Kraig's left, with Shanna now in between, and the girls to his right. Melissa thought it wise to alert Kraig to the change, but Jessica beat her to it. "Hey. My turn to talk to Kraig."

Actually, Melissa was a little relieved. She'd noticed as they walked that every time Shanna so much as shifted her ears, Kraig's attention was diverted to her, giving their conversation a fragmented feel and leaving her tired from the effort of maintaining communication.

With the breeze in her ears, and the gentle crashing of waves just a few yards away, Melissa couldn't hear everything Jessica said; yet, from Kraig's responses, she was able to follow the general flow of conversation.

"Four cats!… Yes, I like cats…. No, I don't have any cats right now…. Shanna is six and a half…. I've had her five years…. She's my third guide dog…. No, I don't have any other dogs, just Shanna…. Yes, I think it would be fun to ride a horse on the beach…." So it went, and too soon, they had retraced all of their steps and were again in front of the rented cottage.

Kraig signaled Shanna to sit, and Emily bent to stroke her head and ears.

"Let's go in, Em," Jessica said. "Bye, Kraig."

Emily went without protest, and Melissa sensed a conspiracy to leave her and Kraig alone together. She watched them climb the stairs, sand falling from their sandals with each step, and heard the screen door screech closed.

Kraig sighed in the silence their departure left. "Don't let them grow up too fast."

"It's too late. They already have."

He laughed, then sighed again. "You should be proud."

"I am."

He looked contemplative.

"I hope you didn't mind," Melissa said. "I mean, maybe you wanted to go for a nice, quiet walk."

"Don't be ridiculous. Why would I mind? Shanna's great company, but sometimes the conversation drags."

She laughed, he laughed with her, and as his eyebrows rose and fell, she noticed for the first time a matched pair of tiny scars at the outer corners of his eyes.

"Melissa?"

"Yes?"

He raised his right hand until it was level with her shoulder, then placed it firmly but gently. "Melissa, let's do this again tomorrow. I'd like it. Very much."

"Yeah. Yes. I'd like it, too. *We'd* like it."

His hand slid down her arm to her wrist, where he held her. He turned as if to reach for Shanna's harness handle, yet still held her wrist. He turned back to her. "Melissa?"

"Yes?"

"Instead of meeting here, would you walk down to my place? It's the Wildflower Inn, and it's two-tenths of a mile north of here."

"The Wildflower Inn. Is there a sign facing the beach?"

He looked blank for a moment, then laughed. "I have no idea. But I'll be waiting on the porch. So just go two-tenths of a mile, and look for me on the porch." He still held her wrist. The breeze blew his hair away from his face. "Thank you, Melissa. I'll see you tomorrow." He turned to take Shanna's harness, letting her wrist slip from his hold.

"Bye, Kraig." Melissa turned toward the stairs. *I should have said "thank you" too.*

§

Melissa closed the screen door as quietly as possible behind her and went over to her easel where she'd propped it the day before. She adjusted her drawing pad and opened her pencil box. She turned around, and as her eyes adjusted to the low light of indoors, she saw her daughters in the window seat, both looking expectantly at her.

"Well?" Jessica said.

"Well, *what*?"

"Well, we know you're not going to work on that right now, because you said this morning that we'd leave for the museums and stuff as soon as we got back from our walk. *So*, don't pretend like nothing happened after Em and I came inside."

She joined her daughters in the window seat. "What do you mean, *happened*? He asked us to meet him again tomorrow. Big deal. But—" she lowered her voice, "there's something wrong here."

"What do you mean?"

"No man *that nice* flies all the way across the country, just to take a vacation, all by himself, for no particular reason."

Jessica gave her the that-is-so-dumb look.

"No, really. First of all, what does he do with the rest of his day? Not drive around sightseeing, like us, *obviously*. Maybe—maybe he's visiting someone. And, he shows no interest whatsoever in my personal life. How does he know I'm not married or something? Which makes me think it doesn't matter. Which means either—"

"Mom," Jessica interrupted, "get a grip."

"Yeah, really." Emily added. "You don't know what we told him when you weren't there."

Jessica elbowed Emily.

Melissa went back to her art bag and put the pencil case away.

§

Chapter 3

Tuesday morning broke mostly sunny and clear, with just the right chill to remind Melissa that she was in Maine. A lively breeze filled the sails of two sailboats on the water and pushed her along as she turned north. Anxious not to upset the morning's plans, Melissa was tempted to get an early start on finding Kraig's place. Yet, she reasoned with herself, if she started *too* early, he might not be waiting yet, and she'd miss him.

Unsure exactly how far two-tenths of a mile was, she slowed down after the first few inns and cottages and began peering up staircases and onto porches. After a few minutes, one inn looked particularly promising. As she drew closer, she could see the familiar man-and-dog team near the top of the stairs. Kraig appeared to be talking to Shanna, and as the dog noticed her approach, she picked up her ears and began to wiggle. Kraig turned toward the beach.

"Good morning, Kraig," Melissa called out as she mounted the stairs.

"Melissa," he answered. His unselfconscious smile awakened in her a joy that had so long lain dormant that she'd forgotten about it, and she felt herself break into a spontaneous grin of her own.

"Hi, Shanna." Melissa stopped and petted the dog. Kraig reached for her hand, and when she gave it to him, he took it in both of his. It was then that she saw that Shanna had only the lead, without the harness, its loop around Kraig's wrist.

"Melissa, I hope you don't mind, but I thought we could talk more easily as we walk if I'm not focusing on working with Shanna."

Wishing she could think of something wordier than "Sure," as she rather liked the feel of his hands around hers, and did not want him to let go, she began to stammer. "Yes. Sure. Just, you know, tell me what I'm supposed to do."

He chuckled. "You'll be fine. Just remember, you are the eyes for two people." He slipped his hand into the crook of her left arm and urged her toward the stairs, about a half step behind. He looked more prepared for a beach walk today, wearing a dusty-teal polo shirt and gray corduroy jeans. It was the first time she'd seen him in anything more casual than pleated khakis.

In front of the cottage, where Jessica and Emily waited, Melissa could discern smugness on Jessica's face. When Jessica began gesturing in American Sign Language, Melissa made out the word "cute" before turning away for fear of bursting into giggles. How cute Kraig was, or how cute they looked arm-in-arm, she wasn't sure.

"I want to go first," Emily said, as soon as Kraig offered the lead up for grabs.

"O-*kay*," Jessica said, rolling her eyes.

"Is there anything they need to know, Kraig?" Melissa asked.

"When she's not working, she's just a dog. I'm sure you know how to walk a dog."

"Sure, we walk our neighbors' dogs sometimes," Emily said.

"Great. Just never let go of the lead."

Without Shanna to set the pace, Melissa did her best to maintain the same speed as the day before. Kraig turned his face to the breeze and inhaled deeply, his face reflecting her own sense of wonder. "Tell me what the ocean looks like this morning, Melissa."

"Oh...." She thought of her empty sheet of canvas paper back at the cottage. "Just acres and acres of blue, stretching out to the horizon. And beyond."

"Ah. Just the way I remember it."

When she turned to look at him, positioned between her and the sea, the hue of his shirt blended pleasingly with the palette of the seascape behind him. "What do you like to do, Kraig? Besides walk on the beach?"

"Mm. Good subject. I like music. And I like to take care of the babies in the church nursery." He turned toward her, his eyebrows raised, and leaned closer. "You're surprised."

"No. Not surprised, really. I..." she chuckled. "I like that." She looked at his hand on her arm. *Big, strong...yet supple and dexterous.* She couldn't help smiling. "What about the music? Do you play an instrument? Or sing?"

"Mostly sing. In the church choir."

"Wow. I always wished I could sing. You're...." She was going to say "so lucky" but changed her mind.

"We can't all have the same gifts now, can we? I'll never be a graphic artist."

"No, I guess not." She laughed, leaning into him, surprising even herself at how relaxed she was by the easy flow of conversation. He was right—it was much easier to converse without his continual interactions with Shanna. She looked back at the girls. "Jessica and Emily seem to be doing fine with Shanna."

"Of course."

"Do you ever sing solo?"

"Yes. Sometimes." Something in the smile he turned away from her made her believe this response was delivered with a hefty dose of modesty.

"Hey—I don't suppose you happen to have any recordings with you—of one of your solos?"

He frowned. "Hmm. I might. I have some CDs in my briefcase, back at the inn. I use them to practice songs the choir will be doing. Yes, I probably have a solo on one of them."

"I'd like to hear it. If you don't mind."

"No. I don't mind. We can do that when we get back this morning."

Melissa searched for a clue as to whether this was an acceptable request, but found nothing.

"What about you?" he said. "What will you be doing this week—besides walk on the beach?"

"I'd like to fill my time here with as much hiking, biking, and canoeing as possible."

"And?"

She looked at him, surprised.

"You're an artist, Melissa. I don't believe *all* your hobbies are outdoorsy things."

"Well, I like to eat out. And go to art museums. I love the American realist painters and folk artists. Especially landscapes and seascapes of Maine."

"Those artists and their work have been invaluable in recording the history of Maine. Especially before cameras were around. Don't let *me* keep you from enjoying the visual arts, Melissa."

Melissa was beginning to get the feeling that very little ever escaped Kraig's notice, and she vowed never again to make a fool of herself by trying to withhold anything from him.

"What kinds of music do you like?" he asked.

Melissa took a deep breath, certain that this was a matter of great weight, and eager to please him with her answer. "Oh, well, I like pretty much any nice, uplifting music." She looked at him; he was clearly expecting more.

He nodded a little.

Disappointed, Melissa looked down at her feet and decided not to ask what *he* liked. Her steps were matched with his for a while, but his strides were longer, and eventually she fell out of step with him. Several more steps, and they were again walking in sync. A long moment later, her curiosity got the better of her. "Okay, what do *you* like?"

He nodded. "I like nice, uplifting music too. But I'll tell you what I *really* like." He turned toward her, and she held her breath. "I like dramatic music, anything with a high emotional content. Hymns, traditional Jewish music, gospel, opera, *love songs*. Nothing held back. Music with honesty and depth, the kind that brings tears to your eyes." He took a deep breath, held it, and let it out. He appeared to search for other words and not find them. He leaned closer, squeezing her arm a little. "Do you know what I mean, Melissa?"

She then realized her error. In her effort to provide the "right" answer, she had failed to show any enthusiasm at all. "Yes. I see."

He seemed pleased at last, and Melissa reflected on how, in just over two days, Kraig had begun to feel like an old friend. She discovered from one minute to the next how much they had in common, and it was so much easier to talk with him holding her arm, their words reaching one another's ears before the breeze could blow them away. He'd graduated from a small Catholic college in southern California, she learned, where he'd majored in English with a minor in American History; he'd written for the school newspaper and sung in the men's choir.

"Don't you ever think of moving back to Maine?" Melissa asked.

"I have. Many times. Especially right after my divorce."

Melissa tried not to react to this little revelation about Kraig's past. Yet she couldn't help wonder. *Who? When? Why?* "Well, maybe you will some day."

"Maybe I will." He slowed and stopped, slipping his right hand free to check the pedometer. "This is the turnaround spot, isn't it?"

"Yes." She sighed, in spite of herself, but noted that he sounded as reluctant as she felt.

He turned his head one way, then the other. "Where are they? I don't hear them."

She turned, and saw Jessica, Emily, and Shanna ambling more or less in their direction. "They're coming." Just then Melissa noticed something colorful near her feet. She held Kraig's hand while she stooped to pick up a piece of beach glass. "Look at this." She opened his hand and placed the bit of glass in his palm.

He caressed it with his fingers. "Almost perfectly smooth. What color is it?"

"Aqua."

He seemed to muse over the word, and Melissa wondered if he had any idea of what color meant. "You can tell a lot about beach glass by the color," he said. "What it originally contained, and when it was produced. Some beach glass that started out clear became colored with time because of the metallic additives."

"Really! I have a huge collection of it at home, but I didn't know that."

"You should keep it." He cradled her hand in his, pressed the glass into it, and closed her fingers around it. He put his hand over hers; his nails were smooth and trim.

"Hi," Jessica said, feigning breathlessness. "You guys walk fast. Okay, tell Emily it's my turn for Shanna."

Emily appeared in no hurry to catch up and turn over Shanna's lead to Jessica. She stopped a step short, leaving Jessica to reach for the lead.

"Emily," Melissa scolded. "Remember, that is not your dog."

Jessica snapped the lead from Emily's grasp, rolling her eyes.

"Okay, then, it's my turn to talk to Kraig," Emily suggested.

"Fair enough," he agreed.

Good thing he's a good listener, Melissa thought as they turned around and resumed walking.

Again too soon, they were back in front of the rented cottage. Jessica handed the lead back to Kraig.

"You've done a fine job, girls," he said, as they turned to head inside. Quiet fell again.

"Well, now you've had the full treatment," Melissa said, by way of apology.

"No. No. They're delightful. Articulate, animated…."

"Just say it. *Talkative.*"

Kraig laughed, a laugh that warmed her all over like splashes of sunshine.

He was standing close to her, his eyes half open as usual. *Gray-green. His eyes are gray-green.* Remembering her blank canvas, Melissa wondered if she had a watercolor pencil just that color, and what its name would be. She realized she still needed to walk him back to his place.

"Melissa?"

"Hmm?"

"Forgive me for saying so, but…you don't seem that old. Old enough to have a grown son, I mean."

Melissa cleared her throat. "Well, that's because I'm older than you think. Not because I dropped out of high school to get married. I…I'm sure I'm older than you."

"I'll be thirty-nine in October."

"I'm forty-five."

No reaction whatsoever. What a gentleman.

"You look younger," he said after a moment.

She felt her face turn pink. "Well, everyone says that, and I always feel like I have to tell people how hold I am, so they don't think—"

"I'm sorry. I didn't mean—"

"No, it's okay. But how—"

"You have a youthful voice, and you're tall and fit."

"Okay."

He chuckled, as if reading her unspoken question. "Well, we've been walking quite fast, and talking, and you've never been out of breath. And I've had my hand on your arm for almost an hour."

It occurred to Melissa that, with his hand where it was, those times when she pulled her arm in close to her side bordered on intimate contact. Now she was sure she had turned full red, and was glad he couldn't see it. "Okay, then. How tall *am* I?"

He put his hand on her shoulder, then touched her chin. "Five-foot-ten."

"With sandals on, that'd be just about right."

He turned his face to the breeze again, and it blew his hair away from his broad forehead, giving him a rugged, boyish look. "Melissa?"

She had to clear her throat again. "Yes?"

"After I've known someone for a while, I begin to have an idea of what they look like. But I'm not always right. I like to find out before I get the wrong picture in my mind."

What else is there to tell? "Brunette," she offered.

He held out his hands, palms turned slightly upward. "May I?"

All at once she understood. Taking his hands in hers, she guided them to her face. His fingertips furrowed her hair at the temples, his thumbs on her eyebrows, and then his fingers glided over her face with the gentlest pressure. His fingers came to rest on her lips, and she willed them not to tremble. Suddenly aware that she had been holding her breath, she forced herself to breathe, too, and when she inhaled, she took in the moist, salty, clean smell of a morning shower followed by a walk on the beach.

She studied his face for a reaction. The corners of his mouth turned up just a little, and he sighed. *What does that mean? Can he really tell what I look like? Is he pleased? Does it matter?*

"The CD," she said, remembering suddenly. "I'd like to hear it. If you don't mind."

He nodded and drew her arm around to turn her northward.

"You could do that with the girls, too—seeing what they look like. They'd get a kick out of it."

In the deep porch of his inn, he handed her Shanna's lead and directed her toward a table with chairs. He slipped inside through the French doors and, returning a moment later, slid a leather briefcase onto the table. As he snapped it open, she noticed the brass initials on it—KBD.

"Oh—I didn't know you spelled your name with a K."

"Yes. My brother, Kevin, is almost ten years older. Maybe my parents thought we'd have more in common if we had the same initials." It sounded sort of like a joke, but there was an ironic edge to Kraig's voice that suggested some mixed feelings about Kevin.

"Do you have other siblings?"

"No. Just Kevin."

"Where does Kevin live now?"

Kraig pulled out a wicker chair and sat opposite her. "He stayed in L.A. He's a personal injury attorney. A *big, successful* one." The words did not convey much admiration.

Melissa chuckled in spite of herself. "I was just thinking. I'm not sure if 'Dobrovsky' fits into one of those long law-firm names."

"He changed it. It's Kevin B. Dobb, Attorney-at-Law."

"Oh."

"My parents weren't happy about that. But Kevin does as he pleases."

"Oh. I see." Sensing that this was a touchy subject, she searched for something else to talk about while he sorted through some CDs. "What does the B stand for?"

"Kevin doesn't *have* a middle name. It *was* a family name, from my dad's side. But he legally changed it to 'B'."

"Oh. But I meant *yours*."

He smiled a half-smile. "It's a family name, from my mom's side."

"Something French?"

"Yes. Maybe I'll tell you some time." His fingers paused on the Braille label on one of the CDs. "Aha. Here's one." He lifted a CD player out of the briefcase, snapped in the CD, pushed buttons until he found the right spot.

The intro gave way to the vocal, and a rich tenor voice filled the air with a song that she had heard once, many years before.

"This is you?"

"You're surprised."

"No! Not surprised. I—I'm—I'm awed. You're very good." She closed her eyes and let his voice be the only thing in her consciousness. She opened them just in time to see his hand hovering over the "stop" button. "Please." She put her hand on his wrist and gently moved it away. "I want to hear all of it."

He moved his hand away.

"Wow. Thanks," was all she could think of to say when it ended.

She thought she detected a faint smile as he put his briefcase back in order, clicked it shut, and slid it out of the way. He didn't appear eager to have her leave.

Melissa took a deep breath and held it. "Tell me about Kevin." *Either he will, or he won't, and either way, I'll learn something about Kraig.*

"There isn't much to tell. He's too busy being successful to be a part of my life. The last time my parents saw him, he put them up in a luxury hotel suite in some elite section of L.A. They saw him exactly twice—when he picked them up at the airport, and when he took them back." Kraig was quiet for a moment. "I found out later, it was because he didn't want them to know he'd become separated from his wife. But still. He could have handled it differently.

"And *then*, after my parents had died, Kevin invited *me* to go on a trip with him to Russia. At *his* expense. He hadn't taken a vacation in years. Why did he wait so long? *After* my parents died, mind you, not while they were still living. My dad would have loved a trip like that."

"Did you go?"

"No. I wrote him a letter with my answer. In Russian." He then reeled off a sentence or two of Russian, which Melissa took to be an excerpt from the letter. "I was angry, Melissa. Kevin messed up, and I was not about to enable him to use me to assuage his guilt. I never found out whether he went to the trouble of translating my letter, but he never brought it up again."

She watched his face, not daring to speak until his eyebrows relaxed and his mouth returned to a soft line.

"I'm sorry. That sounds difficult."

"There are much nicer things to talk about than Kevin." He looked thoughtful. "I do have to give him credit for one thing, though. He always managed to maintain the appearance of a marriage while my parents were living. Even after he'd separated from Carol, they never knew." He paused, but Melissa didn't dare speak. "Perhaps it wasn't the most honest way to deal with it. But I'm glad they didn't know. It would have hurt them deeply. They'd set a good example. Somehow, neither of us got it right."

Melissa put her hand on his wrist, just above his watch. His ring finger bore no imprint of a wedding band; it must have been some time. "Hey, cancel the guilt trip. How long has it been, anyway?"

"Fifteen years."

"Fifteen *years*?" It was incomprehensible that this warm, sensitive, delightful man could have remained single for so long. "I think you've served your guilt sentence. Guilt has its place, but after a while, you just have to forgive *yourself* and move on. Believe me. I know."

"Tell me, where does guilt come into being a widow?"

Melissa was stunned. *How did he know? Is this what Jessica and Emily told him? How could they have had time to explain everything?*

She let go of his wrist before her fingers had a chance to turn clammy. "It's a long story. I'll tell you some time. It was never a good marriage, I'll tell you that much. More like a slow death. Sometimes closure is better than slow death, whatever—whatever and however."

Melissa watched his face for a long time, his eyes half closed, his lips parted ever so slightly.

"Um, Kraig," she said, eager to change the subject. "Um, I don't know if you have a lot of things planned this week or not, but I was thinking, we have a rental car, and we go out and do things every day, and tomorrow we're planning to do some sightseeing in Fog Harbor. I'd like to invite you to come with us."

"Art galleries?" he asked with a mischievous smile.

"Uh, no. But lunch, yes, and maybe a boat ride."

"And what would your kids say?"

"Oh, well, the girls would *love* to have you come along. And Matt—*if* I can get him to go—well, sometimes we just don't worry about what Matt says."

"I see. In that case, I'd love to."

"Oh, and I was thinking, too, that since we'll be doing a lot of walking in Fog Harbor, the girls and I probably won't go for a walk in the morning. But if you need to exercise Shanna at a particular time, we can be flexible."

"I'll work it out. Name the time, and I'll be ready."

"Nine-thirty?"

"Nine-thirty. I'll be ready."

Saddened as she was by the idea of missing her beach walk with Kraig, it seemed wise not to invite some misunderstanding or unsettling revelation that might come up in conversation to cast any dark clouds over a potentially perfect day.

"Oh—one more thing. I'd like to take a look out front, so I can recognize this place from the road."

"Certainly. I'll walk you through."

Inside the French doors, Kraig unleashed Shanna and pointed the way to the front door. He moved around with ease, even without Shanna's guidance. When Melissa returned from looking out front, she found him standing next to a bookcase, the fingers of one hand resting thoughtfully on the edge of a shelf. She went over and stood before him.

"Melissa," he said, raising his head only a little, "have you ever done this before?"

She looked at him, waiting for an explanation. When none was forthcoming, she was puzzled for a moment, then understood. *He wants to know if I've ever had a blind friend.* She looked out the window at the lightening sky. *I should be getting back.* She turned back toward Kraig, but didn't raise her eyes to his face. "No."

"You seem very at ease."

"Oh, well, I—" she stammered, flustered at the unexpected compliment. "I just—why wouldn't I be?"

"You'd be amazed, Melissa. Most people find it awkward, at least at first."

"I find that hard to believe."

"That's because you're naïve. And I mean that kindly," he added quickly. "As a compliment. I'd like to see more of that kind of innocence. Instead of the other side of human nature."

Melissa just nodded.

He laughed softly, perhaps sensing her perplexity, and his laugh put her at ease again. He held out his hand, not as for a handshake, but palm-up. She placed her hand on his. "Melissa, you just keep being yourself. And expect nothing less than total honesty from me." He pressed her hand between his two, and the warmth that spread through her almost brought tears to her eyes. She had an urge to leave quickly, before her confused emotions got the better of her, but he was still holding her hand tightly, and she did not really want him to let go. "I'll see you tomorrow," he said at last, opening his hands.

She wasn't sure how long she'd been standing there, her hand still on his, free to go. "Yeah. Yes. See you tomorrow. Goodbye, Kraig."

Melissa broke into a run as she reached the sand, certain that her daughters would be wondering what had happened to her. Kraig's words tumbled around in her mind as she tried to make sense of them. *What exactly was he trying to say?*

She fingered the piece of beach glass she'd stuck in her pocket. The memory of his hands around hers sent warm shivers all over her.

In a flash of understanding, everything made sense. *It's the touching. It's because he's blind.* Along with the knowledge of mutual romantic availability came a certain responsibility, and he did not want this so-far innocent touching to become a license for inappropriate behavior. *That's all.* At the foot of the cottage steps, she took a few deep breaths, raked her fingers through her hair, and paced herself to arrive at the door completely collected.

Inside, no one seemed to have noticed her long absence. Someone had turned on the radio. Jessica looked up from her book, briefly, with an expression of studied disinterest. Emily appeared to be drawing in Melissa's small sketchbook. "I hope you don't mind, Mom. I'm drawing all of our cats."

"So, are we going sea kayaking?" Jessica asked, without even looking up this time.

"Sure. You could go get ready. I need to talk to Matt."

She went and tapped lightly on his closed door, unsure whether he would even hear it over all his electronic gadgetry. "Matt?" She opened the door a crack to see him sitting on his bed, plugged into music, laptop computer before him. "Yeah," he answered, without looking up.

"We're going out in a little while."

"You're not expecting me to come." It wasn't framed as a question.

"No, I'm not. *But*—Matt, could you take out the earbuds for a minute?—when we go out tomorrow, I *do* expect you to come. *And* I invited someone to go with us."

He paused his music, leaving the earbuds in. "You *invited* someone. *How? We don't know* anyone here."

"We—the girls and I—met a guy on the beach. We told you. The guy with the dog."

He yanked out the earbuds. "Let me see if I have this right. You invited a *total stranger*, and a *dog*, to go on an all-day outing with us."

"Okay, if you want to put it that way, but what's your point?"

"There won't be room for five people—*and a dog*—in the rental car. I don't mind not going." He reached for the "play" button.

"Wait. You *like* dogs, remember? You were the one who always—"

"Okay, I like dogs. That doesn't mean I want to ride in the car with one. Dogs smell and drool."

"Matt," Melissa said, keeping her voice steady, "I want you to come, and I expect you to be polite."

Matt shrugged. "Yeah. Whatever." He put the earbuds in and pressed "play."

"The girls and I are leaving in a few minutes," Melissa said, her voice rising to be heard. "See you later." She closed the door.

In the privacy of the sleeping porch, Melissa sighed deeply as she jerked open a dresser drawer to find something to wear sea kayaking. *There's something behind this, of course.*

Jeff.

Jeff had been a lay youth leader at church; Melissa had met him through Matt. Auburn-haired, boyish and athletic, a natural leader among kids, but with a shyness that made him irresistible, Melissa had liked him immediately. And things had gone very well…for a while. Matt had always given himself credit for bringing Jeff into their lives, and never let Melissa forget it wasn't *his* fault Jeff had left.

As if it's mine.

"Mom, Jessica and I are ready. Is this outfit okay?"

Melissa turned to see Emily standing in the doorway. "Yes, that's fine, and if we don't get going, we're going to run out of daytime."

"So, does Matt have a problem?" Jessica asked as they gathered at the door.

"Yeah. We'll talk about it in the car."

She turned to open the door, and her daughters almost bumped into her as she stopped abruptly. "Wait. I have to do *one thing* before I forget what the sky looked like this morning." She went over to her art bag, took out her new box of watercolor pencils, and selected a few shades of blue, lavender, and gray. *Oh—and this gray-green one. Perfect!* She set them aside so she wouldn't forget.

§

Chapter 4

When Wednesday morning's first rays of sunlight burst into the sleeping porch, it seemed to Melissa that sleep had come only a few moments before. She had gone to bed early enough, pleasantly fatigued from a half day of kayaking, but the roiling of disturbing thoughts had kept her mind active most of the night.

First, Matt didn't want to go. "I didn't want to come on this trip in the first place," he'd reminded her so many times that it played like a tape loop. "I could have saved you a lot of money. There are a lot of things I'd rather do...." And so on, and so on.

Then there was Matt's prejudice against Kraig, which would put her in the awkward position of impartial mediator.

Finally, there was the seating arrangement for the day's outing. She could let Matt drive; that would give him something to do. But she definitely didn't want to force upon Kraig Matt's unwilling company by seating him in the front passenger seat. Yet, with his height, what choice was there?

Maybe Matt was right. Maybe this is all a bad idea. Five people and a dog won't fit in the car, we will all be miserable, the day will be a disaster, and Kraig won't want to see us again. And another thing—he is, in fact, a stranger.

Such was her state of mind when they pulled into the driveway of Kraig's inn later that morning. "You guys stay here. I'll go get him," she said, almost *expecting* an argument.

She had hit upon a possible solution some time in the wee hours of the morning. Sacrificing her own comfort, she would slide the front passenger seat all the way forward and seat him behind her. "I thought you'd enjoy sitting with my lovely daughters," she said now, holding the door for him. "Matt will be driving. I hope you and Shanna will be comfortable enough."

"It's not a problem, Melissa. We do this all the time." He climbed in, called Shanna after him, tucked in her tail, and closed the door.

Melissa heaved a sigh of relief and determined to ignore her own discomfort as she squeezed into her seat, her knees against the dashboard. She began to relax, listening to the easy conversation going on in the back seat. She marveled at how quickly Kraig had learned to distinguish the girls' voices. *Sometimes I can't even tell them apart!*

"Who named Shanna?"

"That's a good question, Jessica. Guide dogs come to us already named. The mother dog's host family makes suggestions. Shanna's siblings were Savannah, Simpson, and Samuel."

"Do guide dogs always have people names?"

"No, Emily, sometimes they have names like Legend or Rocket."

"Rocket! That's a kooky name for a dog. Why do some guide dogs have such kooky names?"

"Well, no two guide dogs can have the same name, so sometimes they run out of names that aren't kooky."

In no time at all, Matt was parking the car in downtown Fog Harbor.

§

"Whatever you ladies want to do is fine with me. I'm just enjoying the company," was Kraig's typical response to her inquiries about what he would like. She watched him closely for signs that he might be becoming jaded or impatient. He *seemed* to be having a good time, and she began to think that perhaps she wasn't interfering with whatever other plans he might have had, after all.

Matt, on the other hand, generally stood in one spot—usually on the sidewalk outside of whatever establishment the rest of them were in—listening to his music, exploring all the capabilities of his cell phone, making alterations on his pocket organizer. *At least he's keeping busy.*

"I see a place we need to go," Melissa said. "This place will have things that smell good, and the sign says they have gourmet fudge."

She watched Kraig's face as he took several deep breaths of the fragrant atmosphere. She wondered what memories were being revived by the blueberry, balsam, and other Maine smells. She wondered if there was enough power in them to make him feel the yearning of moving back. "Wait a minute," she said, having a sudden inspiration just as they were leaving. She hurried back inside, took care of some business, and caught up with the others.

Over lunch, Kraig was telling about a movie review he'd recently had published. "It's a good illustration of how the male and female leads in a movie don't have to be, shall I say, romantically involved in order to have an interesting relationship. The chemistry is obvious, but above all, the relationship is one of mutual admiration. The movie makes a special point of showing us that the couple *isn't* sleeping together. It's rather refreshing."

Out of the corner of her eye, Melissa could see Matt gesturing to get her attention. She ignored him for a while, but the girls were losing their struggles against fits of giggles, much as they wouldn't dream of making Kraig uncomfortable.

"Yes, Matt?"

He began to sign something in American Sign Language. Melissa concentrated as the question unfolded. "How...does...he...see...movies...if...he...is...blind?"

Of course, this type of question was inevitable. "Matt, I don't think Kraig knows sign language. He knows some other languages, though, so how about we choose a language everyone knows. Like English."

Matt said nothing.

"Kraig, Matt was asking about your work as a movie critic. Could you—"

Kraig seemed to have heard the question before. "Movie theaters have special decoding equipment you can borrow. Newer television sets have this feature, too. You wear a headset to receive a narration track that explains anything you might otherwise miss."

"Oh. Wow." The girls looked impressed, and it occurred to Melissa that a person would probably have to be fairly intelligent to follow a movie in this way.

Matt didn't seem to be paying attention.

When Melissa thanked the server for the check, Kraig reached for Melissa's arm and tried to slip it from her grasp.

"Oh, no," she protested.

"I insist." He peeled her fingers loose. "I'm having so much more fun than I would just sitting around the inn with Shanna." He pulled out his wallet and removed a credit card from it. "Would you do something for me?" He handed the card to Melissa. "Place it so the top edge is even with the signature line." He then signed his name, using the edge of the card as a guide.

"Thanks," Melissa said feebly. "Hey, there's a 45-minute harbor cruise that I thought would be fun. We have just enough time to get there." She turned to Kraig and whispered, "And you can keep your credit card in your wallet for the rest of the day. I wouldn't want you to think we invited you along so you'd pay for everything."

He just smiled.

Settling into her seat on the boat, Melissa found herself sandwiched between Kraig on her left, and Jessica, then Emily, on her right. Matt found a seat in another part of the boat.

"Squeeze closer, Mom, it's crowded," Emily said.

Melissa slid as close to Kraig as she could, her elbow settling into the crook of his arm, then looked for Emily's okay. Then she did a double-take—there was plenty of room on Emily's other side. Emily managed not to giggle out loud, and Melissa decided to stay where she was.

"Melissa, would you do something for me?" Kraig asked, holding out his right hand to show her a large splinter embedded in his palm. "I got it from the railing."

"Ouch. That's a big one. But I've done this before. Just tell me if I'm hurting you."

"I'm not worried."

Melissa massaged the skin until she had worked the splinter out far enough to grasp it with her fingernails. "There!"

He flexed his hand. "Much better. Thank you." At rest in his lap, his hands could have been the work of a Renaissance sculptor. Yet, when pressed into service, they commanded all five senses. *No wonder he can read Braille and rock babies to sleep!*

As the boat chugged away from the dock, Kraig closed his eyes, or so it appeared. Melissa closed hers, too, wanting to share whatever it was he was experiencing. She felt him breathe deeply and did likewise. *Oh, yes. There is nothing more evocative than the smell of the sea.*

"Did you hear that, Mom?" Emily shouted over the wind and the roar of the engine. "The guide said we might see eagles, ospreys, seals, and porpoises."

Well...I wouldn't want to miss that. She opened her eyes again, and looked out at the little islands bumping up from the horizon, dark and expressionistic, their pointy evergreens growing right down to the water's edge. She thought of her still-blank artist's pad back at the cottage.

§

Back at the car later that afternoon, Kraig pulled Melissa aside. "Melissa, you can't have been very comfortable up there. Why don't you let one of the girls ride in front on the way back?"

Jessica, overhearing, volunteered.

A deep satisfaction, mixed with relief, engulfed Melissa on the drive back. None of her fears had been realized: she was sure Kraig had had a good time, Matt hadn't caused too much trouble, and, yes, she almost certainly would see Kraig again. *All that lost sleep for nothing!* Her sense of peace, and the motion of the car, lulled her into a profound relaxation.

§

"There it is, Matt." Jessica's voice coming from before her jolted her awake. They were in front of Kraig's inn. To her chagrin, Melissa saw that she'd dozed off and was leaning heavily on Kraig's shoulder. He must not have minded, however; he'd adjusted his position to favor her comfort.

"Turn off the engine, Matt. I'll be back in a minute." She stepped from the car, grabbing her daypack. "Be sure to wash your hand carefully, where I took out the splinter," she reminded Kraig, following him inside.

He nodded.

"Which room is yours?"

He turned and gestured toward the room nearest the kitchen.

"May I see it?"

He didn't answer, but dug the key from his pocket and unlocked the door.

"Oh, lupines!" she said, swinging the door open. "I love lupines. They're maybe my second-favorite flower, after irises. What gorgeous shades of purple, blue, and green."

"They told me it was called the Lupine Room," he said. "Now I know why."

35

He was sort of squeezing her out of the way as he pulled the door closed, which seemed rather strange, until it occurred to her that her being in his room was making him uncomfortable. She stepped out of the way. "I have something for you."

"Melissa," he scolded.

"No, you'll like this." She pulled the little pillow from her daypack and pressed it into his hands, squeezing them around it.

"Balsam," he sighed with an unexpected intensity as the woodsy aroma worked its magic.

"I thought you'd like something to remind you of Maine once you got home."

"I will. Thank you. And for inviting me today. I enjoyed myself…more than you know."

"I'm glad you came. I'll see you tomorrow…here."

Matt was rolling down the window as she approached the car. "Gosh, how long does it take to baby a splinter wound and say goodbye?"

§

• Chapter 5 •

Thursday morning. My second-to-last day of knowing that Kraig is just down the beach.

Standing on the porch as usual, he looked so at home against the classic Maine backdrop, the sea breeze ruffling his light brown hair with its faintest hint of gray and a bit of natural wave.

"Good morning, Kraig."

"Melissa."

She reached for his hand to receive his warm welcome squeeze. He wore a monogrammed polo shirt and moderately worn charcoal gray jeans. His casual attire suited his comfortably large build, which she just now found a way to describe. *Huggable. Not muscle-bound...not portly...just huggable.*

"I like your shirt. That's a good color on you."

He put his hand to his chest. "Thank you. My 'plum heather' shirt." He looked thoughtful again. "Melissa, tell me. What does 'heather' mean? Is that a color?"

"Not really. It just means it has little specks of some other color in it. Like jeans. They always have little white specks in them."

"Oh." He laughed softly. "I remember what a plum looks like, so I supposed 'plum' meant some shade of purple. 'Heather' was a mystery, though." He laughed again. "Thanks for explaining that to me."

"Sure. Well, *someone* with good taste must be involved with your wardrobe. I noticed that right away."

"Ah, yes. Helen," he said with undisguised affection.

"Helen?" Melissa tried to sound nonchalant.

"An older lady at church. She does all manner of wonderful things for me; not just help with grocery shopping and choosing clothes, but noticing when some dust bunny under my bed is getting to be the size of a—a *real* bunny, or when some forgotten leftover in the back of my refrigerator is beginning to look like a science experiment. And when I need a new shirt. Or a haircut." He stopped and ran his fingers through his hair. "That's one thing I meant to do before this trip. But I had to take Shanna to the vet unexpectedly. It turned out to be nothing, really. But things became a little tense in the final preparations for this trip, and I didn't want to go until I was sure Shanna was all right." He stroked the leather of Shanna's lead between his fingers. The corners of his mouth turned up into a smile again at a more pleasant thought.

"Once I was changing the battery in my watch, and I dropped the new one on the kitchen floor. I searched all over. Shanna was no help. I had little choice but to call Helen. She came right over and found it in a crack at the edge of the vinyl flooring. She says her eyesight isn't very good, but what can I say? It's better than mine. She has such a servant's heart. I don't know what I'd do without her."

"Well. *That* must be nice. *I* drop things all the time," Melissa said with a breeziness she hoped didn't sound as forced as it was. "Shall we walk?"

As she started down the steps with the familiar, comfortable feel of Kraig's hand on her arm, she mulled over the less-than-pleasing thought that Kraig had just made the longest speech of their acquaintance, and the subject was another woman—"older" though she may be. *What am I to think about this Helen? What does "older" mean? I'm older too!* Melissa reminded herself that she really knew next to nothing about Kraig, including why he was here, and that she should be careful of investing too much emotionally in him; or, more foolishly, sketching him into her future in Maine.

It's too late. I already have.

"Ah, it's a glorious Maine day, isn't it?" Kraig said as they stepped into the sand and turned south. She caught a glimpse of his eyes. *Gray-green, one of the many moods of the unpredictable sea.* "Are the girls coming?"

"Yes. They're in front of the cottage, and it looks like they're going to make us hurry to catch up." She sneaked a sideways glance at him, pushing disturbing thoughts toward the back of her mind. *At this moment, he's here, with me.* "I've been thinking, Kraig. You're a writer. You could live anywhere, right? So why have you never moved back to Maine?"

"Well, Melissa, that's a short question with a long answer."

"We have time."

He took a deep breath and let it out. "When I finished college, my parents were ready to retire, and they moved back here that year. I'd planned to go with them; I'd always assumed I'd come back here to live. But...then I thought it might be a good time to do something different. So, I decided to move to New Orleans. That's where the French Canadians went after being driven out of Maine and the Maritimes, and that's how the Cajun culture began—the Acadians became the Cajuns. In case you didn't know.

"Anyway, I was immediately drawn into the lifestyle. Oh, Melissa, the food, the music, the language. If you haven't been there, you ought to go sometime. Later, I saw it all as so worldly, but at the time, it was very exciting. I got a job singing in this establishment that had live entertainment. That's where I met Celeste—my former wife. She was the manager of this place, and she hired me on the spot. There was a definite chemistry between us. She was French Canadian, petite buxom blonde...an incredible cook. I soon learned to love Cajun cuisine, and I do to this day.... Are you still with me, Melissa?"

"Yeah, go on."

"Well, I was raised conservative Catholic and Jewish, and I knew better, but I'm as human as the next guy. The truth is, *she* came on to *me*. I share the blame, I know. But I had the distinct disadvantage of not seeing it coming—literally—and...Melissa, I do not now, nor did I then, believe that this scenario is ever excusable, but..." he was clearly struggling with how much to tell. "She engineered a very vulnerable situation for me, and before I knew what was happening, we had done it. If you had been there, Melissa, you would understand how difficult this was for me."

She was beginning to understand why moving back to Maine was such a loaded topic.

"I thought I loved her, as unbelievable as that may seem now, and thought that all would be right if we were married. Remember, Melissa, I was only twenty-two. So we were married in a simple civil ceremony, and I moved into her place. It didn't take long for me to see what a mistake I'd made. She didn't love me. She just wanted to own me. I found out *later* she'd been married before. That really hurt, Melissa. I was too young for all this. She was jealous, possessive, and suspicious. She didn't like my *dog*, Melissa; that should have been my first clue."

So that's why he responded so warmly when we approached him that first day!

"Then one day, rather suddenly, she needed me to leave. That's another story for another day. I didn't have a lot of options; she controlled my employment and my residence. I didn't go back to

39

Maine because I was too embarrassed to face my parents. I gravitated back to southern California; at least I knew some people there. The people I connected with urged me to make things right with Celeste. That's another story too. You asked why I haven't moved back to Maine, not how I became a Christian.

"When I tried to call her, a man answered the phone, and told me Celeste had nothing to say to me. Other people tried to call her on my behalf. It was always the same. Think of it, Melissa, she was still married to *me*. Well, I certainly had grounds for divorce, but she beat me to it. It was just as well. I may have had the guilt of beginning the marriage wrongly, but not of ending it. And *now*," he released her arm to squeeze her around the shoulder, "you know more about me than most people do, and possibly more than you really *wanted* to know."

Jessica and Emily were still ahead, and Kraig still had Shanna on the lead. Melissa slowed her steps, wishing she knew what to say after such a story. Not to mention the "other stories" he'd hinted at! She looked into his deep-set, half-closed eyes, and tears came to her own as she thought about how this gentle, sweet man had been hurt by a selfish, scheming woman whom she hated without even knowing.

"Melissa," he slowed still more, "it was a very long time ago. I'm just glad I didn't hook up with someone else on the rebound. I guess God had something else planned for me."

"Yeah. Marrying in haste is a really bad idea." She laughed, knowing it sounded fake.

"Melissa," now he came to a full stop. "You don't have to tell me everything. But I can't help wondering, what led you into a marriage so unhappy... I've been thinking about what you said the other day."

"You mean, a slow death? Compared to your story, I guess it wasn't *that* bad. Not abusive, really. Just lonely. *Really* lonely."

"Why, Melissa?"

She shrugged. "I never believed in myself enough to think I had any good choices. You know the saying, 'don't marry someone you can live with, marry someone you can't live without'? Well..." she shrugged again. "I thought the best I could do was settle for someone I could live with. And the sooner I settled, the sooner I could stop worrying about it."

"Melissa," his eyebrows came together into a full frown. "I don't understand that."

She shrugged yet again, but said nothing, fearing she'd betray a tremble.

His hands rested on her shoulders, and he stood close enough for her to breathe in his wholesome, clean smell. His lips were slightly parted, and he looked as though he wanted to say something. *Or.... What an absurd thought. He's far too well mannered to kiss me after such brief acquaintance.* She shook her hair out of her face, and Kraig raised his hand to brush it away for her.

"How's your hand?" she asked.

He held it out for inspection. She touched his palm; his fingers closed reflexively around hers. She was going to say something inane about how much better it looked but didn't trust her voice, and just when she thought that nothing would be more natural than to fall into his arms, she heard Emily's voice from a little ways ahead.

"Mom! We're almost to the turnaround place."

Kraig smiled and nudged Melissa forward.

"I almost didn't have them," Melissa said impulsively. "Three kids, I mean. When I saw that I'd made a mistake in marriage, I thought I shouldn't have children. But I was lonely, and I really *wanted* children. Then, when nothing happened for a long time, I struggled with all those questions…am I meant to be lonely forever? Is God punishing me for marrying foolishly? Divorce didn't really occur to me. Before I knew it, I had three kids, and now I can't imagine *not* having them. They're all very bright, and as soon as they could talk, I could see I'd always have interesting company. They've really filled the void. I know my marriage wasn't what it was supposed to be, but…."

"I know, Melissa. Don't beat yourself up." All at once, they had reversed roles.

Jessica and Emily had been keeping pace, just out of earshot ahead of them, giving them time to finish talking. Now they were all together again.

"Kraig, may I take Shanna?" Jessica asked.

"Certainly." He handed her the lead.

Jessica gave Emily a smug look.

"Emily," Kraig said, "come here please."

41

She stood directly in front of him. He put his hand on her shoulder. "About five feet tall."

"Kraig is going to see what you look like," Melissa explained.

A look of awe came over Emily's face—a look Melissa understood well.

"She's pretty," Kraig said as he touched her delicate features, "although I'm not sure she looks like you, Melissa."

"She has big gray eyes and golden-blond hair. So does Jessica, but Jessica's hair is a little more red, and her eyes more green. Go ahead, Jessica, it's your turn."

"Five-foot-seven," Kraig said. "You'll both be tall, like your mom, and just as pretty."

"Wow, that's good, Kraig," Jessica said, stepping back a bit. Melissa sensed her daughter was thinking what she often felt—that Kraig could read everything with his fingertips. *Including perhaps my mind.*

"I wouldn't try that with Matt," Emily suggested, and they all laughed.

"Well, then, maybe you could tell me what he looks like. I've never even been close enough to guess his height."

"He's six-foot-two."

"He looks more like Mom," Jessica added, "dark hair and eyes. But Matt's hair gets all sun-bleached in the summer."

Kraig nodded, filing every bit of information. "Shall we walk?" he suggested after a moment.

Melissa turned, and had taken several steps before noticing that Kraig was keeping pace without actually touching her. Stopping so that he bumped against her, she figured something out—he hadn't actually needed her help on these walks.

"Hey," she said, and immediately sensed that he knew what she was thinking—that it had been nice anyway. He laughed, and she knew in that moment that she would never get tired of hearing his laugh.

"Melissa," he said after a silence, "do you have a story behind your name?"

"I...I know I do, but I don't remember it right now." Just then, a painful memory burst to the surface.

"It's a Greek name. So, that's my picture of you. Tall, slim, dark-haired Mediterranean beauty."

"Well, I *have* been mistaken for Italian," she said. "I'll take it as a compliment."

They were, sadly, more than halfway back. "Jessica, maybe you'd let Emily take Shanna for a while," Kraig suggested.

Jessica obliged.

"Melissa, what's wrong?" Kraig asked suddenly after another silence.

"What do you mean?"

"You're walking unevenly. You weren't doing that before."

"Oh! A couple weeks ago, before we left on this trip, I was out for a walk right at dusk. I noticed a little owl on a telephone wire. So I was walking along, watching this owl instead of where I was going, and stepped on a rock and twisted my ankle. It had started feeling better, but with all this walking on dry sand, it's hurting again."

"Why, then, are we walking on dry sand?"

"You're wearing shoes."

"Melissa, they're *deck* shoes. It's all right if they get wet." He leaned against her to steer her toward the water. "Straighten us out when we're on the right kind of sand."

"Thanks," she said feebly.

"Don't be ridiculous. No need to sacrifice your ankle for my shoes." Kraig was surely the only person she knew who could call her "ridiculous" and make it sound nice.

They were nearly in front of the cottage. "My turn wasn't as long as Jessica's," Emily said.

Kraig laughed. "There will be another day, Emily."

Two more days. Two more walks.

"Let's go in, Em," Jessica said, and, unless it was Melissa's imagination, there was a definite sigh in her voice. *That's just how I feel.*

"Kraig," Melissa said quickly, before she could change her mind, "would you like to come for dinner tonight? I mean, if you don't have other plans."

"No, I don't have other plans. And yes, I'd love to come to dinner. You name the time."

"We'll probably eat about seven. But come earlier, and we'll visit. Would you like one of us to come over and get you?"

"No need. We'll just show Shanna the approach to your place, and she'll know where to go tonight."

"Okay. I don't know for sure what we're having—I thought I'd pick up some fresh fish in town."

"Whatever you choose is fine with me."

"Okay. Great. Well, let's show Shanna, and I'll walk you home." She started to turn, then stopped. "Kraig, um—I don't mean to put off your question about—you know. *You* told *me* everything. It's just…."

"I know. Difficult to talk about."

"Yes." *And with Matt's negative contribution, I don't want to give him anything else to dislike about me. Our fledgling relationship should be asked to bear only so much.*

§

Melissa had the salmon steaks marinating and a bottle of white wine chilling as she sat down to look at the local paper. Just as she was getting up to turn the steaks over in the marinade, Emily rose to her knees in the window seat. "They're here."

Melissa screeched open the screen door. "Hi, Kraig. Come in."

"Melissa." He paused and held out his hand; she returned his squeeze. He was wearing the plaid shirt from Sunday, but it must have been sent to the laundry mid-week, as it now looked freshly pressed.

"Nice shirt. Those are good colors on you."

"Thank you. You notice everything, don't you?"

"It's my job. I'm an artist."

She screeched the screen door closed; Kraig removed Shanna's harness.

"Here's a good chair for you," she said, taking his hand and placing it on the back of an empty chair. Jessica and Emily moved from the window seat to the sofa where they could face him. "Matt will be joining us for dinner. I'll go put the salmon steaks under the broiler. Glass of wine?"

He appeared to think about it. "I never drink and drive, but Shanna knows the way home, so that would be nice."

She laughed. "I'll put it on this little table here, but let me move my easel first."

"You must be working on something."

"A watercolor of the coast of Maine."

"Mom wants something to remind her of Maine," Emily said, "so she can think about it every day until we move here."

"Are you going to move back to Maine, too?" Jessica asked. Melissa groaned inwardly.

"Maybe some day. I'm pretty content in Oregon. What did you girls do today?"

"Went bike riding," Emily answered. "We rented bikes and rode that bike path that goes for miles along the coast, then back. It was *so* fun."

"And went out to lunch," Jessica added. "We had lobster strudel. It was *so* good."

"Do you ever cycle?" Melissa asked.

"I had a bike when I was a kid. My brother fastened the handlebars to his, and we could ride all over our property that way. But he went away to college when I started third grade."

"You haven't ridden since *then*?"

"Oh, a few times. My buddy Dave and I have rented a tandem bike."

"Dave sounds like a good friend."

"He is. I've been blessed."

"Excuse me while I go turn over the salmon steaks."

"Salmon. I believe I came on the right night."

"I was hoping you'd like salmon."

"I'm pretty easy to feed. But there's nothing like wild Atlantic salmon. I try to get it when I can at home."

"Would you believe, I didn't know till today that there's a difference between wild and farm-raised salmon."

"*Big* difference, Melissa."

"You forget, Oak Hill is way-inland, and we don't always have the best seafood selection."

"I suppose not."

Melissa was about to say, "That's one thing I really look forward to about living in Maine," but Kraig began to speak.

"How long have you lived in Oak Hill?"

"I grew up in an affluent suburb of The City—"

"Which means San Francisco where you're from."

"Yes it does. I'm surprised you knew that. But anyway, I always dreamed of living in the country. But, just starting out, you know, you sometimes just end up where you end up. Where you get a job and all that. Much later, when I was head of the household, it was a good time for us to move. I can't imagine what our lives would be like now if we'd stayed..." she shuddered.

"I know what you mean." He nodded thoughtfully.

"But now, it's kind of another turning point. Another good time to move. Here."

"Is Matt going to college here?"

"No. Bible college in Michigan. He got accepted to a couple schools here, but he didn't want us to move, so he chose a school in the middle of the country. Just to make things difficult. He'll go there straight from here."

Kraig nodded thoughtfully again. "What are you planning to do next week?" he asked after a while.

"More of the same. But longer day trips. I want to see more of the state."

"To see where you might want to live."

"Yes. Also to look around at cemeteries and historical societies—genealogical research."

Melissa really didn't look forward to the actual *dinner* part of dinner—Matt would be there. Eventually, though, it was time.

The salmon turned out well, as did the steamed zucchini, sourdough bread, and mixed green salad served with a variety of dressings in nostalgic little pitchers. Matt did all his communication in sign language, and Melissa thought that by never looking at him, she could force him to talk, but his perseverance proved extraordinary. He could always get one of his sisters to get him what he wanted. Wednesday's outing had been a pleasantly surprising success, but now the field was not so level, as Kraig was a guest in their temporary home.

Of course, it was the first time the use of sign language had ever been questioned. She'd always encouraged them to communicate in any language, real or invented, that the others would understand; it stimulated their intellect, she believed. Yet no one had

46

ever tried to do it in the presence of a guest who didn't speak the language. Until now.

Melissa was beginning to get flustered, and Jessica and Emily were trying to give Matt "looks" and mouth words at him to knock it off, but certainly Kraig already knew what was happening, and Melissa decided she would have to ask Matt to leave.

Just then, Kraig put his hand palm-up on the table next to her. A bit puzzled, she put her hand on his.

"Matt," he said in a reverence-inspiring voice, "my mom died a number of years ago, and I still miss her very, very much. I would encourage you to treat your mom with as much respect as possible, as long as you're fortunate enough to have her still with you."

Matt said nothing. Neither did he sign anymore.

I wish his father had spoken to him so authoritatively.

Kraig gave Melissa's hand a squeeze and released it.

She breathed a sigh of relief. "I'll make coffee," she said. "It'll be decaf. Maybe we could play a game."

"Oh! I saw a Trivial Pursuit® game in the cupboard," Emily said, and went to get it.

"That would be perfect," Melissa said.

"Mom and Kraig against us kids," Jessica suggested.

No one protested, so Melissa moved her chair around the corner of the table to make conferring easier.

"The family rule," Emily said, "is, if you don't know an answer, you make up a funny one. It doesn't help you win, but it makes it more fun."

Kraig laughed. "I think I'll enjoy this."

In the end, Kraig and Melissa won.

"It's been fun," Kraig said, pressing the button on his watch to check the time. "But I do think Shanna and I should be heading back. May I help with the dishes first?"

"Oh, no, we never let guests help with the dishes on the first visit," Melissa said.

"There's only room for two people in the kitchen anyway," Jessica said. "Come on, Em."

"I'll walk you out," Melissa said as Kraig harnessed Shanna.

The shadows were creeping across the sand, merging into a continuous darkness; the sky was streaked with purple and lavender, pink and coral.

"An East Coast sunset," Melissa sighed. "Beautiful, but no sun sinking into the ocean."

"As we have on the West Coast. But here, you can watch the sun *rise* over the ocean."

Melissa laughed regretfully. "So far, I haven't gotten up early enough." In fact, she'd forgotten about getting up to see the sunrise.

"Yes, sunrise does come early here in the summer," he said quietly.

"Kraig, I'm so sorry about Matt's behavior. He—"

"No need, Melissa. He's never said an unkind word to me."

"He's never said *any* word to you."

Kraig laughed, but quickly became serious again. "Melissa—" he took a deep breath and started again. "Melissa, Matt just reminds me too much of my brother. And for that very reason—" he took another deep breath, "for that very reason, I'm going to try *very hard* to like him."

"Oh—" but she couldn't say more, for fear of betraying her emotions.

"I'm sure he's been a challenge to raise." The unspoken word *alone* hung heavily in the air. "You should give yourself a lot more credit, Melissa." Kraig signaled Shanna toward the steps.

"Kraig, the other day, I gave you credit for knowing a lot of languages. But do you…."

"I speak French fairly fluently. Russian and Hebrew, a little. They're a bit more difficult, you know, because they have their own alphabets."

"Wow. I only know a little Spanish, which I guess most people born and raised in California do."

Kraig laughed. "*Most* people. You're too modest, Melissa. Remember, I lived in *southern* California, where almost everything has a Spanish name, and most people *I* knew could speak less Spanish than *I* do. And *I* don't claim to speak *any*."

They stepped into the sand at the bottom of the stairs, and the smoky, seaweedy smell of a clambake wafted over with the faint notes of a guitar accompanying some indiscernible singing.

48

Kraig sighed deeply and signaled Shanna to sit, dropping the harness and letting the loop of the lead slide onto his arm. He reached for her hand. "Melissa." He pressed her hand into the deep warmth of his, and she was sure he could feel her pounding heart. "I have had a *truly delightful* evening." He took a step closer so that her hand touched his shirt front. "I want you to know how much I've appreciated your sharing your vacation with me this week. I know it hasn't all been without its complications for you. It's meant a lot to me." He paused, but his furrowed brow suggested there would be more.

"I didn't know what this week would hold for me when I came here, but this has been more than I would have asked." He squeezed her hand more tightly. "I'd like to believe, Melissa, that you aren't just being charitable to a lonely bachelor." He raised her hand a little, and she thought for a moment that he was going to kiss it, but he didn't. His head was tilted down, his eyes mere shadows in the failing light.

"I've enjoyed it just as much," Melissa said when the silence became uncomfortable. "I'm sure I speak for the girls too."

He nodded, squeezed her hand, and released it. "Good night, Melissa."

"Good night, Kraig. I'll see you in the morning."

Kraig spoke to Shanna, turned, and headed north along the beach. For a while, she could hear him talking to her, but soon the softly crashing waves muffled the one-way conversation. Without thinking about what she was doing, Melissa put her hand—the one he had held—to her face. She breathed in the smell of soap and just a hint of well tended leather.

§

"We're almost finished with the dishes," Emily announced.

"Did he kiss you?" Jessica asked.

"Of course not!" But she wasn't sure she sounded as indignant as she meant to. She remembered plenty well what it felt like to anticipate a first kiss.

She put away the Trivial Pursuit® game, chuckling to herself at some of the funny answers people had come up with.

§

Chapter 6

Friday morning came quickly, but not as quickly, Melissa feared, as it would fly away again.

"Melissa," Kraig said as they stood on the porch of his inn, "I'm going to do this first, so I can stop worrying about it. Will you let me call you, once we're both back home on the West Coast?"

"Sure," she said, with no doubt that he could hear her smile.

He took from the pocket of his weathered-sea-green polo shirt the smallest recorder she had ever seen. "Just say your name, address, e-mail address, whatever phone numbers you have—clearly," he instructed.

She did; he replayed it twice, looked satisfied, and put the recorder back in his pocket.

As they turned to start down the beach, the wind ruffled his hair; he turned his face into the breeze and took a deep breath of the sea air. "There's no place like it, is there, Melissa? I could be bound and gagged and dropped from a plane, and I'd know I was in Maine."

"Are you sorry you're going home tomorrow?"

"Yes...and no. I'm sure you know what I mean."

"Yeah. Our second week here will go by just as fast." Another thought came to her. "How are you getting to the airport?"

"In a taxi."

"Oh, Kraig—will you let me drive you?"

"Melissa," he sighed, "you've done so much. I really don't want to take any more of your time away from whatever you have planned."

"Actually, Saturday is sort of our 'buffer day'—an extra day in case we ran out of time. So we really didn't have anything else planned. Really."

He smiled, perhaps not fully believing her.

"Oh, come on. You don't want to finish your vacation in a taxi."

"Not really," he admitted.

"Good. Just tell me what time we need to leave."

"I'll have to check my notes again. It's all here." He patted the pocket that held the recorder. "Melissa," he said slowly, his face turned away, "as a writer, I'm used to working with the written word, which can be contemplated almost indefinitely before it's let fly. I hope I've not said anything this week that's confused or offended you."

"Kraig, I can't even *imagine* you saying anything offensive."

"That's very kind of you, Melissa. I just need you to know…. Touch is a very powerful thing for me. I even *dream* of touch sensations. Most people dream in visual images, you know. It's important to me that touch be as honest as words. I can't help wondering, sometimes, who or what I'd be if I'd had my sight all these years. And I suppose that should be a scary thought, since God doesn't make mistakes."

Melissa opened her mouth to protest, but something in his pensive demeanor hinted that she was about to gain some deep insight into this complex, fascinating man.

"Although occasionally I *would* like to pull back the curtain and take a peek at what's out there…" he turned to her, the corners of his mouth turning up into a smile, "most of the time, it's just an inconvenience."

Melissa shrugged. "It doesn't make any difference to me. In case you were wondering."

"I know, Melissa. I've seen that it doesn't." He reached into his pants pocket. "I want to give you this."

Whatever it was, he seemed determined not to reveal it until she put out her hand. He cradled her hand and pressed into it something smooth. There, in her hand, was a piece of dull green beach glass.

"Oh! Where did you find this one?"

"I've had it for many years. I brought it with me."

Holding it up to the light, she saw that it was almost exactly the same color as his eyes. "Thank you, Kraig. I'll add it to my collection." A moment later, it occurred to her to wonder about the significance of this particular piece, such that he would have brought it with him, but decided not to ask.

With all the stops and starts, Jessica and Emily were now far ahead; and although Melissa felt sure that sooner or later one of them would double back and ask for Shanna, for now it appeared they were content to give her and Kraig some aloneness.

"Kraig, there's something I need to explain to you. It has to do with Matt, and why he's the way he is. There was a youth leader at church. He was thirty-eight when I met him, too; this was a few years ago. He was Matt's friend first, but Jeff and I began dating, and for a while things looked perfect."

Kraig nodded.

"Jeff came from an unchurched background, like me. His parents became Christians when he was a teenager, then his older brother and sister. But Jeff—who had always been a good kid—rebelled. One day, he said, he just looked at his life, got totally disgusted, and turned it over to God.

"This was all *way* before I met him. I was ready to forgive him for everything; I believed in him. But he seemed determined to shock me with every gory detail of his past—drugs, alcohol, promiscuity—until he got the reaction he wanted, I guess. Maybe he thought I was too 'good' to understand where he was coming from. He just couldn't forgive himself and move on. It really put a damper on our relationship."

"Guilt seems to be the universal affliction," Kraig said. "God forgives us...yet we insist upon carrying around our burdens of guilt."

"Yeah, well, it's not always that simple. At that time, I'd just found out for sure that I was a widow."

"I know you have a story, Melissa, but now might not be the time to tell it."

True to prediction, Jessica and Emily now stopped and waited for them to catch up.

"Kraig—" Melissa turned to face him, not wanting the girls to hear anything, yet anxious not to leave things in such a precarious place.

He put his arm around her shoulder. "It's all right, Melissa. There'll be another time."

Reassured, she turned and resumed walking.

"Mom, Jessica and I need turns walking with Kraig and Shanna," Emily said. "We're running out of days to walk with them."

As if I need to be reminded.

"Here you go, Emily," Kraig said, handing over the lead.

"Shanna's pretty good-sized for a female golden retriever, isn't she?" Melissa said.

"Yes, in fact, she's the first female guide I've had. There's an ideal size for a guide dog. A dog too small can't body-block her human partner from stepping in front of a bus, for example; but a very large dog isn't comfortable in cars and public transportation. Then there's the person's size to take into account, so I've always had a relatively large dog."

"We always wanted a dog," Emily said, "but our dad didn't like dogs, so we never got one." She glanced at Jessica. "Oh, yeah. We already told you."

Jessica gave Emily a look, then quickly turned to Kraig. "Tell us about the other dogs you've had."

He motioned them forward. Melissa reached for his hand to put in place on her arm—not because he needed it, but because she liked it.

"I'm always pleased to talk about my dogs. Markus was my first guide. He was a black lab, and I got him when I was sixteen, the age when you can get a guide dog. I had him through college, moving to New Orleans, and moving back to southern California and then to Oregon. He worked with me for eight years, through a lot of big changes. Hartley was next. He was a German shepherd, and I had him until about five years ago."

"What happens to the dogs after you have them?" Emily asked, crowding in from her outside position.

"When they need to be retired, I'm free to keep them as pets, if I choose, although I've never done that. It doesn't seem right to keep an aging dog, who's been such a faithful partner, at home alone when I'm gone to work all day. So they're offered back to the family who raised them. There are always people who are eager to have such a well-trained dog."

"How much longer will you have Shanna?" Jessica asked.

"I don't know, Jessica. That's always hard to think about. She's six and a half now. I hope to have her several more years."

"Maybe you'll get to keep her," Emily said. "I mean, after you get your next dog."

"Maybe, Emily. We'll see."

For a while no one spoke, and it was delightful to discover that they didn't need to speak to enjoy one another's company. Melissa watched the coarse, wet sand squish up around their feet with each step, and then surge back into place as each foot was lifted again. The sea was dotted with sailboats and fishing boats; the ombre sky, whitish at the horizon, deepening to blue overhead, was dotted with gulls and clouds. She remembered, with a pang of guilt, her blank sheet of canvas paper back at the cottage. She had not yet rendered one single line on it.

"Tell me what it looks like today, Melissa," Kraig said after a while.

"It looks…it looks like a background on which you can paint anything you want."

"Hmm," he nodded. "I like that."

They reached the turnaround point; Shanna's lead changed hands; the quiet conversation began to feel like a farewell. They found themselves in front of the cottage.

"Girls," Melissa said, trying to sound cheerful, "we're going to drive Kraig to the airport tomorrow. So you don't have to say 'goodbye' until then."

"We can come?" Emily asked.

"Of course you can come."

"Good," Jessica said. "So…we'll see you tomorrow, Kraig. Bye, Shanna. Come on, Em." She handed the lead to Kraig and jogged up the steps toward the cottage, Emily close behind.

"Maybe you should check on your flight time," Melissa suggested.

He took out the tiny recorder and pressed some buttons. Melissa heard airline, flight number, time, gate, and seat in a voice that wasn't Kraig's. "Be there or you're in deep doo-doo, buddy. I don't want to have to come all the way to Maine to get you," the message finished.

Kraig smiled at the familiar voice of his friend. "I asked Dave to read the ticket aloud on the recorder for me. He has a certain style, doesn't he?"

Melissa laughed. "What time shall I come for you?"

He made some mental calculations. "Eleven-fifteen."

"I'll be sure to get gasoline in town this afternoon on the way back from hiking."

"Good. Travel makes me nervous enough."

"Me too. Is someone picking you up on the other end?" Somehow, she already knew the answer.

"Dave. I'll be back in time for the evening service. There's a special music program I don't want to miss."

"Do you want to go for a walk in the morning?"

He looked thoughtful again. "I think we should. Shanna and I will be confined long enough."

"Maybe we should get started a little earlier than usual. So you'll have time to pack, and everything."

"Yes." He sounded relieved to have *her* suggest it. "Come by maybe fifteen minutes earlier. If you don't mind."

"I don't mind. Well...let's...."

He nodded. "Get back to my place. So I can let you get on with the rest of your day."

§

Chapter 7

"I have to tell you," Melissa said as soon as greetings had been exchanged Saturday morning. The day had a hurried feel to it, shadowed by the knowledge that the last leisurely walk together on the beach was already in the past. "He didn't come home from work one Friday night. We were still living in the city then. I didn't give it much thought, to tell you the truth. Our communication had never been very good. Maybe he'd told me he was going to be late, and I wasn't listening. But by the next morning, I knew something was wrong.

"It was investigated as a missing person. I heard myself telling the authorities, 'Well, no, things *haven't* been very good between us,' and 'Well, yes, we *did* argue recently.' So, they said, 'Sometimes people just walk away.' I *knew* that wasn't what happened. He just wouldn't have done that. If nothing else, he was boringly predictable. But that's what they decided. In a way, I wanted to believe it.

"Over time, I put together bits and pieces of information... his parents said he'd asked them about taking care of the kids some weekend, and someone from his office said he'd been asking around for ideas for a weekend getaway. It would have been a *little* out of character for him to do something like this as a surprise, but he *was* more interested in saving the marriage than I was.

"Well, three winters went by, and when the snow in the foothills melted for the third time, someone was out hunting wild turkeys in a remote area at the bottom of a steep incline, hidden from the road by this rough terrain. They were poaching, so they didn't tell anyone right away. Well, they found the car, and whatever there was to be found. By then, whatever evidence there had been was long gone. It had been two and a half years. He probably either fell asleep at the wheel or swerved to avoid a deer. If there were any skid marks, they were long gone. We don't even know which direction he'd been going.

"So, I figured he'd gone to check out some weekend getaway place, and never made it, or never made it back. This was during the time I'd been really anxious to move out of the city, so I felt like it was my fault. Maybe if I'd thought sooner that something was wrong.... Sometimes people live for days after an accident like that. Later, people said I should sue the law enforcement agencies for doing a bad job. Then, I felt guilty because I just wanted to get on with my life.

"But for those two and a half years, I didn't know if I was a widow, or if I'd been abandoned. After that, just knowing what had happened...."

"Was a tremendous relief, I'm sure. Now I see what you mean by a slow death."

"In the meantime, we'd moved to Oak Hill. There was no reason not to, now. There, no one knew us before, and I didn't feel the need to explain everything to everybody. But when it was solved, and this bizarre story was all over the papers, it kind of started all over again. Maybe I imagined it, but after that, I always felt like people treated me differently. But it *was* my fault. And Oak Hill has never felt as much like home since then."

§

Arriving comfortably early at Kraig's place later that morning, Melissa found the front door ajar. She pushed it open and peeked in. "Kraig?"

"Melissa. Come in." He sat at the large oak dining table, his briefcase open, his hand on the page of a Braille Bible. His back was to her; Shanna stood to greet her. Melissa spoke softly to her, not wanting to interrupt whatever Kraig was doing. She sat across the table from him, scratching Shanna's head; she thought she saw his hands tremble ever so slightly as he closed his Bible and organized his briefcase. His suitcase stood on the floor, his jacket folded neatly on top.

"Thanks for being so prompt, Melissa. I feel better already."

"I'm sorry you're leaving, but I'm glad you don't have to take a taxi."

He smiled weakly as he stood and began to fasten Shanna's harness.

"Shall I check your room, to make sure you haven't missed anything?"

"Sure. Thanks."

She did; he hadn't. Looking around the room, Melissa rested her gaze on the solid oak double bed, now left unmade, in which he'd spent a week's worth of nights. Resisting the urge to straighten it, she hurried out of the room. "Everything's okay in there. Can I carry your briefcase and jacket?"

"Sure. Thanks," he said again. "Are Jessica and Emily here?"

"They're waiting in the car. Oh, your jacket feels so soft! What kind of fabric is this?"

"It's microfiber. I liked the feel of it, too. Helen said the color is called 'weathered spruce,' and that it'll go well with almost everything I have."

"Oh." She had conveniently almost forgotten about Helen, and now was not the best time to be reminded. Six days had gone by, filled with miles of conversation, and she had never discovered Kraig's reason for being in Maine. Nor did she know Helen's exact role in his life. She suddenly realized, too, that somehow he had failed to greet her with his customary hand squeeze on this last day, and she missed it. All of this, combined with Kraig's subdued mood, plunged her into a melancholy of her own. She was privately glad for her daughters' company, certain that their cheerful chatter would keep the awkward silence at bay.

"Kraig," Emily said brightly after he'd settled himself and Shanna into the car, "my mom says you might come see us when we get home from here. Will you really?"

"I hope so, Emily." The sparkle was back in his voice, and Melissa's spirits lifted just a bit.

§

"Mom, we're going to go watch the planes take off. Come on, Em."

At the check-in desk, Kraig requested pre-boarding. They settled into moderately comfortable chairs, and Kraig checked his watch.

"We'll be thinking of you next week," Melissa said, "when we're out sightseeing and everything."

"I look forward to hearing about it."

"I'll be happy to tell you about it. If you call me."

"I'll be thinking of you, too, while I'm sitting at my desk, maybe wishing I were still in Maine. And I *will* call you, Melissa. I said I would, and my word is good."

Great. Now I've insulted him. She looked to see what Jessica and Emily were doing; they seemed to be amused by something happening outside the window.

"Melissa," Kraig said, sighing deeply. "I really am not my best self today. I didn't sleep well last night. When it gets to this point in a trip, I really do look forward to getting home."

"Yeah, I know what you mean." Melissa relaxed a little, leaning until her shoulder rested on his. People scurried along the concourse, some one way, some the other. *Everyone is in a hurry to get somewhere, or to get home from somewhere. I alone want to freeze time at this very moment.*

The first pre-boarding announcement came. Kraig rose heavily from his seat, letting the loop of Shanna's lead slide down his wrist, and sighed deeply again. Melissa pressed the jacket into his hands.

"Thanks," he said, and put it on, explaining, "one fewer thing to carry." He put his hands to her face, as if taking a picture of her, and she remembered not to hold her breath. In the next moment, his arms were around her, and the force of his embrace took her breath away. She hugged him back, hard, inhaling deeply, wanting to imprint him on her memory.

The second pre-boarding call came, and still he held her tightly. She hoped she could remember exactly how it felt, to comfort and reassure herself when he was gone and she began to miss him. And she would, oh so intensely, miss him.

He released her partway, putting one hand on her cheek, then her lips. It was just as good as a kiss, Melissa decided. He held her hand as he bent to grasp Shanna's harness, but a moment later he released it to pick up his briefcase. He straightened and faced her, sighed deeply once more, then said simply, "Melissa."

He turned and walked toward the waiting plane, just as a ridiculously cheerful-looking flight attendant approached, probably to remind him it was time to board. Melissa watched him disappear into the tunnel.

She joined Jessica and Emily at the window. They watched his plane pull away from the terminal, taxi, take off, turn westward, shrink into a silvery dot, and disappear. She said a silent prayer. Then she said, "Well, I guess we can go now."

"You should have seen it, Mom. It was *so funny.*" Emily was talking animatedly as Melissa simply tried to focus on working her way through the crowd to the exit. "Jessica and I were watching this guy load packages onto this trailer thing, and he kept dropping them. He dropped, like, five packages. After a while, he picked one up, and whatever was in it was broken. We could tell because something was dripping out of it—" She stopped abruptly, her mouth still open, her face turning to anguish. "I forgot to say goodbye to Kraig!"

"It's okay, Em," Jessica said gently. "So did I. Remember? We're going to see him again."

On the drive back to the cottage, a gloomy silence prevailed. Melissa thought she would welcome a cloudy sky, or even rain, so she wouldn't feel obligated to go out and do something.

"Mom, maybe you can start on your picture today," Jessica said.

"I was just thinking about that." Sitting in front of her easel with a steaming cup of coffee or tea, perhaps with a fire in the fireplace, seemed just the thing for this kind of day. The thought of getting to work on her seascape at last lifted her spirits considerably. She had a few postcard-sized prints she'd picked up over the week, which she could refer to as she created perfect clouds. *Puffy, cotton-ball clouds against a blue sky.*

"Jessica, Emily," she said after another silence, "what was it that made you run over to Shanna that first day on the beach?"

In the rearview mirror, she saw them exchange blank looks and shrug. "I don't know, Mom," Jessica said. "I just remember seeing this guy and this dog walking along, and I thought maybe they were someone we wanted to talk to."

§

Chapter 8

Before she opened her eyes, Melissa knew there was something wrong with the day to which she had just awakened. Then she remembered, and was surprised by the power of the memory to overwhelm her with sorrow. Tears formed at the corners of her eyes, rolled over the bridge of her nose, and disappeared into her pillow.

It's Sunday. I won't see Kraig on the beach today. Or tomorrow, or all week. Or...maybe ever.

She sat up and looked out at the incongruously blue sky. *I've missed a whole week of sunrises and hardly given it a thought. What was I thinking? Have I forgotten why I came here?*

Melissa looked at the old alarm clock on her bedside table that was really a stool. She turned it over, wound it, adjusted the alarm time, and tested it. *It works! Now I have no excuse not to get up in time for the sunrise all week.*

Cheered by simply having something to look forward to, she went to the kitchen to make a pot of coffee. While it brewed, filling the cottage with its comforting aroma, she studied her progress on her seascape. She had made only a few tentative horizontal pencil lines. Mostly she'd spent Saturday afternoon listening to the radio and looking at travel literature, trying to get excited about the day trips planned for the second week, trying *not* to look anxiously up the beach for someone who could not possibly be there.

She rearranged the postcards along the bottom of the easel.

"Hi, Mom."

"Oh, morning, Emily."

"Are we going to church today?"

"Oh! It's Sunday again. Uh, no, I never got around to looking for one."

"Going for a walk?"

"Maybe. Later. We have all day, not much planned."

Emily looked wistful. "I hope our cats are okay."

"I'm sure they're fine. It's still dark at home, you know. The pet sitter will be over later."

"Hi, everybody."

"Morning, Jessica."

"No church, walk later," Emily told her.

"How about breakfast?" Melissa said. "We have all kinds of stuff to choose from now."

§

It's Monday morning. I'm at the beach. It was a dream.
It wasn't even much of a dream; more like a still photograph. It was of Kraig, and he looked happy. It was so real, it lifted her out of her doldrums. She reached for the clock to take a closer look.

Then she realized, it was the alarm that had awakened her. *The sunrise! I'm up in time for the sunrise!* Melissa hurried to the kitchen to brew some coffee to enjoy while she watched the sunrise.

By the end of the day, she had all the pencil lines sketched in on her canvas pad.

§

Tuesday morning, Melissa was again awakened by the alarm clock, but in the darkness she sensed someone standing over her. "Emily?"

"Hi, Mom," Emily whispered back. "I heard your alarm clock and decided to get up and watch the sunrise with you."

The sunrise watch had replaced the beach walk as the focus around which her life revolved. With the longer day trips, farther up the coast and farther inland, there really wasn't time to do both *and* work on her seascape.

Some day. Melissa mused, cup of coffee in hand and Emily by her side as she watched the sunrise, some day she would have a studio in her home with a window that faced east. She could watch the sun rise over the ocean...or a lake, or a meadow, or through the pine trees...as long as she could see the sun rise any day she fancied, she would be happy. Every day would feel like a new beginning. She would be surrounded by her cats as she worked. *And a dog! I will have a dog when I live in Maine. I'll get an older dog, already trained.*

The sun was up, her cup was empty, and she was eager to work on her masterpiece.

§

Melissa held the piece of gray-green beach glass in her hand. It didn't look the same without the sun shining through it. She set it on the easel, next to the postcards.

"That's coming along nicely," Jessica said, looking over Melissa's shoulder. "Are you going to put any people in it?"

"No. It's a seascape. No people."

"Oh. Just wondering."

§

Getting up earlier was easier now.

"Hi, Mom," Emily whispered. "Jessica's going to watch the sunrise with us today."

"I thought I should, since we're going home in three days," Jessica said.

Melissa switched on the bedside lamp.

"Hey, look, Mom. Your sailboat bedspread is just the same as Jessica's and mine, except yours is green, mine is lavender, and hers is blue. So we each got a color we like."

"What color is Matt's?"

"Beige," Jessica answered. "I almost forgot Matt was still here."

"Yeah," Emily agreed. "He's been so quiet since you stopped making him do things he doesn't want to do."

"Hmm…you're right. Well, let's go watch the sunrise!"

§

Melissa held up the gray-green watercolor pencil with the picture window behind it, searching for a place to use it in her masterpiece.

"Hey, you're almost finished." Jessica looked over Melissa's shoulder again. "I still think you need something down in this corner. It looks kind of unbalanced. What do you think, Em?" She stepped aside to let Emily see.

"Yeah. A person. Or a dog. Or just a seagull."

"I'll think about it."

§

65

Seated at her easel Thursday afternoon, Melissa looked up from her canvas at her daughters in the window seat. "Tomorrow's our last full day, girls. Saturday we'll just be packing and flying home."

"Yeah." They both looked out the window.

Jessica looked back toward Melissa. "Do you think you'll have your picture finished?"

"I think so. I'm just doing the finishing touches. And I have to decide what to do with this corner you don't like."

Jessica and Emily came and looked over her shoulder again. "Hmm. We'll let you know if we get any good ideas."

"Yeah," Emily agreed. "Maybe a seashell."

The girls went back to the window seat, Jessica to her book, Emily to her sketching.

Jessica looked up from her book. "Mom?"

Melissa looked up from her picture. "Hmm?"

"Did Kraig ever tell you why he's blind?"

"No. I never asked."

"Oh."

Melissa looked out the window. "I suppose he hasn't always been blind, though. He said something about remembering…things."

"Oh. Okay."

Melissa went back to her picture, Jessica to her book.

Melissa looked over at Jessica again. "Why? Does it matter?"

Jessica shrugged. "No. Just curious." She raised her book, then put it down again. "Weren't you curious?"

"Hmm. I never really thought about it. But now that I think about it…maybe I don't *want* to know. Maybe it's something sad."

Jessica frowned. "Yeah. Maybe."

Melissa applied a watercolor pencil to her picture.

"Mom?"

"Yes?"

"Did you ever find out why he was in Maine?"

"No, never did. Maybe it was just like you thought—he was just on vacation, same as us."

"Yeah. Probably."

Everything was set for a smooth departure in the morning. Melissa had her art folio packed with her tabletop easel, canvas pad, sketchbook, pencil box, and watercolor pencils. Her finished masterpiece was securely tucked into the middle for the trip home.

One more sunrise. One last walk on the beach.

She put her art folio by the door so she wouldn't forget it.

§

• Chapter 9 •

Home.

As soon as she'd dropped her bags just inside the door, Melissa looked at the display on the answering machine. "That must be a record number," she said, mostly to herself. She took a piece of paper and pen and pushed "play." *Messages from work...church...the kids' friends...Matt saying he'd arrived at college safely....*

"I'm sure there's one from Kraig," Emily said.

"It's okay if he didn't call," Melissa said. "He knew we weren't home yet."

Last message. Beep. "Melissa, Jessica, Emily. This is Kraig. Welcome home. I'll call you in a few days when you've had a chance to get settled. Talk to you then."

"Yes!" Emily said.

"I told you he liked you," Jessica said.

Monday, arriving home from work, she barely had the door open when she heard both girls call out, "Mom, something came for you."

On the dining room table she found a long box—a florist's box. Jessica and Emily appeared as she began to open it.

Inside was a single purple iris.

"How did he know you like irises?" Emily asked.

Melissa thought for a moment, back to the first week at the beach. "I guess I mentioned it." She was astonished that he could have remembered her passing mention of iris being her favorite flower. The card read simply, "Thank you again. Kraig."

"See? I *told* you he liked you!" Jessica said again.

As life returned to its familiar routine, the time spent with Kraig in Maine began to take on that dreamlike quality that fondly remembered vacations tend to do in retrospect. Several more days went by, with no call from Kraig.

Some part of her hoped he *wouldn't* call. There was something enticingly easy in thinking of that episode of her life simply being over. *Like a painting, once finished, is framed and hung on the wall, to be gazed upon with satisfaction. Or a good book, once read, is put on the shelf, lovingly recalled but not read again.*

He had called; he had kept his word. It would be okay if he didn't call again.

Melissa's thoughts turned to Jeff. Jeff was a comfortable subject on which to dwell, a story with a known ending. Perhaps she could call him! He'd want to know how Matt was doing; that he'd just left for college.

But, no. A closed book should stay closed.

§

A few days later, Melissa felt caught up enough on work to take a longer lunch and shop for framing materials. On a whim, she decided to frame her picture after the girls had gone back to school, then hang it while they were away, and see if they would notice.

Saturday, Melissa mowed the long-neglected lawn. It had been Matt's job, so she was surprised to see a low-hanging oak branch he hadn't complained about. *If he could dodge it, then so can I.* Yet somehow it seemed best to cut it off. She went to look for a pruning saw.

One week after the return home, the phone rang at about eight o'clock in the evening. Melissa answered it.

"Melissa. It's Kraig. I always call people at eight o'clock because I believe most people have had dinner by then but haven't gone to bed yet. Is this a good time for you?"

"Kraig. Hey," Melissa laughed, and the moment she heard his voice again, she couldn't believe she'd ever *not* wanted him to call. "Yeah. It's a good time." She pulled a chair over and got comfortable.

"I've been trying to work out the details of your visiting up here," he explained, "particularly where you'd stay. How would it be if I came down there first?"

"Sure. We have a guest apartment with a separate entrance. The previous owners had finished all but the flooring and paint down there when I bought the house. It's kind of snug, but you should be comfortable."

"Sounds perfect. So let's talk about *when*."

A weekend about a month hence was settled upon, right near the beginning of fall.

"We can go out to dinner, take a canoe out on the lake, go to church on Sunday…" Melissa said. "And *everything* is my treat."

As she hung up, she suspected another possible reason for Kraig's suggestion of traveling to see her first. *He hasn't told anyone in Oregon about me. And he won't, pending some degree of certainty that there's something worth telling.* Helen came to mind again. Since Melissa's family already knew about *him*—and with Matt in another time zone—there would be no major complications to her hosting him.

§

The girls were back in school. Arriving home before they did one day, Melissa took the opportunity to frame her seascape. She hung the finished work on the wall in the dining room, where she would see it every day.

"Oh!" Emily said as they gathered for dinner. "Your picture!"

"It looks really real," Jessica said.

"What's this down in the corner?" Emily asked.

"It's beach glass, can't you tell?" Jessica said.

"Oh. Yeah. Look at this glow on the sand where the light shines through it. How did you do that?"

"I put some grains of sand in the watercolor."

"That was a good idea."

"Yeah," Jessica agreed. "I like it."

§

Chapter 10

The hour-plus drive to the airport gave Melissa plenty of time to fret. In her mind she went over the list of essential tasks accomplished in anticipation of Kraig's visit. *Guest quarters aired and scrubbed top to bottom...sheets and towels washed and freshened with linen spray...all impediments removed from the floor, everywhere in the house...Jessica and Emily at home, keeping an eye on dinner preparations....*

Kraig was the first one off the plane. She must have burst into a grin, because the flight attendant turned and said something to him, at which he smiled. He then spoke to Shanna, who made a straight path for her.

"Kraig." She slipped her arm around his waist, but the crush of deplaning passengers pushed them along, preventing a more complete greeting. The crowd soon fanned out; Kraig signaled Shanna to stop, dropped the one bag he carried, and faced her. His left arm around her waist, he put his right hand to her face. Melissa was warmed by his touch and comforted by the thought that, whatever happened this weekend, he would always be a friend.

"Melissa." He hugged her, she hugged him back, and it was as if no time had passed at all. He was exactly as she remembered him. *Almost.*

"You got a haircut."

"Actually, I've had *two* haircuts since you saw me."

"It looks nice. Very nice."

In the parking lot, Melissa unlocked the side door of her minivan. "I think Shanna will be more comfortable in here than in that rental car."

"Melissa." He surprised her by hugging her again. "I'm glad I came." This last part was a little muffled by her hair, and as he continued to hold her, she felt—as she often did—that there was more he wanted to say.

"I'm glad too," she said, when she got her breath back. "I hope you have a nice shirt for dinner and church in your bag."

"You'd be amazed at what I can fit into here," he said as he heaved his bag onto the rear seat and instructed Shanna to get in.

About halfway home, Melissa's cell phone rang. The display indicated home. "Hi," she said.

"Mom?" It was Jessica. "Don't put me on speaker, okay?"

"Okay, Jessica, go ahead."

"I forgot to ask before you left. Do you think it would be okay if we hug Kraig when he gets here?"

"I'm sure it'll be okay. We'll be there in a little while." She smiled to herself as she hung up.

"Is everything all right?" Kraig asked.

"Yeah. Fine."

Kraig smiled at his memories of them, but a moment later grimaced and put his hand to his temple. "We must be gaining some altitude."

"I'm sorry. I should have told you. The Sacramento airport is at about sea level. We just passed 1,000 feet. By the time we get to my house, we'll be above 2,000. When we go into town for dinner tomorrow and church Sunday, we'll be at about 3,000 feet."

"I see. Well, it always takes me about a day to adjust."

Melissa's heart sank a bit; she hoped Kraig's suffering wouldn't hamper his enjoyment of all she had planned.

She parked in the driveway—a much more decorous entrance than the garage—and at the door, took Kraig's bag from his hand in anticipation of the girls' greeting. They rushed him, just inside the door, and hugged him together, and he hugged them back, and Melissa thought with mild horror how she would not have been the only one to miss out had she decided not to see him again.

They then turned to Shanna and gave her the same greeting.

"We can show you your room later," Melissa said. "Would you like a glass of wine now?"

He bent to unfasten Shanna's harness. "Oh...I *would*, Melissa, but right now I'm dealing with this altitude headache."

"Oh. Well...mineral water?"

"Perfect. Thank you."

In the time it took her to pour it, Jessica and Emily had him seated between them on the couch. She stood holding his glass, unsure of how to place it, as Emily waxed eloquent with her description of their cats. In time, she stopped to take a breath.

"Melissa?" Kraig said.

"Here's your water," she said, suddenly feeling foolish, because it would have been so easy just to take his hand and put the glass in it.

"Thank you," he said, "and when will I meet Buster, Chester, Snowflake, and Diana?"

"They're hiding from Shanna," Jessica said. "They've never had to live with a dog."

"Yeah, we never had a dog," Emily added.

"He *knows*, Em," Jessica said.

"Mom finished her picture!" Emily said.

"Tell me about it, Emily."

"Well, it's a seascape, and it looks like the beach where we were in Maine. And it looks totally real, and there's a piece of beach glass down in the corner, and it looks like the sun is shining through it."

"Your mom must be a talented artist."

"She is. I like to draw, too, but I'm not as good."

"Some day, maybe you will be."

"I got out my collection of beach glass," Melissa said. "I thought you could tell us something about it."

"Aha. Well, I'll bet the color you have the most of is aqua."

"It is!"

He took the jar as she placed it in his hands. "Is the piece I gave you in here?"

"No, I wanted to keep it separate. This is my California collection."

He selected a few pieces. "Here's something you'll notice. See these two? I'm guessing you didn't find them on the same beach. One is smoother than the other, so it's probably from a sandy beach, while the more frosted one is from a pebbly beach."

"Oh, yeah!" Jessica and Emily leaned in, impressed.

"Show me the biggest piece you have."

Emily dug it out with her slender fingers and placed it in his hand.

"About the size of a quarter. A *really* big piece you know has been in a protected place."

"What about the black pieces?"

"If you hold them up to the light, Jessica, you'll see that they aren't really black, but very dark green. They contain lead to protect the contents of the bottle from light."

"What about brown?"

"Brown pieces could be from a beer bottle or a bleach bottle, Emily. Fishermen used bleach in glass jugs to clean their boats. Do you have any red?"

Emily dug some more. "No, no red."

"Red is pretty rare. It contains copper or gold. Any pastel colors?"

"Yes. A lot," Melissa said.

"That's probably Depression glass, inexpensive glass made in the 1930s."

"Wow! I never dreamed there was so much to know about beach glass. I just thought it was pretty."

"It's all history, Melissa. Of course, everything I just told you is East Coast history. West Coast, I'm not sure."

"That reminds me! I wrote down all the French names we saw, sightseeing, after you went home from Maine, in case any of these people are related to you. I can tell you about it later. But right now, how about if we show you your room? And Shanna—well, we don't have a fenced yard—"

"Not a problem. She can 'relieve' on leash."

"We can help him with all that," Jessica said. "I know how to open the sofa bed."

"Sure. But don't leave it open yet. It fills up most of the room. Well, I'll go see how dinner's doing."

"I believe we're having lasagna," Kraig said.

"Right, as usual."

At dinner, Melissa asked Kraig to say the blessing. It was the first time she'd heard him pray, and if she had a list of "tests" for him to pass, he would have just passed another one. For he prayed with sincerity and originality, without a hint of rote recital, which was for her a critical characteristic of a man who knows how to be the head of a household.

"Isn't it nice without Matt?" Emily said suddenly.

"Well, Emily, I don't know that I'd put it that way," Kraig said.

"I kind of miss him," Jessica said.

"Yeah…" Emily agreed, "he *is* pretty funny sometimes."

"He'll turn out all right," Kraig said. "Just be on the same team; that's the most important thing. Do you have grandparents?"

Melissa cleared her throat. "My dad died a few years ago. My mom lives half the year in Florida, the other half in Europe, and I haven't seen her since my dad's memorial service."

"I'm sorry," he said after a moment. "That's hard for me to imagine. I was close to my parents and I miss them a lot."

"I do miss my dad. My mom never tried to pretend she really wanted kids, and now she's *more* mad at me because after my dad died, she found out he'd made some investments in my name. Not that *she* needed all of it. She just didn't want *me* to have it."

"I figured as much, since you just said she lives half the year in Europe."

"She never even sends us birthday cards," Emily said. "Grandpa always sent us birthday cards."

"Well, *I'll* send you birthday cards," Kraig said.

"Oh," said Emily, disappointed, "mine just went by. I'm eleven now."

"Then I'll send you a late one as soon as I get home."

§

Saturday morning, Melissa descended the outside staircase to the guest apartment as the leaf-filtered morning sunlight slanted across the yard. Kraig sat in a deck chair outside the apartment door, Shanna by his side, a cup of coffee held steady on his knee.

"Morning, Kraig."

"Melissa." Setting the cup under the chair, he stood to greet her. This time, she remembered not to try to talk until after he'd finished hugging her. She'd never known anyone to hug as hard as Kraig did, and it felt good.

"How's your head?"

"My head. Well, I'd forgotten about it. The sofa bed was comfortable and I slept like a log. I'm sorry about last night, though."

"What do you mean?"

"I would have enjoyed a glass of wine with you, if not for the headache."

She laughed. "There will be other times. Although I'm sure Jessica and Emily's non-stop talking didn't help with your headache."

He frowned, and she immediately knew she'd said something she shouldn't have. "Melissa, I wish you wouldn't say that. I live alone, you know, and I'd rather have their company, non-stop talking and all, than eat alone, any day."

"You're right. And I know it will be too quiet when they leave, and *I'll* be the one eating alone."

"None of us knows the future, Melissa."

She decided to be more careful not to say stupid things. "I see they showed you the coffee maker."

"Yes, they showed me everything." He stooped to retrieve the cup from under the chair. It was the first time she'd seen him wearing shorts, in this case a pair of Bermuda shorts she hadn't seen in Maine, with a gray T-shirt, gray athletic socks, and running shoes. *Not bad.*

"Shall we go for a walk before breakfast?" she asked.

"We should."

"It's not the beach, but there's not a lot of traffic in this neighborhood, either."

"I did notice that. I've heard very few cars since I've been here."

"Well, this is life in the country. You saw how long our driveway is."

"I could get used to it." He handed her Shanna's lead, taking the outside position as they reached the road.

The familiar rhythm of walking and talking together quickly returned; the conversation nearly picked up from where it had been left on the beach.

"Now tell me the part about how you got from southern California to Oregon," Melissa said.

"Ah, that. Well. All right. When Celeste asked me—rather *told* me, somewhat forcefully—that it was time for me to go, I was in a pretty bad way, emotionally, financially, every way. I headed back to southern California—as I told you, I knew some people there. Actually I wanted to re-connect with this girl friend. Not a *girlfriend*, really, just a female friend…but maybe I was hoping for more, a shoulder to cry on, maybe more."

"Mm," Melissa nodded.

"Well, she seemed pretty happy to see me again, and she said she was sure this group of guys she knew who shared a house would be happy to let me stay with them for as long as I needed to. It turned out that one of them was her boyfriend…so I got the shoulder to cry on, but nothing more." He paused. "It was probably a good thing. I think perhaps I was looking for the wrong thing, being on the rebound, and that I would've ruined my relationship with her and distanced myself from God even further.

"As it turned out, all of them—the girl, the boyfriend, the group of guys—were Christians, and it was they who led me to the Lord. They had a weekly Bible study going in their house, and I had to go—not that I *had* to, but it would have been impolite *not* to—and it was through this that I became a Christian."

"Aah. So then what happened?"

"After I got my bearings a little, emotionally anyway, I wanted to get out of the city. One of these guys had connections with a church in Portland, and they said they could help me get a job, a place to live…get settled into this church…. I liked the idea because I thought the Northwest would be more like Maine. It was then, even more so than now."

"How did you get from music to writing?"

"At the same time I made this move, I decided it was time to get into something more mainstream. Singing in a nightclub just wasn't for me, and I didn't really want to pursue it further. I thought about teaching…but the writing just seemed to click."

"Then you met Dave, started running, and lost twenty pounds."

"You *do* have a mind for detail. Yes. Once I got off the Cajun fried food and started running, the twenty pounds fell off rather easily. And I met Dave, and Helen, and everyone who became my surrogate family, especially after my parents died a few years later."

Melissa stopped at a crossing, thankful for a chance to catch her breath. "Tell me about Dave."

"Dave. The best friend anyone's ever had. He was still in college when I met him, in an internship program to take over the leadership of the single adults' group. Now he *is* the leader. And his 'other job' is sales director for a big educational materials publisher."

"A bachelor too?"

"A bachelor too; probably the most eligible bachelor in church, as you'll see right away when you meet him."

"I see. Well. That probably makes for a better friendship than one with a married guy."

"No doubt. Although I've never really figured out why he's not married yet. Sometimes I get the feeling that he's waiting for someone…someone really special."

"You mean, someone in particular—someone who isn't available right now?"

"I'm really not sure, Melissa. We'll see."

"Well…you've been single for a long time, too."

He didn't say anything; she decided to change the subject. "There are always rocks in the road, where they roll down from the embankment," she said. "If I suddenly give you a push, that's why."

"Now I understand how you turned your ankle. There are a *lot* of rocks."

"Plus, I'm not famous for being graceful."

"Really." His brow furrowed. "I wouldn't have thought that."

"You'd better believe it. I once rammed my grocery cart into an end display of shampoo and knocked down fourteen bottles. Three of them broke."

He stifled a laugh. "I wish I'd been there. —To help you clean it up, I mean."

"Sure you did."

"Melissa," he said after a moment. "I've been thinking about what you said last night, about your mom. I'm trying hard to imagine what that would be like. I didn't grow up in a Christian home, *per se*, but I always knew I was wanted and loved."

"And I grew up knowing I wasn't supposed to be here."

"I'm so sorry, Melissa." He was quiet again, and Melissa realized she had never before felt so wonderfully, painfully transparent. Tears welled up in her eyes. "Melissa," he began again, "I'm going to…." She wanted desperately to hear what he was going to say, but, sensing her struggle, he decided not to. Instead, he put his arm around her shoulder and squeezed her, knocking her off balance; he stopped, holding her by the shoulders until she was steady again. "We'll talk about it another time, Melissa." And they walked on.

He was quiet again, but, hoping in a way that he would return to whatever it was he'd started to say, she said nothing. "Do you have any brothers or sisters?" he asked.

"One sister, Lori, three years younger."

"Are you close to her?"

"We get along okay."

"I see. What is Lori doing now?"

"Picture a two-career childless couple in a 4000-square-foot house overlooking San Francisco Bay; vacation home in Aspen. We hardly ever see each other. Our lives don't overlap much."

"I see," he said again. "Do you have *any* relatives you're close to?"

"I have an aunt and uncle and cousins who are Christians, but I don't see them very often, either."

Kraig took a deep breath. "Now I know how you stay fit. It's from walking up and down these hills. It's going to be a warm day, isn't it?"

"I *so* look forward to fall. Indian summer lasts such a long time here. At this time of year, I always want to be back East, where it really *feels* like fall."

"I know what you mean."

"But some day soon, I am going to *live* in Maine." She steered him around some rocks. "Kraig…could I ask you something?"

"Of course you may, Melissa."

"You never had kids, did you?"

"No, I never did. I would have loved to." His face clouded over in an expression rather unlike any she'd seen before. "At least, none that I know of. Celeste…I wouldn't put anything past her."

Melissa wasn't at all sure what he could have meant by that, but decided to let it go.

Back at the house, after a breakfast of scones made from some of the mixes she'd bought in Maine, Kraig said he had to go downstairs to do something for a while. Disappointed, as she'd looked forward to a leisurely second cup of coffee with him on the leaf-canopied deck, she just said "okay," and proceeded to tidy up the kitchen. She was mentally beginning to go through a list of things he might possibly need to do—work? Practice music? Pray?—when he came up behind her, held her shoulders, and said, almost in her ear, "I'm really looking forward to going canoeing. Come down and get me when it's time to go, all right?"

"Sure." Her spirits lifted instantly at his touch. "I'll come down around eleven."

§

Melissa went to knock on the apartment door just before eleven, and Kraig said, "come in" before the first knock even landed.

"Tell me about this lake, Melissa," he said as she pushed open the door and stepped in. She saw that he was already tying his shoes.

"It's a man-made lake. This is California, you know, not Maine. It's about a half-hour drive. We're borrowing a canoe from some friends. They're leaving it at the dock for us, with a life vest—I didn't have one that would fit you."

"I'm glad the girls wanted Shanna to stay here. I've taken her boating—I have a life vest for her—but it'll be easier not to worry about her."

The car radio was playing. After a minimum of fiddling, Kraig had mastered the controls, and as he adjusted the volume up or down according to what song played, she learned a great deal about his taste in music. The intro to Louis Armstrong's "What a Wonderful World" came on, and Kraig said, "oh, yes," and turned up the volume.

"I never thought he had much of a singing voice," Melissa said.

"Ah, but you miss the point, Melissa. Louis was one of *the* greats in American music history. Jazz is *the* music of America. And this is one of *the* great songs."

"Okay. But I think I'd enjoy it more if he just played it on the—" she thought for just a moment—"trumpet. And left the singing to someone else." He merely smiled that mysterious smile and appeared to lose himself in the song.

§

As she pushed the canoe away from the shore, Melissa's eyes traveled from Kraig's strong, graceful fingers, wrapped around the oar handle, up his arm to his shoulder, where the contours of his muscles gave form to his shirt. "That's a good color on you, that dusty green. You look good in those muted tones."

His eyebrows came together thoughtfully. "Muted tones. I thought that was a music term."

"Maybe it is. If I could paint what you hear, it would all be in color, wouldn't it?"

"Yes." He nodded slowly, seeing something, a memory perhaps, in his imagination.

She watched his face as thoughts and emotions played upon it, transforming his strong, masculine features from one interesting picture into another. She never could figure out what he was thinking, yet she never tired of trying, either.

"Melissa," he said after a moment, "you don't ask a lot of questions."

"I don't?"

"I mean, you ask me all the usual things, about what I do, where I've been, what I like. I don't mean to say that I don't think you're interested in who I am as a person. I know you are. But..." he shook his head a little and gave the oars a hard pull, "you don't ask...and this is what drives me kind of nuts about you, mostly in a good way...you don't ask the kinds of questions that other people ask. And usually much sooner than this."

"I don't get it."

"Even *I* would have wanted to know this about you by now, were the roles reversed. As much as I believe in respecting other people's privacy."

"What is it you want me to know?"

He rested his oars, pulling them together in his lap. "Most people want to know how I became blind. And when. And how I do this or that. *Everyone* wants to know something. And I've heard some amazingly stupid questions, believe me. Like, 'How do you know whether it's night or day?' and...Melissa? I appreciate that you don't ask stupid questions. Trust me, I do. But...Melissa?" He tipped his head. "Do you see what I mean?"

She shrugged. "I always just thought it didn't matter."

He lowered his voice. "It doesn't. But it's a part of who I am, and I want you to know."

Oh dear. Here it comes.

"It was the summer before I turned four. I was playing hide-and-seek with my brother and some other older kids. I thought I'd found the perfect hiding place—our apple orchard. Some of the trees were very old…huge. I decided I was going to impress the other kids and climb higher than anyone had ever climbed before.

"I don't know how long I waited, but they didn't come and find me. Maybe they even forgot about me, and went on to some other activity. Maybe they left me there as a joke. I don't know what happened because no one ever talked about it. But I remember getting tired from holding on. I didn't want to climb down, though; otherwise no one would ever believe how high I'd climbed.

"The doctors said later I must have landed on my head when I fell. I may have hit a branch on the way down. No one really knows how far I fell, or how long I lay on the ground. It was getting dark when someone found me. I'd been unconscious for several hours."

Melissa let the tears flow; they evaporated quickly from her sun-warmed face. She didn't dare speak until she was sure his story was finished. As Kraig went on with the medical aftermath of the accident, key words registered on her consciousness. *Detached retinas. Cerebral hemorrhage. Damaged optic nerve.*

"They were able to reattach the retinas right away. Doctors could do that, even then. But they couldn't repair the nerve damage. That's an area the medical community is exploring now. Maybe someday they'll be able to do this. Maybe even for people whose injuries happened long ago." He spoke very gently.

She pulled over her sleeve to wipe her cheeks and took a deep breath, as silently as possible.

"Melissa?" Kraig set his oars in the bottom of the canoe and rose from his seat, wobbling the canoe in the process.

"Oh—" she cried out, lunging to steady the canoe, succeeding only in making it rock harder.

"Melissa, it's all right," he said, steadily lowering himself into the bottom of the boat in front of her, taking both her hands in his. "Talk to me."

She didn't trust her voice just yet, but, seeing his face up close, remembering the little scars at the outsides of both eyes, she slipped one hand free and put an index finger on one of the scars, inviting him to tell her more.

He nodded. "From one of the surgeries. I've had several, some more recent than others." He took her hand again. "I want you to know as much as anyone knows. Ask questions, Melissa. I need to know that you *want* to know everything about me. Just as I want to know everything about *you*. Don't worry about sounding too nosy. It's because you don't ask…that I want you to know."

He maneuvered back into his seat, picked up his oars, and began to row, seeming not to mind that she hadn't answered him.

He stroked steadily, toward where, Melissa wasn't sure; after a while she gave her face a final wipe with the hem of her shirt, put her oars in and began to row too. She felt her gaze riveted to his face; everything she learned about Kraig just created more mystery, more desire to get to the bottom of this complex, captivating man's heart, mind, and soul. She took a deep breath, aware that its ragged quality betrayed her crying spell.

Kraig laughed a little, but without scorn. "Melissa," he said, "I could tell you some stories. You'd be amazed at human nature, and not in a good way. And *you*, Melissa, are just so refreshingly…" he searched for some time for the right word, "different." He checked his watch. "We've been out here a long time. I don't know about you, but I'm getting hungry."

§

Melissa planted her oar in the sand while Kraig swung the other end of the canoe toward shore. "You first," she said.

He stepped in ankle-deep, lake water covering his deck shoes. He held out his hand and, when she took it, lifted her effortlessly out of the canoe, too quickly for her to gain her balance, and caught her as she literally fell into his arms. He embraced her so hard she heard her back make a cracking sound, but it felt so good she wanted it to last forever. He smelled of clean cotton and sunshine and fresh air, and when he breathed, and laughed, and spoke, she felt it more than heard it. "It's all good, Melissa."

Unpacking the picnic basket at a table in the picnic area, she gave him a bottle of mineral water to open and a pair of plastic glasses. Then she watched as he poured into them, stopping one inch from the top, not spilling a drop.

"So tell me a story," she said.

He took a deep breath. "Ah. One time, when I was in college, I went to get a haircut. There were several stylists, and I usually went to this rather more mature woman. On this particular occasion she wasn't there, so this hot young babe did my hair instead. As she was brushing me off afterward...picture this, Melissa, I had just stood up, and she was brushing the loose hair off of me with her hand...she gave rather too much attention to my rear end. I have no doubt it was intentional. I felt violated. But what could I do?"

"Well, that could have happened to anybody. She'd probably seen you come in all those other times, and found you attractive."

"I can laugh about it now. And it certainly could have been worse." He paused, and when the image became fully formed in her mind's eye, she blushed. "I definitely can appreciate how vulnerable a woman feels when something like that happens.

"But there are other things. My 'favorite' is when people talk in front of me, instead of addressing me directly. I'm *blind*, not *stupid*." He swirled the water in his cup, pausing periodically to let the fizz die down. The water just reached the top, yet never spilled over.

"People feel awkward because they can't make eye contact," Melissa said, being bolder than she would have just an hour before.

"Somehow I suspect it's not quite that simple." He continued to swirl the water in his cup, and she just watched him, fascinated by the movement of his hands. "Thanks for being different, Melissa."

On the drive back, Kraig was scanning the radio stations, stopping whenever he found a good song. Melissa was amazed at how often he could sing along with them, even decades-old songs, not only getting the words right, but every note, every vocal inflection an exact imitation of the song as it played.

§

"Mom, two of the cats came out when Shanna was in the room," Emily said the moment they walked through the door. "Diana even went over and sniffed noses with her. Shanna is so nice and polite, I think the cats are getting used to her."

"Cool," Melissa answered. "Let's go have some raspberry lemonade on the lawn."

As Kraig followed her to the lawn furniture, Melissa saw what an extraordinarily fortunate inspiration it had been to cut off that low-hanging oak branch. An enormous pitcher of raspberry lemonade disappeared in record time, and the sun retreated to the west, slipping behind the house and leaving the lawn in shade.

"This is a nice time of day here," Kraig said.

"Oh, yeah. But you should be here in the spring, when the pond is full of frogs. We can hear them at night, when we're going to sleep and the windows are open." It occurred to Melissa that life in the country would pose some difficulties for Kraig, reliant as he was on such urban amenities as public transportation.

Kraig checked his watch. "It's time for Shanna's afternoon potty break."

"Can I come?" Emily asked.

"Em!" Jessica said, horrified.

"I just want to find out how you can *tell* a dog to go potty," she explained.

Kraig laughed. "You're welcome to come, Emily. This is actually a good thing to learn."

Emily gave Jessica an I-told-you-so look.

Task accomplished, they rejoined the others on the lawn.

"It's almost time to get ready for dinner," Melissa said.

"Is Shanna staying with us again?"

"That's up to Kraig, Emily."

"That would be great."

"Would you like me to iron your shirt, Kraig?" Melissa asked.

"Delighted. I don't even own a travel iron."

§

"I'd love to hear *you* read the menu," Melissa said after the hostess propped a dry-erase board next to their table and left them to ponder it. "Most of the names are in French."

"What have you had that's good?"

"*Everything* I've had here is good. Oh, here's what you'll want—the salmon with spinach one."

"*Saumon aux epinard,*" he said. "Indeed I do."

"Then I'm going to have the chicken and Brie ravioli." Melissa found herself staring at Kraig in the flickering candlelight. "That shirt is absolutely stunning on you."

He smiled. "Thank you. Helen says so too. It's called 'mallard plaid,' but somehow the knowledge that a mallard is a duck doesn't help me much with what a mallard plaid shirt looks like."

"Mallard is...well, actually the color 'mallard' is just another word for teal, although the green on a mallard duck is—"

"A very brilliant green, like an emerald. But a teal is also a duck. So I'm still confused."

"Well...I guess I can't really help you. Somebody decides these things, and then they just *are*, whether they make sense or not."

"Good thing you're the artist, and I'm not."

When the server came, Kraig gave her Melissa's order, and then his own—something that no one had done for her since she'd last dined with her father, and she basked in his chivalry. She wished—not for the first time—that Kraig had come along much sooner.

Sitting across the table from him, she studied the contours of his face where the low light left areas in shadow.

"Tell me what this place looks like, Melissa."

She glanced around. "Exposed brick walls. Pictures of the French countryside. Flowers and candles on every table. The tablecloths have a rose pattern on them."

He nodded. "I like it."

Melissa suddenly remembered something. "Thank you for the iris! Sorry, I forgot. Thank you."

"You're most welcome."

"I could hardly believe you remembered."

"Oh, you're going to be surprised at the things I remember."

"I'm sure I am."

He seemed to be waiting for something more, then after a moment, frowned a little and said, "I think I'm detecting a slight lack of enthusiasm for being sent flowers."

Mildly flustered at his uncanny ability to read her mind, she said, "Oh...it's just that flowers die little by little, so I have decide when to throw them away, and that makes me kind of sad. I'd rather have chocolate. That, I can enjoy, and when it's gone, it's gone."

He nodded, no doubt filing this bit of information.

The server came and poured the wine. Kraig took a sip, gave his approval, then rested his glass on the table, his fingers lightly on its pedestal. "Tell me about Matt. I have sort a half-formed picture of him."

"Oh, he's a pretty good kid. Really. He's never given me any *real* grief."

"But?"

"Well, he's always been a challenge. He's a bright kid, he's the oldest, he's the only boy, and he never had the role model he needed."

"Given what you've already told me about certain key events, I'm guessing that the lack of a role model was an issue even when his father was alive."

"You'd be right about that. Matt knew, from very early on, that he could outsmart Dad, and could somehow always get what he wanted. That *has* to be a frightening thing for a kid—"

Kraig nodded. "To have so much power."

"Yes."

"I saw that at home, with my brother. Not that my dad wasn't a strong leader. He *was*. But back when Kevin was little— keep in mind, this was before I was born—my dad worked long hours, seven days a week, building his business. He wanted us to have *more*, like a lot of parents who are children of immigrants. He just wasn't around when Kevin needed to be shaped into the right kind of man. So he grew up selfish and controlling." Kraig took a thoughtful sip from his glass. "I think Matt will turn out better."

Melissa felt tears spring to her eyes again.

"There's just one more thing I'd like to know, Melissa. Why wasn't Matt's father able to be the right kind of dad?"

She shrugged. "He just never seemed comfortable in the role. He couldn't appreciate the unique personalities of three kids— three *bright* kids, who were always doing and talking about all kinds of off-the-wall things—the unique needs and quirks and idiosyncrasies and..." Melissa shrugged again. "You know what I mean. To *me*, that's what made them such fascinating people. But he just couldn't deal with it. Every little thing just drove him nuts."

"And then there's the other thing you told me about when we were in Maine. Something about a guy named Jeff."

"You *do* have a good memory. Yes. Matt really liked having Jeff be the man in our lives. Partly because Jeff was kind of a big kid himself; partly because it was Matt who brought Jeff into the family. But it was Jeff who broke off the relationship, not me." She took a sip from her glass. "Anyway, that's partly why Matt reacts to you the way he does. Because *you* weren't his idea."

"I can live with that. Don't worry about it, Melissa." He started to raise his glass and put it down again as the server arrived with the salads. "Thank you," he said, and then to Melissa, "The guitarist is good, isn't he? Or she?"

"He. Yes. They don't always have live music."

"Remind me to leave him a tip on the way out."

"I will. And that reminds me of something I *have* wondered about. How do you distinguish between different denominations of money?"

"That's a good question, Melissa. I'll bet you never noticed, but the ink on American currency is actually raised quite a bit, and I can read the face of a bill with my fingertips."

She was just about to say, "*Really?*" when something in his smile gave him away, and he laughed.

"Just kidding. No, it helps to know what I have in my wallet to begin with, and then keep a mental list of what I've spent. Sometimes I fold the bills in different ways—fives in half, tens in quarters, and so on—or put them in certain positions in my billfold. Most salespeople are pretty helpful. No one's ever cheated me that I know of. And now, there's a movement afoot to get the treasury department to make American currency more user-friendly for visually impaired people."

"Well, that's a great idea. But I almost believed the part about being able to read them with your fingertips."

"When I was younger, I convinced quite a few people."

The entrees arrived. "I think we should trade bites," Melissa said.

"Maybe I should—" he rose from his seat, and she slid over to make room for him on her side of the table. It was so much nicer, having him next to her, being able to talk in low voices.

She decided to broach a subject that had nagged her since Maine. "Kraig, when we were in Maine..." she began tentatively, "I kept wondering…if maybe you were there…to visit someone. You know, like a girlfriend or something."

He looked a little surprised. "No, nothing like that. There hasn't been anyone like that in a long time. Although Dave did try to get me interested in one of his sisters a few years ago."

"What happened with that?"

"Dave and I, and his two sisters—Amanda and Brenda, both younger—and Hartley, my guide dog then, went on one of those Mississippi riverboat cruises."

"Oh, *that* must have been fun!"

"It was. We had a wonderful time."

"Then what?"

"Then, nothing. Dave's sisters are both lovely young ladies, tall slim beauties, like your girls. His whole family is cut from the same cloth—wholesome, hospitable, absolutely genuine Midwestern folk from Wisconsin. But that was all. We remained friends. They're both married now."

"Oh."

"Everything is good here, Melissa, just as you said. Tell me, what are you wearing?"

"A short-sleeved knit dress."

"What color?"

"Green. Emerald. The *real* mallard color."

He nodded. "You always notice what I'm wearing. I need to begin learning these things about you—what kinds of clothes you wear, what colors you like."

The evening dissolved in the warmth of candlelight and companionship, shared food and morsels of intimacy.

The server came with the dessert tray.

"Oh, for sure! That dark chocolate mousse cake, please. Kraig?"

"I'll just be having a bite of yours." As the server retreated, he put his arm around her shoulder. "This must be a fine cotton. Your dress. It feels very nice."

"It is. I love to wear cotton and natural fibers."

"I do too. Tell me, Melissa," he said, squeezing closer to close the small gap between them, "what is the story behind your name? You said you didn't remember, but I didn't quite believe you."

That day on the beach, she had felt too vulnerable to share it with Kraig, yet now she felt strangely relieved. "My mom wanted me to be a boy, so she could name me after *her* father. At least, that was the way *she* explained it. If I *had* been a boy, she probably would have had some other reason for not wanting me. Anyway, when I turned out to be a girl, she said she couldn't name me, because she didn't have a girl name picked out.

"Well, my dad—he was in the importing and exporting business, and he'd just been on a business trip to Europe…. I don't remember it *exactly*, so what I told you was pretty much the truth…but he'd met a family with a little girl named Melissa, and he decided that if he ever had a daughter, he would name her Melissa. So he had a name ready for me."

Kraig nodded.

"After he died, I asked my mom to tell me the story, so I could remember it right. She said she didn't know what I was talking about. She never would tell me." Melissa paused, not trusting her voice. "*She* always called me 'Missy'. Which I absolutely despise."

"I solemnly swear never to call you 'Missy'." He gave her shoulders a squeeze. "I love your name, and I like to say it often."

The chocolate mousse cake arrived. "The first bite is yours," she said, forking off a piece.

"No, you first. Tell me if it's good."

She laughed. "Okay. Mm. Yeah, it's good. Here you go." And she put her hand on his cheek as she guided the fork.

He nodded as he chewed. "If I were a chocolate connoisseur like you, I would definitely like this."

Melissa wrapped the corner of her napkin around her finger and wiped away a bit of chocolate lingering at the corner of his mouth. She leaned into him, thrilled with how natural it felt, how easy conversation became, how quietly she could talk to him and still be heard. For, although his hearing was just as good as hers, he lacked lip-reading skills, which, she was just beginning to be aware, sighted people depend on quite a bit for communicating in a noisy environment.

He raised his coffee cup—using his left hand, as he had his right arm around her shoulder, with ease—and she watched his face up close as he drank, as he ate, as he spoke. "This is a turning out to be a delightful evening, Melissa," he said, his lips just an inch from her ear. "Thank you for bringing me here." Each word was weighted just right to land on her ear surely and softly, and she was certain she would never get tired of hearing his voice.

"Wouldn't you be disappointed if you never got to move back to Maine?" she asked.

He stroked the side of his coffee cup thoughtfully with his thumb. "Yes…and no. I've always dreamed of moving back. But the people I know in Oregon are like family to me now. It's important to be in a place you love. But *people* are more important. It would be hard to leave. It just wouldn't make sense now. Maybe some day…. Well, I hate to say it, Melissa, but…one can only drink so many cups of coffee. Even if it *is* decaf."

"Hey, let's take a stroll up and down the block before we go home."

"Sounds good to me." He reached for his wallet.

"Don't you dare," Melissa said. "Remember, everything is my treat."

"But you *are* going to let me tip the musician?"

"Oh! Of course."

He deftly removed the bills he wanted. "Do me a favor, will you? He must have a basket or something for tips."

Back at the car, Melissa unlocked the front passenger door, and was about to open it for him, when Kraig took her hand firmly and eased the car keys out of her grasp. Saying nothing, he circled the front of the minivan, his fingers lightly touching the hood, and unlocked the driver's door. Melissa stood waiting, but still he said nothing, just held the door for her. Then, suddenly recognizing the simple act of chivalry, she went around and got in. He firmly pressed the door closed, retraced his steps, opened his own door, got in, and held out the keys for her.

"Thanks." She started to turn the key in the ignition, then stopped. "Kraig?"

"Yes, Melissa."

"I have this feeling that I keep doing stupid things."

"What stupid things, Melissa?"

"Oh…I don't know. But this morning, and in the canoe, and just now, and a lot of times, I've just had this feeling that I keep doing and saying stupid things. Tell me if I do something stupid, okay?"

"Give me your hand."

Puzzled, she obliged. He held it palm-up, and she felt warm all over as he traced the creases of her palm with his fingers. "I see no stupid things in your future." He placed her hand back in her lap.

Melissa burst out laughing.

"You didn't know I could read palms, did you?"

She laughed some more, and he was smiling too, and trying not to laugh.

§

They returned home to find Jessica and Emily, each with a cat in her lap, and Shanna, forming a little circle on the living room rug.

"Look, Mom and Kraig! Diana and Buster are just sitting here with Shanna, not minding her at all."

"I believe I'll need to meet these cats and learn to tell them apart," Kraig said.

"We can start right now," Emily said.

"Maybe not now," Melissa said. "Kraig might want to turn in early."

Initially miffed at his booking a mid-afternoon flight— whether by choice, to avoid overstaying his welcome, or not, she didn't know—she now saw the advantage of his departure while they were all still having fun, not jaded or exhausted.

"I'll walk you down," she said, as Kraig collected Shanna and headed for the door. "Do you need help opening the sofa bed?"

"No," he answered with unexpected firmness. "Thank you. I can manage. We'll say good night here." Outside on the deck, she fell into his embrace, having come to expect it, to the point of feeling incomplete without a fairly regular hug from Kraig. "It would not be a good thing for me to have you in my bedroom…temporary bedroom that it is," he said, his lips touching her ear.

"Oh. I'm s—"

"No, it's all right. But I need to ask you to just respect this, weird as it may seem."

Melissa relaxed in his arms, and, when she returned to the house, really had no clear idea of how long she'd been outside with Kraig. Yet she was beginning to feel at ease with her time with him, to lose that sense of urgency, that fear that time would take him away from her.

§

"He hasn't kissed you yet, has he, Mom?" Jessica asked the moment Melissa walked through the door.

"No. He hasn't."

"I wonder why not," Emily said.

"I don't know. But—"

"I think I know, Mom," Jessica said. "Remember when we took that seminar at church, about waiting until marriage? I remember learning that some people think kissing—you know, kissing on the lips, that kind—is one of those things that should be saved until marriage, or at least a serious relationship. Maybe Kraig believes that, too. He seems kind of old-fashioned like that, don't you think?"

"Yeah. That could be it. But you know what? It doesn't matter." Until tonight, the possibility had nagged her that he wasn't as romantically available as she had allowed herself to believe. But he had said, unmistakably, there was no one else like that in his life, so she would no longer worry about it. Helen? "Older," he'd said. "Like family," he'd said. And she had no reason to disbelieve.

"But you *do* think he's cute—don't you?" Emily asked.

"Yes. I do." And she turned away as a spontaneous grin took over her face.

§

Standing next to him in church Sunday morning, Melissa was delighted, yet no longer surprised at this sort of thing, that Kraig could sing every hymn, even to the third and fourth stanzas, despite having no Braille hymnal. When they were seated after the last hymn, he leaned over to her and whispered, "Am I going deaf in my right ear, or were you not singing?"

"I wasn't singing," she whispered back. "I only wanted to hear *you*."

§

95

"There's a great little lunch spot about halfway to the airport," Melissa said. "Right about where you noticed the elevation change on the way up."

"I'm glad you told me not to eat much breakfast. Otherwise I wouldn't be hungry yet."

"Well, at *least* you have to have some of their iced tea."

They were seated on the patio, and as Kraig got Shanna situated under the table, Emily asked, "Why doesn't anybody mind when you bring Shanna places?"

"It's the law, Emily. Stores, restaurants, pretty much all places of business have to allow any kind of service dog on the premises. As long as she's wearing her harness, it's never a problem. Besides, most people *like* dogs. Shanna makes it a lot easier to talk to people. Total strangers who might feel awkward about talking to *me* will walk right up and start talking to Shanna." He paused. "Of course, it really helps if they ask first, so I know what's happening."

Melissa looked at her daughters, remembering that first day on the beach, and they returned her knowing look.

"That wonderful smell must be the tea you were telling me about," he said. "And I *am* starting to get an appetite. Although I'll feel better if I don't eat too much, right before my flight."

As they waited for the tea to arrive, Kraig unbuttoned his cuffs and rolled each one twice.

"I'm sorry," Melissa said. "I should have suggested you bring a short-sleeved dress shirt."

"I don't own any. Dave tells me a short-sleeved dress shirt screams 'geek'."

Melissa laughed. "I didn't know that. You could take off your tie, anyway. Most people don't even wear a tie to church in the summer around here."

He loosened it, but kept it on.

"Nice tie. That medallion print looks very nice with that striped Oxford."

"Thank you. Tell me what *you're* wearing."

"A sleeveless purple-and-beige plaid dress."

"Mom looks really good in purple," Jessica said.

"Do you have one of those tweed jackets with the leather elbow patches?" Melissa asked. "*That* would look good on you."

"Dave said the same thing. No, I don't. Next time I need a blazer, I'll keep that in mind. Right now the thought of a tweed blazer makes me feel faint."

"I told you it gets hot here. I bet it's much cooler in Maine right now."

He sighed a little wistfully.

"Hey, I'll get you a bag of that tea to take home," Melissa said.

Back at the car, Kraig examined the keys on his key ring, searching for the suitcase key.

"I just realized, I'm making you open your suitcase again," Melissa said.

"Don't be ridiculous. Everything will smell like cinnamon-orange tea when I get home. It'll remind me of this weekend."

At the airport, the melancholy that had prevailed over their parting in Portland, Maine was conspicuously and happily absent. Jessica and Emily took seats, with Shanna and Kraig's bag at their feet. She stood with him a few feet away, planning a visit with him in Portland, Oregon.

"Melissa, will you ask the girls to come over for a moment?"

She motioned them over, and he gathered them into a huddle. "Jessica, Emily, first of all, I want to thank you for helping me have such a great time this weekend. Especially for being so good with Shanna. Now, here's the thing." He lowered his voice conspiratorially, and Melissa stepped back, staying close enough to hear what he said to them. "I want your mom to come and visit me in Oregon next month. And I want you both to do whatever will make it easier for her. All right?"

"We're not invited?" Emily asked.

"Not this time. But I'll tell you what. If your mom has a good time, you both can come next time."

He hugged them close, and both looked perfectly content just to absorb the warmth of his embrace. After a long moment, he eased them away. "Now, remember what I said, will you?" He hesitated, then pulled them close again, one at a time, kissed them each on the forehead, then released them again. "Melissa?" The girls returned to their seats, she to his arms.

She fingered the silkiness of his tie, considering the aesthetically pleasing combination of the tan-on-teal medallion print with his teal-on-white Oxford shirt; she looked into his face and saw what a striking complement these were to his eyes. And she felt with a deep sense of joy how comfortable it was just to be held and not have to say anything.

"Melissa," he said after a while, "I want you to stay in Portland as long as you can. Choose a weekend when you have nothing else planned. If you can leave work early on Friday and come in the afternoon, leave late Sunday evening, whatever you can do to make your visit longer, I can be flexible. I don't want to cause you any inconvenience. I just want to spend as much time with you as I can. I would have stayed longer this weekend, if I'd…you know what I mean. I just didn't know if it would be the same as it was for us in Maine. As it turns out, it was better. But I didn't want to expect too much…."

"I know what you mean." Her voice came out barely above a whisper. "How about the weekend closest to your birthday?"

"All right, but no big surprises; remember, it'll be *my* turn to treat. Even your plane fare. I mean it, Melissa, all right? My birthday is the twentieth."

"Four weeks. I'll get busy planning."

"I'll find a place for you to stay." He pressed her head to his shoulder, and she breathed deeply, relishing his familiar wholesome smell, a pleasingly masculine blend of cleanliness only mildly compromised by the warmth of the day. "Melissa, I need to tell you one more thing." Her head was still against his shoulder, so she couldn't see his face, which was probably his intent. "This is what I was going to tell you when we were walking yesterday morning." He breathed deeply before he began. "What I wanted to say was, 'I'm going to do my part to make you feel wanted and loved.'"

She felt tears fill her eyes yet again, but was not embarrassed. He understood; she could feel him continuing to breathe rather more deeply than normal. She stayed in his arms, not speaking, until, inevitably, his flight was called. He cupped her face in his hands, turned her head a little to the side, and kissed her on the cheek. His lips lingered there for a long moment, then slipped ever so slightly closer to her lips before moving to her forehead, where he kissed her again.

"I have to go," he said at last.

"Girls," Melissa said, "we need to finish saying goodbye to Kraig and Shanna."

"I'll call you in a few days," he said.

And a moment later he was gone.

§

Melissa was silent as she walked with her daughters out of the airport, her mind too a-swirl with the weekend's events, and all the things she would have to do to get ready to go out of town, to allow the formation of any organized thought.

"Mom, is Kraig your boyfriend now?" Emily asked.

"Oh, I don't know, Emily, I—"

"He kissed you, finally."

"Well, on the cheek and on the forehead; I don't know if that really counts."

"It looked like a kiss to *me*," Jessica said.

"He *is* younger, you know."

"Does he care?"

She shrugged. "He doesn't seem to."

"So it doesn't matter."

"Oh, and I found out…how he got to be blind."

"Is it sad, like you thought?"

"Yeah, it's pretty sad. But you should know, since it looks like Kraig's going to be part of our lives. I'll tell you in the car. Oh, and I also found out, he wasn't in Maine to visit someone."

"So, why *was* he?" Jessica asked.

"That, I still don't know. But I'm not going to worry about it."

§

Chapter 11

On Tuesday, a padded envelope arrived by overnight delivery. Inside, Melissa discovered a CD. She smiled to herself, thinking it would be a recorded message, like a letter. Putting it into her player, she quickly recognized the intro to Louis Armstrong's "What a Wonderful World." *Is he teasing me?*

When the vocal began, it wasn't Louis Armstrong. It was Kraig. Melissa laughed out loud with surprise and delight.

Wednesday night, he called. She hardly gave him a chance to greet her.

"That was awesome! Is there no end to your happy little surprises?"

"I hope not." She could hear the modest smile in his voice. "I think I have everything covered for your visit. Helen will come with me to pick you up from the airport; Dave and I will take you back on Sunday. And Helen says you're more than welcome to stay at her place."

"Really? I mean—I'm a total stranger."

"Not at all. You're a friend of mine, and she'll be delighted to have your company."

"Okay, then."

"How are things going on your end? Do the girls have something planned for that weekend?"

"Yeah, they can stay at some friends' house…. Kraig, this might sound funny, but Emily calls you my boyfriend now."

"And…what is funny about that?"

"Oh…I don't know…'boyfriend' sounds so…kind of… adolescent or something. What do *you* think?"

"Well, there's 'gentleman caller'… 'significant other'… 'partner'…. Melissa, there are some truly dreadful terms out there, none of them having the warmth, spontaneity, and innocence of 'boyfriend' and 'girlfriend'."

"Then you're comfortable with 'boyfriend'?"

"Yes, Melissa, I am perfectly comfortable with 'boyfriend'."

After she hung up, she reflected that Kraig had seemed to have no problem working out the details of her visit—which confirmed her suspicion that he hadn't even *tried* the first time around. But it didn't matter. He didn't really *say* he'd tried; in his mind, anyway, the obstacles had been real.

§

Melissa could see Portland coming into view below, a city defined by highways and waterways. She found herself exploring the softness of her sweater, and wondered what it would be like to be hugged in it…and what it would feel like for Kraig when he hugged her.

Entering the terminal, Melissa looked around and quickly picked out of the crowd the man she'd come to see. At first, she didn't see the woman standing next to him—petite, gray-haired, a little stooped. *Helen.*

Helen smiled when she saw Melissa, and stretched to say something to Kraig.

"Kraig. Hey," Melissa called out when she was close enough.

He broke into a smile, and she dropped her carry-on bag, planning to kiss him on the cheek. For she'd decided, on the flight up, that she'd try to appear more formal and distant than she would if he'd come alone, not wishing to embarrass him. Not that it made any difference—he embraced her as he always did, squeezing the breath out of her, not seeming to mind that no introductions had yet been made.

"Helen," he said when he released her at last, "Melissa Melvin from California. Melissa, Helen Kovalik."

"Kraig has told me so much about you, all of it good," Melissa said, taking care not to clasp the older woman's hand too tightly. "And Shanna!" she said, suddenly remembering Kraig's loyal companion, waiting for her bit of attention.

"Do we need to go to baggage claim?" Kraig asked, bending to pick up the bag she'd dropped with a thud.

"I'm afraid so. I just can't pack quite as efficiently as you do."

"Not a problem," he laughed.

As they waited at the carousel, his arm around her, Melissa whispered to Kraig, "Helen seemed to recognize me right away. What did you tell her?"

"I just told her to look for a tall, willowy, gorgeous brunette about my age…" he leaned closer and said into her ear, "wearing a very flattering sweater." She blushed and giggled, deciding it wasn't important to know how much of this was fact and how much flattery.

§

Helen left Melissa, Kraig, and Shanna at the entrance to Kraig's townhouse complex. Melissa followed the pair through a self-closing wrought-iron gate into a brick courtyard—an inspired feature, she thought, for if Shanna were to slip out the door of Kraig's unit unnoticed, she would still be contained within the gated courtyard. Kraig's unit was on the second floor, and at his door was an intercom box.

As Kraig held the door, she stepped into his well-ordered world. Almost Spartan in its neatness, the townhouse was at once relaxing and inviting. She soon identified what made the place so comfortingly familiar—its smell. All the smells entwined with her memories of him were there to greet her—the balsam pillow, the cinnamon-orange tea, a clean dog, *him*. An open window admitted a breath of northwestern flora-scented air.

"I like it."

"I'll put this in the spare bedroom," Kraig was saying, taking her suitcase to a room somewhere behind her.

"Sure. I'm just looking around a little."

The décor was mostly in neutral shades of beige and tan, yet saved from dullness by artfully placed spots of color. A large quilt, probably heirloom, filled the far wall behind the sofa with rich hues of blue, green, red, and brown. A throw blanket and several pillows echoing these colors decorated the sofa. Numerous large, healthy houseplants occupied spaces high and low. *A woman's touch, no doubt.* Melissa smiled, thinking of the worry she'd wasted on Helen.

In the corner, behind a loveseat set at an angle, towered the only extravagant thing in the place—an entertainment center crammed with state-of-the-art stereo equipment and the most intimidating collection of recorded music Melissa had ever seen outside of a music store.

Suddenly remembering the birthday gifts she had tucked into her carry-on bag, she felt with a dreadful certainty that he must already have the CD she'd chosen for him. In a bit of a panic, she explored her options.

"You can use the guest bath here, off the entryway," Kraig said, rejoining her.

"Okay, thanks. Um…do you mind if I look at your music collection?"

"Be my guest. Choose something to play if you like. Glass of mineral water before we get ready to go for dinner?"

"Please."

"Slice of lemon?"

"Sure."

Upon closer inspection, Melissa saw that the recordings were arranged according to a library-like system. Each column was labeled—with both block lettering and Braille—according to style. *Jazz. Classical. Opera. Popular. Christian.* Within each style were subgroups by artist, arranged alphabetically. Scanning down the columns, she determined, to her amazement, that he did not have the CD in question after all.

Kraig brought her glass.

"Thanks. This is impressive—your music collection."

"Did you find anything you want to hear?"

"Uh, no, you go ahead and choose something. I'll be right back." She set her glass on the coffee table and went to retrieve the gifts.

Kraig was putting some selections on the stereo when she returned.

"Oh, that's nice," she said as some jazz began playing.

"Nice. *This* is nice," he said, putting his hands on her shoulders, caressing the softness of her sweater. He put his hands on her waist. "Is it cashmere?"

"No, just cotton and silk."

"It feels like cashmere. What else are you wearing?"

"A denim skirt," she said, still trying to hide the packages she was holding. "I hope it's fine for where we're going."

"It's fine," he said, and she had the distinct feeling he'd like to explore further; that if he were a different kind of man, he wouldn't give a moment's hesitation to indulging his desires to put his hands in other places. In a way, she wanted him to. *But, no. To encourage that would be a violation of who he is.*

He looked quizzical as the packages she was holding made a telltale crinkling sound. "What's up?"

"Happy birthday."

"I was hoping you'd forget."

"You were not!"

He smiled, sort of shyly. "Have a seat."

Melissa was surprised to see that the rough-looking texture of the sofa's upholstery was actually rather velvety; then, upon reflection, she realized that he would have chosen it by feel, although someone else might have weighed in with an opinion on color or style.

"This one is from the girls." She placed a soft, amorphous package in his hands as he sat next to her, and watched his fingers reveal its contents.

"A stuffed cat. Well, maybe the girls can help me name him. Or her."

"They'd like that. This one is from me." She handed him the wrapped CD. "You don't already have it. I checked."

"Did you? That was clever of you." He removed the wrap, expertly pried off the factory seal and shrink-wrap, rose to put it on the stereo; then picked up the remote control, returned to his seat next to her, and pressed a button to start the music.

"Ah, yes. I do like this." He smiled. "Thank you. And I'll write the girls a little note, too."

She leaned into him, wanting to sink into the softness of the sofa and the warmth of his embrace, which she'd so looked forward to since their last goodbye. Instead, he turned his body toward her, somewhat awkwardly, she thought, in effect keeping her at a distance. Thinking this rather odd, she looked at him; he suddenly looked shy, and she realized: it was the first time they'd been together, completely alone and in private, not to mention on a very comfy piece of furniture.

"Oh, hey, what time do we need to leave for dinner?" she asked.

He checked his watch. "We should go out to catch the bus in about half an hour. It's a few blocks' walk. But you don't mind walking."

"No, I wore sensible shoes. It was so good to meet Helen, finally. I'm *so* looking forward to meeting Dave, but the way you have the weekend planned, it sounds like I won't get to till Sunday."

"That is correct."

"I just meant…you've told me all these wonderful things about him…I thought it would've been fun to include him…." Melissa could see that the conversation had taken a strange turn, and she hurried to end it. "But that's okay. Never mind. Hey, could I see your watch?"

He held out his wrist. Closing her eyes, she explored its Braille display with her fingers.

"Watch this." He pressed a button, and a computer-generated voice announced the time. "I can set it to announce any number of different times throughout the day; even different times for different days of the week."

"Wow. That's neat."

"Speaking of time…do you need time to get ready?"

"I guess I should go freshen up my makeup."

§

"How long has it been since you rode a public bus?" Kraig asked as they took their seats.

"Oh…years. I don't even remember."

"It's a great place to people watch, isn't it?"

"Yes. It'll be fun." Tentatively, Melissa settled herself against his side. He put his arm around her. *In public…no problem.*

As the bus stopped here and there, she watched the passengers board. A couple of rough-looking men—either dressed in black, or wearing clothes so dirty they *looked* black—got on, and just at that moment Kraig squeezed her closer. Just as she realized that she was probably staring at them, the one in front made eye contact with her, and she turned away quickly. She still felt his gaze on her as he and his companion took seats a few rows ahead. Melissa let out her breath.

A few stops later, a couple of younger guys boarded, one a wannabe tough guy and the other sort of nerdy-looking. Melissa immediately recognized the pairing: a troublemaker-leader and an impressionable follower. These two, she didn't feel afraid to watch;

she was surprised to see the nerdy-looking one staring at her unabashedly as he and his leader-friend took seats only two rows in front of them. Then the nerdy one said to the tough one in a very audible whisper, "Check it out." She couldn't hear the whole communication, but there was no missing the words "blind dude." The second guy then turned and looked, then whispered to his friend something Melissa couldn't hear. They both laughed hysterically.

She shook her head, stupefied at the blatant rudeness. She was half-hoping, against all logic, that Kraig hadn't heard. When she sneaked a sideways glance at him, he was smiling. He pulled her closer and whispered into her ear, "Welcome to my world." Then he kissed her on the cheek. Melissa toyed with the idea of initiating a very public display of affection, just to give the stupid people something to talk about, but decided against it.

A moment later, another reason occurred to her for Kraig's easy acceptance of such idiotic behavior by other men: it was confirmation that the woman he was with was, indeed, found attractive by sighted people.

Getting off the bus downtown, they had to pass both unsavory pairs. As they passed the younger two, one made a crude comment to the other, with no pretense of privacy, and they both laughed like maniacs again.

Kraig turned to take her hand as she stepped from the bus. "Not *everyone* in this city is so Neanderthal," he said.

"Thank goodness. I was beginning to wonder."

§

"I've just submitted this piece to *Light of the World* magazine," Kraig was saying as they sipped from glasses of wine, waiting for their meals. "It's a commentary on the murder of that gay student, with liberal thinkers saying he was the victim of a 'hate crime' and that we need more laws to protect certain groups from hate crimes. Not that Christians would ever be on the 'protected' list. But some extremists are blaming people with traditional values for creating an atmosphere of hate that led to his murder. The point I tried to make is that through the ages, Christians have been the most ardent supporters of religious freedom for everyone. And religious liberty is the foundation for all other freedoms."

"Wow. I'd be interested in reading that."

"I'll send you a copy. I always get a few free ones." He looked pensive for a moment. "Tell me what this place looks like, Melissa."

She looked around, then went on to describe every detail as he nodded.

"I've been here many times, and certain things I know. I know we're sitting in a very high booth, and that the light is low."

"How do you know that?" She watched his face as he contemplated her question.

"That we're in a high booth, because of the way the sound carries. And people talk more quietly when it's dark. They move differently when it's hard to see. It's a different atmosphere." She continued to watch his face as he continued to look pensive. "Nobody describes things the way you do, Melissa. When you describe things to me, it's not just words. You make me *see* them." He put his hand palm-up on the table for her to place hers in his. "I love that about you. Not many people can really get into my world. Not many *try*." She smiled, probably blushed; he reached across the table and touched her cheek. "Forget this," he said, "I'm coming over there." And he circled around the table to her side of the booth.

"I love that about you"…he sort of, almost, said "I love you."

§

"We have about an hour till Helen comes," Kraig said with a sigh as he selected some music to put on the stereo.

"I hope we're not keeping her up too late." Melissa settled into the soft depths of the sofa, safely on what she judged to be her side.

"Generally I try to avoid asking her to drive at night. I'd originally planned to escort you over on the bus, but she said, 'Don't be silly.'" Kraig said this in what Melissa took to be an imitation of Helen's voice and mannerism, and she laughed. It occurred to her that Dave could have handled this job, but since Kraig seemed to be deliberately keeping him out of the picture for the first part of the weekend, she said nothing. "It won't be long, though," Kraig continued, "before she can no longer drive at night. Or at all."

"Hey," Melissa said, suddenly having an idea, "do you have a photo album? Pictures of you when you were younger?"

"In fact I do." He sounded a little surprised, perhaps equally delighted, that she should ask. He finished fine-tuning the stereo, disappeared into his bedroom, and returned a moment later, placing the large volume in her lap. "My mom put this together for me. She thought I might someday have someone in my life who'd be interested." His voice lowered a bit. "I never even took it out of storage when I was with Celeste. Good thing. I packed fairly hastily, and it would've been horrible if I'd left it there."

Melissa opened it and saw that each picture was labeled with both neat print and Braille captions. He put his arm across the back of the sofa, behind her shoulders, his fingers on the first caption. "This was my first studio portrait. I was three months old."

"Oh," she breathed, "what a beautiful baby. Such intelligent eyes."

As he turned the pages of the album, she watched his life unfold. *Kraig, age four, no longer focusing on the camera. Kraig now taller than his dad. Kraig at sixteen, confidence manifest in the firm set of his chin, posing with his first guide dog.*

"Kevin!" Melissa said at the next turn of the page. "He looks pretty much as I imagined. Your dad looks very determined. And your mom…was beautiful." Melissa studied the images of Kraig's family, trying to form a fuller picture of who he was and where he'd come from. "This reminds me. You've never told me your middle name."

"Bourgoine. My mom's maiden name. As you probably guessed."

He put his fingers on the caption of his mom's portrait and, Melissa thought, looked a little wistful. She was suddenly overcome with affection for this sweet man, surrounded by people who cared about him, some no longer with him, but having left him with good feelings about himself; yet in another way, alone, longing for someone to fill a void. And suddenly, overpoweringly, she wanted to be that person. He felt it, too; Melissa clutched the book as it started to slide off her lap, yet he made no move to catch it; he put his arm around her shoulder, the other hand on her face. He put his fingers on her lips, caressed them, leaned closer. Melissa had felt fairly sure, until this moment, that he had no plans of kissing her; yet now, she was certain that he was going to, and she leaned into his embrace, ready to receive his kiss.

Looking pained, he leaned away again; surprised, Melissa let the album slide to the floor.

"Melissa...."

"I'm sorry," she said, picking up the photo album.

"No. *I'm* sorry. Let's..." he said, but apparently was not sure what he was going to say. "How about I put that away." She handed him the heavy book; he left the room and returned a long moment later without it. He stood before her, looking as though he might have splashed some cold water on his face during his absence; he held out his hand, offering to help her up, and she let him.

"I'd like to show you some things." His hand on her shoulder, he turned her toward the spare bedroom, which, she'd noticed earlier, served as his home office. She felt something in his touch, some unspoken consolation; she tried to act as if nothing was wrong, but in fact, her feelings had been hurt. One of them had done something wrong; she knew neither who was guilty, nor of what.

"Have you ever seen a talking computer?"

"No, I haven't."

He pulled out the chair for her to sit in front of this marvel of technology, then put his arms around her to reach the keyboard as he stood behind her. "It reads the words back to me as I type. I can do all kinds of things. I can scan the newspaper, my mail, anything. I can convert print to audio, print to Braille, or audio to Braille. It even has a feature to convert sheet music to Braille." He began to demonstrate.

Melissa's eyes wandered around the work area as he did, and she was drawn to a pair of small wooden bird carvings on the shelf above the desk. They were not finely detailed, but as she lifted one, she felt its surface, polished to a high gloss. The rich wood grain was striking, almost iridescent; she wondered if he held these often and rubbed them in his hands, polishing them yet more over time. Turning it over, she saw KBD on the bottom. "You made these? The little birds?"

"I did. Many years ago. It was sort of therapeutic for me at that time in my life."

"They're beautiful."

He stopped what he was doing on the keyboard. "Why don't you choose one to keep? I'd like you to have it."

"Really? Thank you." She took down the other one, compared them, and settled on the one she'd held first.

"Let me see which one you chose."

She placed it in his hand.

"Ah, the female chickadee. Good choice."

"Chickadee?"

"Maine's state bird."

"Oh! Of course." Next her gaze fell upon a paperweight on the desk; just able to reach it from her chair, she lifted it for inspection and saw that it was a plaster cast of a puppy's paw print. "Is this Shanna's paw print?"

"It is. Her puppy raiser gave that to me."

"That was thoughtful."

He finished what he was doing on the computer and handed her a Braille printout. "See what this can do? It's a real life enhancer."

"This is Braille music?"

"It is."

"Wow," was all she could think of to say. The complexity of it was bewildering; anyone who could understand *that*, she thought, was surely a genius. She looked at him, admiration swelling in her heart, and felt her spirits begin to lift as each little part of Kraig's world revealed more of him to her.

"And now," he said, checking his watch, "I think we should go out to wait for Helen. I don't like to make her walk up here in the dark alone."

Kraig put Shanna on just the lead, without the harness; he didn't really need her just to go out to the parking lot, but he liked her companionship just the same, Melissa noted with great tenderness. The evening was cool, and he put his arm around her shoulders as they waited. She longed to be content with just that, but her unsettled emotions wouldn't quite allow it. She was almost glad to see Helen drive up; spending some time with her might help.

§

111

Melissa stirred her chamomile tea as she sat in a chintz-covered chair in Helen's living room. She didn't know whether Helen always had chamomile tea at bedtime, or whether she'd sensed Melissa's troubled spirit, and offered it as a balm; but Helen said it was soothing and good to have at bedtime, so she'd gratefully accepted.

Helen's place had a cozy oldness to it; great care had been taken with the details, the handmade curtains, the well maintained Oriental rugs and a few heirloom pieces; yet, looking more closely, Melissa could see that many of the larger pieces of furniture were simple and inexpensive-looking. Not a speck of dust could be found anywhere. Helen, sitting across from her and stirring her own tea, seemed pleased to have company, just as Kraig had said.

Melissa rested her spoon on her saucer. Not knowing if she'd get another chance, she forged ahead with the questions she'd yearned to ask of Helen. "How long have you known Kraig?"

"Oh…."

Melissa's heart sank; she wondered if Helen's long-term memory would serve.

"Fourteen years. As long as he's been in Portland."

"Well…then you know him as well as anyone. Whatever you think is okay to tell me…."

"Anything, dear."

"Is he what he seems to be? As nice? And mannerly? And sweet as I think he is?"

"Why, yes." She seemed puzzled that Melissa should ask.

"Well—" She struggled for the best words with which to express her question.

"Let me tell you how I came to know Kraig," Helen said. "When he came up from California, you know, he didn't know anyone here…although I do remember something about some of the young people being friends-of-friends of his. I had just started coming to church, too…." And she went on to tell about how the leadership of the church thought she could fill a need by helping him get settled, keep an eye on his mail, and so forth. And how what had begun as a service to a fellow churchgoer deepened into a friendship and then into almost a familial relationship, especially after his parents passed away and he no longer went back East for holidays. "Kraig is very dear to me. I can't open jars. When we go to the grocery store, he opens all of my jars that I'll be needing in the next few days. He changes my light bulbs. He can do that without even standing on a chair!" In Helen's face she saw the same depth of admiration she'd felt upon seeing the Braille sheet music.

"You can trust Kraig to do the right thing," Helen concluded. "That much, you can be sure of." She looked as though she'd suddenly remembered something. "Have you met Dave yet?"

"No! I thought it was strange, but Kraig planned it so that I'd meet him Sunday at church."

"That *is* a little strange. Well…I'm sure there's a reason. But when you meet Dave, you'll feel better about everything."

Melissa looked into her now-empty cup and swirled the residue around in the bottom. "I also think it's a little weird that he's been single for so long. I thought maybe I was missing something."

"Hmm." Helen looked thoughtful. "Well, maybe. Kraig does tend to get settled into a comfortable routine and try to avoid change. Maybe that's what you're seeing. In any case, he'll make everything right. I want you to know, dear, we were all so happy when Kraig told us about you. And we've been happy with *everything* he's told us about you since."

§

It was more anticipation than apprehension that Melissa felt as she waved goodbye to Helen the next morning and turned toward the wrought-iron gate. Soothed by Helen's companionship and the tea, she had slept well.

Kraig was leaning against his front door frame, and a smile spread across his face as she approached.

"Morning, Kraig."

"Melissa." He held out his hands at shoulder level, and she fitted herself into his embrace. "Melissa. Before anything else, I want to tell you I'm sorry about last night. I know we had some awkward moments. I know what happened, and why, and I know how you must have felt. But I want you to know that I want what's best for both of us, and I want you to trust me."

"I know. I do. It's okay."

"I love you."

113

Melissa squeezed her eyes closed, savoring this moment in which he first said, "I love you." She hesitated only a moment before saying, "I love you, too."

He squeezed her long and hard, pressing her head to his shoulder, his face to her hair.

"I guess I should tell you, Kraig, I've never put that much value in the words 'I love you.' A lot of the time, I think people say that just to manipulate other people. I hate it when people use words meaninglessly. I can tell whether someone loves me or not."

In his silence she heard the unspoken question.

"I can tell that you do," she answered.

He took in a deep breath and let it out, then released her and held her at arm's length. "Today is going to be a good day." He tapped the toe of her shoe with his. "I see you wore good walking shoes. Good. We'll be doing plenty of walking."

He ushered her inside, closed the door, and took Shanna's harness from the entryway closet along with a daypack. "Do you have anything you want to put in here?"

"No, thanks. I usually carry a little daypack; I prefer it to a purse. This one has straps that zip together, so I can wear it as a shoulder bag."

Shanna sat obediently as Kraig harnessed her, and he hummed to himself as he went about the task.

§

"I think you'll like this place," Kraig said as he held the door for her at the deli-café where he'd said they should eat breakfast.

"Oh, dear," she said a few minutes later, beginning to peruse the menu.

"Melissa?"

"I mean, too many choices. What do you usually get?"

"An omelette. Or Belgian waffles. Or a breakfast burrito. Sometimes a fruit smoothie. Or an espresso drink. Or all of the above."

"That's helpful," she laughed. "Well, what are you getting today? Shall I read you the whole menu?"

"They do have a Braille menu here, but I have a better idea: look at the chalkboard above the deli counter and read the specials."

"Ah! Well, I see what I want." She settled on a giant pecan roll and a fruit smoothie; he decided on an omelette with smoked salmon, Tillamook cheese, and sun-dried tomatoes.

"All their espresso drinks are great," he said, mentioning a few with a convincing Italian accent, "but if we just get coffee, we can linger over refills."

"I suppose you speak Italian too?"

"No, of course not. But I like the way it sounds."

Melissa shook her head. "You amaze me." He looked a bit shy again, she thought; she wondered if he thought she was flattering him, but surely other people noticed his vast repertoire of talent, and commented on it often.

She looked around at the high, open-beamed ceilings, with their colorful, screen-printed banners; at the booths and tables, filled with pairs and groups of people, bustling with conversation; then out the window to the street scene. The mid-morning sun reached down between the buildings to the sidewalk, promising a bright day. She looked back at Kraig, and he was smiling, filling her with a certainty that it would, indeed, be a great day.

He held out his hand palm-up on the table. She put hers in it, wondering how long it would be before he gave up the effort at cross-table conversation. Just before their plates arrived, he said, "Forget this," and moved around to her side.

"Much better," she said.

§

"Now we walk," Kraig said as she took his hand and stepped off the bus at Forest Park. "This is the biggest city park in North America. We could spend the day here and not see it all. Helen loves the rose garden. Dave comes here to run cross-country. Shanna and I like to walk the trails. With company, whenever possible. A lot of people go to the zoo, but I prefer not to take Shanna there—it makes her a little nervous and it's harder for her to concentrate."

"Well, I'm just glad I didn't eat any more than I did, or I wouldn't be *able* to walk."

"Ah, but you'll be hungry again after this."

They walked, explored, crossed bridges, stopped often to examine things. Kraig identified an impressive number of plants by

115

their smell. Even different varieties of roses, he could distinguish with little trouble.

"I never even noticed that different varieties of roses *have* different smells," Melissa said in wonder.

"Then I shall have the pleasure of teaching you. You won't even need to know the names—just that certain colors have certain fragrances. You'll be good at it."

§

Melissa took a sip from her bottle of mineral water. Kraig rested on his back, his head on Shanna's side, his fingers twisting a blade of grass as he summarized for her a recent movie review. She loved times like this, just listening to him, as he poured out his thoughts freely, almost, it seemed, forgetful of her presence.

"Some conservative critics are calling this movie 'politically correct' or even 'pro-gay,' but I disagree. The central character knows he's dying from a condition he's brought upon himself by his lifestyle. He knows he's hurting his loving, supportive family. He's not expecting any reward in the next life. To me, it's a call for compassion."

He brushed his hair away from his forehead; it was turning out to be a warm, mostly sunny day. Looking at him lying on the grass in his gray corduroy jeans, she couldn't help notice the way his pants fit him very nicely; yet as soon as she caught herself looking, she looked away. Still, she reflected with surprise...she *had* noticed.

"Oh, and the music in this movie," Kraig continued. "I think you would call it haunting. I believe the music can either make or break a movie, don't you? Melissa?" He rose on one elbow. "Are you still with me?"

"Every word."

"Oh. Good." He sank back down onto Shanna's side. "One advantage of being a writer is that if your audience leaves, you usually don't have to know about it." He plucked the blade of grass he was twisting, tossed it, and began twisting a new one. "What are you wearing, Melissa?"

"Stretch-denim leggings and a tunic-length striped polo shirt, teal and purple."

He nodded, then looked a little apprehensive. "Melissa, I've been wanting to ask you something. Tell me the truth, now."

"Sure, go ahead."

"Is my hair very gray?"

She laughed. "No, not very. Maybe just enough to keep me from looking older than you. You could call it 'brown heather'."

"Brown heather," he laughed. "I like that. I've been worried about that for…I don't know, a long time. I never knew whom to ask …it just sounded so vain." He plucked the blade of grass and tossed it. "Melissa, you don't worry about that other thing, do you? About being older?"

"Well…a little."

"Don't, Melissa. Please. I never even *think* about it. It just doesn't matter at all."

"Okay. I'll try not to."

§

Back at the townhouse, Kraig put Shanna's harness and the daypack in the entryway closet and took out a caddy filled with dog grooming tools. Shanna followed him enthusiastically as he sat on the love seat in the corner, where there was room for her to sit in front of him. Melissa watched the procedure from the sofa.

As he brushed every inch of her, Shanna held as still as her ecstasy would allow. Kraig put the brush back in the caddy and ran his fingers through her fur, now glowing like burnished copper, around her ears and neck, down her chest and back, between her toes. Melissa watched his strong, sensitive fingers complete the task, and if ever a dog had gazed more adoringly upon her master, Melissa could scarcely imagine it.

"You're so lucky," she heard herself say, without taking the time to think how it would sound.

He turned toward her. "Me? Or Shanna?"

"Both. She's such a good dog. You're such a good master."

"Ah, yes. When we were at the guide dog school, being matched with our partners, each person seemed to think he or she got the best dog. Including me. Except that I *know* I got the best dog." He held Shanna's head between his hands and kissed her. Then he put the tool caddy back in the closet and washed his hands.

117

"Now, Melissa, I want to show you something." He took her by the hands and directed her to the love seat, went behind it to put some CDs on the stereo, and fitted a set of expensive-looking cordless headphones on her. "Close your eyes." Some nightclubby-sounding instrumental music came on. Partway through the song, he leaned down and said, close to her ear, "Now you can see music the way I do. Can't you?"

She nodded.

Toward the end of the song, he took the headphones off of her, and in the next moment, he was standing before her, his hand extended, as if asking for a dance.

"Oh, no, not that. I told you, I'm not very—"

"It doesn't matter." He found her hands and pulled her up, against her half-hearted protests. "Relax," he said, placing her hands in their proper positions, even as she struggled to remember them. The music changed to a slow instrumental tune. *He must have planned this!*

Melissa forced herself to breathe.

"You're doing fine," he whispered into her ear. As the saxophone melody came in, he clutched her right hand to his chest. A few bars later, he pressed her hand into its place and slipped his around her waist; following his lead, she slid her hands around behind his shoulders.

She relaxed and let him lead her. He was right: it didn't matter. It wasn't about dancing; it was about the closeness, the movement, the togetherness. She breathed more deeply, and every intake of breath brought to her senses the warmth and fragrance of his nearness. For five magical minutes, this was her whole world: her hands on his shoulders, her body touching his, his lips slightly parted, his breath on her face.

The song ended, and the next one was too lively. Still, he held her close, his cheek against her forehead. "That wasn't so bad, was it?"

"No," she said, hearing her voice come out sort of giggly.

"You did fine. No more about you not being graceful." He still held her. "We should take ballroom dancing lessons. Learn to tango. Wouldn't that be fun?"

"Do you really think I could?"

"Of course you could." Still he held her, and as he brought his hands together behind her, she wondered if events were leading up to another awkward moment. When she heard the electronic voice of his watch, she realized he was merely checking the time. "I say… it is time to go make dinner."

A little disappointed, a little relieved, she began to follow him into the kitchen. She nearly bumped into him as he turned around suddenly. "Wait. We need dinner music. How about…opera?"

"Um…."

"I heard that utter lack of enthusiasm. I know you've never mentioned opera among your favorite types of music. It isn't the most upbeat kind."

"Besides, for those of us who speak only English, it doesn't make sense."

"Oh, Melissa, how much you miss! You don't have to understand the *words* to feel their *meaning*. You'll like this guy. He's young—our age—fresh, original, and brilliant. And handsome." He held up the CD case for her approval.

"I'll take your word for it. Go ahead, put it on."

In the kitchen, he took from a drawer an apron that had probably been his mother's, and, judging by the creases in it, hadn't been worn in a very long time. He proceeded to tie it on her—not from behind, the way she had tied her daughters' sashes over the years, but facing her and reaching around. Her hands fell naturally on his shoulders. So, the evening progressed like a continued dance, Kraig moving around his kitchen with ease, Melissa following his lead, occasionally bumping into him; but mostly on purpose, as he always stopped to give her a squeeze, as if to make sure she was all right.

"What are we having?" she asked.

"Bachelor food."

"Bachelor food!" she laughed. "If I didn't know you better, I'd be worried."

"Seriously. You'll get to see what I eat when you're not here. There's a package of shrimp in the refrigerator; could you get that out?" He took a package of pasta from the cupboard and handed it to her. "Check this for foreign objects, will you?"

She turned the bag over, examining the contents. "I have a feeling there's a story here."

"There is. Once I was eating some pasta for dinner—just like tonight—and one particular bite just didn't feel right. Upon inspection, it turned out to be a well-cooked piece of paper. Turns out it was a coupon that I didn't know was in there, so I cooked it along with the pasta."

Kraig was smiling, so Melissa felt free to laugh.

"Dave laughed harder than that, when I told him about it."

"I'm sure he did. No coupons today, though."

"Well, how boring. How about a glass of wine?" He got out a bottle of white Zinfandel and two glasses. "You're not one of those purists who have to have a certain wine with a certain food, are you?"

"No, whatever you've chosen will be perfect."

He suddenly checked his watch, as though he might have forgotten something important, but didn't say what it might be.

Soon they were sitting across from one another over plates of pasta with shrimp, mushrooms, and red bell peppers; on the side, steamed zucchini with butter and garlic.

"If this is bachelor food, I'm not *too* concerned. You can cook for me anytime."

"I'd like to." He put his hand palm-up on the table; she put hers in it. She liked the way it looked there. He skillfully lifted his wine glass with his left hand.

"How do you do that, use your left hand so easily? I couldn't."

He smiled, setting his glass on the table, resting his fingers on its pedestal. "Melissa, you are not as graceless as you think you are. In my mind, you're an elegant woman."

"Thank you." She was glad he couldn't see her blush, yet she knew it was betrayed in her voice. She caressed his fingertips. "But I do not understand how you can read Braille. I've tried feeling those dots with my eyes closed, and they all feel the same to me. And your fingers are so much bigger!"

"I learned young. In a way, I was fortunate. You could learn if you had to."

"Maybe."

"How do you like the music?"

120

"You were right. I like it. But he's no more original or brilliant *or* handsome than you."

He tipped his head down; she guessed it was his turn to blush. He looked up again. "Oh, Melissa, I live in fear of the day you figure out that I'm not as smart or talented or anything else as you think I am."

"Never. I see it more clearly each day."

He nodded slowly, as if carefully considering something. "Then...I think...everything is going as it should." He checked his watch for maybe the fifth time. She found this sudden obsession with the exact time puzzling; but, since nothing else seemed amiss, she dismissed it as a quirk she hadn't noticed before. After all, he was not free, as she was, to sneak a glance at a wall clock.

"For dessert," he said, "one of your personal favorites—chocolate chip cookies. You can be in charge of this project. Helen tells me I have everything we need. The recipe is on the bag, right?"

"Usually. If not, I think I have it memorized."

"How about if you get organized while I tidy up a bit?" He picked up their plates from the table.

Melissa tore the corner off the chocolate chip bag and, by force of habit, ate a couple of chips. She soon noticed that he was aware of what she was doing.

"Are you one of those people who eat cookie dough, too?" he asked.

"Actually...I am."

"Not at my house, please. I don't want to feel responsible if you get food poisoning. Once they're baked—dig in. Since you seem to be able to do so, and keep that girlish figure."

Waiting for the cookies to bake, they sat across the table once again, her hand on his. "How do you tell when they're done?" she asked.

"That's *your* job."

"I mean, when I'm not here?"

"I don't bake cookies when you're not here."

"Oh." The timer beeped. "The top tray is finished," she announced. "Probably two more minutes on the bottom tray." She reset the timer.

The timer beeped again. Kraig checked his watch.

"Yes, perfect, just as I thought. We should wait for them to cool off, though."

"Let's wait in the living room."

There was a tightness to his voice, an ominous creak as he rose slowly from his chair, that made Melissa turn to look at him. At the sight of his drained face, she felt the color leave her own. She tried to swallow but her throat felt hollow. Suddenly the memory of last night, and all the other awkward moments in their brief history together, came back to her in a rush. *Dear God, what now?*

He reached for her hand as they sat on the sofa together. "Melissa...this has been wonderful, hasn't it? All the time we've spent together?"

"Yes?"

"But you must know that this long-distance relationship won't work forever."

I can't be hearing right. She didn't trust her voice for an answer.

"A relationship whose lifeblood is long-distance phone calls, overnight mail, and interstate flights...is weak and won't survive. Don't you see that?"

"It's been worth it to *me*." Her voice had a strange, strangled sound, and she really just wanted to burst into tears, yet she didn't want her emotional weakness to be the thing to change his mind about whatever he was going to say. She pulled her sweaty hand away.

A second later, seeing his hurt, lost expression—and not *really* wanting to hurt him, for he'd promised to do what was best for both of them, and she'd promised to trust him—she gave him back her hand. She turned away as he continued.

"Oh, yes, *more* than worth it. I wouldn't give up my memories of these times together for anything. But—"

Melissa could barely see through a mist of tears as she tried to blink fast enough to hold them back. "Kraig, whatever it is you're trying to say, just say it."

Suddenly, he was in front of her, on one knee, gathering both of her hands in his. "Melissa, will you marry me?"

She must have gasped. His raised eyebrows, his open mouth, his statue-like pose reflected her own astonishment. She repeated the words a couple times in her head, just to make sure there was no other possible interpretation. "Yes!" She threw her arms around his neck, nearly knocking him off his balance, and she hugged him, not caring that her tears would be discovered. For in an instant, they had turned to tears of joy.

He stood, pulling her up with him, and pried her arms loose from his neck. He cupped her face in his hands, and he kissed her, fully on the lips, deeply and long.

It was a minute or two before either of them could put any words into any semblance of order.

"I rewrote and rehearsed that speech...you have no idea how many times."

"And yet...it still ended up sounding like you were trying to say goodbye." Her voice was still shaky as she spoke and laughed and cried all at the same time.

"My God, Melissa, to think that I would let you go..." to her surprise, he laughed. "Well, I *told* you I was better with the written word. Melissa, I love you *so much*." And he hugged her until she felt her ribs give, so that she knew he didn't expect a response in kind. "Come over here and sit with me." He pulled her toward the love seat, pulled her down next to him, pulled her close. She drew up her legs so that her knees rested on his leg.

He took in and let out several deep breaths. Now, it seemed *he* was the one in need of comfort.

"You poor dear. Have you been fretting about this all weekend?"

"Oh, Melissa, much, *much* longer."

"I'd love to give you a back rub."

"I think that would not be such a good idea right now."

She blushed, taking his meaning, and took his hand—the one from which she'd removed the splinter some two and a half months before—and rubbed it between hers.

"Even that does it to me, Melissa. There will be a time for all that." He turned her so that her back nested against his chest, his arms around her, and spoke into her ear. The idea was probably to hide his face from her; that was okay. "I've spent a great deal of time thinking about how my life would change if you said 'yes.' You need to know—and hold me to this, Melissa—that not much is going to change in our relationship between now and the wedding date. Of course, I do *so* look forward to making love to you. I've tried not to think about it too much. Now, it's all right to think about it, as long as I keep it where it belongs—in the future."

"Well, I should tell you, I always saw that in you. And that's what attracted me to you more than anything…I always felt safe and respected with you. And that feeling that you were holding something back, that you would always have something new for me to discover."

He sighed, squeezed her, kissed her cheek. "Dave was right. He's always telling me, 'You gotta stick with it, buddy. Somewhere in the world is a sweet Christian lady who's someday going to be very glad you saved it for her.'"

"I have to ask you something. Several times I thought you were going to kiss me. Especially last night. Yet you never did. Why not?"

"I *was* going to. But I just couldn't do it. Years ago, Dave and I made sort of an 'accountability pact' that neither of us would kiss a woman until there was a commitment to marriage. I think it was mostly for *my* sake; he probably didn't really need that, but he did it for me." He turned her to face him. "You could have asked me, you know."

"You could have just told me."

"Do we have a communication problem?"

"I always felt like you could read my mind."

For only a moment, he looked surprised, then reflective. "If I can, it's because you're honest. What you do and say and think are always the same. That's another thing I love about you."

Melissa sighed deeply, mostly with contentment, also with the daunting prospect of all there was to accomplish. "We have a lot to talk about."

"Do you want to call the girls?"

"Hmm…if I tell them while they're at their friends' house, their entire peer group will find out before Matt does."

"Ah, yes. Matt."

"Do you think Kevin will come?"

"I think he will. Unless he's too busy. Or forgets. Or comes up with something more important to do. No…I think he'll come. What about your family?"

"My mom, I don't know. I think Lori and Gordon will. And the other relatives."

"And then there are the 'wheres.' We should have the wedding at your church; that's only right. And, Melissa, I've given a lot of thought to where we should live."

She held her breath. He always said he wanted to move back to Maine "some day"—was *this* "some day"?

"As you said, Melissa, I'm a writer. I can live anywhere. I'm prepared to move to California to be with you and the girls. You have a house there, and your job...the girls are in school...it would be the least disruptive thing. At least at first."

She was too excited about the prospect of living with him *anywhere* to be disappointed about not moving to Maine immediately. "Some day" was still there.

"Then there's 'when'," Kraig went on. "I was married in the summer the first time, and I'm adamant about making this as different as possible."

"Summer's a long time off, anyway. For me, it was spring the first time."

"Then how about the last Saturday of winter?"

"Five months. So far away...and yet so close. We have *so* much to talk about."

"I've invited Dave to go out to lunch with us tomorrow after church. His support will be invaluable."

"Are you going to tell me why I'm not meeting Dave till tomorrow?"

Kraig looked pensive for several long seconds before he began to formulate an answer. "I've sort of told you already. Dave is probably the most eligible bachelor in church. If you were to notice that, you certainly wouldn't be the first."

It was another several seconds before Melissa began to comprehend his answer. "Kraig...are you—"

"Jealous? No, just realistic."

"I was going to say, 'serious'."

"Absolutely."

Melissa just stared at him, half-expecting him to confess that it was a joke, yet he did not.

"It was never his fault," Kraig continued. "In that sense, he's the best friend I could have. But...well, I'll tell you about this one time. Long story short: I asked out this lady I met at church; made the mistake of asking Dave to drive us somewhere; he was supposed

125

to drop us off and disappear; she started acting like *he* was her date instead of me; that was the last I saw of *her*. He wasn't interested in her. Or at least pretended not to be. But, I'm sure you can see, having Dave around can be, shall I say, a distraction."

Melissa felt tears begin to gather.

"Melissa? What's wrong?"

"That makes me feel like you don't trust me."

"Melissa, I'm sorry." He gathered her in his arms and squeezed her tight. "It's not even about you, really. After that happened, I told Dave he was never again going to meet someone I was interested in until the relationship was fairly well along. I shouldn't have said that, but I did. Then, *he* said I wouldn't dare get serious about a girl without his input. I know he meant it in a loving way, but I chose to take it to mean I couldn't do anything without his help.

"If you had been there, Melissa, you would have seen a side of me that is not my best side. It was the worst moment between us. I've long since forgiven him, and he's probably totally forgotten about it. But that doesn't mean I could go back on my word."

She wiped her tears away. "Oh, my gosh, what a weekend."

"I'm sorry," he said again, kissing her.

"No, really, it's okay. It's actually kind of funny."

"I guess it is." All of a sudden, Kraig checked his watch for the first time in maybe an hour. "Helen will be here soon. We should wait outside."

"Oh, no, I'm leaving you with a big mess in the kitchen. Maybe we could—" She bolted from her seat.

"No, Melissa," he said, catching her. "I'm going to need something to do after you leave. I have a lot of nervous energy to burn."

"The cookies! We forgot about the cookies."

"Take some home with you. I just didn't feel the need for cookies tonight. If things had turned out differently, I probably would have eaten them all at once."

§

Sunday morning, Melissa closed the courtyard gate as quietly as she could, wanting to catch a glimpse of Kraig in his

126

doorway before he knew of her arrival, but to no avail. He was already smiling, standing there wearing a pale periwinkle, shadow-striped dress shirt, a dark striped tie, and gray suit pants. He looked so handsome, she felt herself go tingly, and she wavered between hurrying to greet him and slowing her approach to gaze at him longer.

"Morning, Kraig. You look nice."

"So do you." He put his hands on her shoulders. "Tell me what you're wearing."

"A teal-green linen blazer and skirt and a peach silk blouse."

"Peach? That's a color?" He took her into his arms, but gently, so as not to wrinkle her outfit. Melissa found that she had begun to draw strength from these hugs, magical moments of contact that infused every fiber of her being with warmth, energy, and the joy of life.

He motioned her in and closed the door. Just inside, he put his arm around her, the other hand on her face. "Are you wearing lipstick?"

"Lip gloss. It's—"

He pressed his lips to hers.

"Helen's waiting," she said quickly when she got the chance.

"She'll understand." He kissed her again. He released her, taking her hand and leading her into the kitchen. After a few steps, he turned around abruptly and caught her as her momentum carried her into his arms. He kissed her again. "We don't *have* to go to church today," he whispered into her ear.

"Kraig, I—"

He put his fingers to her lips. "Never mind. I just remembered—we do."

He called Shanna, fastened her lead, and picked up his suit coat from the back of a chair where it hung in neat folds.

"I have your Bible," Melissa said, picking it up from the table. "Wait—" She darted into the guest bath for a tissue. "Hold still. Do you know what happens when you kiss someone wearing fresh lip gloss?"

"It was worth it. I hope you have more in your purse—I mean your shoulder bag-daypack thing."

"I do. It's in the car. That is, if Helen hasn't given up and gone on without us."

127

"Don't be ridiculous. We're going." At the door, he stopped again and put his hand on her cheek. "Melissa, I wish I had time to make a better speech. The fact is, we are on the threshold of a whole new life. I want us to think of our engagement as an unrepeatable five months of our lives. I want it to be fun. Let's make it fun, all right, Melissa, love of my life?"

"Of course."

"Good, then. Let's go." He kissed her yet again.

§

Inside the Sunday school classroom, Melissa put the Bibles in empty chairs in the front row. As she stood holding Kraig's arm, people came over and greeted them; he always introduced her as "Melissa Melvin from California," with no other qualifier, and no one seemed surprised nor curious about her presence; she wondered what briefing they might have had before her arrival. She found herself looking toward the door every time a shadow came over it.

Soon a young man—strikingly handsome, tall, although not as tall as Kraig, and leaner, of a more athletic deportment—paused on the threshold. His brown hair swept back from his forehead, and he moved in the breezy manner of people who are always busy, but happily so; he smiled broadly as he waved to someone in the back of the room. Melissa watched him as he scanned the room, and his eyes locked on hers with an unmistakable look of recognition.

She continued to follow his movement with her peripheral vision as he strode to the front of the room and dropped a stack of books on the lectern with a thud. When she looked at Kraig, his little smile confirmed what she suspected. *Dave.*

He walked over and shook Kraig roughly by the shoulder. "Well, buddy, this must be Melissa and she must have said 'yes'."

"Good morning to you, too, Dave," Kraig said with the exaggerated patience of one who has endured years' worth of a friend's good-natured teasing. "Melissa, this is Dave Budd. Dave, Melissa."

She offered her hand, and he clasped it in both of his, heartwarmingly reminiscent of the way Kraig had done early in their relationship.

128

"Something gives me the feeling that I wasn't the first to know about it," Melissa said, for Helen's response to the news had contained some element of expectation as well.

"No. Not even close. Melissa, I'm delighted beyond words to meet you, especially under these circumstances, rather than… those *other* ones."

Melissa looked at Kraig.

"Kraig didn't tell you about Plan B?"

Melissa shook her head.

"Another time, Dave, please," Kraig said. "And you can let go of her hand now."

"Sure thing, buddy."

In any other setting, Melissa would have judged Dave less favorably. With his effortless good looks, exclusive-men's-store suit, and almost excessively friendly manner, she might have taken him for pretentious or shallow. But behind his stylish wire-framed glasses, deep in his blue eyes, she saw the loyalty and genuine concern that had made him such a priceless friend to Kraig over the years.

She saw, too, what Kraig meant about his being the most eligible bachelor in church.

"Well!" Dave said. "As much as I'd love to stand here and chat, we'd better get busy with the day's teaching." He went to the lectern, which everyone took as a signal to be seated. "Show of hands, please, class. Has anyone here *not* met Kraig's fiancée?"

A ripple of delighted sounds went through the room, and the collective goodwill for Kraig—and by extension, for her—made her glad all over again to have said yes.

"That's right, ladies and gentlemen, the lovely Melissa Melvin, soon to be Mrs. Dobrovsky, right up here in front. If you have not met her, your assignment is to meet her before you leave this room today.

"Now let's get started. Today we're taking a little break from our study of the book of Romans to discuss Philippians 4:7. 'The peace of God will guard your hearts,' it tells us. But 'guard your hearts' does *not* mean we shouldn't fall in love. So please open your Bibles…."

The lesson consisted of solid Biblical teaching interspersed with deadpan humor, mildly corny Bible jokes, and silly chalkboard illustrations.

Melissa leaned toward Kraig to ask him something, but Dave interrupted her. "Reading your thoughts, Melissa, I am *not* always like this, regardless of what my buddy Kraig there may tell you. Today just happens to be a good day for me. It's not every day I get to see my buddy get engaged and sit there looking so happy and, I suspect, not paying any attention to me whatsoever.

"Next week," Dave said in conclusion, "our very own Judy Breuner is going to share with us her experiences on the mission field, and how God led her back to the States. Judy…it is good to have you back." His gesture toward the back of the room suggested that Judy was present, perhaps the person he'd waved to as he entered. "Melissa, you're probably wishing you'd come next Sunday instead of today. Of course, you're more than welcome to come back. Remember, everyone, come up afterward and give Kraig and Melissa your blessings. Let's close in a word of prayer."

Dave stacked his materials and joined them. At the sight of Melissa holding Kraig's Bible, he shook his head. "Kraig, the guy with the biggest Bible in town. I tell you, if God judges us by the size of our Bible, you have it made, buddy. But it doesn't count if you make your girlfriend carry it." Dave took it from her and added it to his pile, bending his knees under a pretense of great weight.

Kraig suppressed a smile. "Dave will go with you to the sanctuary, Melissa. I'll join you when I'm finished singing with the choir."

Motioning to seats at the end of a pew, Dave explained that it was the best place to sit, "so Shanna can find us without making Kraig step on a bunch of people." Melissa chuckled at the lighthearted way Dave seemed to handle being Kraig's best friend as she began to peruse the morning's bulletin. Dave followed her gaze rather intently, and it occurred to her that it might be rude to read the bulletin when she should be paying attention to the people around her.

"Dave, who's your guest?" someone behind them asked.

"This is Melissa Melvin from California. Kraig's friend." He introduced her to a couple of women whose names she promptly forgot. *Why did he say "friend" instead of "fiancée"?*

She missed having Kraig by her side during the hymn singing. The choir did their number, then, as they faded out, someone from the front row came forward, picked up a cordless microphone, went to the back row where Kraig was, brought him forward, and gave him the microphone.

He has a solo? She looked at Dave, who returned to her a look of feigned innocence. She looked at the bulletin, and there it was—under "solo," Kraig's name.

As he sang, Melissa was torn between closing her eyes and being carried away by his voice alone, and watching his handsome, expressive face. She wondered how many of the weekend's events had a "Plan B." *Kraig's proposal? Dave's lesson? Kraig's song? What else?*

As the song ended, she looked at Dave, not trusting herself to speak, not knowing what to say anyway, and Dave winked at her.

"Thank you, Kraig," the music director said as the choir filed out. "And if anyone happens to notice that Kraig seems to have an especially radiant smile this morning, or more bounce in his step than usual, it's probably because he has his fiancée with him today. Kraig, when you find your seat, will you please have your fiancée stand and introduce her to us?"

As she stood with Kraig and heard herself being introduced to the entire congregation, a ripple of applause surrounded her with still more goodwill.

She'd planned to say something to Kraig about his awesome surprise solo, but the morning's events seemed to follow so closely one upon another, she simply didn't have time to react to everything.

§

In the parking lot, Melissa watched with a mix of emotions as Dave moved her bags from Helen's car to his. Adequate words to thank Helen, and then say goodbye to her, eluded her completely. *What a bittersweet time it must be for Helen: her joy over Kraig's happiness surely overshadowed by her sadness at his departure from her daily life.*

§

131

Arriving at their table, Melissa took Kraig's hand from her arm and placed it on the back of a chair. Once oriented, he pulled out her chair, then waited for her to be seated before taking his own seat.

"You two look like you've been practicing that for years," Dave said as he took his own chair.

"She's a natural," Kraig agreed.

"As good as Shanna?"

"Oh, at least. Especially where my wardrobe is concerned."

"I think *you* should be the one to tell him dogs are colorblind, Melissa."

She laughed as she opened her menu. "Oh, this place is very California," she said, intending a compliment.

Dave scoffed. "No, Melissa. Oregon. We're in *Oregon*."

"If you have something against California, you might want to get over it before your best friend starts living there."

Dave neither responded nor looked up from his menu, but there was something in the blank way he was now staring at it that made her uneasy. *Kraig hasn't told Dave about his plans to move to California.* If she thought it would help, she'd give Kraig a scolding look.

After a long moment, Dave closed his menu and laid it on the table, carefully lining up its bottom edge with the edge of the table. He turned to Melissa with a smile that looked forced. "I hadn't even thought of that. I guess it makes sense. You and the kids wouldn't have to move...Kraig could do his writing from down there."

Melissa tried to smile back, but suddenly the thought of separating these two best buddies had taken some of the joy out of her future. She looked back at her menu and blinked hard.

"No, no, it's okay," Dave said. "Of course, the music department at church will go to pieces, and the babies in the nursery will never stop crying."

"Please," Melissa said, now on the verge of real tears.

Kraig took her hand. "Dave, you're not helping."

"Just kidding. Well! What's everybody having?"

"Kraig, shall I read you the menu?" Melissa offered, anxious to be useful.

Just then the young waitress arrived, announcing that it was her first day on the job, with a plea for patience.

"You're doing fine so far," Dave said.

She smiled, maybe even blushed, as she began to list the specials. Melissa ordered a Caesar salad with grilled chicken; the guys each ordered a pasta dish; they all settled upon raspberry tea. Every time the waitress came, Dave had some encouraging words for her; she never failed to giggle.

"She thinks you're flirting with her," Kraig said as she retreated from delivering the main dishes. "*And* she likes it."

"I'm going to give her a big tip," Dave said.

"That's very nice, Dave," Kraig said, "except that you're not paying for lunch—I am."

Dave shrugged. "Well, then, whatever you leave her, I'll match it." Dave looked at Melissa. "Melissa thinks I'm flirting with the waitress, too. But I'm not. Really. It's just that I worked as a waiter in college, and I know what a difference it makes to have customers treat you nicely."

"I can picture that."

"He was good," Kraig added. "One of the few who could remember everyone's order without writing it down."

"I'd be *amazed* if his memory is better than yours, Kraig."

"And his attention to detail," Kraig continued. "People started requesting to be seated at Dave's tables. Eventually he won a promotion to this really classy place downtown, owned by the same people as the place he worked. Dave was singled out for his outstanding waiterly talents."

"Waiterly?" Melissa repeated. "Is that a word?"

"If Kraig says it's a word, it's a word. By the way, Melissa, how many new languages has this linguistic genius taught you?"

"None, yet."

"But she could spell my name on the first try," Kraig said.

"Definitely a good omen."

"Oh, you guys, this is great," Melissa said. "The food...the company."

"Uh-oh," Dave said, suddenly thinking of something. "Melissa, are you a good cook?"

"Yes," Kraig answered for her.

"I hereby transfer to you the grave duty of keeping Kraig in shape. Take good care of him. Love handles...barely acceptable. Maybe. Definite paunch...no."

133

"I'll do my best."

"I believe you will."

"And on that note," Kraig said, "I think I'll decline dessert."

"How about a round of lattes, then?" Dave suggested. "My treat. Whatever you like. Indulge."

"Well..." Melissa said, "a mocha does sound good."

"Non-fat, low-fat, or regular?"

"Low fat, please."

Kraig leaned over and whispered, "Go ahead, Melissa, make it *really* complicated."

"Go for it," Dave agreed.

"Okay, then, I'd like raspberry flavoring, chocolate and cinnamon sprinkles, and no whipped cream."

"You got it. Kraig?"

"Low-fat cappuccino without whipped cream. Please."

"Meet you at the take-out counter."

Kraig shook his head, stifling a chuckle, as Dave walked away.

§

Dave unlocked the car and held Melissa's drink while she got in. "Next stop, jewelry store?" he asked.

"Oh, Kraig, I didn't know—"

"We don't have to. I just thought, since you're here...."

"Well...sure. That would be fun." Dave handed her her drink, and she took care not to spill it on her linen skirt or on his nice velour upholstery.

Dave seemed to know exactly where to go, and Melissa had the definite feeling that few of the weekend's events had been left to chance.

On the sidewalk in front of the store, Dave clasped Kraig's shoulder. "Buddy, do you want me to take a hike around the block or something?"

"No way. You're my best man. I want you here."

Melissa hadn't given much thought to what kind of ring she would want to wear if she got another chance. Yet when she saw the smooth yellow-gold band with a row of five small diamonds, she knew it was the one.

"We have one for men that makes a nice match," the salesman said.

The ring, with its row of three tiny diamonds, looked as if it were made for him. Melissa felt tears fill her eyes yet again as she looked at her hand, clasped with his, their wedding bands in place, even if temporarily. She looked over at Dave, but he looked away quickly, pretending to be looking at something else.

§

"Come in for a minute, Dave," Kraig said, back at his townhouse.

"Okay. A *minute*. You two need some time alone."

Inside, Dave washed his hands at the kitchen sink, then went to the refrigerator and took out a couple bottles of mineral water.

"Do help yourself, Dave," Kraig said. "I'm going to change."

"Don't hurry back." He turned to Melissa. " 'Generous guy,' you're thinking, right? Fact is, Melissa, I'm the one who put these drinks in here. Would you like yours in a glass, with ice?"

"Sure," she laughed.

"Let's have a seat." Dave motioned toward the living room sofa. He set his drink on the coffee table, loosened his tie, and sat, stretching his arms out across the back of the sofa. Melissa waited for him to speak first. "Melissa…I doubt there are many guys on this planet whose love lives have had as much prayer coverage as Kraig's. We are now seeing the amazing results of those prayers."

"Tell me. Please." She saw her chance to have a lot of things explained.

"Going *way* back…I'm sure he told you about his ex. *Celeste*." Dave shuddered. "From what he's told me, he really took a beating. Emotionally and otherwise. Be patient with him on this subject. I think the whole picture will come to you in bits and pieces. Not that he's going to hide anything from you—there's just a lot to tell. You might need to pry a little. I suspect there are some things that even *I* don't know about. Anyway, I think it put him off serious relationships for a while."

"For *fifteen years*?"

135

"Well...no. There *have* been others during that time. No *good* ones, really. One or two he could have lived with, maybe, but none, really...."

"That he couldn't live without."

"Exactly." He looked thoughtful. "Kraig seems to have this idea in his head that I somehow sabotage things for him. Maybe not on purpose. But...well, did he tell you about this one date disaster, after which he swore he'd never...?"

"He did. But go ahead. I want to hear it from *you*."

"Well, you already know how it turned out. So I said to him, 'Any woman who starts making eyes at your buddy while she's on a date with you is not the right kind of woman.' He said I was missing the point. That was a couple years ago. We sort of had it out...moved on...I thought he'd forgotten about it. I guess not."

"So you knew I was coming this weekend, and that you weren't going to meet me till this morning, and that was okay with you?"

Dave shrugged. "What could I do? Barge in here and insist upon checking you out? I mean, I *thought* about it, but...no. Not seriously. This was something Kraig had to do his own way."

"Well...when did you first know...."

"About you? Good question. When he came home from Maine, he told me he'd met some nice people, had a chance to do some things with them, that sort of thing—not a lot of detail about who these 'people' were. Obviously, though, he'd had a good time.

"So a month goes by, and he tells me he needs a ride to the airport to catch a flight to Sacramento. *Sacramento? Who do we know in Sacramento?* He didn't say, so I didn't ask; I didn't really connect it to anything that had happened in Maine. When I picked him up that Sunday, he was very upbeat.

"Well, just so you don't think I'm *too* dumb, Melissa, I remembered this sort of 'look' from when he came back from Maine. My 'new lady friend' radar picked up on all these clues. He filled me in on some of the details then: yes, it was a woman; yes, the same one he'd met in Maine, who does, in fact, live in California. And he liked her a lot.

"Then, over the next couple weeks, he got kind of moody...broody...weird. He does that sometimes. If you haven't seen that yet, you will. I stopped by after evening service one

Sunday, after he'd said he didn't feel like going with me. He was in his sweats, and I imagine he'd been sitting there—" Dave gestured toward the love seat, "listening to music, hour after hour, thinking, praying. I kind of put the screws to him. 'You have to tell me what's going on here, buddy.' He shared that he really wanted to ask you to marry him, but it all seemed so complicated, the long distance, the short time...

"I suggested we share it with at least one other person, and we started with Helen, and then a widening circle of friends and confidants...and it began to look as though it were meant to be. Starting with the very circumstances of his trip to Maine.

"I told him he didn't have much choice; he could ask, and be rejected, but if he didn't ask, he'd never know what he might have missed."

Melissa tried to keep a mental list of all the things she would need to find out from Dave eventually. "Were you surprised by the suddenness of it?"

"Yes...and no. I'd prayed for *years* that somebody wonderful would come into his life. Kraig's not a simple guy. He wanted a long-term relationship, but the fear was there...he craves the closeness, but I could see him getting into a relationship that wasn't really going to be good for him in the long run. You know what I mean. So I kept telling him, 'You gotta save it for that special Christian lady who's out there somewhere waiting for you.'"

"He told me."

"And I know without asking," Dave said, looking at her very intently, "that he did not kiss you until last night."

"You're right." Melissa was beginning to feel she'd never again have any control over her emotions, as she felt her eyes fill with tears for what seemed like the hundredth time that weekend.

And unless it was her imagination, Dave seemed on the verge of choking up himself. "So I walk into the Sunday school classroom this morning, and I see Kraig standing next to this really nice-looking lady, and both of you wearing these big smiles...I just sent up the most heartfelt prayer of gratitude ever."

Melissa stole a glance toward Kraig's bedroom, for he seemed to have been gone a long time.

"You know," Dave whispered, "I think he's just going to *stay gone* till we're finished talking about him. —So, anyway, I told him, when he had it all planned, to let me know what time he was going to do the asking, and I would clear my calendar and be on my knees in prayer from fifteen minutes before until fifteen minutes after the appointed time."

"Oh! That explains why he was checking his watch so compulsively last night!" She let out a huge sigh.

"I think a lot of things are going to start making more sense to you. Well!" Dave said, somewhat more loudly than necessary, leaning back and clasping his hands behind his head. "That's Kraig's love life in a nutshell."

As if on cue, Kraig entered wearing pleated khakis and a polo shirt.

"Yes, Kraig, you can come back now," Dave said. "We're pretty much finished talking about you."

"Just between you and me, I'm guessing *you* did most of the talking."

"Melissa's a good listener. You are one lucky dude."

"I am." He sat on her other side, putting his arms around her shoulders in a loose circle.

"Yep," Dave said, seeming to like the way they looked together, "she's a keeper."

"Before you go," Melissa said, "what was this Plan B?"

"Oh, *that*," Dave said. "You want to tell her?"

"*You* tell her. You brought it up."

"Okay. It was this: If you'd said 'no' last night, I was to pick you up and take you to the airport. It would have been our first and last meeting."

"At night? Would you have done it?"

"You bet I would have. Of course, I'd have waited with you till you could get a flight back to Sacramento. But it wouldn't have been as nice a scenario as this one." Dave finished off his drink and stood quickly. "Well, I'm out of here. Now that I've been here *way* more than a minute. I'll be back in—" he looked at his watch, "less than two hours. Make the most of it. See you two later." He put his glass in the dishwasher on his way out.

Melissa stared at the door for several seconds after Dave's departure. Then, all she could think of to say was "Wow. What a guy."

"Yes. He is. Everything you think of him…is right."

"The thing that strikes me is…everything you said, and everything he said, it all matches. That makes me feel really good, to know that you have your convictions, and you have him to support you and your convictions."

"If you're thinking I wouldn't be who I am without him to help me *be* that person, you'd be right. In fact…I didn't tell you this before, but it was largely on Dave's advice that I went into writing, instead of singing and playing piano in nightclubs. He pointed out that it seemed to attract the wrong kinds of women to me."

She turned to face him and leaned on his arm. "You didn't tell me you play piano."

"You need to ask more questions."

"I think I *did* ask. Back when we first met. But I can see that I need to probe deeper, because you have a tendency to be modest."

He just smiled.

"Well, I'm going to go change into something more comfortable."

§

The two hours had flown. Melissa knelt to lock her suitcase, her linen suit and silk blouse folded carefully inside. The chocolate chip cookies and the thank-you note for the girls were tucked securely in the middle. There was a knock at the door, followed by "It's Dave" through the intercom. Kraig let him in. Dave had changed to jeans and a dusty-blue polo shirt that complemented his eyes stunningly.

"Ready?" he asked.

"Pretty much," Melissa answered.

"But not *really*, right?"

She looked up at him, grateful for his understanding.

Shanna hurried to greet Dave, as if she hadn't seen him for days, and he crouched to scratch her head and speak to her in that exaggerated way that people do when talking to dogs. "*No*, Shanna doesn't like to be separated from Kraig *either*, *does* she? Shanna came to *my* house when Kraig was in the *hospital*, and she couldn't *wait* for Kraig to come *home*, *could* she?"

Melissa looked at Kraig in surprise. "When were you in the hospital?"

Suddenly a tense, uncomfortable silence invaded the atmosphere. "Last spring."

Melissa looked at Dave for help, but he was pretending to be absorbed in his interaction with Shanna.

She stood. "What for?"

"Eye surgery. Experimental nerve repair." His tone was strangely flat, as if to avoid telling her how to react.

Melissa was stunned. For it had never occurred to her, not for one fleeting moment, that regaining his sight was still a live possibility for him. Obviously, the surgery had not been a success. She looked at Dave again; this time he met her gaze with a look of empathy mixed with contrition.

She looked back at Kraig, standing there holding Shanna's harness, and she was filled with an unfamiliar complex of emotions. The boundless love and admiration she felt was now somehow mixed with a pity that she didn't like to acknowledge, didn't know what to do with. When those surgeries were in the distant past, she felt safe from their implications; now, knowing they were in the very *recent* past, she'd have to look at him as a man who considered himself not quite whole, who wanted to be something he wasn't.

What do I say? "I'm sorry" didn't seem right, nor did "It doesn't matter." She simply wouldn't be able to say anything until she had a chance to find out how Kraig felt about it. She went to him and hugged him. He hugged her back, but she felt in his hug a whole unexplored realm that would act as a wedge between them until they worked through it.

She excused herself to the bathroom and flipped on the ceiling fan, wanting its hum to protect the privacy of whatever Kraig and Dave had to say to one another. She could imagine their exchange. *I'm sorry. I didn't know she didn't know. That's all right. It's not your fault.*

When she returned to the living room, Kraig was gone, presumably to his own bathroom, and Dave stood there looking sheepish. "I'm sorry. I shouldn't have said anything."

"No, it's okay. It's just a surprise. It's just *different*, thinking of him as wanting to be…not…you know. I've always thought of him as complete."

"I know. That's why he loves you. And this all makes me think—" he glanced over his shoulder and lowered his voice, "you don't really know why Kraig was in Maine, do you?"

She started to answer, but just then Kraig reappeared. Dave gave her a knowing look and put a hand on each of them. "You two need to talk."

"But we have to go," she protested.

"We have the whole drive to the airport." He picked up her suitcase.

At the car, Kraig held the front passenger door for her.

"No way," Dave said. "Both of you in back. I'm just the chauffeur."

Melissa chose the middle position, allowing Kraig the extra legroom of the place behind the front passenger seat, and Shanna the floor space on the other side. He put his arm around her as she pressed close to his side. Just as she leaned to receive a kiss from him, Dave turned to look over his shoulder as he reversed the car out of its space. "Yeah, that's good. Just pretend I'm not here."

Melissa felt herself blush.

"When you're finished with that," Dave said, "Kraig, buddy, Melissa needs to know why you went to Maine. She won't have a complete picture of how providential this whole love story is until you tell her that."

Melissa suddenly thought of the piece of gray-green beach glass he'd given her, and for a panicked moment couldn't remember where she'd put it. *Oh, yes. On the bathroom windowsill, where it catches the light.*

§

Kraig's explanation filled in the one thing that had been missing from their story as a couple since the day they'd met; the one thing that she had, oddly, forgotten about once she'd fallen irrevocably in love with him.

"I'm going to put it on tape to send to you," he said. "Don't dwell on it too much until you get it. I need to sort my thoughts and put it all in perspective with what's happened since then. Now, let's think of other things. Our time is so short until you leave."

Dave's presence at the airport was a comfort to Melissa. They could have managed the trip by taxi or bus; but, as she'd seen, most vividly since her arrival in Oregon, Dave's companionship was incalculably precious. She couldn't bear the thought of Kraig going home alone; she could trust Dave to be there.

Dave took from his shirt pocket an index card and began to write on it. "Prayer reminders," he explained.

"He never goes anywhere without it," Kraig added.

"When I get home, I copy them into a notebook. I fill in the answers when they come. It's incredible to see what happens over time. Admittedly, sometimes it's a very *long* time. And it's not always what we expect." He thought aloud as he wrote. "Your name is actually already on my list, in quite a few places. I have your kids' names, too. I don't know all the details—but God does."

Too soon, Melissa's flight was called.

"We're not sending her off without a prayer huddle," Dave said.

Her arms around the waists of these two dear men, their arms around her shoulders, overlapping each other's, she felt a sense of security more profound than anything she'd ever before experienced.

"Now, you two finish saying your goodbyes," Dave said. "Buddy, I'll be waiting over here."

Her eyes met his. "Dave—" she started to say, but he was already coming to give her a hug. "Thanks for everything," she blurted out before her breath left her, for, as it turned out, he hugged *exactly* like Kraig did. It seemed impossible that she'd known him a mere half-day.

She turned back to Kraig and held him until the last possible moment.

§

Chapter 12

Monday, the phone rang at eight o'clock; Melissa answered it on the second ring, trying not to appear as anxious as she was.

"Melissa. What did the girls say?"

"Oh, they were basically jumping up and down and shrieking."

"Did you call Matt?"

"Not yet."

"Call him. As soon as you hang up. Promise me you will?"

"Okay. I will. Did Dave say anything?"

"Nothing new. He thinks you're wonderful. But you already knew that."

"Oh, Kraig, he is *so sweet*, and you are *so lucky* to have people who care about you so much."

An hour's worth of conversation flew by. "The tape I told you I'd send should arrive tomorrow. Listen to it right away, will you?"

"I will."

And so it did; and so she did.

§

"Melissa, love of my life," it began. "I'm sorry our wonderful weekend together had to end that way, with that tension between us. Dave is sorry too, but it wasn't his fault. I need you to know I never meant to deceive you in any way.

"You already know all the pieces of the story, but let me tell it again, from beginning to end.

"I had this experimental surgery at the beginning of April, selected out of a large number of blind people whose optic nerve injuries happened long ago. They were very optimistic about the outcome. So was I.

"The first of August was the soonest they would let me travel. When I planned the trip to Maine, I fully believed I would go as a sighted person. I had so many plans. I would drive past the house where I grew up; I would go slowly, see who lived there, decide whether I should stop and ask to look around. I would drive past my schools, my friends' houses, all the places I knew. Of course, I don't have a driver's license, so I would accomplish all this from the back seat of a taxi. But it didn't matter. I *so* looked forward to this trip.

"You know now that the surgery didn't succeed as expected. The only lasting results are the scars and the headaches; both should go away with time. I was going to cancel the trip; why go? Dave insisted I go anyway; he even offered to go with me. I wouldn't hear of that…but I *did* let him talk me into going. 'You never know what it might do for you,' he said.

"When I met you, it seemed far too good to be true. I thought that somehow I'd forced the hand of Providence, manipulated events …or perhaps the whole attraction between us was a product of my imagination, of my deep desire to see something good come out of the whole ordeal, and that you were just being kind.

"When I came down to see you last month, I went with considerable fear and trepidation. In a way, I wanted to leave well enough alone and not see you again. It felt like a dream, and I might be jolted awake; if I never saw you again, I could go on dreaming, imagining what *would have* been.

"As it turned out, the time we spent together last month only deepened my resolve never to let you go. And you know the rest of that story, too.

"If I hadn't had the surgery, I wouldn't have planned the trip. If I didn't have a guide dog, you and your girls probably never would have noticed me on the beach that day. So, you see, I had a purpose for the trip; God had a different one. And this outcome is better than the one I had envisioned.

"One more thing. Remember the piece of beach glass I gave you? I was going to leave it on the beach, as close as possible to the location where I'd found it as a sighted person. You'll recall, I was a very little kid at the time, but I do remember the day I found it. Under the circumstances that happened in reality, I gave it to you.

"Melissa, I never told you this before because I so loved how you accepted me as a whole package, completely and unquestioningly. That was so new and refreshing to me. I didn't want to take that away from you, from our relationship. Melissa, you are the best thing that ever happened to me. I love you…*so much.*"

Kraig's voice began to waver around "the best thing" and cracked completely in the middle of "I love you." Melissa put her head down on her desk and let the tears flow.

§

She was sitting by the phone, breathing deeply, trying to calm herself, when it rang at eight o'clock.

"Melissa."

"Kraig." And she started to cry again before she could say any more. "I'm sorry. I feel like I've been on an emotional roller coaster. I never cried this much—until recently."

"Go ahead and cry, Melissa. I could never love someone who doesn't cry. People who don't cry either aren't honest with their feelings...or don't *have* feelings, which is worse."

This only made her continue to cry, but eventually she took a deep breath and gained control of her voice. "Thanks for the tape. I loved it. And I want you to know that if you want to try again, you know, with the surgery, that's okay with me. If you don't, that's okay too. I just wouldn't want it to change you. If it worked, I mean. I wouldn't want it to make you a different person. Otherwise it doesn't matter."

"Thank you, Melissa. The doctors said afterward they think they know what went wrong, and what to do differently if I were to try again. In fact, they said they could operate again in the summer— but by then I'd already decided to make the trip. And then...my life took another turn." He breathed deeply. "Let's save all discussion of that for another time. We have so much more to talk about."

"Then there's something else I've been wanting to tell you. I know you say this age difference doesn't matter, and I believe you. But...I know how much you'd love to have children, and with me, it just isn't going to happen."

"I know, Melissa. I've thought about it. It really, truly doesn't matter. Some day we'll have grandchildren. That'll be good enough for me. Don't worry about it. Did you call Matt?"

"I did! Last night, like I promised."

"Well? What did he say?"

"It wasn't as bad as I thought. He really didn't say much."

145

"And that is another answer to prayer. So…where should we begin?"

"Well, I think we could keep this whole thing kind of low-key. I mean, since it's the second time around."

"Not for me."

"Um—what?"

"I mean, of course I was married before, but not with all the frills. It was just a simple civil ceremony—no big deal over clothes and flowers and music and food. Deep down, I don't think I ever really felt married. This will be a completely new experience for me."

"Well, for me, too, in a way. I *did* have a big church wedding. But that's just it—my goal was to *get* married, not to *be* married. Do you know what I mean?"

"Of course I do. So let's keep in mind that it's not the wedding that's really important—but the marriage."

"Oh, Kraig, I'm still re-living the events of the weekend. I meant to tell you how much I loved your solo on Sunday, and how proud of you I was…everything happened so fast…so many things, I never had a chance to say."

"And that reminds me. Dave insists that you and I talk on the phone every single day that we aren't together, until the wedding. He says he's paying the phone bill as a wedding gift. So unless it's urgent, let me call you—it's easier to keep track that way. Now, could you give me Matt's phone number? I need to call him and ask him to be an usher at our wedding."

§

Later in the week, a letter arrived. There was something familiar in the neat handwriting, although Melissa couldn't quite place it until she looked at the return address: David J. Budd.

"Dear Melissa," she read. "First, Kraig knows I'm writing you this letter.

"Second, I just want you to know how happy I am for you and Kraig and that I think you're absolutely right for each other.

"Third, I want you to know I'm here for you. Of course, my first loyalty is to him, but as long as you're on the same team, I'm here for you, too.

146

"Make the most of the next five months and get to know each other as well as you can. I can say with confidence that I don't expect you'll have any rude surprises, but of course there will be adjustments. As much as you love each other, you will be able to work through whatever comes your way. If there's anything I can do for you, just call.

"Your friend, Dave."

§

"Melissa. Did you get Dave's letter?"

"Yes. It was nice." She struggled to hold her emotions in check; it was not easy, for she'd never before felt surrounded by so much love and support. "Hey, you know what I thought of? We need to decide what we're doing for Thanksgiving."

"I was just thinking of that, too. It's been a long time since I traveled on the holidays, but Dave goes back to Wisconsin often, and he says the airport can be a real zoo. Now that I think about it, it would probably be best if I came down there. Will Matt come?"

"I hope so. I'll have to call him again."

"And while we're planning holidays, Melissa, I've already committed to a part in the children's Christmas musical here at church. It's something I do every year. There's always an adult part, and I somehow fell into that role. Melissa, it may be my last time participating in this, so I really want to do it, and I'm hoping you and the girls will be here. And Matt, if he'll come."

"The girls and me, you can count on...Matt, we'll see."

§

A whole week had gone by since her return from Portland, and, as promised, she had talked with Kraig every evening, usually for an hour. Just as the days of that first week in Maine had been measured from one beach walk to the next, now her life was divided into the twenty-three hour periods between phone calls.

Monday evening, Kraig's greeting seemed a little breathless.

"What is it, Kraig?"

"Melissa, Dave has a serious love interest."

147

She tried to remember everything Kraig had told her about Dave's love life, in order to respond properly to this news, but she knew she was somehow too slow in grasping its significance. "Oh! Well, that's nice, isn't it?"

"Melissa, you'll recall that Dave is probably the most eligible bachelor in church." He sounded mildly annoyed. "He's thirty-five and hasn't had a serious girlfriend in something like ten years. Almost as long as I've known him."

She began to understand. "So, you get engaged, and all of a sudden he has a girlfriend, and you're wondering if he's maybe rushing into something that's...."

"Well, no. That's what I *would* think. Except that I know Dave. He has too much sense for that."

"So...what do we know about her?"

"You might actually have met her when you were here. Judy Breuner, the missionary who recently retired from work in Sudan because of health problems, who was—"

"I remember! She was sitting in the back of the room, and I don't think I saw what she looks like, but Dave said she was going to speak the next Sunday and that I should come back."

"Yes! That's right."

"Well, how long has he known her?"

"Now that you ask, let me think.... If she's thirty-two...she was here for college, but he wouldn't have known her until she came into the young single adults' group...she left for the mission field about a year later...so he's known her about ten years. And she's been gone most of the time for nine of those.

"But he's always been a big admirer and supporter of hers, even from a distance. I always *thought* it was her work on the mission field that he so loved and admired. I'm sure that's the basis of it, but clearly there's more.

"So on Saturday, the day before she spoke to the group, he took her out for an all-day sightseeing trip, to get her more comfortable with the idea—I guess she was hesitant about telling her story—and help her organize her thoughts. This is how he explained it to me, anyway.

"Melissa, I was sitting next to him as she spoke. The guy was *riveted*, Melissa, and while her stories about war and disease and orphaned children were pretty fascinating, I feel certain there was another level of emotional response happening."

"What about *her* health problems?"

"A while back, she began experiencing strange symptoms, weakness in one arm or leg, loss of coordination, things like that... then she suddenly lost sight in one eye. Temporarily, but still, it was terrifying for her. So she came home on medical furlough and was diagnosed with multiple sclerosis."

"Oh. Dear me. Well, do you think Dave's feelings for her have anything to do with, you know, just wanting to help her, sort of out of respect for the sacrifices she's made?"

"Maybe. Partly. But...I've never seen him respond to a woman quite this way, and you know that I've known Dave for most of his adult life."

"I just remembered what you said about how he was maybe waiting for someone special. Do you think he's just been passing by all these other women, waiting for Judy to come back?"

"Maybe. But if that was it, he might have waited forever. Who knew she'd have to leave the mission field?"

"So...she can't go back? Ever?"

"Not really. She tried, at first, but the heat aggravates her symptoms, and the medications she has to take don't combine well with the immunizations. From what she said, I gather it was a difficult struggle, emotionally and spiritually, and she's still trying to sort it all out. She believed she'd been called to the mission field, and now this.

"And...I think she wanted to keep Dave at arm's length for a while, because he'd been so supportive, and she felt she'd failed him. I'm reading between the lines, of course, but you know how Dave can be. When she first got sick, he was full of ideas on how she should improve her lifestyle, diet, everything. What he didn't know at first was that, as much as anything, she was suffering from depression, and his 'help' was only making things worse."

"But somehow, they got from there to a budding romance."

"Well, again, you know Dave. He's a pretty sensitive guy. He went to pick her up from the airport, when she came home for good, and I imagine everything was forgiven in a hug."

"So...what are *her* feelings for *him*?"

149

"From what I can see, exactly what you'd expect. Probably what any woman would feel if a good-looking, intelligent, successful, funny, *really nice* guy had sat waiting for her to come home from the mission field. And doesn't mind if she has an incurable illness."

"Yeah. Wow. Well. What's Judy going to do now?"

"Dave helped her get a job in a Christian bookstore. Some people we know here own this store, the biggest Christian bookstore in town. Some other people we know—retired missionaries, in fact—have an in-law apartment and a car she can use. She's basically re-writing her life plan. She said in her talk that, when she was growing up as a missionary kid, she wanted to go into missions work herself, but that she didn't really want to raise a family on the mission field. I think, deep down, she felt kind of torn between the two. So now, God has shown her a different path."

"Well, looking ahead, will she be able to have kids? I mean, is that something she can do, while she's dealing with her illness?"

"I don't know. But if not, she wants to adopt anyway. Even as a single person, she said. She'd like to adopt a child from Africa who's been orphaned by war or disease."

"Wow. What a lot to think about. And pray about."

"Why don't we pray about it right now? Pretend we're sitting together, holding hands. We'll pray for Judy's health, for her and Dave's relationship, and for her to put her future in God's hands."

So they did, and after "amen," Kraig said, "Do you realize, Melissa, love of my life, that we've been talking for over an hour?"

"No. I never watch the clock when we're talking. It always seems like it's five minutes, but you always say it's an hour."

He laughed softly. "Indeed. And we will talk again in less than twenty-three hours."

§

"Great news, Kraig. I called my cousin Marilyn to spread the news around that part of the family, and she invited us for Thanksgiving. They're all having it at my youngest cousin's house, down in the valley. Except my aunt and uncle, who'll be in Europe. But she says they'd all love to meet you."

"Wonderful. Will your sister and brother-in-law be there?"

"No, they always go to their vacation home in Aspen for the holidays. They never liked spending holidays with the, you know, conservative branch of the family. I can see why. We always talk about things they neither know nor care about. But *you* will fit right in. Oh, Kraig, it'll be so great! Most of these people are teachers and medical professionals. We'll have so much to talk about. Oh, and the best part! Marilyn has a new grandbaby, two months old. I didn't even know about him till now."

"That is a lot to look forward to. Oh, I got a flight Tuesday evening, returning Monday morning. The *best* part will be spending five and a half days together."

"Oh! It'll be almost—" she was going to say, "almost like being married," but changed her mind. "It'll be heavenly."

"Will Matt come?"

"He *said* he would. I need to tell him about the invitation from my cousins. If anything, it'll make him want to come. I'll let you know tomorrow night."

§

"Tell me how things are going, Melissa."

"Mostly pretty well. Matt says he's coming, but his flight comes in late Wednesday evening, which is the best he could do, he says, and he's going to take the bus from the airport."

"Bus? Where would the bus leave him?"

"Downtown Oak Hill. Then he'll take a cab from there."

"Why don't we just pick him up?"

"It'll be really late at night. He said he'd rather do it this way than inconvenience us. So we'll see him in the morning. He'd hate it if I got up and made a big deal of it when he came in."

"Well, that should work out all right. Oh, Melissa, I'm bringing a video of last year's Christmas program with the kids at church, so you can get an idea of what we do. I think you'll enjoy it."

"I'm sure I will. Oh, I almost forgot. I got our wedding on the church calendar, no problem, but something I forgot to think about—our church staff requires premarital counseling. It's supposed to be six sessions, but under the circumstances, they've agreed to do three with just me, and three with both of us, if you'll do three at

151

your church; then the church staffs can communicate. I made an appointment for the Saturday after Thanksgiving."

"You know, Melissa, I think I'll enjoy that. I've never done anything even remotely like that before, but I think it'll be a good thing."

"Well, I'm a little nervous about it. I *did* do it, the first time around, and I can't say that it helped a bit."

"This is different, Melissa. Because you *know* that I love you."

§

Tuesday before Thanksgiving, her first glimpse of Kraig as he emerged from the plane created a rush of emotions—the anticipation of his embrace, the mixed feelings about introducing him to her extended family, the apprehension of Matt's response, and the almost unfathomable deliciousness of having him near for the better part of a week.

"You've been baking," he said as he hugged her.

"Pies. Apple, pumpkin, and pecan, to take on Thursday. I am *so* looking forward to this time. Hey, did you by any chance bring work to do while you're here?"

"In fact I did; why?"

"I brought home some work, too. It'll be sort of like, you know, in the future…just going about our lives, but together instead of separately."

"Starting with going to baggage claim. I couldn't quite fit everything for a longer stay into a carry-on."

"No problem. Let's get going. And I had an idea—let's stop at the place we had lunch that Sunday and get some hot tea to go. It's raining here—lots different from last time you came."

§

Thanksgiving morning, the car was filled with holiday spirit and the fragrance of pies as Melissa climbed into the back seat with Kraig.

"I love driving on holidays," Emily said. "There aren't very many cars, and everyone you *do* see is happy because they're going somewhere for Thanksgiving."

With Matt driving, and the girls in the middle seat, she had Kraig's company pretty much to herself. She soon noticed that he seemed unusually fidgety. When riding in the front passenger seat, he would endlessly finesse the car stereo and heat-and-air systems, as well as provide commentary on the music. Now, he had nothing to do; worse, it was Matt's music playing.

Melissa tried to imagine not being entertained during a long car ride. She could lose herself just looking at the scenery—the infinite shades of gray of a cloudy sky, the way different colors of cows and horses stood out against a green background, the perfect symmetry of trees reflected on a glassy pond. The miles would fly by.

This time was better still—she didn't have to drive, and she had Kraig beside her. She was content just to be content. But considering the monotony and the elevation change, he probably wasn't having much fun. Soon Sacramento began to take shape through a light fog—the marker for the trip being half finished—and she realized they had hardly spoken.

She studied his face and saw telltale little signs of distress. "I'm sorry. This is pretty boring, isn't it?"

He smiled. "When I travel alone, I bring something to listen to. When you're driving, I have the accessories to take care of. Sitting in the back seat, I have you for company."

"Sorry. I was just enjoying…just being here, just being with you."

"Tell me what's out there."

She began by describing the cityscape—a building with a mirror-like exterior standing in contrast to one that looked like rust, the tangle of freeways, the riverfront parkway. These gave way to suburbs, then flat countryside. She saw his face contort with discomfort, but he said nothing about it. She noted the herds of cattle, the vineyards, the occasional winery.

"Why don't you tell me who's going to be there today? Just a little about each person, so we'll have something to talk about when I meet them."

Melissa took a deep breath as the anxious feeling about seeing her cousins again returned. "Okay. Keep in mind I haven't seen them much in the last few years. But here goes.

"Marilyn is my oldest cousin. She's a nurse. She's easy to talk to. Ben is her husband. He's a college professor, kind of quiet and studious.

"Brian is my middle cousin. He's a medical researcher. Very intellectual, but laughs easily if you say something funny. His wife is Barbara. She's a music teacher. She's Asian, very petite.

"Christine is my youngest cousin. She's a physical therapist but a stay-at-home mom right now. She plays the piano beautifully. Maybe you and she could play something together. Her husband is Tim. He's a pediatrician, very friendly, athletic."

She took another deep breath. "Next generation. Joanna is Marilyn and Ben's daughter. I haven't really known her as an adult. She married right out of college. She's very intelligent and quiet like her dad. Her husband is Dan. He's a junior high teacher. I've met him only once, briefly, at their wedding. The baby's name is Teddy, and he's almost three months old. I've never seen him.

"Brian and Barbara have two daughters about Jessica and Emily's ages, Kay and Lorraine. Kay is very musical, plays the violin, and Lorraine is very academic. Christine and Tim have three boys younger than Emily—Ethan, Kenyon, and Jordan. That's everybody, as far as I know. Oh, and a couple of dogs."

He nodded slowly. "All right. That's a good start."

For her part, Melissa hoped the time spent with her cousins would recapture the fun of their shared childhood, in the days before she married, became unhappy and withdrawn, and forever after felt the judgment of her Christian relatives. For somehow, she had failed their expectations to create a successful Christian marriage from scratch, and to be an example to the rest of her family.

§

When the door opened and Melissa faced a crowd of people she supposedly knew so well, she realized that in the couple years that had passed since she'd seen them at all—not to mention the many years since she'd really spent time with them—they had changed. The kids had grown older, some now taller than their parents; adults had changed hairstyles and other details of appearance; and she would have to catch her breath before she could introduce everyone correctly. Her bewilderment must have shown on her face, for everyone began to laugh, then hug her and her kids and usher them inside.

Someone pointed out that Matt was surely the tallest in the family; Melissa did a double-take and, sure enough, he was now at least as tall as Kraig, who was an even six-foot-three. People commented on how good she looked, how tall and pretty Jessica and Emily were becoming, how well mannered Shanna was, and all manner of positive and affirming things. As the re-acquaintance progressed, Melissa began to feel silly for thinking that anyone would begrudge her newfound happiness with Kraig.

Kraig, for his part, was at ease and in his element, moving gracefully from one topic of conversation to another, earning everyone's admiration for his ability to remember names and recognize voices. Over dinner, Melissa observed that he was even more adept at this than she'd had the opportunity to notice before, as he would field comments made from various places around the table, then respond to the speaker by name, seemingly never missing a thing. Of course it didn't hurt matters a bit that he never failed to say something complimentary about a particular dish, ask who made it, and compliment her or him directly.

Kraig's biggest moment came when, after dinner, everyone was relaxing in the living room with coffee, and Joanna was trying to get Teddy to go to sleep. As parents and grandparents, doctors, nurses, and teachers all offered sympathy and advice, Kraig said simply, "Will you let me have him?"

In response to the puzzled looks, which Kraig could no doubt hear, Melissa said, "Kraig's really good with babies. He works in the nursery at his church. Let him try."

Joanna looked at Marilyn, who nodded her approval, and gave the baby to Melissa. The people sitting on the couch with Kraig scooted to make room for her beside him, and she handed over the baby.

The effect was immediate and magical. Kraig placed the baby on his shoulder and began to massage his back. He whispered something into his ear that Melissa couldn't understand, either because it was too quiet or because it wasn't English; Teddy's face looked as though he'd just been told some enchanting secret. He stopped fussing and took a couple of deep breaths; his eyes fluttered closed; he sighed deeply and was sound asleep. All the adults in the room, who'd been holding their collective breath—or so it seemed—began to breathe again. "Wow," several people said, and Melissa nearly exploded with pride.

"Melissa," Kraig said softly, "would you please put my coffee cup in my hand?"

Everyone laughed quietly, and the conversation resumed in low tones.

After about an hour, Melissa sensed Kraig becoming fidgety again, and Teddy, who may have sensed it too, began to stir.

"He'll be hungry now," Joanna said, and Melissa eased him off of Kraig's shoulder to pass him back to her. "That helped a lot," Joanna said. "Thank you."

Kraig stretched and stood.

"How about we go for a walk?" Melissa suggested.

"I would love that," he said, then whispered into her ear, "after we go to the bathroom."

She smiled as she realized that Kraig had undoubtedly sacrificed a great deal of comfort to hold a sleeping baby, and that the coffee probably hadn't helped matters.

"They love you," Melissa said as they stepped outside into the cool, crisp air. "You should have seen their faces."

"Melissa," Kraig said slowly, "I have a sense that there's a history of *something* here."

"What do you mean?" she asked, stalling for time as she sorted out her thoughts.

"Well, at dinner, someone, and I think it was your cousin Marilyn, said something like, 'Kraig seems like a solid Christian man,' which sounded to me like a compliment, and you said something like—"

"I know," she said, more abruptly than necessary. "That's because they're trying to make it sound like it's my fault that I was miserable in my first marriage."

"It just sounded a bit more defensive than necessary."

"That's because you haven't been here until now. You don't know the whole story."

"That's why I'm asking, Melissa."

She felt her anger begin to rise, although not really at Kraig. "Somehow I was supposed to know how to choose a person I'd want to spend the rest of my life with. Somehow I was supposed to be the 'example' to my non-Christian family. Somehow I was supposed to fill in the gaps for a dad who couldn't quite fill the role himself. Somehow I was supposed to do all this without any help from anyone."

Kraig stopped suddenly and faced her, cupping her face in his hands, a gesture that never failed to melt away any harsh feelings and create in her a feeling of bondedness to him that she'd never felt with anyone else. "Melissa," he said, "remember, I'm on your team. You don't have to tell me the *whole* history. Not now, at least." He smiled a little mischievously. "In fact—don't. Then I can act as if I don't know what they're talking about, because I don't. You can tell me at home. We can talk about it in the counseling sessions, if it seems important enough. The *really* important thing is, you mustn't feel like you don't deserve to be happy. You *do*. All right?" He put his arms around her and squeezed. "You've done a great job— without much help from anyone, I gather. You deserve a lot of credit for *that*."

"Matt hasn't said anything to you all day, has he?"

"No…but then, it's been easy not to—he got home late last night and slept in, then we left, and talking in the car would have been difficult. And here, there are so many people he hasn't seen in a long time, and so much to talk about." He looked pensive. "You know, I have the feeling he isn't purposely avoiding me."

"He certainly was, when we were at the beach."

"That was different. Being away at college, having his own life, will balance things out for him. He was pretty easy to talk to that time I called him about being an usher. I think it just feels a little awkward now. Everything will be fine. You'll see." He squeezed her tightly. "Take a deep breath, Melissa."

She did.

"Now, let's walk," he said. "What are they growing here?"

"Almonds…grapes. They make their own raisins. They send me some every year. The chocolate-covered ones are incredible."

"I imagine so."

Back inside, Melissa was delighted to see Christine seated at the piano. "Oh, let Kraig play something with you."

Everyone looked at Kraig. "You play piano, too?" said at least two people.

"*And* he sings," she said.

Luckily for him, he was at that moment bending to take off Shanna's lead; Melissa was sure he'd blushed mightily. "I'll sing," he said as he straightened, "if everyone else does."

"Okay," Christine said, "I have a nice hymnal here. What do you know?"

"All of them," Melissa said, steering Kraig toward the piano bench.

He shook his head, trying hard not to smile. "Just choose some of your favorites, and I'll do my best. And don't believe everything Melissa says about me."

Melissa, for her part, was thrilled to have someone to be proud of; someone she liked and loved and respected and admired, in equal portions; someone she was romantically and physically attracted to; someone who, no matter what the future brought, would always have something to draw her in. She stepped behind him and squeezed his shoulders.

The afternoon fled; leftovers were brought out for snacks; darkness fell; it was time to go home.

Making the rounds of goodbyes and hugs took longer than the greetings, mostly because everyone had something to say to Kraig.

"I'm sorry my parents weren't here to meet you, but they planned this trip to Europe a long time ago."

"You'll meet them at the wedding."

"Maybe we can get you to sing at the *next* wedding."

"Come whenever there's a new baby."

"And bring your dog," one of the young boys added, and everyone laughed.

§

On the return trip, in the privacy of the backseat, Melissa felt deliciously alone with Kraig, like teenagers in a movie theater.

"What is there to see now?" he asked.

"Nothing. It's dark," she said, pressing close.

"What kind of moon?"

"Just a sliver more than a new moon." She turned his face toward her, hoping for a good kiss, but letting him decide.

She was not disappointed, for he responded with a true movie-theater kiss. "I love you, too," he said, even though she had not said it first.

§

The remainder of the weekend stretched ahead, gloriously free of obligations, just as gloriously filled with Kraig. With a little free time before dinner Friday evening, Melissa suggested watching the video from last year's Christmas program. The girls were interested; predictably, Matt was not. Just as it began, Matt came into the family room.

"Mom, did you count me in when you made the dinner reservation?"

She pressed "pause" on the remote control. "Yes, I did."

"I can't go. I'm going out with some friends."

Melissa tried not to sound too disappointed. "Okay. Well, I hope we'll get a chance to see you a *little* while you're here."

Matt's gaze shifted toward Kraig, and Melissa could imagine his thoughts. *It's not my fault if you don't.*

"Well, have fun," she said with an effort at cheerfulness.

"Oh, and my flight back to Michigan is tomorrow night."

"Tomorrow night! Why—"

"I wanted to do some stuff with some school friends before classes start again. It's okay. I can take the bus."

As he started to leave the room, Melissa searched for some conciliatory words. "We'll work something out. Have fun. Don't stay out too late."

"Okay, bye."

Melissa and the girls exchanged looks of mild despair.

"Melissa," Kraig said, one arm around her shoulder, the other hand on her cheek, making sure she faced him squarely, "Here's what you're going to do. Tomorrow night, you and the girls are going to take Matt to the airport. And you're going to go out to dinner, as a family, without me. Yes," he said, as she started to protest, "you are. Shanna and I will be fine, I promise.

"Think about it, Melissa. From Matt's point of view, I came along at an awkward time. Here's a guy who's just left home, and wants to be independent, but at the same time, wants home to still be there for him. I was once an eighteen-year-old guy. I know what I'm talking about.

"But home isn't home anymore, because I've taken his place, in a way, and you have no reason to miss him or be happy to see him, because you have *me*. Trust me. This is what he's thinking."

She couldn't help it: every time Kraig touched the heart of a matter in that way that he had, she felt her deepest self being touched, and she began to tear up.

"Melissa," he said, almost in a whisper, "everything will be *all right*."

She let him press her head to his shoulder and shed a few tears. "I'm glad you're here."

"Me too. But life is never perfect, and my presence is going to cause some adjustments all the way around—some easier and more fun than others."

"I have an idea. Why don't we put your couch in here when you move in? It's nicer than this one. You might have some other things that are better than mine, too."

"Sure," he said, laughing softly at her sudden change of subject. "When you come up at Christmas, you can take a look at everything I have and see what you like."

She looked at the girls. "That'll be fun, won't it?"

Kraig looked thoughtful. "I should list my townhouse for sale right after the holidays. One nice thing about it—there's no mortgage. I was able to pay it off with what I inherited from my parents. So if we need to do any improvements here, to accommodate an extra person—or dog—we can."

"Oh, maybe a fence for Shanna would be nice. And fixing up the downstairs apartment to be an office for you. And whatever else would make you more comfortable."

"I think we should to go to Europe," Jessica said. "Wouldn't Kraig be great? He knows so many languages."

He nodded slowly, deep in thought.

"I think we should watch the video," Emily said.

They laughed, and Kraig reached for the remote control and pressed "play."

§

When time came for Kraig to head downstairs for the night, a light rain was falling. "Let me walk you down there," Melissa said. "I put a towel just inside the door for Shanna's paws."

He nodded. Surely by now, Melissa thought, they knew each other well enough to be alone together without the awkwardness.

Inside the apartment, she watched him hang his sport coat and Shanna's harness in the tiny closet, letting him make the first move toward her. He did, enveloping her in a hug so warm and tight that she heard herself make an "mm" that sounded more sensuous than perhaps it should have.

"It's time for you to go, Melissa, good night," he said, although he didn't noticeably loosen his hold on her.

"I love it when you hold me like this. I love it when you touch me. It's not a sexual thing. It just feels good."

"Melissa," he said, stepping back and holding her by the shoulders, "that's wrong. It is. It *is* a sexual thing. All these years I've been afraid to fall in love with someone I was physically attracted to. It's difficult to explain, but it will all come out in the counseling sessions. But you have to trust me. I *know* you trust me. In a way, that's the problem. You have to trust me when I tell you that this is more difficult for me than it is for you. Melissa," his voice took on a new tenderness, "I've been single most of my life, and now, with some suddenness, I'm looking forward to a life of companionship and intimacy. I'd love to skip all the formalities and just go right there.

"But that would be wrong. You know it would. And it would ruin it for us in the long run. I don't know whether your convictions are as strong as mine, or whether you just don't struggle with it. Maybe you never enjoyed sex in the first place. That, too, will come out. This is part of why a long courtship would not have worked. Melissa, I love you, and as we go through our lives together, I want to look back on this time and know that we did everything right." He took her in his arms again. "You know what else I love about you? I love it that you cry."

Which was, of course, all the invitation she needed to do just that. "You probably don't believe me, but I hardly ever cried until I met you. I don't know why—"

"I do. You weren't in touch with your emotions before. But you can't fall in love with the right person until you're honest with yourself about who you are and what you want. Someday, you will have cried all the tears you've held back for so long." He reached into his pocket and brought out a handkerchief, which he pressed into her hand.

"A real handkerchief," she said, laughing a little as she dabbed at her eyes. "Hardly anyone uses one anymore."

"Nor do I. But I thought of this monogrammed set I had, sitting unused in my drawer, and decided that I would begin to carry one. With you in mind."

"Thanks," she said, and tried to give it back to him.

"No, you keep it. Give it back another time. Now, it *is* time for you to go."

Reluctantly, she slipped out of his embrace and out the door.

§

Saturday morning, she sat holding his hand in the pastor's office for the first counseling session. The pastor scribbled furiously as the two of them gave their answers to his question as to what they'd like to cover. Usually more than six sessions are recommended for a second marriage, he said, as often there are issues from the first marriages that need to be dealt with before the couple is ready to begin building the foundation for the new marriage relationship.

Melissa looked at Kraig as her mind raced to find a place in the schedule for two more counseling sessions.

"How about tomorrow afternoon?" the pastor suggested.

"Great," Kraig said, "Melissa?"

"Sure," she said, relieved. "And maybe the same when he comes in January."

"You know, maybe we could do a couple of conference calls, too," Kraig said, "after I've returned to Oregon."

The pastor looked up from his scribbling. "That's a good idea."

Melissa squeezed Kraig's hand.

"Now," the pastor said, "I'd like you each to tell me what it is that attracted you to the other."

Melissa sensed Kraig shifting in his seat, ready to give his answer, but the pastor asked Melissa to go first. She happily poured out her feelings for Kraig as she held his hand. Then she held back tears, as much as possible, as he did the same.

The pastor nodded as he made notes.

The topics flowed from one to another: what blame each carried for whatever went wrong in the first marriage; what blame they placed upon the partner; what they would do differently to make this one better; and so on.

When the pastor asked what each would do differently from the other's first spouse, Melissa didn't wait for permission to go first. She had since learned more about Celeste and the ways in which she'd abused Kraig, verbally and psychologically as well as physically, and her anger at this unseen, unknown, horrible woman vented itself as her words tumbled out. "She taunted him about not being a 'real man,' as if that was the reason for his resistance to her advances. As if moral values had nothing to do with it. They didn't for her, I guess." She looked at Kraig. "I hope you don't mind, Kraig. But I think this is important."

He squeezed her hand and said softly, "It's all right."

"And the moral values are one of the things I noticed first about him. I know I can trust him. And that's so important to me. It just really hurts to think that someone would use that against him." The pastor continued to scribble furiously as Melissa talked almost faster than she could think clearly, and with the other hand, pushed a box of tissues across the desk.

§

"That was fun," Kraig said on the way back to the car. "I look forward to tomorrow afternoon. And all the other ones. Really, I wish we had time for more. And I had a thought—maybe we could fit one in with *my* pastor when you come up at Christmas."

Melissa laughed at his enthusiasm even as she continued to dab at her smudged makeup.

163

"I had another thought," he said. "What time is Matt's flight tonight?"

"Late. The girls and I won't be back till about eleven."

"Oh. That *is* rather late. I was thinking we might go out for coffee and debrief the day's events."

"Oak Hill isn't exactly 'happening' at that hour."

"Neither am I. Well, how about *now*, then? Maybe we can find a quiet corner in an espresso shop. Failing that, we can get our drinks and talk in the car."

"That does sound nice. But, Kraig, tonight—"

"Melissa," he said, sounding exasperated, "what *about* tonight? What's the problem? Do you have food in the house?"

"Yeah, we'll find something for you."

"Then I'll be fine. I promise to stay inside with the doors locked. And if anyone calls I won't tell them I'm home alone."

"Okay," she laughed. "Hey, I thought of where we can go for coffee. And we can walk there from here, if you don't mind walking a ways. Things tend to be spread out around here."

"Of course I don't mind."

§

Returning from the airport, late as predicted, Melissa was anxious to sit with Kraig and hear how his evening alone went, but Emily spoke first.

"Look!" She did, and the focus of Emily's excitement turned out to be Kraig, seated on the couch, with Shanna at his feet, one cat in his lap, another beside him.

"Hey, that's pretty neat."

"They've been with me most of the evening. But come here, Melissa, and tell me how things went."

She sat beside him and began to pet the cat in his lap, letting her hand stroke his in the process. "We went to one of those all-you-can-eat salad bar places, had a nice time, got him on the plane, no problem. He let me hug him goodbye."

"What about the other things? The attitude?"

"Well…it was pretty much like you thought. He's having a great time at college, has a bunch of new friends, new places to hang out, new hobbies, everything. It was almost like he didn't remember

164

the time at the beach and not wanting you to be a part of the family. He's okay with it now, I guess."

Kraig nodded slowly, looking satisfied.

"And that's as close as you get to saying, 'I told you so,' isn't it?"

"Usually."

She pressed close to him, relishing being near him, absorbing his body heat and his smell, which by now she found nothing less than intoxicating, and kissed him on the cheek. As she did so, something he'd said about sex, in a low voice over coffee that morning, came back to her. And in a moment of confused yet powerful thoughts and feelings, her memory of that conversation blended with her love for him, and with the excitement of being near him, and she felt—with an unprecedented intensity—a genuine desire to be with him sexually. For he'd been right: she'd never really enjoyed it. But suddenly, she could imagine enjoying it.

"Melissa, I have something I'd like to give you. It's in my suitcase."

"Don't get up!" Emily protested. "The cats are comfortable!"

"Then perhaps you could get it *for* me. Open my suitcase, and look in the pocket in the back for something wrapped in tissue paper."

"And *don't* rearrange anything," Melissa added.

"She'll do fine."

"No problem." Emily returned a few moments later, looking pleased, and put a small package in Kraig's hand. "Here you go." Then she turned to Jessica and whispered something.

"I want to tell you about it first," he said, keeping it hidden. "This belonged to my mother. My brother's daughter Carlie has most of my mom's things, for no other reason than that she's the only female descendant. But I managed to keep this one piece that has always been special to me. I'd like you to wear it on our wedding day. If you would." He gently pressed into her hand a little bundle of something wrapped in rosebud tissue paper.

Unwrapping it delicately, she discovered inside the fragile paper an intricately carved cameo pin. "Oh," she breathed "my goodness, it's beautiful. It's all ivory—the design *and* the background. It's mounted in gold with a beaded edge. It looks very old. Of *course* I'll wear it." She handed it off for the girls to look at, and, finding herself with nothing to say more meaningful than the obvious "thank you," studied his face for any sign of a story that longed to be told.

"If you're wondering why I still have that—" which she was, in fact, for he might have given it to Celeste, "thank Providence. It was still at my parents' house when I was living in New Orleans. It came to me after my parents died and Kevin and I had to decide what to do with all their possessions." He still looked thoughtful. "That was one time when I came very close to moving back to Maine— after my dad died, and my mom was alone. But she basically talked me out of it. I was pretty well established in Oregon by then, and she didn't want to upset my life. Six months later, she was gone, too."

"Mm," Melissa nodded, pressing close to him.

After a long moment, he seemed to be finished, and the girls had since drifted away to get ready for bed.

"Well!" she said. "It's very late, and I am *so* looking forward to going to church tomorrow and introducing you as my fiancé."

A short time later, after Kraig had gone downstairs for the evening, Emily came into Melissa's room. "I didn't want to tell you this when Kraig was up here," she said, "but when I was looking in his suitcase, I noticed that all his underwear is gray. You know, gray like a sweat suit, instead of white. Even the socks and t-shirts."

Melissa smiled to herself, appreciating how funny this must seem to Emily, finding it rather amusing herself.

§

At the airport Monday morning, as they held one another in those precious final moments, he said, "Be watching for a tape from me in the mail. I want to follow up on something we talked about this weekend. Even in five and a half days, we ran out of time to talk about everything."

"I'll never get tired of talking with you."

"I'll call you tonight."

"I love you," she said, surprising even herself.

"I love you too." His voice caught, just a little.

§

Chapter 13

"Love of my life, Melissa," the tape began. "I can't even say when it was that I began to fall in love with you. I don't *remember* falling in love with you…probably because I have no memory of you without being in love. But if I had to choose a moment, perhaps it was the first time I held your hand, that first day on the beach.

"I had a picture of you in my mind almost from that very moment, and I can't even explain my feelings as I discovered, little by little, how close that first impression was. And I cannot begin to express the feelings that came over me when I first hugged you, at the airport. What I felt was far deeper—and far more complex—than an appreciation for your physical attributes.

"In order to understand *me*, you must understand this. For many years I'd believed that physical attraction would get in the way of a solid, Godly marriage relationship. I now know that is un-Biblical as well as illogical, and probably sounds like nonsense to you. Yet I did believe it. You'll recall that beginning a relationship with a physical attraction once got me into a great deal of trouble.

"In a way I wanted *not* to be physically attracted to you, so that I could believe within myself that my love for you was real. You see, I believed that sexual fulfillment within a marriage was something that grew directly out of the love. But as that week at the beach went by, and I spent more time with you, I saw that this was not to be.

"During the week that I was home and you were still in Maine, I had a couple of talks with my pastor about this very thing. This is something I should've done a long, long time ago. But after that, I sort of gave myself permission to be in love with someone *and* be physically attracted to her—*you*—at the same time. And now I know that this attraction will add to and strengthen our love relationship, not detract from and weaken it. You must imagine what good news this was for me.

"But it also made my life considerably more complicated. Because the more deeply I fell in love with you, the more I desired you, physically. And the more I felt free to express my love for you, the harder I had to work to keep my 'other' desires in order. And maybe you now see, more clearly than before, why a long courtship might have caused the breakdown of our relationship.

"So, at this point, we have four months to get to know each other as well as we can. I look forward to our wedding day, and every day that God gives us together after that. But I also want to savor these four months that we will never have again.

"I love you lots! Call you tonight."

This last part was delivered in such a lighthearted way, in contrast to the intense, serious tone of the rest of the message, that, just as she thought she was going to burst into tears, she burst out laughing instead.

The phone rang before dinner, and because Kraig was foremost on her mind, her first thought was, *It's too early. I hope it's not bad news.*

"Melissa?" said a vaguely familiar voice.

"Yes?"

"This is Jeff Lannon."

"Jeff!" she reached for a chair and sat.

"Say, um," he began hesitantly, "I know this is a surprise. I hope it's a good one."

"Of course it is!" Melissa sought to assure herself as well, for she didn't yet know the reason for Jeff's call.

"How've you been?"

"Fine. I mean, a lot has happened in the last three years. Most of it good. Fine. Really. How have *you* been?"

"Oh, pretty good. Melissa, I just want to say, before I get to the real reason I called, that I'm sorry about how things turned out. I know you've moved on, and so have I, but I really didn't do right by you. I know that. And I just want to say I'm sorry if I hurt you. I never meant to hurt you or the kids."

"Oh, well, no, I know that."

"Listen, there's a reason I called," he said, rescuing her from her verbal fumbling. "I hear congratulations are in order."

"Yes! Thank you."

It turned out a mutual friend had conveyed the news. "Well, then. Congratulations. I hope he deserves you."

"Well, thanks, Jeff."

"Listen, there's something else. I hear your fiancé likes to run. And that he could use a partner."

"Well...yeah...."

"I'd like to do that. If it's okay with you. *And* him."

"Oh! Well, sure."

"Great. So, how's Matt with this development?"

"Well, at first, it seemed like it was going to be a big battle. Like he was going to make me choose between him and Kraig—"

"Kraig! I couldn't remember your fiancé's name. Sorry, go ahead."

"But when we saw him at Thanksgiving, everything seemed okay. He's away at college now, you know."

"I know. So how's he doing?"

"Great, it seems. He's having fun, anyway. We'll see how his grades turn out."

"Oh, he'll do fine. Listen, would you mind if I called him?"

"No, not at all. He'd be happy to hear from you. He's in Michigan, you know."

"No problem. Hey, could I ask you to pray about something for me?"

"Sure, what?"

"I'm seeing someone new, and I really want to know God's will for this relationship."

"I sure will. And hey, I'd like to invite you both to our wedding. That may be the first time you get to meet Kraig."

"Looking forward to it. Hey, say 'hi' to the girls for me, okay? Maybe I'll stop by some time."

"We'd love to see you. And I'm so glad you called."

§

"Melissa," said her favorite voice, at eight o'clock sharp. "Did you get my tape?"

"Yes, but wait till I tell you about the phone call I got earlier this evening. Jeff called."

"Jeff? The old beau?"

"Yes, *that* Jeff. This is great, Kraig. I hadn't seen Jeff in three years—he changed churches or something—but this friend of his, Bob, who'd been leading the youth group with him at our church and still goes there, apparently told him the news. So he called to say 'congratulations'—and also to offer to go running with you."

"Really." He sounded mildly amused.

"No, really. And you'll like him. He's athletic, like Dave, but not as tall. And quieter, more reserved. He's an environmental engineer. But he does have this playful side, when you get to know him. If I told you anything about him, when we were at the beach, that made him sound bad, forget it. You'll like him."

"Well, that's great, Melissa. I'll already have a friend when I move to Oak Hill."

"Sorry. I just realized you asked about the tape, and I've been babbling on about Jeff. It was just such a positive thing to hear from him, though. But the tape. Yes. I agree. What you said about the next four months, and making the most of it."

"Melissa, it goes without saying that most of the planning will fall on you. But I'd like to take care of two areas, if you'll let me—the music and the honeymoon."

"Gladly."

"And anything else I can do to make it easier for you, let me know."

"Well, I was going to ask you what you thought we should wear. I know you have at least one nice suit, and so does Dave; it would make sense to me if you both just wore something you already have. Do you have any other nice suits?"

"I have a double-breasted one I haven't worn in a long time."

"What color?"

"Charcoal gray."

"Oh! That would be stunning on you. With a lavender shirt."

There were a couple seconds of silence before he responded. "Problem. Dave says big guys don't look good in double-breasted suits."

"Let me guess—that was before you lost the twenty pounds. And he probably wasn't talking about *you*. Has he ever *seen* you in this suit?"

"No."

"Well, get his opinion. He'll tell you the truth. And you should be able to get it altered, since it won't fit now. Check into it, anyway."

"All right. What are *you* going to wear?"

"Ahh…I'm picturing a Victorian or Edwardian, tea-length gown, probably lavender, with a high neck so I can wear the cameo brooch."

A couple more seconds of silence went by, and she realized, in a moment of incredible tenderness, that he was becoming a little emotional, picturing her in her wedding gown.

"Kraig?" she began hesitantly to change the subject. "Something's been nagging me these last couple days."

"What is it?"

"Well…when we were at those first two counseling sessions, we brought up the subject of Celeste and how she treated you…I'm sure you're sick of this subject, but as I've thought about it, I realized that I did most of the talking. And I don't know if I have the whole story. Is there anything else I should know?"

"Bless you for asking, Melissa. To be honest, I *am* rather sick of the subject. But you're right, there is more you need to know." He took a breath and waited for her go-ahead. "For many years, I told no one this except Dave. When I first got out of that relationship, and tried to talk about it, people sort of scoffed, so I stopped. But she was very abusive to me. You know that…but not all of it. She was physically as well as verbally abusive. I know—'How can a five-foot-two woman hurt a six-foot-three man?' But she did. She took advantage, quite literally, of the fact that I couldn't see it coming.

"That's the way she approached me sexually, the first time, and other times. I should've known this wasn't a good sign, but part of me—the male ego part that I'd rather not acknowledge—found it flattering in a way.

"Later, she used the same approach, with physical violence. Melissa, you, of all the people I've ever known, can picture this in your mind and imagine what it was like for me. I know I had bruises because people commented on them. But I had to make up explanations because, as I told you, people wouldn't have believed me. This was fifteen, sixteen years ago; it might be different now. But I couldn't defend myself, and I could hardly hit her back; you know that's not my style.

"There were other things. She'd leave things in my path, rearrange the furniture without telling me, move my personal things. Imagine how distressing that is, Melissa, not to be able to lay my hands on something I need, something that my dog can't help me find, so that I'd be at her mercy to get it back.

"The Christian young people I connected with when I first moved back to California, they tried to get me to reconcile with her. I don't blame them; they didn't have the whole story. By then I'd decided not to *tell* the whole story any more, because of the way people reacted.

"Melissa? Trust me, this is more difficult for you than it is for me, because it's new to you. But you needed to know, and I want you to be glad you asked. I don't want anything in my past, anything that I have ever told *anyone*, to be hidden from you. Melissa? We need to pray. Close your eyes and imagine I'm holding your hand."

She did, but her mind wasn't fully on what he was saying; she was forming a vow never, ever to approach him—even with a hug, a kiss, or a sweet word whispered in his ear—without giving him a moment's notice.

"Now, Melissa, I want you to take a deep breath, thank God for bringing us together, and go shopping for that gown. Make sure you get just the one you want. You're going to be the most beautiful bride...." and he laughed, a bit forcefully, and she laughed too; for he did not want to end this conversation with tears over something in the long-ago past, and neither did she.

§

At lunchtime the next day, Melissa stood on the sidewalk, gazing at the gown in the display window. *Is it possible that the very first dress I see is the one?*

For this wasn't even a bridal shop, just a store with vintage and specialty clothing; but she'd always admired the beautiful, exquisite things she'd seen there. She turned the brass doorknob and entered. "The dress in the window," she said breathlessly to the saleswoman, "do you have it in a size ten?"

She could hardly contain her excitement as she tried it on, for it was indeed a perfect fit, a perfect look, the perfect thing to be wearing the day she married the man of her dreams.

"I'll be back Saturday," she said as she prepared to leave with the precious gown, "with my daughters, to look at bridesmaids' dresses."

§

"Have you found it yet?" Kraig asked first thing in that evening's call.

"Yes! It's perfect. I can hardly—"

"Melissa, I was *joking*," he laughed. "You really have your dress already?"

"Yes, they don't have to alter it or anything, it's from this vintage clothing store downtown that always has the most gorgeous stuff in the window, and I thought I'd just—"

"Slow down, Melissa," he laughed again. "Take a deep breath and tell me about it."

"Okay. It's lavender, with antique lace and beadwork, and a high neck so I can wear the cameo brooch. And Saturday we're going to go back and look at dresses for the girls. They're *so* excited. Oh, did you ask Dave about the suit?"

"I did. You were right; he thinks it will be quite salvageable."

"What exactly did he say?"

"That a tailor could whip it into shape, no sweat. And that I'm going to be one dapper dude wearing this suit. He's going to go with me to the store where he buys his suits and help me explain to the tailor what we need. He's better at this sort of thing than I am."

"Thank goodness for Dave."

"I do. Every day."

"How about you and I go shopping for a shirt and tie when I come up for Christmas? We'll make sure we get the right shade of lavender, whether the suit is a warm gray or a cool gray."

"That all sounds rather bewildering to me. I'd be more than happy to have you go shirt-and-tie shopping with me."

"Fun. Hey…you know what I've totally neglected to ask you about these last couple weeks? Dave and Judy. How are Dave and Judy? How's Judy's health?"

"They're great, mostly. Judy is thriving under Dave's loving care. Although I don't know where he finds the time or energy to do all that he does. He just moves faster to fit it all in, I guess. But she sounds perkier all the time, and I've never seen Dave so happy."

"If Dave is happier than he was when I met him, he must be just about bouncing off the walls."

"You'll see what I mean when you come up."

"I look *so* forward to being with them at Christmas. Tell them I said 'hi,' okay? And Helen too. Now, tell me what you like to wear to bed."

He laughed softly, and Melissa was glad for the geographical distance, allowing him to react to her question in private. "Boxers and a t-shirt. Just boxers if it's hot."

"Cotton boxers?"

"Yes. Flannel in winter."

"Hmm. I'm getting an idea of something I'd like to get for you to wear on our honeymoon. It won't be anything silly or racy, I promise. Just something comfortable, something I'd like to see you in."

"All right, then…what are *you* going to wear to bed?"

It hadn't occurred to her until that moment that what *she* wore would be just as important to him—and that the way it *felt* would be the critical factor. "I'm not sure. I'll find something… nice."

"And we have covered a lot, as usual. Tomorrow I hope to get to work on planning our honeymoon. Any thoughts?"

"Oh…well, I guess we should save any *big* trips—say, Europe, like Jessica was saying, or even Maine—for another time, when we can all go…I suppose we could just stay close to home; there are lots of nice bed-and-breakfasts in Oak Hill."

"But that wouldn't be fair to you, Melissa. We need to go someplace that'll be exciting to *you*."

"Well, we want to avoid altitude changes and long drives—"

"Oh, don't worry about that. I'm usually fine after the first day or so. Tell you what: I'll check into it, see what I come up with, and let you know."

"And I'm going to go shopping for a nightgown tomorrow."

§

"Melissa. I asked around and got a great idea for a honeymoon destination. But I want to check with you before I begin making reservations. Several people have told me that the California

174

wine country will be spectacular at that time of year, with things beginning to bloom."

"Oh! That *is* perfect. There are a million bed-and-breakfasts there, and of course that area is famous for great restaurants. And wineries. There are lots of things we could do to fill up a week in the wine country."

"Great. I'll find a place that's cozy but elegant, with some nice amenities but intimate.... Did you find a nightgown?"

"I did. It's peach. That's all I'm going to tell you; the rest you can discover yourself."

"*So* looking forward to it. Oh, Melissa...you need to talk to Matt and find out whether he's coming for Christmas, so we can make airline reservations."

"I did! And no, he's not coming. But he was sort of apologetic about it, saying that he'd already planned this skiing trip with some friends."

"Well. That's pretty positive. Though the apology was a bit more than even I would've expected. What do you make of it?"

"I have an idea. When I talked to Jeff, he said he was going to call Matt. I have no idea what they talked about, but I think that just connecting with Jeff sort of...."

"Gave him the closure he needed, yet at the same time, gave him Jeff as a friend, an ally, a confidant."

"Exactly."

"I'll make it a point to thank Jeff when I meet him. Now, how's your to-do list coming along?"

"With the dresses picked out, now we're working on hairstyles. Next, flowers."

"Purple. Irises."

"Of course. And lupines. In honor of the occasion of our meeting."

"Silk ones."

"Silk? Why?"

"Because of what you said about how real flowers die and make you sad."

"But this is different!"

"Get silk ones anyway. Then we can keep them, as *happy* reminders."

"Okay," she laughed. "Silk flowers."

"What's next on the list?"

"Gifts. For our attendants; for each other."

"And 'no gifts' on the invitations."

"I was just going to say that! Could we put something about 'a donation to your favorite charity in lieu of a gift'?"

"My thoughts exactly. And I had an idea for a gift for each other. Let me run it by the girls and see what they think. They could help me go shopping in January...we could have it delivered just before the wedding...somehow, I'll manage to keep it a surprise for you."

"And then there's Christmas shopping," she groaned.

"I did have an idea for something for Matt. You'll need to get it to him early. When Dave heard about Matt being in Michigan, he reminded me how cold it gets in the Great Lakes. He's going to need a good jacket before he goes skiing. And gloves, hat, socks, long underwear."

"Okay." Melissa let out a long breath. "How about the music?"

"I'm working on some ideas."

"Are you going to sing? I can't imagine someone *else* singing at our wedding, when it could be *you*."

"That's just what Dave said. But I think I would be... emotionally unstable."

"You could lip-sync it."

"Thought of that, too. It would look too phony."

"How about if you record it, and we just stand there and hold hands while it's played? People will know it's you. We could put a little blurb in our program saying so."

"Something like, 'Kraig wanted to sing for you today, but he was afraid of going to pieces in front of his beautiful bride and all of you gathered here, so he took the chicken way out.'"

Melissa laughed. "Something like that."

"Melissa, I want you to look forward to getting the backrub of your life on our honeymoon. Maybe not the first night. Maybe the second. I'll call you tomorrow night. And in two weeks, we'll be together again."

§

176

Stepping into the terminal, Melissa immediately spotted Kraig, Dave on one side, Shanna on the other. Shanna began to wiggle, Dave nudged Kraig, and Kraig broke into a smile. After the hugs and the introductions, Dave said, "Well, buddy, I do believe you'll be spending your days surrounded by pulchritude."

Emily looked puzzled, but, not wanting to expose her lack of understanding, said nothing. "It was a compliment," Melissa whispered to her daughter. Then, suddenly remembering how much she'd been looking forward to meeting Judy, said, "Judy's not here?"

"No," Dave said, "she and Helen are back at Helen's place, up to their elbows in food in various stages of preparation."

"Already? It's five days before Christmas."

"Judy tires easily. I wanted her to be able to enjoy the music programs at church and all the other festivities, and she has to work through noon on the twenty-fourth. I offered to do the cooking, but she wouldn't let me."

"Not that he's not capable," Kraig said. "We'll all be going to Helen's for Christmas dinner. I volunteered *you* to make a salad. You have five days to figure out what kind."

When the door opened at Helen's house, Melissa was at first confused as to who was standing there; a moment later, she realized it could only be Judy, and was ashamed of her unkind thoughts. It wasn't that Judy was exactly unattractive; just that Melissa had expected someone different…perhaps taller, prettier, more stylish.

As Dave quickly went to Judy's side and introduced her to Melissa and the girls, she noticed, for starters, that Judy stood barely taller than Dave's shoulder, although improved posture might have added an inch or more to her stature. She was neither thin nor chubby, but neither did she appear to be very athletic. Her short blond hair was cut without regard to current American fashion, and she wore no makeup. Worse, her clunky glasses obscured what might have been her most striking feature—her eyes. Melissa, desperately hoping no sign of surprise or disappointment betrayed her, took Judy's hand and gushed about how happy she was to meet her.

Dave winked at her, and Melissa knew she had done a poor job of faking.

"This all smells so incredible," Dave said, "we'd better get going or I'm just going to start eating this pie and—" He had stuck a fork into an apple pie and taken a large bite, so the rest of what he said was completely unintelligible.

"Dave," Judy scolded, and he went to work patching up the hole he'd made.

"Go along now, young people," Helen said. "I'll keep an eye on things here."

"Helen isn't coming to dinner with us?" Melissa whispered to Kraig.

"No, she doesn't like restaurants. It's too hard for her to follow the conversation in a busy place. Don't worry about it," he said, giving her a squeeze. "I think she thought we'd all be a bit rowdy for her taste, at least at the beginning of our week together."

Sitting at the table in the restaurant, Melissa watched carefully how Dave interacted with Judy, eager to discover what it was that attracted him to her. It was easy to see *her* devotion to *him*; it seemed that everything Dave said was either the funniest or the most brilliant or profound thing ever uttered.

Whether standing or sitting, Melissa noticed, Dave always had his arm around Judy in such a way that she was positioned slightly forward of him, as if to give her some added importance. She saw, too, that Judy was blessed with a lovely fair complexion, and her hair had a bit of natural wave, so that a skilled stylist could make a huge improvement with a minimum of effort. When Judy took off her glasses for a moment, Melissa was delighted to see that she'd been right about Judy's eyes; they were the green of a bottomless pool.

Suddenly aware that she'd been staring, Melissa said, "Dave, did you ever think of going to the mission field?"

"Who, me? No, I value good food and a good bed way to much."

"Dave," Judy scolded again, then turned to Melissa. "That's not right at all. Some people are called to *go*; others are called to stay home and provide support. We couldn't do what we do on the field without people like Dave, praying and sending money and other things from home. Dave has been one of my biggest supporters. It's made all the difference." Her voice trailed off a bit, and Melissa suddenly felt a kinship with Judy—a sisterhood of women sharing the incomprehensible good fortune of being loved by men such as these.

"But Judy's contribution to the mission field does not end here," Dave said. "Tell them about the other plan."

"Oh," she said, casting her eyes down for a moment. "I want to adopt a child from Africa. My parents—they're missionaries in South Africa—adopted a little boy, my brother Kurt, but this was after I'd returned to the States for college. I didn't get to see him grow up. So I want my own chance to adopt a child. And I'm going to go forward with this, even if I never get married. There are countless kids out there...." Her voice trailed off again.

"I was fascinated with Judy's stories about African music," Kraig said. "Antiphonal harmonies...how one person can play several instruments at one time, using both hands and feet, feeling three or four rhythms simultaneously and independently...."

"Oh, and how they make music from flattened bicycle spokes!" Judy said.

"Don't get her started," Dave said, "or pretty soon, buddy, only you will know what she's talking about and the rest of us will be falling asleep." His arm around her, he eased her shoulder back into his, and Melissa observed that, rather than bouncing-off-the-walls happy, as she'd envisioned, Dave now radiated a deep joy and contentment that could come only from loving, and being loved by, one very special woman.

§

Sunday morning, Melissa arrived at church with Helen and the girls; Kraig had gone earlier, wanting to squeeze in nursery work, his adult Sunday school class, *and* the service. She had worried for him; he would be at church not only all morning, but all afternoon and evening as well, for the children's musical and the adult choir concert. "I've never felt more energetic," he'd said. "Having you here must be just what I need."

Now, she peered over the half-door of the nursery, delighted to observe Kraig in his element for the brief time that her presence would go unnoticed. He was in an oversized rocking chair, in his stocking feet, his shirt collar and tie showing above the neckline of his nursery worker's smock, rocking a baby and talking over his shoulder to a matronly-looking woman arranging freshly washed toys on a shelf.

The woman, noticing her, did a double take. Melissa, certain that by now everyone here knew who she was, just waved, saying nothing.

"Melissa?" Kraig said.

"Aha!" said the woman, shaking her finger in Melissa's direction. "So, *you're* the one!"

"Marguerite, this is my fiancée, Melissa."

Nonplused, not knowing what to make of this greeting, Melissa feebly said, "hi."

"Well, come in," Marguerite said. "Leave your shoes at the door, please. We like to keep the carpet clean for the babies."

Melissa leaned over the door and fumbled with the latch.

"He has the magic touch with these babies, you know," Marguerite went on. "It's surely going to be different around here without him."

Kraig rose, letting the chair settle, and Melissa went behind him to untie his smock as Marguerite took the baby from him. Kraig whispered something into the baby's ear as he let go.

"Your suit coat?" Melissa asked.

"On a hook, behind the door."

She retrieved it and held it while he put it on.

"Shanna, too," Marguerite continued. "She's the only dog who's ever been allowed in the nursery. The older babies, sometimes they climb on her, fall asleep on her...we'll miss her, too."

Kraig took his black wingtips from a cubby by the door and slipped them on. Melissa held the door while he fastened Shanna's lead.

"Well, it was good to meet you at last," Marguerite said.

"Bye, nice to meet you," Melissa said, closing the half-door so abruptly she almost hit Kraig with it. Moving along the hallway with him, she tried to look happy. Many people they passed smiled at her knowingly, and some said "hi" to them. Kraig never failed to return the greeting to each of these by name.

"Melissa," he whispered loudly, leaning toward her, "what's wrong?"

"It just seems like every time I come to Portland, someone makes me feel bad about taking you away from here."

"That's not the best way to look at things, Melissa. Life is full of changes. They'll get over it."

His answer was too simplistic to give her much peace, but this was not a good time to discuss it.

"Where are the girls?" he asked.

"They went to our Sunday school class, with Dave. They didn't really want to go and be with kids they didn't know, and Dave said your classmates would want to meet them anyway."

"Well, that's a good idea." He squeezed her hand.

"What was that you whispered to the baby?"

He thought for a moment. "Oh, that. *Boogalie*. It's a Cajun term of endearment."

"Cajun. Of course." And her spirits lifted considerably as she fixed her mind on the thought of spending her future with Kraig, never ceasing to be delighted and amazed at the things that went on inside his head.

After Sunday school and church, there was time for little more than a quick lunch and clothes-change before he had to return for final rehearsals for the music programs. Dave and Helen and others from church seemed content to do all this driving; yet Melissa looked forward to filling this role herself.

§

The choir kids were dressed in their holiday-best outfits; Kraig wore a plaid shirt with a cranberry-red knit tie. Melissa would have found the kids' performance more interesting had she known any of the kids; as it was, she mostly wanted to hear Kraig sing. After several songs and readings, the kids were seated on the platform steps, the spotlight aimed at Kraig, a guitar melody began, and Melissa held her breath.

As he began to sing, Melissa recognized the story of Simeon, the devout Jew who God had promised would live to see the infant Jesus. At the part in the song where Simeon takes Him in his arms and praises God, two people came out of the shadows; one took the microphone and held it for Kraig, the other handed him a baby. Melissa felt her eyes brim over as she watched this; the way Kraig cradled that baby, it could have been his own, or it could have been the baby Jesus Himself.

181

When, after the last number by the kids' choir, the house lights rose and the kids filed out, Melissa bolted from her seat and rushed to the platform, barely getting out his name before practically leaping into his arms. His embrace lifted her off the floor.

"Did you hear that applause?" she said into his ear, probably too loudly. "You were awesome! Everybody loves you!"

"They were clapping for the kids, not me."

"Everyone claps for their own kids. People don't clap like *that* except for a great performance."

When he released her, she stepped back a bit and looked closely at him. "Are you tired?"

He smiled. "Not really. Maybe a little. The deaconesses arranged to have snacks brought in for all the music people, with the goal of keeping us all at church between performances."

"Who besides you is involved in both?"

"Most of the orchestra, the pianist, the organist."

"Okay, then. So where do you go?"

"The choir room."

Just then Dave came forward with Shanna.

"Well, I guess we'll leave you to do what you need to do," she said. "And we'll be back tonight."

Kraig kissed her lightly on the lips, and as she walked out with Dave, Judy, Helen, and the girls, she noticed after a while that Dave was looking at her with something resembling a smirk, and she realized she'd been walking along wearing a perpetually goofy grin. "I just keep thinking about how lucky I am," she explained.

"Guess what," Dave said in a stage whisper. "He keeps saying the same thing."

§

Awakening later than she'd planned to Monday morning, Melissa needed a moment to remember that she was at Helen's house, her daughters in the next room. With a twinge of self-reproach, she realized that Kraig was probably already on his way to work, and she wasn't even out of bed yet. *And he's the one who should be exhausted!*

Helen, alone at the kitchen table, drinking a cup of tea and reading the morning paper, peered over her glasses as Melissa stood in the kitchen doorway. "Would you like something to eat? A piece of toast?"

"Uh, I think I'll take a shower first. Maybe the girls will be up by then."

"Just help yourselves whenever you're ready."

"Thanks. After that we're planning to take the bus down to Kraig's office and then do a little shopping."

"You don't have to take the bus. I can drive you wherever you want to go."

"No, that's okay, thanks. Kraig gave us bus schedules. He takes the bus all the time; I thought we should get comfortable with it, too."

Helen nodded.

A couple hours later, standing at the bus stop in the crisp, white air of the winter solstice, Melissa suddenly realized with a sinking feeling that perhaps Helen had *wanted* to come with them; that she probably didn't have much else to do. And she sank further into gloom as she began to dwell on the reality that she would be taking Kraig away from a whole world full of people who loved him, who mattered to him; how lonely Helen would be without him; Dave too, not to mention the church choir and nursery. And she thought if only she lived in Portland, all of this pain could be avoided. Kraig had agreed to move to California without any discussion whatsoever; what if she and the girls moved instead? *But, no. That would be such an enormous waste of time and energy, when we'll be moving to Maine sometime soon anyway.*

"Mom, the bus," Emily was saying.

"Oh." Melissa continued her reverie as she followed the girls to empty seats. She gazed out the window as Portland dragged by, her breath making steam on the glass, giving the cityscape a distorted, surreal appearance. She thought about the kids' music program the previous afternoon, and how natural Kraig had looked holding that baby. He'd said it didn't matter at all that they'd never have children together, but how could that be true?

Then, mercifully, Dave's words came back to her. *He keeps saying he's lucky to have found me…only Kraig wouldn't say "lucky," he'd say blessed by divine providence.* And Melissa smiled to herself. Kraig would know what to do about her failure to invite Helen on their outing.

"Mom, it's the next stop, isn't it?" Jessica was asking.

"Yep, next stop."

Melissa braced herself for a reception of unknown nature as she entered the small newspaper office.

"Kraig, your visitors," someone called out after giving them only a cursory glance.

Kraig made the round of introductions.

"I guess Kraig will be in good hands when he moves to California," someone said.

"We're all looking forward to seeing how family life affects his perspective," someone else said.

"Why don't you go ahead, take a long lunch?" said someone who seemed to be the boss.

As the door swished closed behind them, Melissa sighed. "Oak Hill is a much friendlier place."

"That may be. But my boss letting me take a long lunch is friendly, don't you think?"

"Yeah, but what else was he going to do—let us hang around the office, interrupting your work?"

"Melissa, we need to talk, don't we?"

She shrugged. "It's not that complicated. It's just that every time I come here—"

"Someone makes you feel bad about wanting me to be with *you* instead of with *them*. I think most people understand the concepts of love and marriage and of family coming first. Nobody likes change when they're already content. But sometimes change happens. That's *their* problem, not *yours*, Melissa."

"Where are we going, by the way?"

"To a nice little sandwich shop that I know you'll like. Tell me what else is bothering you."

"Helen offered to drive us. I said, no thanks, we can take the bus. It occurred to me later—*too* late—that maybe she *wanted* to come."

He looked thoughtful, then said "Hmm," a bit ruefully. "You could be right about that. But I have an idea. We'll take care of it after lunch."

Inside the sandwich shop, Kraig waited for the girl behind the counter to speak first. "Hey, Kraig."

"Ah, Sally. I'd like you to meet my fiancée, Melissa, and her daughters, Jessica and Emily."

Sally was nodding knowingly as he spoke. "I figured. So I guess we won't be seeing you in here much after, what did you tell me, March?"

"That's right. I'm getting married in March. And looking forward to moving to California to be with my new family," he said firmly, his arm around Melissa's shoulder just as firmly.

"Well, what'll it be today?" Sally asked.

"I'm really not that hungry," Melissa said to Kraig. "We ate breakfast just before we left to come here. I'll just have a bite of yours, if that's okay."

"Of course. Get a mocha or something. Girls?"

"We thought we could share something. We're not that hungry either."

At a little table by the window, Melissa inhaled deeply as the aroma of Kraig's bowl of turkey chili reached her senses. "That smells really good. I think I'll get that if we come here again."

"Pretty much everything here is good. How's your sandwich, girls?"

They'd just gotten out the word "good" when, almost at the same time, their attention was caught by something happening outside. "Hey, it's snowing!"

"Hey, it is," Melissa said.

"Well, there's your salvation," Kraig said. "Now Helen is saying, 'I'm surely glad I let those kids take the bus, because Lord knows I don't like driving in snow.'"

"So what was your idea?"

He smiled. "Flowers. After we eat, we'll visit Judy at the bookstore, and then go choose some nice roses for Helen."

Melissa began to feel a bit sheepish. "Will she think I'm trying to buy forgiveness?"

"I doubt it. I bring her flowers often. In fact," he put his hand palm-up on the table, "when I met you, I was determined to send you lots of flowers, because it didn't seem right to me that I should send another woman more flowers than you. I wanted *you* to have that role."

"Until you found out that I really don't like getting flowers, and that ruined your plan."

"Ah, but that brings us back to the importance of knowing the person on the other end of the relationship. And being happy with who you *are*—not who I expected you to be. And, by the way, the 'no flowers' thing is the only thing I've had to adjust to."

"Maybe I'll be the one to adjust. Because getting flowers from *you* is different from…. When flowers are supposed to make up for the lack of something basic in the relationship, it doesn't work. But when they're a bonus to a *real* relationship…you know what I mean. What were you working on when we got to your office?"

"That'll be a surprise. You'll see it in the paper Christmas Eve morning."

§

Tuesday morning, Melissa made a point of doing two things right: she rose early enough to sit at the breakfast table with Helen, and even help with the dishes. And she invited Helen to go with them on the day's outing.

"Thank you, dear, but I think I'll just stay home and enjoy these roses while they're fresh. And the roads will be icy. You go along without me. And be careful."

She also made a point of arriving at Kraig's office a little later; she didn't want to test the goodwill of one of the few people who'd been polite to her.

"What did Helen say?" Kraig asked as they descended the steps.

"That she'd rather stay home and look at your flowers than come with us."

"Ah. Well. I guess the flowers turned out to be a good idea. What did you three do this morning?"

"We rode the bus all over," Emily said.

"Just to see where it went," Jessica added.

"That could be fun," he agreed.

"For us country girls who never ride the bus," Melissa said.

"Is everyone all right with going to the sandwich shop again?" he asked.

"Sure. We made a point of walking a few blocks, so we're a *little* hungry."

At the table by the window, over steaming bowls of soup and turkey chili, Melissa felt a little better than she had earlier in the week; no one had made her feel unwelcome. *Yet.*

"So, have you decided on a salad for Christmas dinner?" Kraig asked.

"I thought I'd make sort of a winter fruit salad, with apples, pears, grapes, walnuts...."

"That sounds excellent. What kind of dressing will it have?"

"It doesn't really need a dressing."

"Good. If you put mayonnaise on anything, Dave will give you no peace for a long time."

"He eats like a Californian. Strange, considering how he detests California."

Kraig rested his spoon and gave her a strange look. "Whatever gave you that idea?"

"Something he said the first time I met him. At the restaurant when we were having lunch. Or maybe it's just me...."

"Just you he likes to tease. He only teases people he likes. Get used to it."

"What are we doing Christmas Eve?"

"That's tomorrow," Emily said.

"I always go to the Christmas Eve service. I was hoping you'd like to go too."

"Sure," Melissa said.

"I hope it's not at midnight," Emily said.

"No," he laughed a little. "It's at six o'clock. We can eat dinner at my place afterward. I'd like to invite Helen."

"Sure. So I guess we'd better go grocery shopping. Something for the salad, for Christmas Eve dinner, and for Christmas breakfast. What did you have in mind for Christmas Eve dinner?"

"My family had a tradition of having clam chowder and biscuits. I have the recipes. I'm sure we can manage it just fine, although I've never let anyone else use my mom's recipes. Until now."

"Clam chowder?" Melissa asked. "Your dad was Jewish."

"My dad was an individualist. We followed the traditions we liked, forgot about the ones we didn't...." He laughed at a memory. "He liked to put Stars of David on the Christmas tree. Things like that."

"We haven't even *seen* where you live yet," Emily said.

"No, you haven't. But you will. What other errands do you have to do today?"

"Some Christmas wrap. And I just now had another horrible thought. I didn't think to get Helen anything for Christmas. I should have."

"Not a problem. It's taken care of."

"What?" she asked, awestruck at Kraig's ability to solve problems so effortlessly.

"Flowers. Delivered to her door, on the seventeenth of every month, for a year. Since I won't be here to bring them to her. It'll start in March."

"The first month you won't be here. What's special about the seventeenth?"

"Her birthday is March seventeenth."

"Well, that works out great." Melissa shook her head in amazement.

"You can get wrap at the bookstore. Say 'hi' to Judy for me while you're there. Do you know where to get groceries?"

"The place where we got the flowers yesterday looked like a decent-sized grocery store."

"It'll do. And you know how to get there. Regrettably, I need to get back to the office."

"And finish your article. The girls and I can come over on the bus tonight. No way am I going to ask Helen to drive when it's icy *and* dark."

"That reminds me," he said, digging into his pants pocket. "A key to my townhouse. In case you get there before I do."

§

Melissa barely had the door to the townhouse closed behind her.

"Oh! Check out the tree!" Emily exclaimed.

She turned quickly. There, crowding the entertainment center into its corner, was a bushy fir tree, its angel topper brushing the ceiling with its upspread wings. She had taken only a step toward it when she heard Kraig's voice call through the intercom.

"Melissa?"

188

She hurried back to open the door. "Hey," she said, embracing him just inside the door.

He sighed deeply, a bit of emotion showing through. "That is definitely the best welcome-home I've received as long as I've lived here."

"The tree! I didn't know if you'd...."

"Of course I'd have a tree. It's been *years* since I've had family with me at Christmas. How could I not have a tree?"

She had only taken a step toward it when again there was a shout through the intercom. "Pizza!"

She looked at Kraig and laughed. "I didn't even *think* about dinner tonight."

He smiled. "You can carry only so many bags of groceries on the bus," he said, digging out his wallet. "Especially if you're a bunch of country girls who don't usually ride the bus."

"Look at these ornaments!" Jessica exclaimed as Melissa finally made her way across the room.

She examined a hand-painted eggshell on a gold cord. "Where did all these things come from?"

"It's my parents' entire collection. In a way, it's my family history. I've just gotten them out for the first time in many years." He extended his hand toward the tree, finding a tiny violin. "Each one of these things has a story behind it."

"These eggshells are exquisite!"

"Those are a Russian tradition. Some are heirloom; some were sent to us by relatives. The musical instruments, my mom gave me for Christmas one year."

"Here's a Star of David, like you were telling us."

"Yes. The angel on top is an heirloom from my mom's family."

"Here's a chickadee." Melissa smiled, remembering the pair of carved chickadees, one of which was now hers.

"Yes, there's a set of Maine birds—a cardinal, a loon, a puffin...my mom sent me those the year I lived in New Orleans."

"Oh!" said Emily, "I found a guide dog in harness. Only it's not Shanna; it's black."

"My mom gave that to me the first Christmas I had my first dog. There's a German shepherd, too."

"No golden retriever?" Jessica asked.

"No, my mom died before I got Shanna."

The girls exchanged knowing looks, and then turned to Melissa with the same look. She put her finger to her lips, then quickly changed the subject, not wanting Kraig to think they were keeping something from him. "I suppose we should go eat pizza before it gets cold."

"One more thing. Who can find the piece of red beach glass?"

"Here it is," Jessica said. It had a piece of gold braid glued around its edge, forming a loop at the top.

"Once we went to the beach just before Christmas to hear the waves crash. It was our last Christmas in Maine as a family. That's when we found it."

"The elusive red beach glass," Melissa mused.

As they gathered around the table enjoying pizza, Melissa kept gazing at the tree. She thought of her own ornament collection—an eclectic mix of nice pieces she'd bought or been given over the years, mementos from her dad's travels, things the kids had made, a few heirlooms. She thought of hers and his, together on the same tree, symbolic of the blending of their two lives, their two histories. "Can you tell me *now* what your article is about?" she asked, suddenly remembering.

"Funny you should ask," he said. "It's my annual Christmas feature, and it was, in fact, inspired by…" he turned toward the tree, "this. But you can read about it tomorrow."

"What are Dave and Judy doing tomorrow?" Melissa asked.

"They both have to work until noon. Dave is cooking dinner for her at his place. We'll see them at the service."

"No family?"

"No, Dave didn't want to make Judy travel…his folks didn't want to come out, because his sister is expecting a baby soon…her parents and brother are on the mission field…so, it's just them."

"I think we should go see Judy at the bookstore again tomorrow."

"Excellent idea. Which reminds me, you have some wrapping to do."

"I want to help," Emily said.

Jessica shrugged. "Whatever. I'll help Kraig clean up."

Later, admiring the gifts gathered under the tree, Melissa sighed with deep contentment.

"Mom," Emily whispered, glancing over her shoulder to make sure Kraig was still in the kitchen, "Jessica and I had an idea. The golden retriever ornament we got, we should put a harness on it, to match the others."

"Yeah," Jessica said, joining them, "somehow we'll have to do that without Kraig knowing about it."

Melissa nodded. "We'll figure it out."

Kraig came over and gathered them into a group hug. "As much as I hate to say so, I'd like to see you all get going sooner rather than later. At this hour, you'll be riding the bus mostly with commuters. I'll walk you out to the stop."

Melissa suddenly realized that, since their arrival in Portland, she had not enjoyed a single moment alone with Kraig. And while doing things as a family-in-the-making was deeply satisfying, she nevertheless missed being just a couple.

"Call me when you get there, will you?" he said as he hugged her one last time before she stepped onto the bus.

§

"Merry Christmas Eve," Melissa called through the intercom next morning.

"You're nice and early," his voice came back.

"We're not catching you in your boxers, I hope."

"No," he said, opening the door, standing there looking irresistibly huggable in a plaid flannel shirt, corduroy jeans, and moccasins.

She slipped into his embrace.

"You brought breakfast," he said, inhaling the aroma wafting from the bag she held.

"Yes! You'll be proud of us. We got off at this bakery we spotted in our travels, picked out some scrumptious-looking things, and caught another bus. We even got some bottled juice blends. And I see that you have coffee brewing, so we're all set."

"Not bad for a bunch of country girls. I think you might survive in Portland after all. Well, come in and close the door."

191

"Your article!" she said, spying the newspaper on the kitchen table.

"Waiting for you," he said.

Melissa slid into a chair and began to read. "My box of memories.

"It was the smell that came to me first—a blend of evergreen, dust, and time. Then it was the sound, and the feel, of the brittle tissue paper that had guarded my treasures through moves that had taken me to the four corners of the continent. Finally, it was the emotions, as my fingers recognized each precious item and recalled the moments, the phases, the twists and turns of my life they represented.

"A lifetime of memories confronted me. Some were happy, some sad; some humorous, some poignant. Part of me resisted this exercise, this journey through time...."

As she worked her way through it, Melissa saw that the story was, in a very real way, about *her*; about how this memory-laden ornament collection represented a bridge from his past to his future, about how her presence in his life had enabled him to put everything in perspective.

Finishing, she put the paper down on the table. "Wow." The quiver in her voice gave away everything.

"Excuse us for a moment, girls," Kraig said, taking her arm and lifting her out of her chair, putting his arms around her. Oddly, didn't feel like crying; she just enjoyed being in his embrace. He put his hand in his pocket, pulled out the handkerchief, and pressed it into her hand. At this, she laughed a little.

"Take the article home with you," he said. "Read it again later. Now, let's eat something."

"You need to read that, too," she said to the girls, returning to her seat.

Later, as they boarded the bus, Melissa realized that this was the first time her daughters had seen Shanna at work with the bus system.

"How does she know which bus is the right bus?" Emily asked.

"Well, first of all, Emily, it's my job to know where we're going. Dogs can't read signs, even a smart dog like Shanna. But she has a remarkable memory. Usually, we need to go somewhere only once before I can just say the name of the place and she knows how to get there. As for the bus, she can distinguish different buses by their smells, depending upon what part of town they travel in. If I were to tell her we were going to church, for example, and then tried to take her on the bus for downtown, she would hesitate. The thing about having a guide dog is learning to work as a team. I have to learn to trust her, yet I have to do my part, too."

"Kind of like being married," Melissa said.

"It is, in a way. But guide dogs don't share furniture or food with their human partners. Those are bad habits for guide dogs."

"She doesn't sleep on your bed?" Emily asked.

"No, she does not," he said firmly.

"Hey, I had an idea," Melissa said. "Is there an espresso bar near the bookstore?"

"Melissa, we're in Portland. There are espresso bars everywhere. Why?"

"Maybe we can catch Judy on her break and take her out. I don't know if she drinks coffee, but…."

"That's a great idea."

Judy's face lit up when she saw them enter.

"We hope you're not too busy for visitors," Kraig said. "If you have a break coming up, we're here to take you out for a hot drink."

Judy turned toward a woman who was doing some paperwork at the other end of the counter—apparently the store manager—and who, overhearing, smiled and said, "It's been kind of a slow day. Why don't you call it a day, Judy. Go, do something fun with your friends. Have a great Christmas."

"Thank you," Judy said, receiving a hug from the woman before going to get her coat.

"I hope this is okay," Melissa said, out on the sidewalk.

"It really was a slow day. Yesterday was busy. These people who own the store have been really good to me. Thanks for coming, you guys."

"Nice coat," Melissa said. "That turquoisy-green is a good color on you."

"Thanks. That's exactly what Dave said. He got it for me, when I came back from Africa and had no warm clothes. 'Late birthday present,' he said. My birthday is in May," she laughed.

"He's always doing nice things for me and then having some silly excuse for it."

They had reached a corner, and Melissa noticed that Shanna had turned to cross in the other direction. "Shanna seems to know where to go," Melissa said, "and we weren't paying attention."

A wave of warm, fragrant air enveloped them as they entered, and Melissa was glad for Judy's good fortune of having the remainder of the morning free; it would be a good time to get to know her a little without Dave being there to capture all of her attention.

"I know Melissa would like a hot low-fat mocha," Kraig said, "but everyone else, speak up; my treat."

"Kraig is so sweet," Judy whispered to Melissa as the girls gave their orders. "He always remembers what people like."

Melissa nodded.

At a tall table in the corner, Judy leaned over and inhaled the steam from her orange-spice tea. Her glasses fogged, and she took them off. "Don't let me forget these," she laughed, setting them on the table.

Melissa debated over whether to say what she was thinking. *You look much better without glasses. Have you considered getting contacts?* She suddenly noticed that Judy looked pale and dizzy as she struggled to take off her coat. There was a tense moment of silence as Melissa tried to decide whether to help or not.

"Judy?" Kraig said. "Melissa—"

Melissa jumped out of her chair—clumsily, forgetting how high it was, and catching her foot on another chair in the process, making far more of a commotion than she wanted to. She put her hand on Judy's shoulder, gave the sleeve a yank, pulled the coat over the back of her chair, and returned to her own, feeling more shaken than Judy had looked in the first place.

"I'm fine. Thanks," Judy said, more embarrassed than anything, Melissa was sure.

Feeling utterly incompetent, and needing now more than ever to change the subject, Melissa decided to say it. "You look really good without glasses. Are they for reading or...."

Judy nodded. "They're multifocals. I have a pretty complicated correction. I do plan to get some new glasses. On the

194

mission field I just needed something with sturdy frames so they wouldn't fall apart. Getting them fixed was kind of a chore."

"So…I'm sorry I missed the talk you gave to the Sunday school group. I don't want to make you tell the whole story again. But what was the hardest thing about leaving the mission field?"

"Feeling like I left so much unfinished business. Feeling sort of like a failure." Judy looked down at the table, clearly struggling with how much to tell. "And being mad at Dave, wanting to stay there to prove I could do it, but wanting to come home to find out how much he really cared…." She looked a little like she might cry, which Melissa would have totally understood. "He called me, before I'd even decided for sure to come home, and told me about this job that was waiting for me, and the apartment, and the car, and all the things that were ready to help me get settled if I were to come back. Then, I felt like I'd be letting all these people down if I *didn't* come back. It really took a lot of prayer to come to any sense of peace about it."

Melissa nodded, but didn't speak, wanting to make sure Judy was finished. Then, out of the corner of her eye, she saw Kraig reach into his pocket, and unbelievably—for she still had the one from the morning in *her* pocket—pull out a handkerchief. She took it from him and offered it to Judy. Judy looked slightly puzzled at first, but took it as Melissa nodded in Kraig's direction.

Judy understood; taking it seemed to open the floodgates, and she began to cry. "I'm sorry," she said. "So much has happened. I'm still not sure if I'm doing what I'm supposed to be doing. If you guys would pray for me…."

At that, Kraig took Melissa's hand, and Emily's on the other side; they completed the circle and bowed their heads as Kraig prayed for Judy, her health, her relationship with Dave, and guidance for her future.

"Thanks," Judy said, sniffing, then looking at the handkerchief, not knowing what to do with it.

"Keep it and give it back later," Melissa whispered.

"Are you and Dave going to church tonight?" Kraig asked.

"Yes, he's picking me up from work—which reminds me, I need to call him and tell him I'm not there." She took a cell phone from her bag, checking to make sure it was on.

"Neat cell phone," Melissa said, surprised at how high-end it looked.

"Thanks. Dave got it for me. He wants me to be able to get in touch with him at all times, you know. Anyway, he's fixing dinner for me at his place. Will we see you at the service?"

"Yes," Kraig answered. "Helen's having dinner with us at my place after, but maybe Dave could pick her up for church."

"Of course he will." And she looked so wistful that Melissa hoped she wouldn't start crying again, for fear Kraig would think all women were emotionally fragile.

Judy sighed deeply and smiled. "This is really great, you guys. Thanks so much for coming by. It's nice to have friends. When I came home...I mean, I *guess* this is home...I felt like a stranger. I think America had changed a lot in the years I was gone. Or maybe it was just me. Of course, I'd been back a few times in between, but then I was treated like a guest...now, I'm just supposed to fit into a place I don't really know. I grew up on the mission field, you know; my family's there...I came here for college and found a church home, so this is the closest thing to home that I have in the States. If not for the people here, it wouldn't be home at all."

Melissa nodded vigorously as Judy spoke, hoping that her total understanding would keep Judy from wanting to cry.

Judy looked around the table and smiled.

"Well," Kraig said, "now that we're all warmed up, maybe we could do some window-shopping. Judy?"

"Sure. Great. I'll just give Dave a call as soon as we get outside." She slipped her coat on, and Melissa watched carefully, wondering if that was a good idea. Stepping outside into the winter chill, she zipped her own jacket. She glanced at Judy to make sure she had her glasses back on, and saw that Kraig had his hand against Judy's back, to steady her if she needed it. She smiled to herself at his chivalry and was starting to feel giddy about her future with Kraig, when he dropped Shanna's harness and caught Judy as her knees buckled; surely she would have fallen to the sidewalk had he not been prepared.

Shaken, Melissa took Shanna's lead and just stood there watching while Kraig made sure Judy had regained her balance.

A moment later, Judy looked as if she suddenly remembered where she was. "That's been one of the hardest things to get used to," she said, "the climate change."

Kraig stood with his arm around Judy's shoulder for a long moment, while no one spoke and Judy looked dazed.

"Call Dave," Kraig prompted.

She took out her cell phone and pressed a key. "Hi, it's Judy."

Dave's voice came back very loud. "Sweetie, are you okay?"

"Yeah, I just called to tell you I'm not at work." Her voice was a little shaky; certainly Dave suspected something. "Kraig and Melissa and the girls came by and I got off early. ...No, I'm fine. We're going to do some window shopping." She stopped to listen, and Melissa couldn't make out what Dave said. "Okay. Where should we meet you?" She turned to the group. "He's leaving work in a little while." She went back to Dave. "Yeah, the traffic looks kind of bad.... Okay."

Melissa whispered to Kraig, "Has she been like this since she's been back?"

He shook his head. "Not really, as far as I know. But then, it's much colder now than when she arrived."

"Yeah. That's what I was thinking."

Judy said goodbye to Dave and put the phone away. "He's going to call when he gets into downtown. It'll be a while. We still have time to go window shopping."

Kraig and Shanna seemed to have a plan, so Melissa concentrated on staying even with Judy; not an easy task, as her natural pace would have been considerably more brisk. For her part, Judy seemed to have forgotten the falling incident, though perhaps she had the sense that everyone else was worried about her. Jessica and Emily had Kraig involved in a debate over what color bow Shanna would look more beautiful wearing on Christmas morning, so Melissa had Judy's company to herself.

"I thought it was so neat when Dave told me about you and Kraig," Judy said. "Kraig is such a sweet guy, and Dave has been praying for him for such a long time, that he'd find someone really special."

"Yeah, I do feel really lucky. You, too. Dave's a great guy. I felt like I'd known him forever almost as soon as we met."

"Oh…" Judy looked down at the sidewalk. "He's…it's not like that. Not like Kraig feels about you. Dave's just being nice to me. I think. He *worries* about me. But…." She shrugged.

"Excuse me a second," Melissa said, mostly to relieve Judy of the awkwardness. "Kraig, Jessica, Emily, are we going somewhere in particular?"

Kraig turned around. "Fresh flowers for Helen."

"Okay. And if you see any stores you want to go into, just say so."

Emily turned around. "Okay," she said. Jessica nodded without turning around.

"Flowers," Judy said, chuckling. "That's what I mean."

"Yeah," Melissa said, and she was beginning to feel that her lack of appreciation for Kraig's desire to give her flowers was not a constructive thing for their relationship. Deep in her awareness, she noticed, too, that Jessica had been unusually quiet since they'd left the espresso shop; but then, they were all concerned about Judy, so probably that was the cause. *And Judy…definitely doesn't get it about how Dave feels about her.*

A short time later, Melissa was holding the bouquet of red and white flowers, and Kraig was inside paying, when she heard Judy's phone ring.

"He'll be here in five minutes," Judy said, snapping the phone closed. "He says to stay put."

Sure enough, Dave pulled up to the curb five minutes later, giving the parking meter only a quick glance before hurrying across the sidewalk to embrace Judy. "How are you?" he asked, looking at her closely.

"Fine," she said with a puzzled frown. "Tired, actually. We've been walking a lot."

Dave turned to the others. "Don't go anywhere. I'll be right back." He helped Judy into the car, barely giving her time to say goodbye to the rest of the group, then came back with a more serious expression than Melissa had ever seen him with. "What's up?"

Melissa spoke without giving Kraig a chance. "It was amazing. I don't know how he knew—we were at this coffee shop. It was hot inside, and we'd just come in from the cold. Judy started looking sort of pale and shaky, but she took her coat off, then she was okay…. Then we were out on the sidewalk, and she started to fall, and Kraig caught her. I don't know how he knew. But then she was okay again."

He looked thoughtful for a moment, then turned to Kraig. "Buddy?"

"It was pretty much just like that. She said something about the climate change being difficult. Melissa and I thought maybe it was because it's gotten so much colder in the last couple months. I don't think she fainted. I think her legs just failed."

"Right. That's two separate symptoms—the temperature sensitivity and the weakness." Dave muttered something that sounded like a swear word. "It could be the medication, too. I'm afraid they've got her on one of those merry-go-rounds where every problem is solved by a drug that causes some other problem." He looked deeply contemplative, then suddenly remembered Judy waiting in the car. "Hey, thanks for being there." He pulled Melissa and Kraig into a group hug. "You too, girls. Gotta go. See you at church tonight. I'll give Helen a ride," he called back. He and Judy both waved as his car pulled away from the curb.

Later, on the bus, her arm wrapped tightly around Kraig's, Melissa found herself so deep in thought, she couldn't formulate a coherent sentence to start a dialog.

"What are you thinking about?" Kraig asked.

"Judy, mostly."

"Me too. And thanking God for *our* radiant health."

"Yes." It occurred to her that, were she not as fit and healthy as she was, she would see this other side of Kraig—this tender, nurturing persona—on a daily basis. As it was, she would probably have to wait until they had grandchildren to enjoy the experience.

"Kraig," she said tentatively, "was I ever unkind to Judy?"

"Of course not. What do you mean?"

"Well, when I first met her, I was expecting…I know Dave noticed it, and I figured you would have, too…I was just picturing someone different."

"Someone tall, slim, and gorgeous. Because if Dave could have anyone he wanted, that's who he would choose."

"Yeah. I guess that's what I was thinking."

"You'd be forgiven for thinking that. But no. You were never unkind."

She wasn't entirely convinced, but left it at that.

199

§

Melissa stirred the clam chowder, absently scanning the recipe for the umpteenth time.

"It smells exactly right," Kraig said. "The biscuits, too. Good job, ladies."

Jessica retreated to the living room, where Emily was brushing Shanna to a high sheen, and began to peruse the music selection.

Kraig, finding Melissa's hand and releasing the spoon from it, put his arms around her. "I want you to stop worrying about Judy. We'll pray about it."

"I have, for the moment. I was actually thinking about Jessica. Does it seem to you that she's been unusually quiet?"

"Hmm. She has. Do you have any ideas?"

"Not at all."

"Do you think she'd talk to me?"

"I can't imagine why not."

"I'll see what I can find out." He kissed her lightly, and she watched as he made his way to where Jessica stood and put his arm around her. Melissa couldn't hear their exchange, but Jessica smiled and nodded.

"You're going for a walk?" Emily said anxiously. "Are you taking Shanna?"

"Oh, I think we can manage without her."

"Don't be gone too long," Melissa said as they slipped out the door.

"Why are they going for a walk?" Emily asked.

"We thought Jessica had been too quiet. And that she might talk to Kraig." Melissa went back to stirring the soup.

They couldn't have made it more than about once around the block before they were back. Jessica returned to the living room with a look that attempted indifference but betrayed happiness.

"Well?" Melissa whispered to Kraig. "Can you tell me what she said?"

He smiled, still trying to organize his thoughts. "Well, a lot in a short time. Basically she'd decided, over the last few years...that *true* love...was rare and hard to find. And that *she*...would *probably*

200

…just go into a career with *animals*…and not get married." His delivery sped up a bit. "But *then*, after these last couple of months, seeing *us* together, and especially these last few *days*, seeing Dave and Judy, she began to change her *mind* and…." He seemed to be holding something back.

"And?" she prompted.

He groped for the words he wanted. "She said that it was…seeing 'a couple of guys who really know how to treat women' that made her change her mind about what she wanted to do with her life. But she wasn't sure if she might be asking too much to have such a guy, too."

"Wow."

"Yes. It was quite a moment."

"You weren't gone very long."

"No, she seemed more than happy to share this."

"Thanks," she said, wrapping her arms around him.

"Absolutely my pleasure. Now, I think the clam chowder is ready, if you haven't stirred it to death. And I think the biscuits are out of the oven. How about we go wait for the bus? It wouldn't hurt to be at church on the early side."

Inside the church, more than half an hour before the start of the Christmas Eve service, all was bright and warm, fragrant with evergreen, and cheerful with Christmas music playing over the sound system.

"I see what you mean," Melissa said. "It's pretty crowded already."

"Tell me if you see Dave and Judy and Helen."

"I do. They must have gotten here *really* early, because they're in about the third pew. And I think they're saving seats, the way everyone's spaced apart. By the way," she said as they made their way forward, "how is it that you're not participating in this one?"

"The staff and their families usually do the Christmas Eve service. And of course we all join in the carols. You'll see."

Dave gathered the coats that had been reserving their places as they approached. "Hey, here come Kraig and his beautiful women," he said in his usual cheerful manner.

Judy looked rested and generally well, and Melissa, realizing that Judy's health was a long-term concern, decided to follow Dave's lead and try not to worry about it, unless some crisis was evident. By the end of the service, her spirits were so high, she'd forgotten about it.

As they stood in the foyer discussing the details of the next day, Melissa noticed Dave looking preoccupied, and in a lull, he put his arm around Judy and squeezed her shoulder, apparently some kind of signal.

"You guys…" Judy began hesitantly, "I was thinking about what happened earlier today. Thanks for helping me. If you hadn't been there…Kraig…." And she sort of fell onto his chest, not heavily, but in such a way as to receive a hug, which he gave.

"We love you guys," Dave said.

"We love you back," Melissa heard herself say.

On the bus back to Kraig's, Melissa found herself preoccupied with thoughts of Judy again. Helen, on his other side, hadn't said a word, probably because the bus was too noisy; yet neither had Kraig nor the girls.

"Hey," Emily said, more or less out of the blue, "I know what we should do. Don't they make—I mean, train—dogs to help other kinds of people? We could get Judy one of those dogs."

"An assistance dog," Melissa said.

"Yeah," Jessica agreed. "I've seen dogs that pick up things you drop, or just follow you around in case you start to fall down. It would have to be a *big* dog."

Kraig was nodding. "Yes. I'll bring that up with Dave and see what he thinks. In the meantime, maybe we could get her a cat. Just for company."

"*Two* cats," Melissa said. "One would get lonely by itself when she's gone."

He smiled. "Melissa and her family of cat experts. Now, let's look forward to…all that we have to look forward to. Which is a lot."

§

"Let Kraig open the present from Jessica and me first," Emily said immediately after breakfast Christmas morning.

Melissa never tired of watching Kraig do things; the movement of his hands was a thing of beauty in itself. He took the bag Emily handed him and unwrapped the four small items bundled in tissue paper. "Cats," he said.

"Yeah," Emily explained, "they're cat *ornaments*. And we picked these out *before* we knew about your guide dog ornaments."

"There's one more thing in the bottom," Jessica said. "We wanted you to open it last."

"A dog...a golden retriever...guide dog...ornament."

"We added the harness ourselves. We can make a better one later," Jessica said. "We weren't thinking about it being a guide dog until we saw your other ones."

"To complete my collection. Thank you. Now, tell me about the cats."

"They're *our* cats," Emily said. "The gray one is Diana, the white one is Snowflake, and the tabbies are Chester and Buster. We made Chester's paws white with acrylic paint so you could tell them apart."

"If you'll forgive me, I'm still not sure I can tell them apart."

Emily looked blank for a moment, then embarrassed. *She never thinks of him as being blind.*

"Come here, Emmy," he said. She did, and when her knee touched his, he took her and turned her around, sitting her in his lap—something no one had done since Emily was a very little girl. And she seemed to mind not one bit.

"Are you going to have a nickname for Jessica too?" she asked.

"If she'll let me. I could call her Jessie."

Jessica smiled, perhaps reluctant to admit that she didn't mind.

"Jessie, I was going to ask Emmy, but might I ask you to find one from me to your mom?"

Taking the squishy package from Jessica's hand, Melissa immediately thought, *clothes.* And this thought brought with it happy memories of when she was young and her grandparents were alive and came for Christmas. For it was that one time a year that she received pretty clothes, girlish clothes, so different from the practical, sturdy things she always got for school and play.

Inside was the softest, fuzziest sweater she had ever touched. "Oh...my...goodness. It is cashmere?"

"It is. Since you came up in October, wearing this very nice sweater that you said wasn't cashmere, I've wanted to get you a *real* cashmere one. Only somehow I neglected to ask you what color that one was. Helen said she remembered it being a lavender, so I thought you'd like a deeper purple one. I confess I had a lot of help with the selection. Dave knows what's fashionable, and Judy knows what a conservative woman would wear. I wanted to get you something attractive but not...immodest."

"Oh, my goodness, it is *beautiful*," she said, pressing her face into it. She didn't want to think how much he might have paid for it; yet obviously he gained deep satisfaction from choosing such a thing for her, not to mention the satisfaction he would get from her wearing it. She wanted to go put it on right away and get hugged, but that would have to wait. "I'd love to wear it right away...but the only thing I brought that would go with it is a skirt, and I'd rather not wear a skirt all day."

"There'll be another time," he said.

Now, she could hardly wait for him to open her gifts to him—a striped crewneck sweater, an argyle sweater vest, and a couple of Oxford shirts—all in earthy green, brown, blue, lavender, and gray tones. "Now we can be huggable together," she said quietly, for only him to hear.

Kraig's gifts to Jessica and Emily were partly a surprise even to Melissa; she knew only that they had something to do with music. As it turned out, he gave them each a certificate to attend a musical event with him—a concert, ballet, opera, or other production of mutual choice.

"I'm glad we don't have a lot of big things to haul home on the plane," Melissa sighed with relief.

"Ah, but you do have something big still to come. Although it is not big in size, only in importance, so you needn't worry. Emmy, would you go look for three envelopes clothespinned to the back of the tree?"

"I didn't know anything was back here," she said, but sure enough, there they were—one for each of them.

"Emmy...why don't you go first," Kraig suggested.

A look of wonder on her face, she unfolded a letter with two pictures of a cat imprinted on it. "I'm sponsoring a cat at a cat refuge in southern California," she said. "His name is Bootsie. Wow. Here's how he looked when they got him, and how he looks now. So, he's mine, but they take care of him for me. It says he's going to send me letters and pictures telling me how he's doing. How neat. Thanks," she said, hugging the letter.

"Jessie, your turn."

Jessica tore hers open and laughed. "I thought it was going to be the same thing—only mine's a dog! Look," she said, turning the letter around for the others to see. "Thanks."

"Melissa."

"Well, let me guess...a horse," she said, opening her envelope. Her mouth fell open as a picture fluttered out of it. It was not a horse, but a little girl. She dared not speak as she held up the picture of this tiny girl with huge, sad eyes. She swallowed hard. "We're sponsoring a little girl...from Senegal...she's four...her name is...something like 'Kin-ay'...and for about the price of one of these other gifts, we can supply her with food, clothes, and medication for a year."

"Wow," said Emily. "We just got a new cat, a new dog, and a new kid."

Melissa laughed, even as she hugged Kraig's neck. "Thank you," she whispered.

"Dave gave me the idea. He's doing the same thing for Judy. Bring yours when we go over to Helen's, and I bet Judy will bring hers."

§

"Look at the proud moms showing off their new babies," Dave said as Melissa and Judy passed the pictures of their sponsored children around the table.

"Mine is a boy from Kenya," Judy said. "His name is Dominique and he's six. I wanted a boy about that age because that's how old Kurt was when my parents adopted him. Now he's sixteen. I haven't seen him in two years, and I really miss him."

"Is he cute?" Jessica asked, surprising everyone, probably including herself.

"He is," Judy laughed. "I have pictures of him, but they're at my apartment, so I don't know if I'll get a chance to show them to you while you're here."

"He's a good kid," Dave said. "Plays piano, too. Hey, good salad, Melissa."

"Thanks. I heard about the 'no mayo' rule."

"It is good to have you in Kraig's life," he said, and she was about to laugh, but when she looked at Dave, his expression was serious, so she just smiled.

"Did you do the jacket idea?" Dave asked. "For Matt?"

"We did. We sent him other things, too—gloves, socks, long underwear. He should be fine. Thanks for the idea."

"Although it does seem weird for him to be skiing," Jessica said, "instead of having Christmas with us."

Later, after helping with the dishes, Melissa looked forward to settling into the couch, getting dozy against Kraig's shoulder. Returning to the living room, she found Emily in the spot she coveted, looking half-asleep herself.

"Emily, sweetheart," Dave said, "I have a hunch your mom would like a turn sitting next to that handsome guy whose attention you've been enjoying there for quite a while now. Be a pal and scoot over, will you?"

"That's why God in His wisdom made man with two sides," Kraig said. "So a guy fortunate enough to have more than one special girl doesn't have to choose." He slid over with Emily, and Melissa slipped in on the other side.

She sighed loudly, closed her eyes, and pretended to fall asleep on Kraig's shoulder, wearing a huge smile. "Wake me up when it's time to go home," she said.

"You *are* home," he said. "This is where you're staying tonight. Although you'd be more comfortable in a bed."

"I mean *home* home," she said, her eyes still closed.

"You're going to miss some things if you sleep through Sunday."

"Oh. Yeah. Our counseling session. Shopping for your shirt and tie. And church. Oh," she said, opening her eyes and sitting up, "we want to go to all three services with you, and help in the nursery. If that's okay."

"That would be fun."

"One more thing," Dave said. "Judy and I were talking, and saying how Kraig and Melissa hadn't had any time alone together all week, and that maybe Jessica and Emily would like to hang out with

us at my place tomorrow night. We can get a movie, rent a pizza—
no, I mean—you know what I mean. Anyway, Kraig and Melissa
could go out to dinner…Melissa could wear her new sweater….
What do you think, girls?"

"Sure," they agreed.

"An evening with Uncle Dave," Kraig said. "How could that
not be fun?"

§

Chapter 15

When the phone rang at home, eight o'clock Sunday night, Melissa hardly gave Kraig a chance to say hello before she dove in. "Kraig, listen to this. I got a message from Matt, on the machine when we got home, thanking us all for the jacket and stuff. By the way, the gift was from you, too. Anyway, he said he had the best jacket in the group and he was never cold.

"And that's not all! It turns out he didn't go skiing on Christmas *Day*—he went home with one of his skiing buddies whose family lives in the area, and they left for skiing the next day. So he got to have Christmas dinner after all."

"Well, that is good news."

"Sorry. You called me and I'm doing all the talking."

"That's all right, Melissa. I do want to hear what you have to say."

"Now we need to talk about your visit down here in January."

"I need to be at my home church the third Sunday, because that's Sanctity of Human Life Sunday, and that's a cause that's dear to my heart. I usually have a solo that ends up with most of the congregation in tears."

It was so unlike Kraig to say anything even remotely boastful, she couldn't help wondering what was behind this particular comment.

"The last weekend would be best, anyway," he went on, "since your birthday is the first of February...I'd be there on your birthday."

"My birthday," she repeated.

"Melissa?"

"I'm just thinking, I'm going to be seven years older than you again."

"I thought you'd stopped worrying about that."

"I have. Mostly."

"Melissa..." he began tentatively, and something in his voice set her a little on edge. "I have something I've never told you, that I need to tell you. But I'm not going to get into it over the phone. We'll talk about it when I'm there. Just don't worry about it too much, all right?"

"Well, I'll *try* not to." Although, of course, not knowing what it was made it harder not to worry about it.

§

The last Thursday evening in January, Melissa enjoyed every second of the long, hard hug he gave her, and she hoped every single person in the airport was watching and would see how much she loved this guy.

"I'm sorry I couldn't get tomorrow off work," she said when she got a chance. "The girls have a plan to teach you how to tell the cats apart. It should be interesting. Anyway, it'll just be you, Shanna, and the cats tomorrow during the day."

Later, as dinner cooked, she watched with amusement while Jessica and Emily carried out their lesson plan.

"Okay," Emily began. "You've held Diana before. She's the softest and the lightest."

"No, wait," Jessica said. "Diana's the lightest, but Snowflake's softer. Yes, she is—feel her with your eyes closed."

"Okay, then. Snowflake's fur is longer. But Diana is still softer, in a way. See the difference?" She put one of Kraig's hands on each cat so he could compare.

"I'll get Buster," Jessica said.

"Then I'll get Chester, so you can tell *them* apart. They're both short-haired. They're brothers."

"Okay," Jessica said, "this is Buster. He's the heaviest and he growls the most. But he doesn't bite. The girl cats bite if they get annoyed."

"This is Chester," Emily said. "It's kind of hard to tell the boy cats apart. Chester has white paws, but…."

And so it went.

"If you're finished with cat identification lessons," Melissa said, "dinner's about ready. Something we should do after dinner is show Kraig the rest of the house. He'll be here alone as soon as we get back from our honeymoon, and I'm a little worried—"

"No he won't, Mom," Jessica said. "That's our spring break. Em and I will be here."

"Oh! I'd forgotten about that. Well, the kitchen, anyway. He *will* be here alone all day tomorrow."

When Melissa arrived home the next afternoon, Kraig looked very much at home in the kitchen, with the teakettle beginning to rattle on the stove.

"I thought you'd like a cup of tea," he said. "I put it on as soon as I heard your car."

"Wow," she laughed. "That *is* a nice surprise."

"If you want to go change clothes or anything, it'll be ready in about four minutes."

When she came back to the kitchen, Kraig was not there, but just then she heard the door from the garage close. He came into the kitchen and washed his hands; the kitchen timer beeped; he took out the teabags. "Your tires are low by five to ten pounds each," he said. "Let's get that taken care of this weekend. And you should get new ones on the rear before winter is over. Oh, and if you'll show me where the dipstick is, I'll be happy to check your oil."

Melissa was speechless.

"Melissa?"

"Oh—no—it's not that I doubt you could do it. It's just that …no one's ever done those things for me before. Well, no. Matt got pretty good at it after he learned how to drive, but…wow. Thanks."

While she spoke, Kraig's expression had changed from one of domestic tranquility to something approaching anger.

"What's wrong?" Melissa asked, suddenly remembering there was something of some seriousness that he needed to tell, and feeling a little nervous.

"You mean to say that you were married to a man who didn't check your tires and your engine oil?"

"I was. For—" she decided not to say how many years.

"Melissa, that's—" He shook his head as he finished stirring the tea and then just stood there shaking the spoon over the sink for far longer than necessary. He looked as though he wanted to hit someone with it.

"Kraig?" she said, beginning to worry.

"Oh, my God, Melissa, it's not your fault." He put the spoon down and turned toward her; she hurried into his arms and collided with him rather too forcefully. "It just really, really hurts me to think that no one's ever cared for you in the way you should have been. And every time I'm reminded of that…it just makes me want to do my job better." He squeezed her very, very hard. "When will the girls be home?"

She supposed he was feeling a little awkward about being home alone together. "Jessica will be home in about an hour; Emily, a half-hour to forty-five minutes later."

He released her. "Sit down. I'll bring the tea."

Sitting across the corner of the table from her, he put his cup to his lips, found it too hot, and set the cup back down, wrapping his hands around it. He looked thoughtful but didn't speak.

"How are Dave and Judy?" Melissa asked.

"Oh, they're wonderful, mostly. Judy's doing better. They adjusted her medications. No more falling. They both like you a lot, by the way. They said so again, after you left."

"Dave has been a huge surprise to me. If I'd met him, not knowing he was your friend, I would have just dismissed him as some Hollywood-handsome guy, all style and no substance. But of course I could not have been more wrong."

"I should've known...that you'd be different. And for that I apologize."

"Oh, no, it turned out fine. It'll always be a funny story for us to tell."

He nodded, smiling a little, but his mind was on something else.

Melissa took a deep breath. "What is it you need to tell me, Kraig?"

"Something I've never told anyone before. Not even Dave. You're the first. It has to do with Celeste." He took a deep, ragged breath. "I have reason to believe she was pregnant when I left her."

"You mean...you might have a son or daughter somewhere, that you've never—"

"No. Not that. I mean, if she *was*, she had an abortion."

Melissa gasped.

"I can't say how I know this, but I know. Not long before she kicked me out, I had this feeling that she was expecting, and I was excited, thinking she was going to tell me about it at any time... yet a little nervous. Not just about my own competence as a parent, but about the stability of our relationship, and what she would be like as a mother..." the words poured out faster. "But I wanted to believe that this would make everything right, bring us together...that being

212

a mother would bring out some good side of her that I hadn't seen…I *really* wanted this.

"Worst case, I thought, she would relinquish custody to me and I would raise the child alone. An enormous challenge, I realize; but I would've moved back into my parents' house or whatever I had to do.

"I think the urgency she had for me to leave had something to do with this—she needed me out of there before I could find out. But how could I prove it, especially from 2,000 miles away? And who knows, by the time I even got settled in California and had a moment to think about it, it was probably already done. She never let me talk to her anyway; I told you about that.

"And this is why I had to be at church last weekend, and every Sanctity of Human Life Sunday, and do my solo that ends up with everyone, including me, in tears. Because this whole subject is so very close to my heart."

"Oh, Kraig, I—" And as the full weight of his words sank in, and how it must hurt him, she began to cry. Which seemed to give him permission to do the same.

"Melissa, that was *my child*…and I wasn't there." As his tears flowed unchecked, she put her arms around his neck, her cheek against his, his tears warm on her face.

"You know…" she said quietly after a moment, "Dave knows there's something you've never told him. He said something to me about it, that Sunday that I met him, when he and I were talking in your living room. You should tell him. He's the absolutely best friend you could ever ask for."

"He *was*. You are now. But he's still the second-best."

At that, Melissa laughed a little and pulled away to look at him directly. "I love you *so much*," she said, and leaned in again to kiss him.

"Mm," he said, and he got that shy look that she found so endearing. "I love you at least as much."

"Hey, when the girls get home, why don't we go out and shop for that item you need to shop for? I can drop you and the girls off wherever you need to be dropped off, while I go do some grocery shopping."

§

213

Monday morning, Kraig went along with Melissa to work, where she put in a half-day, setting aside some unfinished projects to take home with her. There, Shanna amazed everyone with her skills and model behavior, while Kraig listened to tapes and chatted with her co-workers. In no time at all, it was time to leave for the airport.

"You may be right," Kraig said in the car, "that people in Oak Hill are friendlier than in Portland. I think I could get used to living here."

"Good," she said, yet knowing that many adjustments would still be made.

When she returned home from the airport, Jessica and Emily were there, yet the house seemed eerily empty without Kraig and Shanna. She went to the calendar and studied the potential weekends for visiting him in Portland.

When he called, she remembered to let him talk first; then said, "I want to come up in four weeks," hoping she didn't sound too much like a whiny child. "If I come up for longer than a weekend, maybe it'll only be three and a half."

"Ah, Melissa, I miss you so much already. Were you thinking of coming without the girls?"

"Yes, if that's okay."

"As much as I love them, I do think it would be best this time. And do stay as long as you can."

A couple days later, a box arrived for her. It looked like a florist's box, and for an instant, Melissa thought that maybe he'd sensed her changing heart about the "no flowers thing." But inside were what looked, at first glance, like half a dozen roses, yet they were shiny, metallic, like flowers wrapped in foil. "Dark chocolate roses," she read on the label, and laughed out loud.

§

February's visit to Portland had a hurried feel to it that made her a little anxious, yet the busyness also helped the time pass, and she had reached a point where she really just wanted to be married to Kraig and be with him all the time. He had sold his townhouse, so a fair amount of time was spent on putting things in boxes.

"I'm happy not to have to worry about this, at least," he said as they cleaned out his bedroom closet. "My agent said she thought it would sell quickly, and it did."

"Because it's so neat and tidy. That makes a good impression."

"I was also worried about what I would do if it sold *too* quickly, and I had nowhere to live."

"How could you worry about *that*? You have so many people who love you, it's not as if you'd be left homeless."

"Still, I wonder what it'll be like being at Dave's house all the time for two weeks. I hope we'll still be friends after we've been roommates."

She laughed. "I'm not too worried. I'm glad to be able to help you with this, though, to see what you have and think about where we'll put it. You're not afraid I'm going to find anything I'm not supposed to see, are you?"

"Like what? Letters from old girlfriends?"

"That, or whatever I might find."

"No, not worried. The love letters are all in Braille." He smiled. Then he stopped smiling and looked serious, then sad. "I do have something I want you to see." He went to his dresser and opened the top drawer. Reaching under all the stuff, he slipped out a letter. "Would you tell me what this says?"

Taking it from him, she saw that it had been opened; inside was a handwritten letter.

"I was never able to read it," he said. "But I have an idea of what it's about."

Looking at the postmark, she quickly recognized the part of his life it represented; it had been sent from somewhere in Louisiana to an address in southern California, then forwarded to one in Portland. "It's from a Monsignor McSweeney," she said, and began to read, looking at Kraig between sentences.

He nodded while she read this letter from a sympathetic priest to whom Celeste had gone to confession after having the suspected—now confirmed—abortion.

"She gives me permission to tell you this," Melissa continued reading, "and I regret that I do not know whether your child was a boy or a girl, so that you might have been able to give him or her a name. I pray that you will find peace in the certainty that your child is now in heaven, and that you will be reunited with him or her one day…."

She put her arms around him and cried with him.

"Now I know," he said softly. "I could have asked someone else to read it to me. I guess a part of me didn't want to know the truth. Until I was able to bear it. Until *now*."

§

The long weekend dissolved in a blur of last-time-ever moments. *Last time I'll set foot in this townhouse, where he asked me to marry him and I said yes…and where we had our first Christmas together. Last time I'll go here, do this, see these people.* She would be back in a few weeks to help him move from Portland to Oak Hill, but it would be a brief and hurried visit.

One of the brightest spots was seeing Judy again; Melissa hardly recognized her. Judy's hair had grown a good inch, with the effect that its natural wave was really showing through; and whether it was truly fuller and thicker, or whether she was just spending more time styling it, was hard to say. Her color had gone from borderline sallow to positively rosy. Best of all, she'd updated her glasses to a lightweight, frameless style that were almost invisible at a casual glance. Whether she wore makeup was also hard to say; it didn't seem to matter. She even seemed to stand straighter and stronger.

"Judy!" Melissa exclaimed when she saw her. "You look *great*!" and she meant it. Dave winked at her.

Sunday afternoon, there it was again—the farewell at the airport.

"I bet you're getting tired of this goodbye-at-the-airport stuff," Dave said.

She nodded.

"Guess what. This is *the last time*."

Indeed, it would be.

Dave and Judy stepped a respectful distance away as she finished saying goodbye to Kraig. "I changed my mind about something since I met you," she said. "I *do* want you to send me flowers. *If* you want to. I'd like it."

§

Melissa tried to keep the momentum going as the last few weeks went by, channeling all her anxiety about missing Kraig into making the wedding the best it could be, while remembering his words that the wedding day itself was not as important as all the days that would follow.

"How's everything coming along?" he would ask.

"I think everything's falling into place. Photographer... flowers...music...clothes...hair...."

"What do you hear from Matt these days?"

"Oh, he keeps in touch. He has his life, and he's content to let me decide what to do with mine. I think the hardest part of it was getting him to go get measured for a suit. But that's done. It's all coasting from here."

"Think of it, Melissa. We're almost there."

"Yeah..." she sighed.

"How about the invitation responses?"

"Oh, they're pouring right in."

"Did you hear from your mom?"

"No."

"Kevin?"

"No."

"Well, in Kevin's case, it doesn't mean he isn't coming. It really doesn't mean *anything*. Whoever is meant to be there will be there."

§

Melissa arrived at the Portland airport on the Monday evening before the last Saturday of winter feeling exhausted and anxious. She'd agreed to work over the weekend in exchange for getting almost two weeks off, yet she was not as caught up as she would have liked, meaning that she'd have to go in on Thursday.

Jessica and Emily had insisted it would be all right if they spent a few days at their friends' house, but doubts nagged her. It would feel like an extended slumber party to them, but homework and bedtime and competition for the bathroom would all be real challenges.

217

And then there was the drive down. While she looked forward to this uninterrupted time with Kraig, the weather was always a great unknown. Nothing horrendous was in the forecast, but the Northwest at this time of year could take a beating from bone-chilling wet and cold, ice storms, blinding rain, mudslides, downed trees, and overflowing rivers. A delay of even a day would severely compromise the week's schedule. Dave had offered to come along and help with the driving, but he'd done so much already, it didn't seem right to ask more of him. Besides, she didn't want to take him away from Judy.

As soon as she saw Kraig with Shanna and Dave, Kraig's smile illuminating at least that one tiny corner of the dreary Northwest, she realized that pretty much no matter what, she would be married to him by the end of the week, and nothing else really mattered.

Still several feet away, she nearly flung her bag to the ground and leapt into his arms, managing to get his name out just before her breath was squeezed out of her. Before releasing her, he extended an arm to include Dave, turning it into a group hug. She sighed heavily and suddenly felt a hundred times better. Kraig found her bag and picked it up.

"I'm sorry I won't get to see Judy *or* Helen on this trip," she said as they made their way to the baggage claim.

"No worries. We'll party when we all get down there," Dave said.

"How's Judy doing?"

"Much better. By the way, she says to thank you for being so concerned for her. We're going to check into the assistance dog idea. Right now, though, she's doing so much better...but we'll see."

"I'm so glad to hear."

"You'll be staying in my room tonight," Dave continued. "It's the most comfortable bed, and you're the one who needs a good rest. I've already changed the sheets for you, so don't bother arguing."

"Well, thanks. So you guys are still friends?"

"Thanks to the brilliant invention of two-bathroom dwellings," Kraig said.

"And to Kraig being even more of a neat freak than I am," Dave added.

At the carousel, Melissa pointed out her tapestry suitcase. Dave made a show of reaching for it, then being unable to lift it and being dragged for a few feet before finally gaining control of it and heaving it off the carousel.

"Gosh, Melissa, what do you *have* in here? I spend the weekend putting Kraig's stuff in a *truck*...two hundred boxes of Braille *books*...now *this*...."

Kraig was trying hard not to laugh, but Melissa was laughing so hard she could barely speak. "I packed extra in case we got stranded somewhere."

"Extra, she says," Dave muttered. "Extra *what*? Extra snow shovels...global positioning system...bivouac with solar-powered stove and water heater...."

Melissa was still laughing, and Kraig was still trying not to, as they stepped outside into the bracing air. "It's really not that heavy," she whispered to Kraig.

"I figured as much," he whispered back.

Dave's townhouse complex was a little farther off the main thoroughfare than Kraig's, in a quieter part of town, closer to Helen's older, more established neighborhood. Melissa felt a squeeze on her heart when she saw the rented truck parked out front.

"So...there it is," she said.

"All of Kraig's worldly possessions," Dave said. "And a few other-worldly ones."

"Two hundred boxes of Braille books?" she asked.

"Maybe not quite." He winked at her.

"You guys loaded all this stuff yourselves?"

"Nah, not really. I hired a couple of twenty-somethings from church who were willing to give up a Saturday to earn a few bucks. We mostly just supervised. Think you can manage this thing all the way down I-5? I can still take a couple days off work...."

"No, that's okay. As long as the weather holds out, we'll be fine."

"Good news for you, then. Nothing scary is in the forecast."

Stepping inside the townhouse, Melissa saw that the floor plan was nearly identical to Kraig's, and nearly as neat and sparsely furnished. *No wonder it's been so easy for Kraig to be here.* "Nice," she said.

"So, this is your room for the night," Dave said, putting her suitcase in the master bedroom. "I shouldn't have to bother you...I got out the clothes I need, and I'll buddy up with Kraig on bathroom usage...one more night and one more morning, and he's all yours."

"Thank goodness," Kraig said, smiling.

"Well—*almost* all," Dave said, and Melissa was surprised to feel herself blush.

Tuesday morning, Melissa heard the guys in the kitchen even before she opened her eyes. She rolled over, trying to get oriented and read the clock radio display. *Five-thirty! No wonder it's dark!* She clicked on the lamp, pushed back the covers, plowed through her over-packed suitcase for some clothes, and dashed for the shower.

In the kitchen, she found Kraig and Dave at the table, a map spread before them, plates and glasses pushed aside.

"We didn't want to wake you," Kraig said, standing to kiss her.

Dave poured her a cup of coffee. "We're just making a few notes for you. Kraig has everything on his recorder. Today should be a pretty easy day, mostly flat and straight. You'll be saving some of the more challenging parts of the trip for tomorrow, so be sure to get rested tonight. When you leave Ashland in the morning, be *very careful*. Siskiyou Summit is at 4,310 feet. It tends to get icy overnight. Just wait till well after sunup to hit the road. Drink lots of coffee to stay awake. Stop frequently and get out of the truck...."

"Dave?"

"Yeah, buddy?"

"It seems to me that if we're drinking lots of coffee, we're going to *have* to stop frequently and get out of the truck."

"Yeah. Right. Well, get something to eat, Melissa. We're just going to put Kraig's houseplants in the truck."

"We saved that for the last minute so they wouldn't freeze overnight," Kraig explained.

"Kraig and his houseplants," Dave said. "He treats them like babies."

It was fully light by the time everything was in order for departure. Kraig took Shanna for a quick walk while Melissa stood on the sidewalk staring at the truck.

"You okay?" Dave said, joining her.

"Yeah. I'm just thinking about...everything."

Dave nodded, then shook his head. "Kraig told me about that letter," he said in a low voice. Looking deep into his eyes, Melissa felt sure that the only thing preventing him from using some very strong words was that the villain in this story was a woman. "You know, don't you, that he's never shared that with *anyone*, till you came along. That really...*really* means something."

Melissa nodded, blinking, turning away. Just then Kraig and Shanna appeared around the corner. Melissa watched him approach, his expression determined, yet his step light.

"Hey," she said when he got close. "Ready?"

"I am."

"Sure you don't want me to come?" Dave asked. "Just say the word...I call in at work with an emergency...I'm packed in five minutes...unlike Melissa, who packs a trunk for a two-night trip.... No. Of course you don't. Well. Then I guess I'll go get ready for work."

No one moved.

"You two'd better get going or you're going to have to stop for lunch before you get out of Portland," Dave said. "Come here. Prayer huddle." After that, Dave grabbed Kraig in a bear hug that looked positively painful. Then, he embraced her. "Take care of each other," he said. "If any conflicts arise on the way down, call me before you make any drastic changes in plans."

Melissa laughed softly, but Dave was still hugging her, and she found such comfort in it that she was in no hurry to go. "Thanks for everything," she said.

"Go on, you two," Dave said at last. "Drive carefully. Stop frequently. Enjoy the trip. I'll see you in Oak Hill."

Melissa turned and waved as Dave walked up the front steps and disappeared into his townhouse. Then she watched in the rearview mirror as the building disappeared from view. Kraig was busy with the contents of his briefcase, arranging things on the seat between them.

"What do we have here?" she asked, trying to put her mind on the task at hand.

"Dave let us borrow his portable CD player. His is better than mine. Look, we can play it through the truck's speaker system. I put some of our favorite CDs in my briefcase so we can listen to them during the drive. The others are all accessible, too, in case we get tired of these. Melissa? This is going to be fun."

Kraig pushed buttons to get to the song he wanted, and as the Smokey Robinson song "Cruisin'" began to play, Melissa smiled and immediately felt more relaxed.

§

The exit signs for Ashland began to appear just before sundown. Kraig suddenly realized they hadn't referred to Dave's recorded instructions since Eugene where they'd stopped for lunch; he now played it to the right spot.

"Ashland, Oregon," Dave's voice said. "This is where you stop for the night. Have a relaxed dinner and get a good night's sleep. And remember," Dave's voice lowered, "separate rooms, buddy."

Kraig tried not to laugh. "Ah, yes, Dave, thanks for that reminder. But next time we come here, Melissa, we'll come for the Shakespeare festival. And we'll get *one room*. Now, let's find something that looks nice, park this thing, change clothes, and go have dinner. I'm ready to sit in a seat that doesn't move. Oh, and maybe we can take a walk in Lithia Park after dinner. We could all use the exercise."

Wednesday morning, they sat on a bench in the park, warming their hands with hot mochas, watching the sun pour over the hills.

Kraig suddenly laughed. "The people at the registration desk were looking at us pretty strangely, weren't they, when we asked for two rooms?"

"Yeah—like we're mad at each other or something."

"When in reality, nothing could be further from the truth. Melissa," he said, turning toward her, his face radiant with deep joy, "I have truly never been *so happy*." He kissed her. "But I'm going to be happier still when we get into Oak Hill. What do you think? Is the sun high enough to have melted the ice over the summit?"

"I think, by the time we put our things together and check out, it will be. At the first sign of trouble, anyway, we can just pull over and wait. If it comes to that."

Just before they got rolling, Kraig reached for Melissa's hand. "We need to pray," he said. "For the rest of our journey...for Dave and Judy and Helen's trip down, too."

As they began the climb up the pass, Melissa could tell by the texture of the road that no ice had been there recently. "It feels like it's been sanded, too," Kraig said. On the California side, they let out a huge, simultaneous sigh of relief. Kraig took the recorder and pressed "play."

"If you've made it to this part of the recording," Dave's voice said, "you've made it safely over the summit. Welcome to California. Enjoy the view of Mt. Shasta. But don't relax *too* much. This part of the state can still see some pretty devilish weather. Have lunch in Chico. Now you're on Melissa's home turf. You should be home free. Unless there's flooding in the Sacramento Valley. But there's no mention of that in any of the news media, so you should be fine. I'll see you in Oak Hill Thursday afternoon. If everything has gone well, that's tomorrow. Love you guys. Call me if you need anything."

"You should call him," Melissa said.

Kraig took his cell phone from his briefcase and pressed a couple buttons.

"Is that a new cell phone?" Melissa asked.

"Pretty new. Dave got it for us specifically for this trip. He said mine was too wimpy to get a signal over these trees and mountains."

"Wow. How nice."

Kraig seemed less impressed. "He's a single guy with plenty of money. He likes to spend it on other people. But yes. It was very nice." Melissa could hear Dave's recorded voice. "Voice mail," Kraig said. "Dave. Kraig. It's nine-thirty Wednesday morning. We're over the summit. No ice. The sun is shining in from the left, Melissa is awesome, and it looks like a great day for traveling. We love you too. Have a good flight and we'll see you in Oak Hill tomorrow."

It was dark when Melissa turned east toward Oak Hill.

"Will Jessica and Emily be home when we get there?" Kraig asked.

"Yes, they were supposed to have gone home from school today. I sure hope everything went okay with them at their friends' house these last two nights."

"I'm sure it did. Have we invited these friends to the wedding?"

"We have. They're coming."

"How about if I call the girls and tell them where we are?"

"Good idea. And tell them not to fix dinner. We can pick up something on the way."

Melissa could tell by Kraig's end of the conversation that he spoke with both of them, and that neither of them gave him much of a chance to talk. He was chuckling when he hung up. "They were glad to hear from us." He continued to smile at some private thoughts for a while, then said, "Hmm," chuckled some more, and put the phone away. Melissa felt tingly all over as she contemplated the quantity of love and attention that the three of them could shower over him, not to mention Shanna.

Jessica and Emily came out to watch as Melissa parked the moving truck in the driveway. "You drove this thing all the way from Portland?" Jessica asked.

"Yeah, and the hardest part was getting it into the driveway. Now that I think about it, I don't know how I'm going to get it *out* of here."

"You won't have to," Kraig said. "Dave'll be here tomorrow. He'll deal with it."

"Where are we going to put all this stuff?" Emily asked.

"That's a good question, too," Melissa said. "The things we've made room for, we can just move into the house tomorrow afternoon when I get home. Dave will be here by then. The other things, in the garage for now, I guess. I'll park my car outside for the time being. We'll have to move fast, because we have to return the truck by Saturday, but really by Friday, because Saturday, obviously, we'll be—"

"Dave said he'd take care of it for us if we get in a bind," Kraig said.

Melissa shook her head in amazement. "That guy is worth his weight in gold. I hope we get a chance to repay him someday."

"I hope we *don't*. Think about it, Melissa. Do we really want to see Dave in a position to need our help? Yet that day may very well come. Let's be careful what we wish for."

Melissa's thoughts turned to Judy, and she realized he was right.

Shanna was wiggling with happiness to see Jessica and Emily again. "Emmy, will you take her for a romp on the lawn?" Kraig asked. Emily happily obliged.

"Jessica, could you take these into the house?" Melissa asked, handing her the bag of sandwiches they'd picked up. "Oh, and drop off Kraig's briefcase in the downstairs apartment on the way. Please."

"Well, it's not really on the way, but I will," Jessica said.

It would be Kraig's last night in the guest apartment; Thursday and Friday he would stay at the local motel with the others. It just seemed right that he should be with old friends in the last days of his singlehood, rather than under Melissa's roof.

"Oh, Mom," Jessica said as they set the table for dinner. "Matt called. I wrote it all down, but he said his flight comes in about eight o'clock on Friday night."

"Eight o'clock. That figures. It's in the middle of the rehearsal. No one will be available to pick him up."

"I say we let him take the bus," Kraig said. "So he'll miss dinner. And life will go on."

§

Friday night, Melissa fell into bed exhausted, yet profoundly relieved that everything had gone relatively smoothly and gotten finished on time. Indeed, her only real worry was Judy. The three of them were already at her house when she'd arrived from work Thursday, having rented a car at the airport. They all stood to greet her, yet Dave seemed to be supporting Judy rather heavily on her right side; when Melissa went to hug her, Dave stepped back but didn't entirely let go. Melissa had tried to give Dave a questioning look; he'd winked at her but otherwise avoided her. Maybe Kraig knew the story; she'd have plenty of time to ask him about it later.

Thank goodness she'd let Dave stay behind in Portland. For now, all she could do was pray.

225

She mentally went over the next day's schedule as she drifted off to sleep.

We all go out to breakfast in the morning. Dave, Judy, and Helen will meet Matt for the first time.

Praise God, Matt's suit fits and looks good. Someone can go over things with him at church tomorrow. It'll be a low-key ceremony... Matt's job isn't too difficult.

The girls and I get our hair and nails done at eleven-thirty.

The truck is empty. Everything fit somewhere. Dave, saying something about learning to drive a tractor on his grandparents' farm in Michigan when he was ten, handily backed it out of the driveway... and we got it turned in a day early.

Dave, Judy, and Helen will be able to go to church with Jessica and Emily on Sunday, before Dave and Judy leave for the airport. Matt can ride with them. Thankfully, Matt's flight and theirs aren't too far apart in time.

Helen will stay the week with the girls. She'll have the minivan, since Kraig wanted to rent a smaller, more luxurious car for the honeymoon. Helen will be driving a bigger car than she's used to... and in unfamiliar territory... but they shouldn't have to go much of anywhere, anyway. And although Jessica doesn't have a driver's license, she knows how to drive well enough that, in an emergency, she could.

Kraig's wedding gift idea is still a lovely surprise. The guys are picking it up and dropping at off at church during our hair appointment tomorrow.

The weather has cooperated so beautifully, so far; I'm not going to worry about what it's like tomorrow, or next week.

I'm not going to worry about anything.

§

Chapter 16

Melissa sat in the front pew between her daughters, fingering the cameo at her neck. Her wrist corsage of baby's breath and statice lay against the lavender background of her gown as she folded her hands in her lap and tried to look relaxed. Early in the planning stages, they'd decided against the long walk down the aisle, in keeping with the low-key theme. "The suspense would make me nervous," Kraig had said.

She looked to her left and right to admire her beautiful girls in their bridesmaid finery, Jessica with her hair up, adorned with flowers, like her own; Emily's hanging long, with a garland of flowers fashioned into a headband.

Clusters of candles, in lavender, sage green, and ivory, filled the sanctuary with their fragrance and glow; silk irises stood elegantly in shades of purple, periwinkle, lavender, crimson, and gold, surrounded by lacy fern fronds. And, of course, lupines.

Melissa willed herself not to turn and look, but from the volume of hushed voices behind her, she guessed that just about everyone they expected was there. The melodies from the organ she recognized as works of Bach, Handel, and Pachelbel, but Kraig's song was still a delicious mystery. Indeed, her whole future with Kraig would be filled with delicious surprises to be discovered one by one.

She tried to sneak a couple of peeks at Kraig, in the front pew on the opposite side, but it seemed that each time she did, Dave noticed, and smiled or winked at her, and she was concerned that Kraig would wonder what was happening and get nervous. Yet she'd caught enough of a glimpse to know that he looked impossibly handsome in his charcoal-gray, double-breasted suit, lavender shirt, and purple, silver, black, and white striped tie.

At his black wingtips sat Shanna, brushed until she glowed, dignified as her role demanded. Around her neck she wore a lavender ribbon from which hung an ivory satin pillow. Its design had been a creative challenge; the rings needed to be secure, as the pillow would be hanging rather than supported by a traditional ring-bearer with two hands, yet not so secure that detaching them would cause frustration. The rings had been in Dave's care since the weekend she'd helped Kraig pack, for Kraig had not wanted the burden of keeping track of them. Melissa was confident that the rings were now exactly where they should be.

She slipped her hand into her pocket and found Kraig's handkerchief. Suddenly, it seemed as if the last five months had flown by; now the long-awaited day was here.

The pastor approached the platform and asked the congregation to rise and join together in singing "How Great Thou Art." Melissa could hear Kraig's voice, strong and steady, from the other side of the church. Then the pastor said an opening prayer, then asked the wedding party to come forward, everyone else to be seated.

For the next thirty minutes or so, Melissa didn't take her eyes off Kraig as she gladly promised to spend the rest of her life with him, and heard him do the same. At the appointed time, Kraig's song began. He took her hands in his; she squeezed them in return. In a couple of places, his voiced cracked a little; she thought of the handkerchief in her pocket, knowing she was beginning to crack, too, but didn't want to let go of his hand to retrieve it.

"You are the love of my life," the song said.

"And you're mine," she whispered to him, hoping he could hear her huge smile.

On the way out of the sanctuary at the end of the ceremony, Melissa kept her focus straight ahead, but she could hardly wait to get to the fellowship hall and see who was actually there.

After her friends from work and church, a few of Kraig's friends from Oregon, and Melissa's aunt and uncle and cousins, came someone else she'd eagerly looked for.

"Jeff!"

"So this is the lucky guy," Jeff said after kissing her cheek. He put out his hand a little hesitantly until Kraig offered his. Then he introduced the attractive blonde he was with, whose name, he'd told her, was Suzanne. "Suzanne's son Brent is here, too. Looking for other kids his age. He's twelve. Thirteen. Sorry. Hey, where's Matt?"

"He didn't want to stand in this boring line," Melissa said. "He's here somewhere. Why don't you go look for him? He'd love to see you."

"I will. Listen, how long will you be gone on your honeymoon?"

"A week."

"I'll give you a call when you get back, and get with Kraig about going running some time." He looked at Jessica and Emily. "I almost didn't recognize the girls." He shook his head the way people do when contemplating how fast time goes by, how fast kids grow up. "Ah, I have to hug them." And he did. Then he went to look for Matt.

Melissa watched him go, then turned back to the line. "Lori! Gordon! Thanks for coming. This is Kraig."

"Of course we came. Mom sends you her best, too." Melissa took that to mean that Mom wasn't there, but she'd anticipated this and decided it wasn't going to matter. Lori and Gordon almost completely failed to acknowledge Kraig, and Melissa realized that they were exactly the kind of people who were so naturally adept at making him feel uncomfortable. "Well, I don't think we're going to stick around too long," Lori said, looking around the room, "I don't think we really know anyone here. But we thought we should come."

"Good to meet you," Kraig said, which seemed overly generous.

The line was dwindling; then came a man accompanied by a boy and girl about Emily's age. He was of average height and solid build, and walked with that chin-up profile intended to make one look taller. It took Melissa only a moment to realize where she'd seen him before—Kraig's photo album.

"Little brother! Congratulations!"

"Kevin!" Kraig exclaimed when he recovered from the shock, not to mention the forceful hug that Kevin gave him. "I'd like you to meet my wife, Melissa."

He kissed her on the cheek. "Kevin Junior and Carlie. Say hi to your Uncle Kraig and your new Aunt Melissa. Sorry we won't have time to visit. We had reservations to fly up last night but I got hung up in court and we missed our flight. I had to coerce a friend with a private plane to get us up here this morning. I didn't realize your airstrip was so small—it doesn't even have a rental car outlet! So we had to call a taxi. And I had to finagle a schedule switch with Carol—my ex—because it was her weekend to have the kids. But we couldn't miss this, so we worked it out. Didn't we, kids?"

Melissa felt her face getting tired from maintaining her grin, which was spontaneous until now, but becoming forced. *He's exactly as Kraig described him.* Kevin looked as if he were about to go on talking about himself, but stopped with his mouth half-open and put his hand to his coat pocket. "Ah, there's my phone," he said, as if this somehow confirmed his importance. He excused himself and stepped away to take the call.

"That was Kevin," Kraig said.

"And, thankfully, that's the end of the line. My face is getting tired from smiling."

A little later, as the guests sat at round tables or stood in little groups enjoying finger food and fellowship, Melissa stood behind the cake table and took Kraig's hands. "I want you to see this," she said, almost not wanting to cut into this masterpiece she'd designed for a fellow artist friend to make. "Don't worry, we're only going to touch the parts people aren't going to eat." She put his fingertips to the real roses—buds and miniature blossoms—of ivory and sterling silver, piled on its top, and the strings of sugar pearls cascading down the sides.

Then, with his hand covering hers, she cut a dainty wedge of the chocolate cake. Making sure the photographer was ready to capture the moment, she put her hand on his cheek as she guided the piece of cake toward his lips. After receiving a bite from him, she took a floral-print napkin from a swirled stack and wiped his fingertips, moving almost in slow motion, wanting each moment to be captured forever.

Emerging from the church on Kraig's arm, Melissa closed her eyes, but turned her face, smiling hugely, into the shower of confetti. Then she stood, wanting to imprint upon her memory the assembly of dear friends and family, looking around to make sure she'd had a chance to connect with each and every one. "Ready?" she asked.

"Where's Shanna?"

"Emily has her on the lead."

"I want to say goodbye to her."

Melissa called Emily over, and Kraig knelt and put his arms around Shanna's neck. "Enjoy your first week in your new home, Shanna," he said, running his fingers through her head fur one last time before kissing her. Then he stood. "One last goodbye to the kids, Dave, Judy, Helen, and anyone else who's stayed to the end...."

Dave handed her a set of car keys. "You're not getting very far without these. And don't forget to check out what's on top."

She turned toward the rental car to see something covered in a tarp on its roof, having forgotten she hadn't yet discovered the surprise gift.

"Can you guess?" Kraig asked, holding her back.

"I'm assuming it's something we're going to use on our honeymoon...."

"Unless it rains every day, we will."

Memories came back to her, and suddenly she knew what it was. "Bicycles?"

"It's a *tandem* bike. Something we'll use together."

"Oh, my gosh, Kraig, that is going to be *so* much fun."

"As will the whole week."

"I'm ready to go. Are you?"

"I am."

She gave him the keys; he let her in, let himself in, and returned the keys to her.

As the photographer aimed the camera through the front windshield, she pressed her cheek to Kraig's and grinned one last time. She put down the windows as they drove away, waving, and no small quantity of confetti made it inside the car.

"Dave said he'd make sure the car decorations were tasteful—one of his jobs as best man. So, how does it look?"

"Tasteful. Some carnations and an artful 'Just Married' sign."

"Good. He said he was paying some kids to babysit the car and make sure it wasn't tampered with. I guess he meant it."

"What kids?"

"Just some kids who were riding their bikes around in the parking lot."

"Ah, what a day. What an *incredible* day."

As she eased the car onto the highway that would take them out of the hills and toward the wine country, the western sky was streaked with watercolor shades of peach and pearly gray. The dark, leafless branches of oak trees stood out like ink drawings against the blue-white background. A light sprinkle of rain dotted the windshield, and the landscape glittered with freshness and newness. Melissa was glad they'd decided to remain in their wedding attire for the trip to their honeymoon destination; she kept stealing glances at Kraig, so elegant in his double-breasted suit, lavender shirt, and striped tie.

"The pictures are going to turn out great," she said. "Oh, and we'll have all those silk flowers to put around the house after we get home. And, hey, can you put in the tape?"

He reached into his inside breast pocket. "I have *three* tapes here. There's the tape of my song, the tape of the entire ceremony, and the tape of Dave's toast at the reception. Your choice."

"You got Dave's toast on tape? Play that first. That was awesome. I thought maybe he was going to go the comedy route, but that was just an eloquent speech. Did you know what he was going to say?"

"Not really. He offered to let me hear it first, and give my approval, but I said, 'No, that's all right, I trust you.'" He selected one of the tapes. "I think this is it."

Melissa watched as he found the slot for the tape and turned it on.

"Ladies and gentlemen, friends and family," Dave's voice said, "it is my honor and privilege to be here today. And it has been an honor and a privilege, as well as a huge joy and a lot of fun, to watch this relationship develop to the place where we are today—gathered here to see Kraig and Melissa be joined as husband and wife.

"As most of you know—at least, you know if you've read this beautiful program that Melissa put together—I've known Kraig for many years. Melissa I've known for not nearly as long. But in these last few months that I've come to know Melissa, who's turned out to be as lovely inside as she is out, I've become more and more certain that this is a relationship that's meant to be.

"I tell you, dear people, God must have smiled on us the day these two met. And Kraig and Melissa have been an example of two people who not only are very fortunate to have found each other, but who have done everything right to make sure that their relationship is honoring to God and to each other."

After this, there was a moment of silence, during which Dave had turned to look at them, his composure failing, and Melissa had whispered to Kraig, "I think we should go up there." And they had, enfolding Dave in a group hug that ended with the three of them shedding unashamed tears.

"You couples out there, as well as those of you who are *hoping* to be part of a couple some day," Dave's voice continued, "you could do no better than to look to these two as an example. And it all began with that important first impression: she liked his dog. Now, dear people, would you pray with me as we send Kraig and Melissa on their journey—life as a married couple."

The three of them had stood, their arms around each other, as Dave prayed. Melissa wiped her eyes, hearing it again. "Now play the song. Please."

"Are you sure?"

"Yeah. I'll pull over if I can't see to drive."

You are the love of my life.

"I hope you're not going to ask to hear the third tape," Kraig said when the song was over.

"Uh, no, we can do that later." Melissa took a few deep breaths.

They were both silent for a while. "You look tired," she said.

"I am, in a *good* way. I look forward to being there, and not having to go anywhere or do anything that we don't want to for a whole week. And *you* not having to drive more than a few miles here or there." He was quiet for a moment. "I'm just looking forward to being there," he said again, sounding tired, too.

Gravel crunched under the tires as she steered the car up the drive to the inn. A mist covered the landscape, lending a soft, cozy glow to the quaint country inn and its surrounding vineyards, rendering the whole scene like an Impressionist painting.

Kraig took the key from her, and as he groped for the keyhole to unlock the trunk—although she would have fared no better, for it was dark—she realized that, in Shanna's absence, she'd need to stay pretty close to Kraig's side all week. Indeed, that had been the thinking behind the decision to leave Shanna home: maximized bonding between the newlyweds.

At the door to their room, Kraig dropped the bags heavily, swung the door open with a dramatic gesture, picked her up, and carried her across the threshold. "I just *had* to do that," he said, grinning although he still looked tired.

233

Closing the door behind them, Melissa reached to help Kraig out of his coat and stepped around him to hang it in the armoire. She kicked her shoes into it, too.

"Help me get oriented, Melissa."

"Oh, sorry, honey. Okay. We're standing at the door. The armoire is to our right. I hung your coat on the far left, but I'll let you put your other things away so you'll know exactly where they are. Next to that is a suitcase stand. Turning the corner is the door to the bathroom. We'll get to that in a minute. Then the bed, with a small lamp table on each side. On the far wall, there's a bay window with a window seat and a little table and a couple chairs. To our left, there's a dresser in the middle of the wall, with a comfy chair on each side. There's some other stuff, but those are the main things."

"What does the room look like? I mean—what colors? What motif?"

"Mm. Very nice. Green and red tropical prints, sort of a Florida Keys look…ivory carpet…a ceiling fan…wooden shutters …wicker…sort of a Hemingway motif."

He looked pleased. "Good. Now the bathroom."

"Okay. We're in the doorway. On our left is a large pedestal sink. On our right is the toilet…far right corner, a stall shower with glass walls…and I'm saving the best for last. We have a sunken whirlpool tub in the other corner, surrounded by glass block, sort of a mini-greenhouse. I suppose you knew about this?"

He just smiled; she supposed he did. He loosened his tie as they stepped back out of the bathroom, and as she was thinking about putting out the snacks they'd brought from the reception, he put his arms around her from behind. She turned to face him and he pressed her into a full-body hug, complete with passionate kiss.

"Ooh, *that* was nice," she said.

"Many more where that came from."

"I think we should eat the food we brought. It's only a little after seven-thirty." She took him by the hand to the little table in the bay window and began to put out salmon-and-cucumber and chicken salad sandwiches, baby carrots and spinach dip, and cut fruit, thoughtfully packed by Helen and Judy and the girls. "Here you go," she said, handing him the bottle of wine and a cork pull.

He poured two glasses while she held them steady; it seemed his hands trembled ever so faintly.

"Wasn't it just a perfect day?" she asked, taking a seat.

"I wouldn't change a thing," he agreed, taking his own seat.

"Your song just blew me away. I was so sure I was going to start bawling."

He smiled. "So did I. I mean—that *I* was."

"Everyone we expected was there. Everyone got along. Even the weather cooperated! Oh, I am just so, *so* happy."

He just nodded, smiling a little.

"Do you know what's wrong with Judy?" Melissa asked. "She seemed to be leaning pretty heavily on Dave."

This topic seemed to bring him to life; he sat up a little straighter. "Dave told me her whole right side hurts. Her head, her arm, her leg—all on the right side. He wouldn't say much. I think he didn't want to cast any gloom over our day."

"Oh. That's sad."

"We'll pray about it." Then he was quiet again.

"Honey, if you're really tired, we could get ready for bed. It's still kind of early, though."

"It's that...and...."

"What?" she said, putting aside her wine glass and leaning close.

"I have been looking forward to this so much, for so long... and now it's here, and I don't know...."

As his voice trailed off, Melissa realized that shyness, plain and simple, had entered the picture at this most intimate of moments. "Oh, honey, it doesn't matter. We could just go to sleep, and save the other things for another night, if you'd rather."

"No way," he said, tipping back his wine glass and standing. "I'm going to go take a shower." So saying, he set in motion a sequence of events that had been planned and verbally rehearsed with meticulous care, in order to make things go as smoothly as possible and minimize the awkwardness of their first night together. He took a hanger from the armoire and a t-shirt and boxers from his suitcase, along with his bathroom kit, and went into the bathroom, closing the door behind him.

Smiling after him, Melissa began to organize her own things in the dresser.

About twenty minutes later, he re-emerged in a fragrant cloud of steam, hung his shirt and pants, put the other items in his suitcase, and, finding the covers already turned back on the side nearer the bathroom door, got into bed. As he lay on his back with his hands folded across his chest, wearing one of his gray t-shirts, Melissa smiled again, wondering if the shirt was a matter of habit or if it represented to him some sort of wedding-night etiquette. No matter; she planned to slip in next to him wearing only her clingy cotton nightie. She hung her dress, showered, and got ready for bed.

Walking around to the other side instead of climbing over him, she slid in and clicked off the lamp. The lamp on Kraig's side was still on; Melissa didn't have much choice but to lean over him to turn it off. "Hey, handsome," she said, deliberately landing sort of halfway on him, "you must have shaved again."

"I did." He put his arms around her loosely.

"Nice." She pressed her face into his neck and inhaled. "Mm. You smell *so* good."

As he rolled toward her, she slipped her hand under his shirt, and at the feel of his bare skin, she realized she'd never had direct contact with any part of him but his face, hands, and arms.

"*This* is nice," he said, examining the satiny straps and plunging neckline of her nightgown, and the way the soft fabric followed the contours of her body.

She hoped that his next move would be to help her out of it, for she longed to feel the full weight of his body on hers, his bare skin to hers. The way the next moments unfolded would have been a disappointment, had the wedding night really mattered more than the nurturing of trust, the development of mutual security and comfort, the year-upon-year building of the relationship.

But it didn't matter that much.

§

Chapter 17

When Melissa opened her eyes in the morning, Kraig was motionless, although it was hard to tell whether he was asleep or awake. She rose on one elbow to look at him. After a while, he stirred, rolled away from her, and dropped his arm over the far side of the bed. Curious, she watched as he stayed that way for a moment, then withdrew his arm and rolled onto his back again. He looked as if he were hovering in that place between sleep and wakefulness, semi-aware that something wasn't quite right.

She understood. *Shanna isn't there.*

His eyes popped open.

"Good morning, handsome. Do you know where you are?"

He smiled. "I do." He rolled toward her, putting his hand on her face. "What time is it?"

"Barely six o'clock. It's still dark. You're not wearing your watch?"

"Not when I'm in bed with you."

"Last night was nice," she said tentatively.

He smiled, a decidedly embarrassed smile.

"No, really. It doesn't matter. I just like being with you."

"My timing was off a bit, wasn't it? I was trying to take things slowly, and everything was going fine...until I discovered you weren't wearing anything under that slinky nightie. Then suddenly, 'slow' wasn't an option."

"It doesn't matter. We have all week to practice."

"Well, I bet that's the first time you've ever made love under quite those circumstances."

"I think it was the first time I've ever made love."

He gave her an odd look.

"I mean, I finally understand why it's called 'making love.' I just enjoy being with you, sexually and otherwise, because I love you."

"I like that. Thanks, babe." He stroked her face with his fingers. "Now...there's something we need to do."

"Get ready for breakfast? You didn't eat much last night."

"Something else first, since they're not expecting us for breakfast until eight." He reached toward the bedside table for his Bible. "We need to pray together. Every day, starting today. We can work out what time of day works best for us…morning, bedtime, whatever, as long as we do it every day."

She watched with bottomless admiration and love for him as his fingers moved over the page and he read aloud to her, then reached for her hand.

§

"Good morning!" A jovial-looking woman greeted them in the dining room. "I'm Lois, your hostess. My assistant must have checked you in last night. And you must be the—" She consulted a piece of paper from her apron pocket.

"The Dobrovskys," Kraig said.

"Ah! Thanks. I wasn't sure what I'd written."

"He's used to it," Melissa said. "And I guess I'm going to *get* used to it."

"Ah, the newlyweds! Congratulations! Sit anywhere, and I'll pour you some coffee. Breakfast will be out shortly. You're among the first, as you can see."

At a table next to the fireplace, Kraig took Melissa's hand with his right hand, cradling his coffee cup in his left. Melissa smiled at this skill she still found noteworthy.

"Breakfast smells good," he said.

"It does. Suddenly, I'm hungry, too."

"Tell me what this place looks like."

"Cozy. Homey. Pine floors, pine-paneled walls, a few pictures of the wine country. Full-length windows to the back yard. Oh, I didn't notice this last night—a wide, covered porch, looking out to a pond, with ducks on it."

He nodded. Then he motioned her to lean closer. "Is anyone nearby?"

Melissa glanced around. "A couple on the other side of this massive stone fireplace. Why?"

He used his hand as a privacy shield for what he was about to say. "What you said earlier…" he whispered, "about having all week to practice. Remember?"

"Okay," she whispered back, "what about it?"

"After breakfast."

She giggled. "Really?"

He shrugged, smiling a smile somehow different from any of his smiles that she'd known before…playful, hinting at mischief, communicating their newfound intimacy. "Why not? It's our honeymoon."

"Okay."

Just then, Lois returned with breakfast, and Kraig's expression returned to a dignified smile, while Melissa still fought back giggles. "Thank you," she said as Lois placed the plates.

"Enjoy," Lois said, and left.

"Blueberry crepes," Kraig said, inhaling deeply. "I haven't enjoyed these in *quite* a while."

§

Later, as they strolled downtown, Melissa stopped abruptly in front of a store with colorful banners waving outside the door. "Let's go in here. This reminds me of that store we went into in Fog Harbor."

"Where you bought me that little balsam pillow, which I put next to my bed when I got home, and smelled it last thing every night and first thing every morning. It made me think of you."

"It was *supposed* to make you think of Maine."

"Ah, but you and Maine will be forever bound together in my mind, beginning right there."

"Good. Oh, here's something." She moved over to a display of soaps and lotions with testers and massaged some into her hands, holding them up for his approval. "What do you think?"

"Rose. Nice. Get some if you like."

"I'll wait. We'll probably come here again."

"I'd like to ask the salesperson about this music that's playing. Will you show me the counter?"

"Sure." Approaching the counter, Melissa saw a stand holding a CD case and bearing a little sign saying, "Now Playing." Aware that, under normal circumstances, Kraig could accomplish his goal very well without her help, she let him go about it in his own way, keeping her observation to herself.

She stood aside as he engaged the saleswoman in conversation about the recording, the artist, and music in general. The woman, who was perhaps a little older than she and moderately attractive, seemed more than pleased to indulge him. Melissa watched her face to try to determine the exact moment at which she realized that this charming man she was conversing with was blind, but that moment never came. Melissa captured the moment in her memory: *This is my husband.*

Kraig thanked the saleswoman, and Melissa moved to his side.

"Are you going to get the CD?" she asked, drawing his arm into the crook of hers.

"Maybe later, when we come back."

As they stepped outside, Melissa said, "Her name tag said 'Marianne,' in case you want to ask for her by name."

He gave her an odd look.

Melissa shrugged. "She liked you."

"I'm on my honeymoon, you might remember. Is anyone looking?"

"Uh, no...."

He embraced her, lifting her off her feet, and kissed her, in full view of anyone who might happen to glance their way, right on the sidewalk. Melissa, still tingly from the after-breakfast encounter, now found herself positively weak at the knees. "What are we doing after lunch?" he said into her ear.

"Getting plenty of exercise. I mean, *walking* a lot," she said, when she stopped laughing.

"Mm. That'll be fun, too."

He turned her by the arm and they continued strolling. Every so often, Melissa sneaked a peek at him. His expression suggested something that she couldn't quite give a name to, but it had something to do with knowing you're with the person you want to be with for the rest of your life, knowing you won't have to search anymore. Of this she felt certain, for she felt exactly the same.

§

After lunch, Melissa settled into the living room sofa next to Kraig with a stack of tourist literature he'd brought.

"Read me whatever sounds interesting to you," he said. "Mark the ones we want to do."

240

"Okay, here we go. Biking, of course. Routes for all ability levels...tree-shaded streets...wineries along the way...."

"Wineries! Yes. Wineries are *bursting* with fascinating history. And the smell! Just the aroma of those places is enough to intoxicate me."

"Really? Well, good thing I'm driving."

"What else?"

"Hiking! Views of San Francisco...islands...birds...oak trees draped with Spanish moss...."

"Spanish moss...now, that reminds me of Louisiana. It's the only species of the pineapple family native to the United States."

"Really? Spanish moss is a species of pineapple?"

"It is. What else do you see?"

"Oh, listen to this. A mill where they sell fresh bread that's baked from flour they grind right there."

"We should get some to take home."

"Definitely. And here's something else: a discovery center with hands-on displays to acquaint you with different varieties of wines."

"Mm. Good one."

"Now, how about this? A bubbling pool of mineral waters ...a hot tub of volcanic mud...followed by a massage."

"*That* sounds good."

She leaned to whisper into his ear. "I'm not too sure about the massage. I don't really like the idea of someone else getting familiar with your body. At least, not this week."

"Nor I yours. All right...mineral water and mud, no massage. What else?"

"Oh! The wine train! Elegant wining and dining as we glide past vineyards and towns. We'll need to make a reservation."

"That sounds like a must-do. What about horseback riding? I'd like to be able to tell the girls we went horseback riding."

"Horses...here we go. Horses in the vineyards...horses in the forest...."

"Any horses on the beach?"

"I don't see horses on the beach."

"Good enough. What about restaurants? I'd like to find one that has live music."

"Okay, the restaurant guides…here we are…aha! Cajun cooking and live jazz."

"Perfect."

"There are *plenty* of good restaurants to fill the week. And if it rains, we can do more museums, shopping, wineries…."

"And other indoor activities." He had that playful smile she'd seen for the first time that morning.

"Yeah. And that reminds me. I want to show you the boxers I got for you."

"Now seems like a good time." He gathered the brochures into a neat stack.

Back at the room, Melissa pressed into his hands the two pairs of boxer shorts. "One pair is dusty teal; the other is dusty purple. I've always liked those colors on you. And I already washed them, so they're nice and soft."

"Mm. Cotton knit. Nice. Thank you." He went to his suitcase to put them away. As Melissa watched, he stopped suddenly. "I've just found something I didn't know was here."

She went to his side. "Well, no wonder. It's wrapped in fabric, not paper, so it didn't make any noise." She looked at the tag. "Have fun, you two. Love, Dave."

"Open it, babe."

"Okay. We have here…lavender aromatherapy bath gel." She laughed. "He must have known about the whirlpool tub."

Kraig shook his head, trying not to smile. "I can hardly wait until that guy gets married."

"Well, this'll be fun. Smell." She took off the cap and held it up to him.

"Ah, yes. That will be."

That night, after a soak in the whirlpool tub with the lavender aromatherapy gel, Melissa closed her eyes to sleep, in her favorite place in the world—nested against her husband's back, her arm around him, his hand clasping hers.

When she opened her eyes Monday morning, Kraig was already awake, intently listening to something.

"What, honey?"

"I heard a puppy. There's a puppy here somewhere."

Melissa listened. "I don't hear it. Maybe you dreamed it."

"No, Melissa, it was a puppy."

"Okay." She smiled, thinking he must be missing Shanna terribly, although he hadn't spoken of it. "Let's ask Lois about it at breakfast."

Later, out in the hall, Kraig inhaled deeply. "Ah. Cinnamon French toast. Sourdough. Something else I haven't had in a long time. I think we came to the right place, Melissa."

As soon as Lois came with the coffee, Melissa decided to ask about the puppy, willing to risk embarrassment for Kraig's sake if he turned out to be mistaken. "Do you have a puppy?" she asked.

"Yes, Benny, our beagle puppy. We crate him at night, and he stays in the sun porch during the day, until he's housebroken."

"I'd like to see him, if it's all right," Kraig said.

"His guide dog stayed home this time," Melissa explained. "He misses her."

"Certainly. He'd be happy to see you, too. Tell you what—as soon as you're finished with breakfast, just go through that door there," Melissa made a note of where she pointed, "that leads to the sun porch. That's where you'll find him. In fact...now, don't tell anyone else, but...while you're here, you can go see him any time you like."

"Thanks," they said at the same time.

"I'll be right back with cinnamon French toast."

Melissa watched Lois go, then turned back to Kraig and smiled. "Some day I'll catch on that you're always right."

He smiled. "Tell me what Lois looks like."

"Middle-aged. Older than I am, I mean. Pretty tall and sturdy looking, like maybe she grew up on a farm. Short, easy-care hair style."

He nodded. "What does the weather look like? I feel a bit of a chill."

She looked out the window. "Yeah, it's a little foggy. When it clears, it might be a good day for a bike ride. By the way, I love you in that argyle sweater vest."

"Well, you're the one who chose it."

"I know what I like on you."

Back at the room, she put her arms around him as soon as the door swung closed. "Wait. I need to hug you for a minute."

He chuckled, a little indulgently, but seemed pleased to be hugged and hug back.

She pressed her face into the softness of his sweater and inhaled deeply. "Mm. *Mm*."

"What?"

"I love how you smell. I *always* love how you smell, but now, your sweater has some of the smells from breakfast, so you smell even better than usual. And besides that, I like to hug you."

"Well, I like that, too. What shall we do before we go bike riding?"

"I was just thinking, we have the bike, but not the clothes. At least we need the right kind of pants. Maybe not shorts, but long ones that fit tight. Why don't we go shopping?"

Later, seeing him in those form-fitting pants, she felt that physical desire for him that, only a short time ago, had been a new and unfamiliar experience. Now, having enjoyed marital intimacy with him, she discovered that the bonding process was self-perpetuating: the more she was with him, the more she *wanted* to be. Now, she could hardly keep her hands off him.

She watched him fiddle with the clasp on his cycling helmet. "Here, let me help you with that. Not that I don't think you're capable. I just like doing things for you."

He closed his eyes as she adjusted the straps and snapped the clasp, taking care not to pinch him.

"You're so cute," she said, giggling.

He looked vaguely amused. "That's exactly what my mom said. I think I was nine at the time."

"I do not believe for one second that your mom was the last person who said that before now. In fact, Jessica and Emily both said it, the week we met."

"Really."

"Yes. Really. I wasn't ready to see it then. But I was, later. Ready to go?"

"I am."

That night, in those tender moments between lovemaking and sleep, Melissa asked, "Did you have fun today?"

"Of course," he said. "This whole week has been like a dream. Although…I *am* a little sore. My legs…and other places. And on that note, I think we should put off the horseback riding for another day."

"Sure. We have plenty of things we can do. Hey, maybe tomorrow's a good day for a mud bath."

He looked preoccupied. "Do you think I'll have a problem with the horseback riding establishment?"

"What do you mean?"

"Think about it, Melissa. Liability."

"Oh." She honestly hadn't thought about it. "Hey. If we *do*, we'll just tell them your brother's a personal injury attorney. A *big, successful* one."

He smiled. "I like that. In fact, I think I still have one of his business cards in my wallet."

"Good. Then I don't think we'll have any problem. How long has it been since you've ridden?"

"A *long* time. I participated in a therapeutic horseback-riding program when I was a child; my parents thought it would help with my posture and balance until I was old enough for a guide dog. They talked about getting me my own horse, but then we moved to southern California and didn't have room for a horse."

"That's sad. Well, Jessica and Emily both want to get horses. If they ever have horses, you can ride whenever you want."

"I'd like that."

"Hey, it just occurred to me—you haven't had any headaches this week, have you?"

"No. No headaches. I never even thought about headaches." He rolled away and snuggled his back to her, her arm around him, her hand in his.

Friday morning, Melissa found herself in exactly that position when she awoke. She raised her head to see whether Kraig was awake; although his eyes were closed, something about his smile suggested he was awake.

"Hey, handsome. What are you smiling about already?"

"I dreamed I spent the night in the arms of a beautiful woman. Then I woke up. And I really *was* in the arms of a beautiful woman. Life gets no better than that."

"Well…today *is* the last full day of our honeymoon."

"No," he said, rolling onto his back, "it's our last full day in the wine country. That's not the same thing. The honeymoon doesn't have to end tomorrow. Or ever. I'm glad we saved dinner with live jazz for tonight, though. I'm looking forward to that."

"Me too. Let's get an early start. We can sit on the porch swing for a while before we turn in."

"And then soak in the whirlpool tub. And maybe you'd like the backrub I promised you. Somehow we never get to that, do we?"

"Yeah. I'd like that. But I've liked *not* getting one, too."

"It makes me very happy that we're in sync in that area, Melissa. Now, let's read from the Bible. You know what else I like? I like it when you lean over me. Will you please get my Bible from the bedside table?"

She did, but as it turned out, her reaching across him triggered a sequence of events that ended not in Bible reading but in lovemaking.

But it didn't matter. There was still time to read the Bible before breakfast.

§

The sun was setting into the hills as she parked the car in front of the Cajun restaurant. She had saved her nicest dress for the occasion, a soft silk, cut low in back and fitted at the waist. Kraig was wearing the same shirt and tie he'd looked so handsome in on that breathless Sunday morning in Portland.

"This is the best blackened redfish I've had since New Orleans," Kraig said. "Your shrimp, too, is excellent. How do you like the wine?"

"I'd be having a third glass, except I'd better not. Maybe later, if we stay long enough." She remembered a subject she's wanted to bring up with him. "Honey," she began tentatively, "I hope you don't mind what I'm doing with my name."

"You mean, the hyphenating?"

"Yes. That."

"Of course not. Why?"

She shrugged. "For a long time, I've wanted to change my name back to Crane. It just never seemed like the right time. The kids—I didn't want them to have people always asking them why their name was Melvin and mine was Crane. They had enough to deal with. Besides, it seemed sort of disrespectful...it would've been different if I'd been divorced.

"But then…when I was going to change it *anyway*, I thought, now is a good time to change it to Crane-Dobrovsky. And it doesn't bother me as much as I *thought* it would that we'll have three different names in the family."

"You know what? It doesn't bother me either. As long as you're married to me, I care not a bit what your name is. Although I always did think Melissa is a pretty name."

"I won't mind, though, if people call me 'Mrs. Dobrovsky.' I'll still answer to that."

"Well, then, Mrs. Dobrovsky. Shall we dance?"

"Is that why you wanted to come here? So we could dance?"

"*Live music*, Melissa. What did you suppose? There *is* a dance floor, is there not?"

"There is."

He stood and offered his hand, bending at the waist, the other hand behind him in a courtly manner.

"How could I refuse?" she said, taking his hand.

"Now, you'll do fine, just as you did that night at my place."

At least she remembered where to put her hands this time. "I was so nervous then. Could you tell I was nervous?"

"I was only thinking about how nervous *I* was, because only *I* knew what I was planning to ask you later."

She held his hand, the light glinting off his wedding band. "You're always the picture of composure. I'm the one who's always struggling for the right thing to do or say."

"Nonsense. Melissa, look around you now."

"Okay. What?"

"See all those people looking at you?"

"No. No one is looking at me."

"Yes, they are. You just don't *see* them looking at you. And they're all wondering how I got to be the fortunate guy who's with this tall, stunning brunette in this gorgeous—" he whispered in her ear, "I forgot to ask what color your dress is."

"Purple."

"This gorgeous purple dress that looks so good on you because you haven't gained a pound even though we've been eating scrumptious gourmet food all week."

She laughed. "If anyone is looking at us, they're thinking how amazing it is that a big guy like you can be so graceful compared to me."

He kissed her on the lips, almost as if to cut off her words. "No. I'm going to have to say you're wrong about that."

She eased her head onto his shoulder, wanting just to be together without speaking for the remainder of the set. Sadly, after the next song, the band took a break.

Returning to the table, Melissa saw something that hadn't been there before. "Honey, somebody left us something."

"*Something?* What?"

"A bottle of champagne, a single red rose, and a note. It says—" she held it closer to the candle, " 'Thanks for reminding us what a married couple in love looks like.' It's not signed."

He held her chair for her. "Well, there you are. I *told* you people were looking at you."

Melissa looked around the room, but no one showed any telltale sign of being the sender. Soon the waiter arrived to open the champagne and fill their glasses. "Do you know who sent it?" she asked.

"Yes, but I am sworn to secrecy."

"Will you please thank them for us," Kraig said.

"With pleasure." He bowed and left.

Melissa moved her chair around to Kraig's side of the table. If the anonymous benefactors were still watching, she thought, they might as well get what they paid for.

He put his arm around her and held his glass up to hers. "To being a married couple in love—*forever in love*." He linked his arm through hers for the first sip, then kissed her, champagne lingering on their lips.

§

Melissa snuggled closer to Kraig on the porch swing.

"Are you cold?" he asked.

"Not really. I just like snuggling with you."

"I was hoping you'd say 'yes.' Because I have a cure for that."

She laughed softly. "We still have time for that."

He sighed with contentment. "Melissa…I've said it before, but I'm going to say it again. The sex thing is not so important in and of itself. You know that I waited all this time for you. Fifteen years, Melissa. That's a long time for a guy in the prime of life to go without it. But I knew that without the lifelong commitment, it just wouldn't be worth the trouble. The emotional damage it would cause, and all that. I've been through enough of that in my life.

"But it does give me enormous satisfaction. I appreciate how attractive you are, apart from how much I love you. Besides the obvious, deeply personal benefit, I like knowing that others find you attractive, but see that you're with *me*.

"And as for sex *per se*, it not only feels good on a physical level, but it makes me feel connected. To you…to life. And when I think…" he paused to take a breath, and she heard a bit of a quiver in it, "when I think *how close* I came to missing this…."

"No." She shook her head. "It only looks that way to us. God knew exactly where He wanted you to be that day on the beach— right in my path."

He chuckled. "Yes."

They were both quiet for a moment.

"Well," she said after a time, "tomorrow we go back to regular life."

"Regular…but new. For me, a new home."

"Everything together instead of separate. Starting with that mountain of dirty clothes in our suitcases. Hey, I've been meaning to ask you something. I was afraid it would seem inappropriate when I first noticed this, but now I can. When you came to visit us in November, we noticed that all your t-shirts and socks and underwear are gray instead of white."

"It simplifies doing the laundry."

"Well, I'd be happy to do your laundry for you. *If* you'll let me."

"I will happily let you do my laundry."

"That works out great, because I don't wear white underwear either. White's boring. I always wear beige, yellow, lavender, mint green…."

"Peach?"

"Yes. Peach."

"Like that slinky nightie you had on the first night, but not much since then."

"I get in bed with it on. *You're* the one who seems to like it better off."

"All right. I admit it. I do." He sighed again. "What do you say we call it a night?"

"I guess we should get a good night's sleep for the drive home."

The swing creaked to a halt as their footsteps echoed across the floorboards.

§

Chapter 18

"Give me a beautiful smile, honey," Melissa said, aiming her camera at the front porch of the inn as Kraig posed. "I want us to remember years from now how much fun we had on our honeymoon." She clicked the shutter release twice. Then she showed him where to stand and aim the camera while she posed.

"Wait," he said, finding the door and disappearing inside. A moment later he returned with Lois. "We were on our honeymoon *together*, right?"

She posed with him for a couple more shots, thanked Lois, and took a last, long look around. After a double-check to make sure the bike was secure on the roof, Kraig opened the door for her. In the back seat were things collected to keep alive the memories of this glorious first week together: twelve bottles of wine, two each from six wineries; two loaves of fresh bread; the music CD; rose soap and lotion for Helen; chocolate; and a few knickknacks for Jessica and Emily and the friends they'd stayed with during that tense time before the wedding.

The two-hour drive fairly flew by. When the front door of home opened, if Kraig were anything less than six-foot-three and two-hundred-plus pounds, Shanna's greeting would have knocked him flat. Jessica's and Emily's greetings were slightly more reserved, but no less heartfelt. Helen looked tired.

Melissa barely had the door closed when she began to think of the dirty laundry needing attention, but Jessica had picked up a small stack of envelopes from the table by the door. "Some things came for you." She handed Melissa the mail, then pointed to a package sitting under the table.

"What kinds of *things*?" Kraig asked. "We *did* put 'no gifts' on the invitation, didn't we?"

"Yes we did," Melissa said.

"This is all stuff from relatives," Jessica said. "Maybe they thought it was okay."

"Something from Kevin," Melissa said. "A letter—on his lawyer letterhead—and a check. It says...we're supposed to buy a piano."

"A piano?" Emily asked, sneaking a peek at the check. "Ooh! Is *that* how much a piano costs?"

"I don't know." Melissa whispered the amount to Kraig.

"That'll buy one nice piano," he said.

"Why a piano?" Melissa asked.

"That's Kevin. I wanted a piano very badly, about the time he went away to college. But then we moved, and…like getting a horse, I guess, it just never happened. Maybe he felt responsible. So here's the piano he 'owes' me."

"Where are we going to *put* it?" Jessica asked.

"We're not," he said. "With your permission, Melissa—it's your gift too—I'd like to help your church—I mean, *our* church—get a new piano. I think they could use one."

"We do have a piano fund. How did you know about that?"

He looked like he didn't have a ready answer, but even if he had, her attention was drawn to the next piece of mail.

"A card from Lori and Gordon. And my mom, it says, although it's all in Lori's handwriting." She wondered whether her mom even had any knowledge of it. "And a gift certificate from a nice department store. Well, I can't think of anything we need from a big department store in the city. I wonder what we should…."

"I have an idea," Kraig said. "Check with church to see if a missionary family on furlough could use some help furnishing their house."

"Good idea. One last thing."

Jessica lifted the box, about the size of a mailbox, out from under the table. "It's from your cousin."

"Christine and Tim. It's heavy."

Emily had run to the kitchen for scissors, and Melissa sliced through the packing tape. "Aha! A five-pound bag of raisins. *And* a five-pound bag of chocolate-covered raisins."

"Now, there's something we can use," Kraig said.

§

Monday morning, Melissa struggled to keep her mind on her work, distracted by competing emotions—joy, of knowing Kraig was at home, *their* home, bonding with his stepdaughters and getting reacquainted with his dog; and worry, with his being in a new and largely unfamiliar environment. Sunday after church had allowed precious little time, between returning the rental car and taking Helen to the airport, for getting him settled, let alone setting up his office in the guest apartment.

Melissa had gone over a few new house rules with the girls, which she now went over in her mind, searching for gaps she might have left. *Never leave shoes or other obstacles on the floor. Always leave doors fully opened or fully closed—never halfway. Never use or move Kraig's things without his permission. Never give Shanna any food or toy without his permission. Always tell him whenever you enter or leave his presence.* They had happily agreed to all these things—but would they remember?

One unresolved problem concerned the cats.

"How will we keep them from getting stepped on?" Emily had asked.

"I don't know. I guess they'll learn to stay out of his way," she'd said.

"But we want them to *like* him!"

And Melissa had had no answer.

For his part, Kraig had offered to wear only socks around the house at first, instead of the hard-soled moccasins he preferred.

Even now, as she consoled herself with the thought that the girls were there to help, she wondered how much help they'd really be. They could probably occupy the better part of the day just organizing his music recordings, and labeling hers to fit into his system. She had agreed to move her stereo out in favor of his, which was better anyway. She'd cleared a bathroom drawer for him, too; no small feat. He'd suggested some changes in the kitchen arrangement, but she'd asked him to wait until she could be involved, which he would, unless Jessica and Emily were eager to carry out his plan.

Melissa focused her attention on her work for the umpteenth time when her phone rang. "Jessica! What is it?"

"Kraig. He fell on the stairs. He might have broken his arm or something. I'm sorry. But could you come home?"

Melissa's heart nearly jumped into her throat. "Of course. And it's not your fault. Is he there? Let me talk to him."

A moment later Kraig came on. "I'm sorry, babe."

"No, honey. What stairs? Inside or outside?"

"The stairs inside the house."

"You didn't trip over a cat, did you?"

"No, it's not the cats' fault. At least...not directly."

"What do you mean?"

He hesitated. "It's your socks-only rule. The hardwood floors are slippery. I just slipped coming down the stairs and fell hard against the wall. And not very gracefully."

She groaned loudly. "I'll be home as soon as I can."

During the twenty-minute drive home, which had never before seemed so interminable, a loop of questions played over in Melissa's mind. *Which arm? Which would be worse—not being able to hold Shanna's harness, or not being able to do anything else? And what about not being able to type?*

She parked out front and Emily opened the front door. "Sorry, Mom. We were supposed to help when you weren't here."

"No, it's nobody's fault." Kraig was seated on the couch, cradling his right arm, stroking Shanna's head with his left. She went over and put her arms around him and kissed him. "Honey, I'm so sorry. Ready to go?"

As it turned out, Kraig's arm was not broken, but heavily bruised, with a broken or badly sprained index finger. Back at home after the trip to the emergency room, they settled into the couch side by side, cups of tea in their hands.

"What are you going to do all week?" she asked.

"Spend time with my new daughters. Maybe I'll show them how my computer works."

"Won't you get behind on your work?"

"The newspaper always keeps articles in reserve for times when people are gone. They'll get along all right. You know," he said, "this isn't really so bad. I'm surrounded by people who care about me...being babied by three pretty women. How bad can that be?"

§

When the phone rang that evening, Kraig answered it—his first time ever answering the phone as a resident of his new house.

"Dave!" he boomed. Then there was a long silence, during which Melissa could hear Dave's voice, although she couldn't make out any words. "Wonderful. The honeymoon was wonderful, the place was wonderful, my wife is wonderful, we had a wonderful time. Then I celebrated my first day in my new home by falling down the stairs and wrecking my arm.... No, it'll be all right.... Yes, everything's great, just great...." Then there was a really long silence, and after that, "No. Seriously? *Really?* Well, what wonderful news to hear my first Monday back. My arm feels better already. Would you like to talk to Melissa?... All right, then, I'll tell her. Let us know if you need any help from us experts.... Give Judy our love, will you?... Talk to you soon.... We love you too."

Melissa heard the phone click into its cradle, then Kraig turned carefully to avoid hitting the kitchen wall with his splinted arm. "Melissa? Dave and Judy are getting married." He looked as if he wanted to slam his fist into his hand, but thought the better of it. "September."

Life soon settled into a manageable routine. That Saturday was a dawn-to-dusk frantic scramble to transform Kraig's office from the haphazard arrangement it had been left in the Friday before the wedding, to a semblance of order, with Melissa and the girls positioning things to his precise specifications. Resisting the urge to "help" by doing things *for* him, she constantly reminded herself— and them—that an aesthetically pleasing arrangement would be useless if he didn't know where things were.

Monday, the girls went back to school. Arriving home from work those first afternoons, she would go directly to his office, calling out, "hi, honey," as she passed the window behind his desk, then open the door and peek in to see how absorbed he looked. If he turned toward her in his swivel chair, she would go in; if he greeted her without his full attention, she would continue up to the house.

There, she would usually find a pleasant surprise in the form of some chore that she had left undone, now completed. Sometimes firewood would be stacked, sometimes the kitchen tidied; without fail, the houseplants were well tended. She had assumed, foolishly, that Kraig's vibrant houseplants had been under Helen's care; now, not only did his continue to thrive—hers looked healthier as well.

Always, she hugged him often and spontaneously, so that her daughters could see what a married couple in love looked like.

And suddenly, so many things that until now had been mundane chores presented one of two blissful circumstances—an opportunity to do something together, or an opportunity for her to do something to make his life easier.

Dave called often; Melissa usually tried to give Kraig his privacy while they talked. When he lowered his voice during these conversations, she *did* wonder what they talked about; yet she knew Kraig would be respectful of her in his choice of what to share with Dave. "You're going to love being married," she sometimes heard him say. "It's a little piece of heaven on earth."

Sometimes she would talk to Dave. "You certainly are making him happy," Dave would say. "I've never heard him sound so happy."

"I don't have to try very hard to make him happy. He just chooses to be happy."

"Well, then you're making it very easy for him to choose to be happy."

As the days went by, and Kraig learned to do everything, from type, eat, and program the stereo, to shower, shampoo, and shave with the limitations imposed by the splint, the pain eased. Eventually, it seemed as if he'd always managed with only nine fingers. Yet, even as his injury healed, Melissa noticed a more disturbing development.

One afternoon, when Kraig came up from his office, he moved so stiffly she couldn't keep quiet any longer.

"Honey…something's wrong. You haven't been standing up as straight since you've been here."

He nodded wearily.

"What is it? Our mattress? Or just not being confident in the new surroundings?"

"No, not that. *Maybe* partly that. Mainly I just haven't been getting enough exercise."

"If Jeff hasn't called yet, we need to call him."

"We have a bigger problem than my fitness, Melissa. I'm not working Shanna enough. If I don't get her out more, we're in danger of losing her training. And this is *after* I've just been away for a whole week. Running with Jeff would help me, but not her."

"Well, we can go for walks together in the evening. She can come. On the harness, not just the lead like we did before."

"That would help both of us. There's nothing like being pulled along at four miles an hour to straighten one's spine."

"Okay. Starting tomorrow."

Hand-in-hand with the fitness and dog concerns went another—Kraig's social life. He no longer went to an office every day; he had nowhere to go on his lunch hour. Other than church and Wednesday night choir practice, he was almost totally isolated. And in an unexpected way, walking together in the evenings seemed to make things worse instead of better. He seemed to be withdrawing from her emotionally; she longed for the days when he'd shared his thoughts so freely on those walks.

Now, Kraig's only friends outside of his own household were Dave—now a long-distance friend—and Jeff, who at this point was a friend only in theory. Profoundly thankful for these two, Melissa nevertheless began to worry about him in ways she never had before.

The third Monday, Dave called. Melissa answered the phone, and some tension in Dave's voice filled her with more despair than she could handle, so she handed off the phone to Kraig as quickly as she could.

After a while, Kraig came to find her. "What did he have to say?" she asked.

"Oh…they're doing all right. Judy's been so fatigued, though, she can't work a full day. The bookstore people have been so good to her; work isn't the real issue. It's just the unknown of where this will go." He looked deeply contemplative. "Melissa, there's something about Dave you need to understand. He's a very giving person—that's easy to see. But Dave feels extraordinarily blessed… he has physical health, a supportive family, a measure of material success. When he gives out of this abundance, he doesn't really feel as if it counts for anything…if there's no sacrifice involved, he shouldn't get credit for it. Like supporting Judy on the mission field, buying people cell phones, paying my phone bill for five months. So what? It doesn't hurt to give those things.

"But I think, as time goes forward, we're going to see a different side of Dave. He's used to being on the giving end. But now…with Judy, and her health issues, and his love for her, and the potential for deep sorrow and loss…we're going to see Dave beginning to give from a place where it *does* hurt. That's not going to be easy for any of us. And we need to be alert to his needs, because he's not going to complain."

257

Melissa studied his face, not wanting to interrupt his thoughts, not knowing what to say anyway.

"We need to pray harder," he said at last.

The next day, on her lunch break, Melissa went out and bought a bright orange vest with reflector strips on it. "Hi, honey," she said, passing by his office window that afternoon, peeking in the door, then entering. "I had an idea. You should go for walks any time of day you like. We can go in the evening if you want to, but you'll meet different people at different times of the day. And look. I got you this vest so you'll be safer on these narrow, winding roads. Lots of people wear these around here," she said, exaggerating only a little.

"Thanks, babe," he said.

She went forward to hug and kiss him, which he received, but he didn't invite her to stay, so she went up to the house. He didn't come up until time to fix dinner.

The next day, she repeated the process, this time with the day's mail in hand. "Hi, honey."

"Hi, babe. I did as you suggested. I went for a walk at lunchtime. And I met some neighbors—a retired couple with three dogs. Perhaps you know them; Wayne and Jean?"

"I do." She beamed. "Great. And look. The proofs of the wedding pictures came."

"How do they look?"

"It's hard to say. They're on a CD. I thought we could look at them on your computer."

He looked blasé. "I'd thought I could leave that to you."

Deeply hurt, but not wanting to show it, she said, "Well...I guess I could do it."

"We could do it together if you want to. How about tonight after dinner?"

Whether he really wanted to, or said this just to please her, she wasn't at all sure. "Okay. Well...I'll let you get back to work."

The next day was pretty much the same, except that Kraig had asked to postpone looking at the pictures. "Hi, honey," Melissa said, peeking into his office.

He turned the computer monitor away from her. "Hi, babe. Any mail I need to see?"

"Not really."

"All right, then. I'll see you at dinner. Wait," he said as she started to close the door. "Jeff called. We're going running tonight, up at the college. I'll eat later."

"Okay."

Dave called while Kraig was gone.

"Oh, you missed him, Dave. He went running with Jeff."

"He went running with Jeff! Well, you know what that means, Melissa. You can tell me *anything you want*. Go ahead. Any behavioral problems or bizarre idiosyncrasies you'd like to discuss with me?"

"Well, no, not really."

"Come on, Melissa. Talk."

"Okay," she said, secretly grateful for the chance. "I guess it's that 'moody, broody, and weird' thing you were telling me about. The honeymoon was fantastic. But since we've been home, he's just …nothing, really, but…well, I just don't know how much space to give him. I love having him here. I get home from work and he's *here*. I just can't get over what a good feeling that is. But I can never tell if I'm going to be interrupting him. And sometimes he acts as if maybe I'm going to see what he's working on, and like it's going to be a disaster if I do."

"That's a writer thing, Melissa. Cardinal sin to let anyone see what you're working on till it's finished. Anything else?"

"Just trying to find that balance. How much closeness is enough…how much is too much. He needs more people in his life. I'm so thankful to *you* for being there."

"Never doubt that he loves you deeply, Melissa. *Never* doubt that. Kraig can be difficult to read. Probably because he thinks deeper thoughts than most of us do. But he responds very well to being talked to in an honest and straightforward manner.

"Melissa…I hope you don't mind my going here, but…I think this is the number one thing that went wrong with any other relationship he might have had during the years that I've known him. Kraig expects people to be what they seem to be…say what they mean, mean what they say…do what they say they're going to do… those sorts of things. And you, Melissa, are apparently the first one to come along who's passed this test.

"So talk to him. Tell him how you feel. Cry if it feels natural to do so. He'll melt faster than a snowball in—Mexico. Really. Everything'll be okay."

She felt tears fill her eyes for the first time in a long time. "Thanks, Dave. Well...you must have called for a reason. Sorry. We've just been talking about *me*."

"No worries. I was just calling to invite you—*all* of you—on an overnight rafting trip this summer with our Sunday school class."

"Oh! Well, that does sound like fun."

"Don't worry about Kraig. His arm should be healed by then."

"What about Judy?"

"A group is going to set up camp at the end of the route, fix dinner for us and so on. Judy plans to stay with that group. Shanna can too. Judy wants me to have fun and not have to worry about her."

"I'll run it by Kraig and let him call you tomorrow night. It *does* sound like fun."

"Excellent. Now, Melissa, don't worry about a thing. I'll be praying for you two. As much as you love each other, nothing will come along that you can't work out. Promise me you won't worry?"

"I'll try not to. Thanks for calling, Dave."

"Love you guys."

Only a moment after she hung up, she heard Jeff's car in the driveway. She didn't hear it drive away immediately; Kraig must have invited Jeff to come in. She went to greet them at the door. "How did it go?"

"Fine," Kraig said, more buoyant than she'd seen him in quite a while. He kissed her, such a public display that she was almost embarrassed, probably a deliberate demonstration of his exclusive privilege. "I'm going to go take a shower."

Melissa and Jeff both watched him go up the stairs.

"Really," Jeff said. "He did great. He's pretty fast for a big guy. I bet he'll shape right up once he gets into it. Depending on how much of a commitment he wants to make, anyway."

"Let's let him take the lead on that. And you know, Jeff, this is as much a social thing as a fitness thing. He needs friends. This is a big adjustment for him, being here with us. So don't push him, as far as the fitness goes, please. Just be his friend."

Jeff nodded. "It's a deal. Hey, are the girls around? I'd like to say 'hi' to them."

"Sure. Jessica? Emily?" she called up the stairs. "Come say 'hi' to Jeff."

Seeing them, he shook his head in wonder. "Pretty girls. Tall. Like Mom, like daughters."

"Oh, one more thing," she said as Jeff reached for the door a few minutes later. "You don't *have* to walk him to the door when you get home. Of course, you're always welcome to drop in. But as long as you park in the same place every time, he'll be okay."

"Good deal. Oh, by the way…things are at kind of a critical point for Suzanne and me. I'm not at all sure about her standing with the Lord. She needs to get off the fence and figure out which world she wants to belong to. You could pray for that."

"I will."

"For me…just pray that I'll have the strength to stick to my convictions."

"I will. *We* will. Jeff—" So much had been left unsaid during their relationship, some of which she still longed to say, most of it now either inappropriate or unnecessary; yet she needed to know that all was forgiven between them. He had kissed her cheek at the wedding, but that was a formality, an expectation. Slowly, watching for his reaction, she reached out to hug him. "Thanks, Jeff."

He hugged her and smiled. Then he left.

As Kraig ate dinner, she told him about Dave's call and the rafting trip.

He nodded. "That sounds like fun. Don't you think so?"

"I guess so. Dave says Judy's going to stay in camp. Shanna can stay there too."

"I hope you're not worried about *me*. My arm will be fine by then. How could this not be fun?"

She shrugged.

"It's not the rafting trip that's bothering you, is it? Come here, Melissa."

She slid her chair next to his.

"Tell me. What is it really?"

"I don't know what you want me to do when I get home from work. I like coming home and knowing you're here. But sometimes I feel like I'm bothering you."

"It all depends, Melissa. Sometimes I'm on a train of thought I don't want derailed. Sometimes I'm not."

"How do I know the difference?"

"You don't. But you'll learn how to tell."

This wasn't terribly helpful. "What shall I do till then?"

He looked thoughtful for a moment, and Melissa began to feel hopeful once again that they were on the same team. "I have an idea. Call me just before you leave work. I'll give you an idea of where I am. If I don't pick up at all, I'm deeply entrenched in some thought pattern. So please just go up to the house when you get home. I'll know you're home. And I promise to try harder to welcome you, either way."

She put her arms around him and let the tears flow.

The next day, she opened his office door a little tentatively, having gotten sort of a lukewarm response on the phone, wondering if this new system would work. "Hi, honey. I have the mail."

"Melissa. See if my paper from Portland is there, will you?"

"It is."

"Come in and close the door, will you?"

She did, handing him the paper as she settled onto the sofa bed. All traces of staleness had been banished from the formerly little-used room; it now smelled deliciously of *him*. He looked so at home here now, surrounded by his books and music; the little carved chickadees, reunited, perched on a shelf.

"Here," he said, handing it back to her. "Go to page four and find my column."

"Okay, here it is."

"Read it out loud, please."

"Not Coming to a Theater Near You," she read. She looked up at him; he had his hands folded behind his head, looking satisfied. She continued reading. "The first scene opens with a man walking his dog on a beach in Maine. The wide-angle shot suggests an aloneness, an emptiness. Honey," she interrupted herself, "this isn't a movie; it's about *us*! Is this what you were working on so secretly?"

"It is."

She continued reading. "The couple has settled in Oak Hill, California," the column concluded, "from where Kraig will continue to write his regular feature. They expect to live happily ever after."

"Honey…I love it. Your readers will love it too." She re-folded the paper and laid it on his desk.

He pulled her into his lap. "When we get the wedding pictures back, they want to do a story for the social page, so everyone can see my lovely bride."

"Then we'll have to work on that this weekend."

He nodded, but he had that look that suggested his thoughts were elsewhere. Then he got that irresistible shy look. "Melissa? Make love to me."

"Um…now?"

"Ever since Thanksgiving, when I stayed down here for the first time after we got engaged, I've dreamed of making love to you here. It's still a little while until the girls get home."

"Mm. Okay. Well, I think the sheets are still on the sofa bed since you slept in it just before the wedding."

"I love being married, Melissa. To *you*. I love being married to you."

§

As the next days went by, Melissa felt more at peace than she had in a few weeks. Something about making love to him in his private, sacred space made her feel more included in his work and his life. He seemed more upbeat, too, as he got to know people in the neighborhood; he began to seem as though he felt at home in Oak Hill.

A few days later, Kraig came in alone after running with Jeff, looking very pleased about something.

"Did you have fun?" Melissa asked.

"Yes. I did. I'm going to take a shower."

Hmm. She went back to reading the paper. A few minutes later, Kraig came back, sitting next to her on the sofa and leaning over to kiss her.

"So," she said. "You had fun."

"I did. Jeff let me drive his car."

She flung her newspaper aside. "Did you just say…Jeff let you drive his car?"

"I did. Not on the *highway*, Melissa; just in the college parking lot."

She stared at him, speechless, for a long moment, then laughed. "I have this feeling I'm *supposed* to be surprised. But somehow I'm not."

"It was fun," he said.

"I'm sure it was. And I suppose that's why Jeff didn't come in?"

"Right. He said, 'Is Melissa going to freak out when she finds out I let you drive my car?' And I said I honestly didn't know. So he said, 'I'm going to let you and Melissa deal with this, big guy.'"

"I see." She mulled over this latest development and its implications. Jeff had two vehicles—a four-wheel drive, which he used for camping trips and youth group outings; and his "nice" car, a mid-size luxury sedan that he drove to work and church. Toward the latter, he had a more protective attitude; he certainly wouldn't let just anybody drive it. "Which car was it?"

"His nice car."

He had let Kraig drive it, splinted finger and all. It was a sign of the deepening friendship between the two, and she couldn't have been more thrilled.

"I suppose Dave has let you drive his car?"

"Sure. Many times. On the road, too. Late at night, though, when no one's around."

"I see. Well...you can tell Jeff I'm not mad at him."

Melissa went to sleep that night feeling greatly encouraged about Kraig's physical and social health, and more empowered to find a solution to the problem with Shanna. Some time during the night, an idea came to her. In the morning, as she showered, she composed a notice for the Women's Fellowship newsletter at church, to be included in that Sunday's bulletin.

"Dear Ladies of Oak Hill Bible Church,

"As many of you know, I have brought my new husband, Kraig, to live with me here in Oak Hill. As he works at home, he has few social contacts outside of church and choir. Would a few of you be willing to encourage your husbands to provide him with some fellowship?

"Kraig has a guide dog and is relatively independent. If any man of Oak Hill Bible Church would be willing to get together with him for Bible study, prayer, social activities, or anything, we would both be very grateful. Kraig has many interests and is fun to be with.

"Thank you!

"Melissa (formerly Melvin) Crane-Dobrovsky."

Of course, she told him what she'd done, so when the phone calls came, he'd know what was going on.

Monday morning, after the item had appeared in the Sunday bulletin, the phone started ringing. By week's end, a number of potential companions had come forward. Several offered to pick him up for choir practice and neighborhood Bible studies; a guy Kraig's age who owned a business in town wanted to meet for lunch any time Kraig could get into town; a retired man would be delighted to come over once a week for one-on-one prayer. He even got an invitation to learn to play golf.

"Are you going to do it?" Melissa asked.

"I might. But this probably isn't a good time to learn a new activity that's going to take me away from home that much. Once you get started, I hear, it becomes an obsession."

"Yeah, maybe when we're older. And I had another idea. Sometimes my office gets writing projects that are beyond the scope of what we do, and we have to turn them away. I bet you could get some work that way…maybe come in once a week. It'd get you and Shanna out of the house."

"That's an idea. I'll think about it. I have some other ideas I'm working on, too. Life is good, Melissa."

It was true, and it became truer over the next few weeks. Kraig was busy and fit, and he was becoming part of the community. Shanna was getting practice. The cats learned to stay out of Kraig's way when he walked across a room, although they trusted him as long as he provided a lap. Wedding pictures were chosen; Melissa's favorite close-up was enlarged and hung in the dining room. The splint would come off soon.

Next time she saw Jeff, he looked a little sheepish when she mentioned the driving incident. "No, really," she said. "I want him to have fun. How are things with Suzanne?"

He cast his eyes downward again. "You know…in praying about it, I came to realize that the main problem was *me*. The fact is…I've been flaky about attending church since you last saw me at Oak Hill Bible. Trying to explain the difference between believers and non-believers is difficult if you're not setting a good example. You're going to start seeing me on Sunday mornings again, starting this Sunday. If she doesn't come with me, it's over. But that, too, will be an answer to prayer if it's meant to be. So... thanks for praying."

The only bad news was what came over the phone when Dave called. Melissa began to feel sad and afraid whenever the phone rang and it turned out to be Dave.

§

Chapter 19

Dave always sounded cheerful when she talked to him, and Melissa was certain he was giving Kraig the worst news, letting him filter it for her. One time, when Kraig went to answer the phone, she heard him say, "Accident? What kind of accident?... Oh. Thank God she's all right." His voice returned to normal volume and she couldn't hear the rest. A few minutes later, when he came to find her, she asked.

"What happened to Judy?"

"It wasn't Judy. It was Helen." He sat next to her on the couch. "She backed her car into her mailbox. She wasn't hurt. But apparently this wasn't the first mishap. She's giving up her driver's license."

"Oh, dear. And I bet Judy isn't driving much, either, since the falling incident at Christmas."

"I think you're right."

Melissa leaned into him. "I wish we could do more for them."

"We could. If we were there."

"There must be people at church who help with these kinds of things. *Our* church has people who volunteer to help with shopping and driving to appointments and things."

"Sure, they do too. But...it's not the same, you know. Helen and Dave are the people who were there for me all these years. Now *I'm* the one with the abundance. I feel as if I should be giving back more."

Melissa didn't know what to say. She could just see her watercolor of the Maine coast from where she sat, hanging on the dining room wall. When they moved to Maine, she thought with a twinge of guilt, they would be *farther* away from the important people in Kraig's life. But...being a family was the most important thing, wasn't it? *And we've both wanted to move to Maine for so long....*

She resolved to be bolder about coaxing the bad news from Dave. It was the least she could do to help Kraig bear the sorrow of not being there to help.

"We're looking forward to the rafting trip," she told Dave next time she talked to him. "I hope everything's going as planned?"

267

"Yes, right on schedule. It's hard to believe four months will have gone by since we last saw each other."

"I know. Kraig really misses you."

"He has a family now, I understand that, Melissa. Don't worry about us. Oh, did I tell you we got Judy a pair of cats?"

"No! Tell me about them."

"I heard it was your idea to get two. Well, we went to the shelter, and there was this pair of cats turned in by the former owner for some reason, ready-made for Judy, it seemed. One short-haired tuxedo cat, one long-haired orange and white, both young adult females. Chessie and Lily. Judy is enjoying their companionship very much. So we thank you for the idea."

"I'm so glad."

"So, what have you two been up to? I usually talk to Kraig, so maybe you have a different take on things."

"Oh, everything's fine. We've signed up to take ballroom dancing lessons. I'm *so* looking forward to it. And Jeff says Kraig is doing well with the running. They're getting to be pretty good friends."

"I heard about the driving." Dave laughed. "I guess I should have told you Kraig has this daredevil race-car driver in him. But he said you were gracious about it."

"Oh, I'm just glad he's having fun with guy friends. It was hard, at first, watching him give up so much of his independence. Now the only hard thing to watch him deal with is…never seeing you."

"Melissa…I know it's difficult for you to watch Judy suffer from a distance. But I want you to remember that nothing is going to happen to her that hasn't passed through God's loving hands. We value your friendship a lot. We wish you were closer, but that just isn't the way it is. Try not to worry, okay?"

"I'll try not to."

§

For Melissa, time passed ever faster as the days and weeks went by. Jessica turned sixteen in May. Soon, the school year was over, and one warm summer evening, the four of them were at the Portland airport, searching the crowd for Dave.

"There he is!" Melissa said, hearing the emotion in her own voice.

Dave had already spotted them. "Buddy," he said, grabbing Kraig in a powerful bear hug. "My gosh, Melissa, he looks great. Have you lost weight, buddy, or is your wife just dressing you better?"

"Both," Kraig answered, without missing a beat.

"And Melissa, you look...younger every time I see you." He sighed deeply as he hugged her, and she felt in his embrace unspoken volumes. "Jessica, Emily. Oh...my...goodness. Kraig, you are one lucky guy." He shook his head before embracing the girls one at a time. "And Shanna, the world's most pampered dog." He bent and hugged her too.

"Where's Judy?" Melissa asked.

"She's back at my place. And she's fine. Mostly. You'll see her soon. Let's go get your baggage. If memory serves, Melissa is a, should I say, very *thorough* packer, so I'm not going to be surprised if we have to make two trips." He winked at her.

"You can carry our new two-bedroom tent," Kraig said.

"I'd feel honored to carry your new two-bedroom tent."

At his car, as Dave finished heaving things into the trunk and slammed it shut, he said, "You know, Kraig buddy, I've been doing a lot of thinking, in these last five minutes since you got off the plane. When our single adults' class sees you, and how good you look, and how *happy* you look...not to mention how happy your *wife* looks...I wouldn't be surprised if there's a mass exodus out of the class. You know what I mean? Everyone's going to see that I've been deceiving them all these years about the joys of singlehood and rush to get married. But you know what? That wouldn't be such a bad thing at all. In September, I'm retiring from teaching the group, and wouldn't that work out just great if there was no group to teach after that anyway."

Melissa held her breath as Dave swung open the door to his townhouse, wondering how Judy would look, wondering if her reaction would show.

"Sweetie, we're here," Dave said.

Judy came from the kitchen where she had been putting together some snacks. "Hey, you guys!" She held out her arms as if to embrace them all at once.

Melissa stepped forward. "Judy!" She hugged her—gently—then stepped back to take a better look. "Hey, you look great."

Judy's hair had grown a couple more inches and shone with a healthy sheen. She looked fit and, as far as Melissa could tell, generally well. She watched Kraig hug her, certain that she would learn more from Kraig's reaction that by any other means. She could ask him later what he thought.

"Okay, people," Dave said, "we can get something to eat as soon as you all get settled. Kraig and Melissa, you're in my room... girls, you're in the spare bedroom; you can flip a coin for who gets the trundle...Shanna can sleep wherever she wants. I'll run over and get Judy early in the morning, so the four of you can spread out and use both bathrooms.... Melissa? When you're ready, how about you and I finish getting some snacks together, so we can let Judy take it easy. We can order pizza later. No one will go to bed hungry."

Joining him in the kitchen, Melissa saw that he had an assortment of wholesome snacks—whole-grain crackers, good cheese, gourmet tortilla chips, homemade salsa, vegetables and tofu dip, cut fruit, nuts. "California food," she said.

He nodded. "Can't argue with that. I like to keep this kind of food handy, so when Judy's here, she doesn't have to do any work to get something good to eat. You know how it is, sometimes when you're tired *and* hungry, you'll eat anything. We need to avoid that."

"So, is Judy going to move in here when you get married?"

"At first. Later we want to get a house somewhere. By the way, I meant what I said about Kraig looking good. I've never seen him so happy and healthy."

"Well, I think married life is good for him. He's very easy to live with, too."

"Those adjustment issues pretty much in the past now?"

"I'd say totally. You and Judy will be just as happy." Just then Judy came in to help carry things to the living room. "Judy, congratulations," Melissa said. "I forgot to say that. Congratulations. That's so exciting, about the wedding."

Judy went to Dave's side and put her arms around him; he kissed her forehead in return. "What's ready for me to take?"

"Here, sweetie," Dave said, handing her a bowl of tortilla chips—the lightest thing available—and it was then that Melissa saw Judy's hands tremble.

After Judy left the kitchen, Melissa turned to Dave and looked into his eyes.

He nodded, acknowledging her unspoken question, but didn't say anything for a moment, and she had a sinking feeling that much was being left unsaid. "One day at a time. The best thing you can do is pray for us." He hugged her briefly, and for the first time in her life, Melissa felt a pang of guilt about her good health.

Conversation flowed as the snacks disappeared. Dave ordered pizza, but before it arrived, Judy said she was tired and wanted to go home.

"I'm sorry, sweetie; what was I thinking? I should have ordered the pizza sooner."

"No, it's okay, I'm not that hungry. I just need to go to bed so I can get up early."

Dave dug some bills out of his pocket. "Here, buddy, tip the pizza guy. I gave them my credit card number, so it's paid for. Don't wait for me. Be back in twenty." He helped Judy put on her sweater and waved as he went out the door.

"We'll get Dave to fill us in when he gets back," Kraig said, reading Melissa's thoughts.

"What impression did you get when you hugged her?"

"She has a tremor of some sort. From what I know, it's a common symptom."

The pizza arrived just minutes before Dave returned.

"Dave," Kraig said carefully, "I don't know if this is what you wanted to talk about, but it's what everyone's thinking about. How is Judy, really? The *whole* truth, please."

"First, everybody get a piece of pizza on your plate. Second, we pray. *Then* we'll talk about Judy."

A minute later, Dave was still fiddling with the placement of his pizza slice on his plate. "You know, I really don't know that much more than you do. MS is such an unpredictable condition. Her symptoms could disappear entirely for long periods of time. She could get worse, then better. She might live to a ripe old age. She might not.

"We *do* know that we should plan on not having any children. Biological ones, I mean. She's always wanted to adopt, anyway, so that's not a big deal. Probably an older child, who doesn't need to be carried around. Oh," he said, looking at Melissa

271

and the girls, "we're checking into the assistance dog idea. That would give me some peace of mind.

"I have some other ideas in the works, too. I'd like to start a consulting business and work out of home. When we get a house, I'll have a home office. Then I'd be nearby if she needed me. I have enough energy for two people. I figure God made me that way for a reason. I can't tell you how grateful I am for your friendship. All of you. That's the best thing …just knowing you're there, and that you care." Dave looked around at them, and Melissa felt tears fill her eyes, as Dave looked not too far from the verge of tears himself. No one spoke, as Dave looked as if he had more to tell.

"I've loved Judy as long as I can remember," he went on, smiling wistfully. "When she came into my Sunday school class eleven years ago…there were several new faces at that time, young people who'd just graduated from college…I asked each of them to go up and introduce themselves. Judy went last. The others all had ambitions that revolved around career goals, timelines for owning things…then Judy gets up there and talks about her desire to go to the mission field. She grew up on the mission field, you know… various parts of Africa…among some of the most deprived people on the planet. And that's what she wanted to go back to.

"I thought…*this is what I want*. This girl just glowed, just radiated God's love for His neediest people. And I thought, if I can't have *her*, maybe I'm meant to stay single. All the years that she was gone, I never prayed for her to come home. That would've been selfish and wrong. I only asked God to make His will clear. In my letters to her, I never hinted at any romantic feelings. I just wanted to be a friend, a confidant, a fellow laborer." He was quiet as he fiddled with his pizza slice.

Melissa dared to speak. "I think that's what she fell in love with. And if you don't mind my saying so, I think it was only fairly recently that she finally figured out what your feelings for her really are."

He nodded. "Well. I didn't mean to make such a big speech. But I want you all to know that, whatever the future holds, I'm going to be a better person for what I will have gone through with Judy. I've led a pretty charmed life. Judy has much to teach me. She's the easiest-to-please person I've ever known. Any little thing you do for her, she acts like you've just given her the world on a silver platter.

"I'm thankful for every day God gives us together. And I'm doubly thankful for every *good* day He gives us together. Come to think of it...*every* day He gives us is a good day. Everything else is pure cream." He looked down at his untouched pizza slice, and around at everyone else's empty plate. "Looks like I'm going to have to microwave this. Be right back. Have another piece, everybody."

During the minute or so that Dave was gone, Melissa leaned to Kraig and whispered, "I have *never* felt so humbled."

"I know what you mean," he whispered back.

Melissa looked at her daughters and realized they'd just witnessed a priceless life sermon.

§

She could still feel the motion of the river as she settled down to sleep Saturday night. Memories of Kraig's beaming face appeared before her; thanks to Dave's foresight and thoughtfulness in getting some waterproof disposable cameras to pass around, she even had some of those smiles captured on film. She chuckled aloud as she pressed close to him in their new double sleeping bag.

"What, babe?" Kraig said, semi-awake.

"I was just thinking about how much fun you were having. How do you feel now?"

"Pleasantly exhausted...clean...comfortable...well-fed... pretty perfect. What about you? Are you glad we came?"

"Totally. Thanks to your contagious enthusiasm."

"Are the girls in?"

"Emily is. Jessica's at the campfire surrounded by a bunch of college guys. Looks like they're all enjoying themselves. Dave said he'd keep an eye on things."

"He'll be the last one to bed...and the first one up. I'd bet money on it."

"Mm." She snuggled closer, arranging her feet around Shanna.

"Babe? Lean over so you can hear me, will you?"
She did.

"Have you ever made love in a sleeping bag?"

"No. Never have."

"What do you think?"

273

"I think we have an eleven-year-old daughter on the other side of a very thin nylon wall, and that this isn't the right time."

"Mm. You're right of course. But it was fun to think about it."

"Rain check. Night, honey, I love you."

It seemed only a few minutes had passed, so soundly had she slept, but Melissa could tell by the glow on the tent wall that the sun was well up. Next, she heard footsteps, which is probably what had awakened her. Then, some very loud gospel music boomed through camp; so sudden and unexpected was it that she burst into laughter.

"What in heaven's name?" Kraig mumbled.

"I'm guessing this is how Dave gets people out of bed on the Sunday morning of a rafting trip."

"Ah," Kraig said, rolling over. "My arms are sore. What do you say we ask him to bring us breakfast in bed?"

"Yeah. *That'll* fly."

After breakfast, Dave led an informal worship service; Kraig led some hymn singing. Then there were a couple of hours of unscheduled time. Melissa sat at a picnic table, people watching, a cup of coffee to warm her hands. It was one of those Northwest summer mornings that were so common, yet so rare for her in Oak Hill—chilly and foggy. Kraig straddled the bench, facing her, a cup of coffee warming his hands too.

Dave and Judy stood a few yards away. She had her hands held out for his examination, possibly to see if the tremor had lessened since yesterday. Melissa couldn't hear their conversation over the roar of the river, nor would she have wanted to violate their privacy by eavesdropping, but just watching them gave her a warm, fuzzy feeling. She smiled, not noticing she'd said "hmm" out loud until Kraig reacted.

"What, babe?"

"I'm just watching Dave and Judy. And thinking about what he said last night. You know, I think she's finally figured out that he's not a hero or a demigod. Just a guy who loves her and will be there for her."

"Just an ordinary—an *extraordinary* ordinary guy who loves her and will be there for her."

"Judy and I have a lot in common."

Kraig turned to her with an odd expression.

274

"At least one *big* thing—being loved by two of the sweetest, classiest gentlemen the world has ever known."

He smiled, and she took his hand, savoring the heaviness of it in hers. He shook his head and got that modest, shy look that made her consider, for a moment, abandoning her cup of coffee and taking him by the hand back to the warmth and privacy of the tent.

"And to think that the guy you fell in love with," he said, "the guy on the beach in Maine last summer—was definitely not the best version of me. God is merciful."

She leaned in to kiss him. Finishing that, she looked up to see Dave and Judy watching *them*. Dave turned to say something to Judy, then came toward them. He pulled over a folding chair to complete a triangle. "It's been a great weekend, hasn't it? I'm so glad the four of you came. It's been tons of fun being together again. Lots of people have come to me and commented on how happy you seem as a couple and as a family. I owe you a lot for setting such a good example."

"I'm so glad we came," Melissa said.

"But now, it is, sadly, time to get ready to go."

"It won't be so long this time," Kraig said. "Two months, we'll be back for your wedding. And looking forward to it."

"Me too." He slapped Kraig's knee. "Now, let's go fold up that new two-bedroom tent of yours. If I don't take you to visit Helen while you're here, she'll never speak to me again. Oh, and speaking of speaking…you're going to have to yell a little. She's lost quite a bit of her hearing in the time you've been gone."

§

Chapter 20

It was that part of the summer in Oak Hill that Melissa thought of as the doldrums—an endless procession of hot, dry days, with no end in sight. It hadn't rained in a couple of months, and the hills were brown and parched. And, just like every year, she yearned for any hint of fall—a cloud, a breeze, a wisp of fog.

"Is this weather *normal?*" Kraig asked.

"Normal for Oak Hill. I bet Maine is green right now."

"Oregon too."

"The first anniversary of the day we met is coming up."

"We'll have to celebrate."

"I wish we could celebrate in the *place* we met."

At the end of July, they went on a camping trip Jeff had planned. Jeff had been confident he could persuade Matt to come, although Melissa wasn't nearly so sure. As it turned out, Jeff was right: Matt took off a couple days from his job at a sporting goods store near college and came home.

"Whoa, check this out," Jeff said upon seeing Matt, "this guy is taller than Kraig!" And it was true—Matt was now six-foot-four.

Jeff, remembering Matt's nineteenth birthday in the middle of July, hosted an impromptu little party in the mountains, complete with a cake he baked in a reflector oven over the campfire. Melissa, remembering that Jeff's forty-third birthday had been in *early* July, insisted they sing "Happy Birthday" a second time. Suzanne didn't go along, but her son Brent did, and Melissa observed, over the course of the weekend, that Matt seemed quite comfortable in sort of a big-brother role.

Dave and Judy's wedding was approaching.

"We need to pray for Judy," Kraig said one evening at bedtime.

"We *have* been. Every day."

"We need to be more specific. Let's pray that she'll have... let's say, one good week. From her wedding day, one week forward, that she'll have no symptoms."

"Okay. Do you know where they're going for their honeymoon?"

"Last I heard, they were considering the islands of Lanai and Molokai; Costa Rica; and the Virgin Islands. They've set aside two weeks for it."

On the last Saturday of summer, Melissa sat in the second pew of Dave and Judy's church—Kraig's former church—in Portland. She, Jessica, and Emily had new emerald green dresses for their roles as guest book and gift table attendants. Kraig looked so impossibly handsome in his best man attire, Melissa had to remind herself, as she clutched one of Kraig's handkerchiefs, that it was Dave and Judy's wedding day. Of course, the groom too was handsome.

As the processional started, Melissa rose, with the rest of the assemblage, to catch the first glimpse of the bride. Judy was indeed beautiful, glowing as she strode, straight and steady, down the aisle on her father's arm.

Melissa had been pleased with her impressions of Dave's and Judy's parents. Jim Budd was lean and bespectacled, with arresting blue eyes and deep laugh lines, like an older version of Dave himself; his wife Lenore was also tall and youthful looking. Dave's sisters, Amanda and Brenda—Judy's only attendants—were just as Kraig had described them: tall, slim beauties, one brunette and one blonde.

George and Charlotte Breuner appeared to be older, and wore the wise, world-weary expressions of people who had seen a lot, yet they impressed her as being completely open and genuine. All of them were warm and welcoming.

It was Judy's brother Kurt who had been the biggest surprise. Melissa remembered hearing Judy say at Christmas that he was sixteen, yet for some reason she'd still pictured a young boy. She could see now, as he stood on the platform, that Kurt was nearly as tall as Dave at six-foot-one.

The ceremony began. Several times, Melissa realized that instead of following the ceremony, she had fixed her gaze upon her own handsome groom of six months; thankfully, the videographer would capture it all. She made a mental note to get a copy of the finished product.

Melissa held her breath. Dave had approached Kraig early on about singing the song he'd recorded for *their* wedding—live. "I think I can do it," he'd said, determination showing in his expression. Now, he had the microphone and the intro was playing. She prayed that he'd make it through—and that if *she* started crying, it wouldn't be so loud as to disrupt the ceremony. A couple of times, Dave turned toward her; once he winked.

Kraig had done it. The song was over. Melissa dared to look around her; many were in tears. It was almost too much—Judy looking well, in answer to their prayers; the abundant love between the wedding couple; her own incomprehensible good fortune in having found Kraig and married him in so short a time, only to fall more in love with him each day.

The ceremony ended; the wedding party filed out, Kraig with Amanda on his arm. Taking Shanna, Melissa met him in the foyer; the girls went ahead to the reception.

"Go get that baby," Kraig was saying to Amanda. "I'll hold him while you stand in the receiving line."

She laughed as she agreed, swinging her shimmering hair over her shoulder as she headed toward the church nursery.

"This is the baby she had January eighth," Kraig explained. "Nathan. He's eight and a half months old now."

"They don't need you in the receiving line?"

"No, family only. I think Dave thought he was doing me a favor. He's right. I'd much rather hold his nephew."

"Here he is, Kraig," Amanda said, returning with a very healthy-looking baby boy. Melissa studied Amanda's face for clues as to how she felt about turning over her child to Kraig's temporary care, but it was obvious: no doubt whatsoever.

As they sat at a little table in the fellowship hall, Kraig bouncing Nathan on his knee, Melissa scanned the room for her daughters. She found them, circulating among the guests, in that timid way that young people do when they feel alone in a crowd. She saw Kurt, too, mugging for the camera—cheek-to-cheek with Judy; with Dave, his arm around Dave in a pretend headlock; horsing around with Amanda's four-year-old daughter and Brenda's three-year-old son; between his parents, towering over them both. And what a presence he had—his café-au-lait complexion; dark, wavy hair; deep brown eyes framed by dark lashes; and one of those smiles that begin on one side and spread to the other, ultimately revealing a set of dazzling white teeth. And smile he did—a lot.

"What do you know about Kurt?" she asked Kraig.

He frowned, trying to recall. "The Breuners adopted him when he was five or six. You knew that much. But before that… orphaned as a toddler, then cared for by an elderly relative, then—mercifully—abandoned at the mission. Not a good beginning. And he was a mixed-race child, with a white father of unknown identity."

"Aha!" she said, for that explained Kurt's color.

"There were some other sordid details that I might be able to recall if I thought about it. But I'd rather not just now."

"Well, whatever horrible beginning he might have had, he seems to have overcome it. What a doll."

"Hmm," Kraig said, and he had that expression that made Melissa think she'd give a great deal to know what he was thinking. "What are the girls doing now?"

She looked around again. "They seem to be hovering around watching the photographer. Oh, now…it looks like *they're* being photographed." She chuckled, watching them. "*Oh,* now, *this* is interesting…the photographer is grouping them with Kurt. Both of them with him…now just Jessica…now just Emily. All with huge smiles."

"Hmm," he said again.

Soon the girls were coming toward them. "The photographer wanted to take our picture," Emily said.

"He wants you, too," Jessica said. "Kraig with the wedding party, then both of you together."

"As anyone can see," Kraig said, "*I* am holding a baby."

"He has plenty of pictures to take," Melissa said. "He'll come and get us when he needs us."

The girls took seats and joined them at the table. "I'll hold Nathan when you go," Jessica said.

"I want a turn too," Emily said.

"And to think, just yesterday, they were fighting over *you*, Shanna," Kraig sighed.

Jessica and Emily were looking around the room. Melissa saw Jessica sign the word "cute" to Emily. "*Who's* cute?" she asked.

They both turned to her with horrified looks, then tipped their heads toward the subject of their attention. She looked where they indicated, and there, not much to her surprise, was Kurt. A moment later, they tried to look absolutely oblivious as he came toward them, carrying a couple of baskets. Arriving at their table, he nodded to acknowledge Melissa and Kraig, then turned to the girls. "Jessica and Emily, Dave and Judy thought you would like to help pass out favors." He offered each a basket, which were filled with little lace bags of birdseed. They looked at each other, then at Melissa as they got up to go with Kurt.

She watched them go before she spoke. "Well, they seem quite smitten."

"Hmm," Kraig said a third time.

"Too bad they'll probably never see each other again. Tomorrow we go back to California...he goes back to South Africa...."

"Ah, but God alone knows the future," Kraig said.

Melissa watched the girls move around the room, seeming to waver between wanting to stay with Kurt and not wanting to be too obvious about it.

"I can hardly wait to see these pictures," Melissa said.

§

Chapter 21

"Melissa!" Dave practically yelled over the phone. "Did you get our postcard from St. Thomas?"

"Dave! Yes we did! It sounded like you were having a great time!"

"We did. We had an absolutely, completely, totally wonderful time. Hey, get Kraig over here. He didn't tell me being married was *this* much fun."

"Yes he did," Melissa laughed. "I heard him."

Melissa got an enormous lift out of hearing Kraig's end of the conversation; Dave's joy was so overflowing that she relived those heady times in the first week of her marriage to Kraig. And so it continued, for a couple of weeks, and life was better than it had ever been before. None of what Dave had to share could be construed as bad news about Judy.

Until one evening when Kraig answered the phone, and his voice was low, so that Melissa couldn't hear what he said from where she was, reading on the couch. She closed her eyes and prayed while Kraig talked to Dave. A few minutes later he came.

"What's the news?" she asked.

He sat next to her and put his arms around her, holding her tight. "Judy's pregnant."

That was about the last thing Melissa expected. "Oh! I thought they weren't...."

"They weren't. I don't know the details, Melissa; it didn't seem right to ask. But the baby's a reality now." He didn't speak for a moment; neither did she. "I guess they really enjoyed their honeymoon," he said at last.

The irony of it was too much. She had to laugh. But that was all right. Kraig laughed too.

So, their daily prayers became more intense, more focused. *Please help Judy and the baby to make it...not just survive, but thrive. And please give Dave enough strength for all three of them.*

Fall finally came to Oak Hill, around Kraig's fortieth birthday.

One Friday evening, Melissa found herself restless and distracted. Kraig was down in his office, working on something of apparent great urgency, having taken a break for dinner and then gone back to it. That was unusual for him, as they usually spent evenings relaxing together. And she had especially looked forward to it.

"Do you *have* to finish it tonight?" she'd asked at dinner.

"Yes, Melissa, it's called a deadline," he'd answered. The sarcasm, too, was rare for him, and she couldn't help wonder what was going on.

Casting about for something to do, she found herself gazing at the watercolor of the coast of Maine. Opposite the sideboard from it was the wedding portrait—her favorite among them. She faced the camera with a huge grin, and Kraig's face was turned toward her, as though he were about to kiss her—or perhaps tell her a secret. She smiled, remembering the occasion.

She looked again at her seascape. Something was not right. *Oh, no!* The grains of sand, which she had so painstakingly placed in the watercolor to make it sparkle where the sun shone through the beach glass, were gone. They must have come loose and fallen down into the frame. She carefully began to lift the frame off the hooks. Then she changed her mind. She probably wouldn't be able fix it anyway, and the wall would look so bare without it. It didn't matter that much.

She began to wonder if Kraig had fallen asleep at his desk, and considered going down to see…but decided against it. She went back to the couch with a stack of mail she'd set aside over the week and began to sort through it. Some time after nine o'clock, she heard the office door downstairs close and Kraig's footsteps on the outside stairs. Then the kitchen door opened and closed. "Melissa?"

"Couch," she said, trying to sound nonchalant.

He came in and sat beside her. "I'm sorry, babe. I just mismanaged my time and didn't get it done when I should have. I'll try not to let that happen again."

"That's okay."

"Thanks." He settled deeper into the couch.

"I've been thinking about Maine a lot," she said. "Now that things have sort of settled down, do you think we could start thinking seriously about moving?"

"To Maine?" he said, as if it were a brand-new idea.

"Yes, to Maine. That's what I've wanted to do as long as you've known me."

He got that deeply thoughtful look, and she got a feeling that whatever he was thinking was not going to be what she wanted to hear. "Melissa, I truly hate to say this, but I have a feeling about Judy. I know people live for years with MS…and she might. Of course I'd love to be wrong. And how much Helen had gone downhill when we saw her over the summer…was truly shocking. You must have seen that."

"Yeah," she said, annoyed that he'd changed the subject, but not wanting to sound selfish by pointing it out.

"Melissa, if you really think about this, you'll see what's the right thing to do."

She was beginning to figure it out. "Oh. I will, will I? And since when do you have a monopoly on what's the right thing to do?"

"Melissa?" He looked genuinely hurt. "That was uncharacteristically unkind."

"Okay. I'm sorry. But what are you talking about?"

"Think about it, Melissa."

She thought about it, but didn't want to say it. "I guess you're talking about not moving to Maine. So why don't you just say that?"

"Because I want you to see it yourself."

"Why is it that what *I* want to do is not important?" She heard her voice rise to a shrill pitch.

"Calm down, Melissa. I won't fight with you. When you calm down, we'll talk."

"*We'll* talk? Or *you'll* talk, and I'll just say 'okay' to whatever you say?"

He didn't answer, and she began to shake as she tried not to cry. She really, truly did not want to cry right now. But she couldn't stop herself. She heard a sob escape. That was all it took. Kraig put his arms around her, and she could feel that he really loved her.

"Melissa. This isn't about what I want, either. It's about what's the right thing to do."

"Which means, you think we should move to Oregon."

"I do. That's the right thing to do right now."

She felt more relaxed as she leaned into him. "I remember, way back when we first met, you said 'people are more important than places.' So… I guess that's what this is about."

285

"It is, Melissa. The people who were there for me all those years…need *us* now. I have you. I have everything I need. And it's *my* turn to give from *my* abundance. The girls will come with us, and Matt is already gone, so it'll make no difference to him. Let's pray about it. All right? I want us both to be happy with what we decide to do."

Melissa drifted off to sleep that night snug against his back, as usual, with her arm around him. She wanted to be angry with him, yet she couldn't. She couldn't find an iota of fault with anything he'd said, because he was thinking of others, not himself. She waited until she was sure he was asleep, then let a few tears slide from her eyes. He still might awaken, as she recalled, smiling to herself, that although he'd told her before they married that he usually wore a t-shirt to bed, he never had, since that very first night. It was always his bare back that she fell asleep against.

Some time during the night, she had a dream. It wasn't much of a dream, just a scene that lasted no more than a couple seconds. But in it, she saw Kraig seated on a train or a bus, she wasn't sure, except that she wasn't beside him, but rather standing on the platform. He didn't even turn toward her as the conveyance began to move and he slipped away from her. She tried to scream his name, and that was when she awoke with a start and realized it was only a dream. Kraig was there beside her and all was well. Except that they wouldn't be moving to Maine.

In the morning, when she awoke, Kraig was gone. Being sure it was Saturday, she wondered where he could be, until she heard him in the kitchen. A moment later, he came up the stairs with cups of coffee.

"Babe?"

"Hi, honey." She sat up.

He sat on the side of the bed and handed her a cup. As he did so, his hand rested on hers for a moment, as though to see how she felt about things before he brought up the topic of the night before. "Are we all right?" he asked.

She felt tears come to her eyes again, not so much tears of sadness over not moving to Maine as tears of joy that she had the love of this wonderful man. "I just want to be with you," she said. "I wanted to move to Maine. *So* badly, for *so* long. But more than that I want to be with you. That's all that matters."

"It'll be the right thing. You'll see. And it doesn't have to be forever. We could still move to Maine some day. Melissa, I had an idea." He was starting to sound excited. "We'll go to Maine. Next summer...maybe sooner. We'll buy a piece of property on a lake. We still have the money from my townhouse—we can do that. Then you'll believe I mean it when I say we can move there some day. What do you say?"

"Yeah," she said, her voice quivering. "I'd like that."

"I had some other ideas, too, Melissa. We can do great things. You know, I worked for the newspaper all those years because I liked going out every day and being with people. Everyone always told me that I could do much better working independently, but I was a single guy, and the money didn't matter to me as much as the fellowship.

"It's different now. I have a family. Not that you weren't getting along fine without me. But...I'm not just responsible for myself anymore, and I can do better. It takes me less than a minute to walk from the kitchen door to my office. I'm at my desk by seven o'clock every morning. Writing my column for the newspaper doesn't take all my time. Even with the other articles I'm doing for other publications. I'd like to expand my business and take on other writing jobs. You said you thought there's a market for that.

"And Melissa—there's more. You could do the same thing. Maybe after I get established, you'll feel confident about being an independent graphic artist. Think of it. We could be a team—an artist and a writer. Then we could live anywhere we want. Even on a lake in Maine.

"But in the meantime...we need to be in Oregon. We don't have to be in the city. We'll get a house outside of town, out in the country. Maybe on the west side, so we could go to the beach sometimes. How could this not be the right thing?"

She couldn't argue with a word of it. "It is," she said.

"I *do* want you to be happy, Melissa."

"I am."

"But...let's not tell Dave and Judy for a while. Let's wait and see how things develop."

"Let's."

§

Matt came home for Christmas and went skiing with Jeff and Brent. Kraig had been invited—whose idea that was, Melissa didn't know—but declined. "I'd just slow them down," he'd said. "But it was nice of them to think of me."

Jeff and Suzanne became engaged and set a wedding date in April. Jeff asked Kraig and Matt to stand with him, along with Brent; Jeff's brother Gary, now the nationally known director of a conservative family-advocacy organization, as best man; and Bob—the mutual friend who'd told Jeff about Melissa's engagement to Kraig. Jeff also asked Kraig to sing his song again. "No problem," he said.

Judy seemed to be doing as well as could reasonably be expected, although she was exhausted all the time and could work only a few hours a day. Dave urged her to quit her job at the bookstore, but she feared being lonely and idle, already unable to drive. The store manager reassigned Judy from floor sales to bookkeeping so she could spend most of her time in the comfortable chair Dave got for her to use at work.

Melissa spent more time on the phone with them than Kraig did these days, finding new joy in being able to share the experience with Judy. She learned that Judy was scheduled to have a Cesarean delivery two weeks before the actual due date—the first week of June instead of the third.

Kraig and Melissa celebrated their first anniversary by spending the weekend at a bed-and-breakfast at Lake Tahoe, leaving Shanna home with the girls. Jessica, now almost seventeen, insisted that she and Emily would be fine on their own. Kraig had agreed, so Melissa went along with it.

"So, are we just an old married couple now?" she asked him.

"No way. Still on our honeymoon." He'd ordered some purple irises and had them delivered to their room at the inn on Sunday, their actual anniversary. She cried tears of happiness.

Jeff and Suzanne were married on a breezy spring day under a Winslow Homer sky. Jeff's family, whom Melissa had not seen in years, greeted her like a long-lost friend. Jeff promised he'd still have time to go running with Kraig.

"Your friendship has meant a lot to him," Melissa told Kraig. "You've been such a good role model...I think that's what made the difference in his relationship with Suzanne."

One evening near the beginning of May, Kraig answered the phone. "Dave," he began, cheerfully enough. Then he didn't say anything for a long time, and the silence was filled with such tension that Melissa just froze, anxious to find out what it was about. From Kraig's posture, it was really impossible to tell whether it was good news or bad, and a strange, uneasy feeling came over her. She went to Kraig's side.

He gave only an occasional one-syllable response, as though Dave were talking non-stop. After a while, Kraig reached for her, pressing her to his side, and she felt reassured that whatever it was would turn out to be more good than bad. "All right, we will," Kraig said at last. "Go back to your wife. She needs you. Thanks for thinking of us in the midst of the craziness. Call us again when things settle down a bit.... Love you too. Tell Judy we love her."

Melissa snatched the receiver from his hand and hung it up. "What?" she demanded.

"I need to sit down," Kraig said, taking a few deep breaths.

"Sit! Talk! What happened?" She grabbed a chair and faced him.

"Judy had the baby. She went into labor while she was at work...someone at the bookstore took her to the hospital...Dave met her there...they couldn't stop the contractions...the baby went into fetal distress...they delivered her by emergency Cesarean...Judy's going to be fine...the baby's fine. And it's a girl."

"Wow."

"Seven weeks early. Four pounds, three ounces. Dave said she was *so tiny*...think of that, Melissa. A baby can be that small and still be all right. My God, what a miracle."

"So...what did they name her?"

"He didn't say, and I didn't think to ask. *You* can talk next time. You'd know all the questions to ask."

Next morning, as they finished praying, Melissa could hardly wait to find out the latest news. "Do you think you should call Dave this morning?"

"No...I imagine he's either busy, or getting some rest. We'll let him call us."

"Okay. But call me right away if you *do* hear from him." She kissed him and left for work.

They were eating dinner when the phone rang.

"You get it," Kraig said.

"Melissa!" Dave said. "Hey, I'm sure you're eating dinner, but I knew you'd all be on pins and needles till you heard from us again."

"We are. You sound happy and tired."

"I am. Elated and exhausted—exactly that."

"So what's the baby's name?"

"That's one thing we need to talk about. Judy and I want Kraig to name her."

"Oh! Well, I'm sure he'd be delighted to."

"Tell him to get right on it, okay? When Judy comes to her senses, she's going to want something to call the baby."

"Sure will. So how are Judy and the baby doing?"

"Ahh," he sighed. "Judy's pretty wiped out. She'll have to stay in the hospital for a few days. The baby will have to stay longer. Nursing is difficult. Just holding the baby is difficult. You can imagine. Hey, I'll let you get back to your dinner. Tell Kraig everything I've told you, okay? And keep praying for us. Please."

"We will. Tell Judy we're thinking about her." She said goodbye and hung up.

"What's the latest?" Kraig asked.

"They want you to name the baby. And Dave said to get right on it."

He smiled, shaking his head. "My guess is that this was Dave's idea, and if Judy was in on it at all, she was in a drug-induced stupor, and when she comes out of it, she's going to say, '*What*? You let *Kraig* name the *baby*?'"

Melissa shrugged. "If she doesn't like it, she doesn't have to sign the birth certificate with that on it. Just think of something."

Drifting off to sleep that night, Melissa was jarred awake by a thought so disturbing, she was surprised she hadn't thought of it before.

"Kraig! I just thought of something awful!"

"Mm?" Kraig said, more asleep than awake.

She leaned over him. "Remember what you said about this being a honeymoon baby? Okay, then she was born seven weeks

290

early. So…think about it. They were married only about seven and a half months when the baby was born."

"Mm?"

"And, so, people are always going to think the baby was conceived before the wedding. Won't Dave hate having to deal with *that* his whole life?"

He lifted his head a little. "I'm sure he'll be thrilled if that's his biggest worry. So how about if you stop worrying about it too?"

"Okay. Well…try to think of a name by tomorrow."

"Night, Melissa."

The next day, she went straight to his office after work. "So, what's the baby's name?"

He turned toward her in his chair. "Camille." *His mom's name.*

"Ahh. I like that. They'll like it too. What's the middle name?"

"Middle name? Was I supposed to choose a middle name, too?"

"I don't know. Maybe you'd better have one ready, just in case."

That night, they'd just finished the dinner dishes when Dave called. "*You* get it," Melissa said.

"Dave…. Yes, we're finished with dinner…. Yes, I did think of a name…. Camille Helen…. And tell Judy it won't hurt my feelings if she doesn't like it."

A few days later, the news was that Judy liked the name but wanted to change the spelling of Helen to Helene. "To make it sound French," she'd explained. "To go with Camille." Soon, Judy was discharged from the hospital, but spent most of her time in the neonatal ICU with Camille. Dave had used his paternity leave, and he wanted to save whatever vacation time he'd accumulated since the honeymoon for the first days with Judy and the baby at home, and needed to return to work for now.

The first week of June, Camille had gained enough weight, and her lungs were developed enough, that she, too, could leave the hospital. Melissa felt bouncy with happiness every time she talked to Judy; Judy seemed so content, so healthy, so happy.

One evening when Kraig hung up from talking with Dave, he looked so weary and sad, Melissa went to his side and put her arm around him. "What is it now?"

He shook his head, struggling with a mix of emotions. "It just doesn't seem fair. I know he loves her. I know he chose this life. But somehow it still doesn't seem fair." Melissa wasn't sure whether he was talking to her, or to himself, or perhaps to God, so she kept quiet. "Judy's in another depression."

"Oh. Is this a symptom of her illness? Or more like postpartum depression?"

"Who knows? Maybe both. But Judy's home alone now, with the baby, since Dave went back to work. He's afraid she's going to go to sleep and fail to wake up and feed the baby. Or that she'll neglect to eat, and Judy and the baby will both suffer. People from church were bringing over meals for a while, but at some point, that comes to an end. Then he hired some college girls to take turns stopping by at different times of day to check on her and make sure she eats lunch. Dave is doing most of the cooking, housework, laundry...he's looking into hiring a housekeeper to take off some of the load. But all of that is just secondary.

"It's just that...he misses so much of what I take for granted. Having a healthy wife. Judy went from being sick, to being pregnant, to being sick again. They've never had the chance to get to know each other under anything resembling 'normal' circumstances. I know God is in control. And I learned more about Dave from that speech he made over pizza last summer than in all the other years that I've known him. But I just can't get past thinking it doesn't seem fair."

"We need to go see them. As soon as school is out."

"We can tell them we're planning to move up there."

"They'll be happy."

A few nights later, Melissa found Kraig on the sofa in the semi-dark living room, listening to music, his hand resting on the page of a book lying open next to him. With his other hand, he stroked a cat asleep in his lap. Deep in thought as he appeared to be, it took him only a moment to notice her, leaning against the door frame, watching him. "Melissa?"

She clicked on a lamp and sat next to him, peeking at the cover of the book—*Woodworking Projects*. "What are you thinking about?"

"I'd like to make this for Camille." He held the book for her to see the page he'd been studying. On it was a smooth little box with a mirror inside the lid. "Does Matt have tools I could use for this?"

"He does…but they're all in storage."

"Never mind. Do you think Jeff could help me with this?"

"I'm sure he would."

"Speaking of Matt…he's been positively nice to me lately. Do you know what's behind that?"

"I think I do. You brought Jeff back into his life. Not only that…by doing so, you brought closure to that other part of our lives."

"Hmm. Yes. Besides that, it was because of me that he got your stereo."

She laughed. "Yeah. I'd like to help you choose the wood for this. And I could put in the velvet lining and the mirror in the lid."

"Sure. And we'd better…get right on it."

§

Chapter 22

This time, no one met them at the airport: they'd rented a car, and would be staying in a motel. Melissa had been to Dave's townhouse twice before, but it was primarily Kraig's verbal directions she relied upon to find it. She never ceased to marvel at what an impressive memory he had.

She tried to stand aside to let Kraig receive the first hug, but Dave pulled her into it, and then the girls, forming a massive group hug. She swallowed hard when Helen came into the entryway; she looked so much older, smaller, and more frail than she'd anticipated. Kraig embraced Helen, but it was more a symbolic embrace than a tangible, physical one—so fragile did she seem.

"Come in," Dave said, "go see Judy and the baby. But, hey, wash your hands first. Judy's kind of paranoid about germs these days. Sit anywhere, and pardon the cat fur. And girls, you're welcome to snoop around and try to find the cats. The black and white one is friendly; the orange and white one is more timid."

"We have something for the baby," Kraig said. "Melissa, open the carry-on bag for me, will you?"

Melissa knelt to unlock the bag. She let Kraig lift from the safety of its very center an artfully wrapped package.

"Melissa and I made it, Jessica wrapped it, and Emily did the artwork on the card," Kraig said, handing it to Dave. "And we used Jeff's tools...and his help."

"Ah, it looks too pretty to open," Dave said. "Let's let Judy do it."

It was impossible to miss the sight of a wheelchair folded up, leaning against the side of the couch; Melissa noted that it was new and shiny—not like a rented one. Judy was seated at one end of the sofa, holding a sound-asleep Camille.

"Hey, you guys," Judy said.

Melissa sat beside her, but the men had not followed, and the girls had gone in search of cats. Helen sat on the loveseat opposite.

Melissa leaned in for a closer look. "Oh, my gosh. She is so pretty."

"I think she looks like Dave, and Dave thinks she looks like me. What do you think?"

"I agree. She looks like both of you." Melissa had never seen so tiny a baby up close, and marveled at the miniature perfection of every feature. "Dave seems really happy." Melissa glanced toward the entryway, where the men still stood talking. "Family life must really suit him."

"It does. There's never been a more devoted husband and father. Every day, I learn something new about him—something he can do, something he knows. He's amazing."

Melissa smiled, for she'd had exactly the same thought about Kraig.

"He's had to do everything," Judy said, a little sadly. "Be not just a husband and father, but sometimes a mommy too. To Camille *and* me. But he does it, and never complains. I'm not totally sure I deserve him."

"Oh…" Melissa said, at a loss for words, "he's happy. Anyone can tell he's really happy." She glanced toward the entryway again. "I can't imagine what they're talking about over there. Kraig could hardly wait to hold Camille."

"Let them talk. Dave has *so* looked forward to having Kraig here. He really misses him."

Melissa suddenly remembered the good news they had to share, and could hardly wait.

Judy looked down at Camille, and without looking up, began, "Most people have no idea how long I've been in love with Dave."

Melissa looked around; she was pretty sure Helen couldn't hear from where she was, and everyone else was still out of the room. This story was for her alone.

"When I first went into the single adults' group," Judy continued, "he wanted me to tell the class about my plans for going to the mission field. Well…he asked *everybody* to talk about what they were going to do…but he gave me a lot more time than the others…asked a lot more questions. He really seemed interested. When I was finished talking, he held my hand and said…" Judy began to tear up, "he said he wanted to support me and write to me. He wrote to me *every week* for *nine years*. No one else did that.

"But at that moment, when he held my hand, for the first time in my life, I wasn't sure I wanted to go. I couldn't help thinking, What will I be missing? But…I realized, it was *because* I was going that he was interested in me. It wasn't even *me*—it was what I was doing."

Judy smiled and went on. "Whenever I came home on furlough, he was *so nice* to me. Like I was a visiting dignitary or something. But...he's so nice to *everyone*; I kept telling myself it didn't really mean anything. I couldn't help dreaming, though." She laughed softly. "Every week for nine years, his letters kept coming. After a while, I realized I was living with this constant fear...each letter, I was afraid would be the last...or that some day, one would bring news I didn't want to hear. You know...like he was engaged or something. But that *never happened*. When I had to leave Sudan for good, I was disappointed, yet at the same time I thought, At least I'll get to see Dave.

"When he met me at the airport, I literally collapsed into his arms. I was a mess—exhausted from the long trip, not feeling well, hadn't eaten in about twenty-four hours. I was too tired even to worry about how I looked. And Dave...he was more handsome than ever, and he just held me until I was okay. In a way, I just wanted him to take me home and leave me alone. But he didn't.

"At first, I thought Dave was going to be disappointed in me for leaving the mission field, after all the support he'd given me over the years...but he wasn't. He just wanted me to get well. After I'd been back a while, and he didn't go away...I started to think it really was me he cared about." Judy looked up. "Did you hear how he proposed?"

"No, I didn't."

"We'd gone sightseeing, and we were on the bridge over Multnomah Falls. He gave me the ring box, but the ring wasn't in it ...he told me later he was afraid I might drop it...but inside the box was a folded-up note saying, "Will you marry me?" She was smiling through her tears, and Melissa realized she was, too. And she realized that, as hearer of this precious story, she had the responsibility of keeping it safe in her memory in case she ever had the sad duty of telling it to Camille in Judy's place.

Jessica and Emily returned to the living room, and Kraig and Dave were looking their way.

"Did you find any cats, girls?" Dave asked.

"Yeah, the black and white one let us pet her, but the fluffy orange one didn't."

"You haven't by any chance rearranged the furniture, have you?" Kraig asked.

"No, everything is just as you remember."

"Hey, Kraig," Judy said as he made his way toward the couch.

He put his hand on her shoulder, then bent and kissed her on the cheek before taking the space on Melissa's other side. "When do I get to hold the baby?"

Just then, Camille began to stir; her face contorted with unhappiness as she stretched, both feet popping free of the blanket.

"Sorry, Kraig, she's going to have to eat first." Judy looked at Dave, as if to ask whether she should leave the room.

"Stay comfortable. You're among friends." Dave sat next to Helen on the love seat, while Jessica and Emily managed to share an armchair.

Judy draped a blanket over the baby's head and began to nurse her. Everyone chuckled as Camille let out a sigh.

"We brought something for Camille," Melissa said, seeing the package in Dave's hand. "Kraig made it."

Dave held it up. "It looks too pretty to open."

"Go ahead, Dave," Judy said.

"I was going to let *you* do it."

"No, you open it."

"Okay, I'll open it." He carefully peeled away the floral-print paper and unveiled the smooth little box. "Hey, this is neat. Look—her initials on top, CHB."

"Look inside," Kraig said. "Melissa did that part."

He did, holding the box so that Judy could see the lining.

"Hey, that's my favorite color for Camille," Judy said of the turquoise green, which Melissa had chosen, thinking of Judy's coat.

"That's true," Dave said. "You should see the nursery."

As Dave turned the box over in his hands, showing it to Helen, Melissa smiled upon seeing the initials carved into the bottom—K & M.

"Nice work," Dave said. "Thanks, you guys. And please thank Jeff for us, too."

"We will," Melissa said. "Now, we're here to help you. If want us to go away and leave you alone...."

"If you want us to take Camille *with* us..." Kraig said, which made everyone laugh. "I mean, so you two can spend some time alone."

"Nah," Dave said. "It's just so good to be together. Kraig and I can go out after a while and get some take-out for all of us."

As Melissa looked around at this gathering of dear friends, she felt a touch of sadness over who *wasn't* there. Dave's family, in Wisconsin, probably wouldn't see little Camille as often as they'd like; Judy's family, having come on emergency furlough when the pregnancy turned complicated, had since gone back to the mission field; and although her parents talked of retiring in a few years, no one yet knew *where*. Matt seemed happy in Michigan, and in spite of the sadness at having him so far away, just seeing him *happy* was good enough. Melissa felt an overwhelming sense of contentment.

"Oh," Kraig said suddenly. "We have some pretty big news."

The room fell silent.

"We're thinking of moving," Kraig continued. "To Portland."

"Portland?" Dave said tentatively. "Portland...Maine?"

"No, Dave. Portland, Oregon. *Here*."

"That is great news!"

"It probably won't be for a year," Melissa said.

"Jessica will be finishing high school," Kraig explained, "and Emily will be starting. This seems the least disruptive to them."

"Wow," Dave said, so obviously thrilled with the news that Melissa felt ashamed she'd ever hesitated to go along with the plan. "This is just great. Hey, speaking of which, we're planning to buy a house. Something with more bedrooms and a yard. Since we're planning to add to our family."

The room fell silent again. Everyone seemed afraid to react, except for Judy, who looked as if she were trying not to laugh.

"Ha! Got everyone's attention, didn't I?" Dave laughed. "Besides Judy's dog that we're applying for, her brother Kurt is going to be moving in with us so he can go to junior college here."

"I'm so looking forward to that," Judy said. "I've never lived in the same house with my brother before."

"Yeah, I am too," Dave agreed. "I've never *had* a little bro before. He's a good kid. Oh, Jessica and Emily, Kurt said he really enjoyed meeting you at our wedding."

Melissa looked at her daughters, remembering the pictures of themselves with Kurt they'd plastered all over their bedroom walls.

"He remembered us?" Jessica asked.

"Yes, he definitely remembered you," Judy said.

"Hey, while you're here," Dave said, "maybe we can go sort of preliminary-house-hunting…get an idea of what areas you like, so we can buy in the same neighborhood."

"We were thinking out toward the west," Kraig said. "So it's easier to go to the beach."

"Yeah, I like that too," Dave said. "Well. That'll be fun."

Judy lifted Camille to her shoulder. "She's finished for now."

"That was fast," Melissa said.

"She has a tiny tummy," Dave explained. "She'll nurse like that every two hours, at least. Could be one reason Judy's so exhausted. That's one thing I can't help with much." He rose from the love seat. "One more maintenance detail and she's all yours, buddy." Dave left with Camille, returning in a couple of minutes and placing the baby in Kraig's arms.

Melissa felt her eyes grow moist as she watched Kraig get acquainted with this almost impossibly tiny person. He stroked the translucent skin of her cheek, her cornsilk-colored hair, her tiny, delicate hands with their perfectly miniaturized nails. He held her with her face close to his, breathing what Melissa knew to be the special smell of a newborn, then pressed his lips to her forehead.

As the late afternoon sun of the summer solstice slipped toward the horizon, it sliced through the window blinds. Not wanting Camille to be disturbed, Melissa rose to turn the blinds. As she twisted the wand, watching the results, something unexpected happened. A flash of sunlight hit Kraig directly in the face, and he blinked. *That's strange. Must be a coincidence.* Watching, she repeated the motion, and he blinked again.

He must have always been sensitive to very bright light, and she'd just never noticed. But the incident brought to mind a promise she'd made him, and with it, a touch of guilt. For, as little significance as she'd attached to his blindness in the almost two years she'd known him, she could probably count on her fingers the number of seconds she'd spent thinking about it in the past year. This was mostly a positive thing, for it illustrated how completely they'd become one. Yet it also reminded her that she'd promised to support him in his pursuit of future surgery, and she'd forgotten all about it. When they moved to Portland would be a good time—they could work with the same doctors.

She returned to the sofa, settling in deeply next to Kraig. As she looked around the room to see if everyone else was as enraptured as she, Dave winked at her. She took a mental picture of each face to keep forever.

She looked back at Kraig with the baby, breathing as lightly as she could to try to interpret whatever magical communication passed between her wonderful husband and this tiny human being, the entire miracle of life captured in this one precious moment.

§ § §

About the Author

Lisa J. Lehr's passion for the written word has guided her life. Throughout her school years, she found English an enjoyable and easy subject. Then, having earned all her college English credit through the Advanced Placement Program, she went on to receive a biology degree from the University of Colorado at Boulder. After working in a variety of fields, including the pharmaceutical industry and teaching, she began freelance writing in 1999.

A big believer in continuing education, Lisa is a graduate of the American Writers and Artists Institute (AWAI) copywriting program. She holds majority credit toward a certificate from Central California Bible Institute and returned to school for a time to study graphic art. Her latest subject of interest is public speaking.

Lisa has hundreds of articles and several short stories and essays to her credit, has co-written autobiographies for private clients, and has edited many kinds of projects for business clients. She now focuses on copywriting and creating information products, specializing in the alternative health, pet care, and self-help niches.

A dedicated community volunteer, Lisa has held lay leadership roles in both adult and children's ministries; volunteered with children, animals, literacy, and numerous other causes; and raised a Guide Dog puppy. When she's not busy writing, she enjoys reading, doing artwork, listening to music, studying Italian, being outdoors, and attending Renaissance Faires and Celtic Festivals.

She's listed in Marquis' *Who's Who in America 2005*®, the definitive source of biographical information on America's leaders and achievers, and *Who's Who of American Women 2006*®.